He shifted his weight and leaned forward.

"Simple," he said. "First things first, we get your sister safe and settled so you don't have to worry any more. Then you and me and the lads, and your lady friend, we do one more job. Then we pack it in, go our separate ways, and they all live happily ever after. How about it?"

Something about the way he said it made my skin crawl. "Just any old job, or have you got something specific in mind?"

"Oh, I expect something'll turn up. Something with no risk and good money." He smirked at me. "I have faith."

"There's a war coming," I said. "A big one. It'll be a storm, and either we find somewhere to snuggle down and ride it out, or we'll get washed away. You do realise that, don't you?"

"War's just another word for opportunity. I'm not bothered about any of that."

Praise for the Novels of K. J. Parker

"Full of invention and ingenuity.... Great fun."
—*SFX* on *Sixteen Ways to Defend a Walled City*

"Readers will appreciate the infusion of humor and fun-loving characters into this vivid and sometimes grim fantasy world."
—*Publishers Weekly* on *Sixteen Ways to Defend a Walled City*

"Parker has created a world full of wit, ingenuity, unlikely tactics and reluctant heroes and there is nothing else quite like it."
—*Fantasy Hive* on *How to Rule an Empire and Get Away with It*

"With a steady pacing, solid, lean writing and variety of twists, the novel keeps on surprising the reader."
—*Fantasy Book Critic* on *Sixteen Ways to Defend a Walled City*

"Parker's acerbic wit and knowledge of human nature are a delight to read as he explores the way conflict is guided, in equal measure, by the brilliance and unerring foolishness of humanity.... Thoroughly engaging."
—*RT Book Reviews* on *The Two of Swords: Volume One*

"A ripping good adventure yarn, laced with frequent barbed witticisms and ace sword fighting.... Parker's settings and characterizations never miss a beat, and the intricate political interplay of intrigue is suspenseful almost to the last page."
—*Publishers Weekly* on *Sharps*

As K. J. Parker

The Fencer Trilogy
Colours in the Steel
The Belly of the Bow
The Proof House

The Scavenger Trilogy
Shadow
Pattern
Memory

The Engineer Trilogy
Devices and Desires
Evil for Evil
The Escapement

The Company
The Folding Knife
The Hammer
Sharps
The Two of Swords:
Volume One
The Two of Swords:
Volume Two
The Two of Swords:
Volume Three

Sixteen Ways to Defend
a Walled City
How to Rule an Empire
and Get Away with It
A Practical Guide to
Conquering the World

The Corax Trilogy
Saevus Corax Deals
With the Dead
Saevus Corax Captures
the Castle
Saevus Corax Gets
Away With Murder

As Tom Holt

Expecting
Someone Taller
Who's Afraid of Beowulf?
Flying Dutch
Ye Gods!
Overtime
Here Comes the Sun
Grailblazers
Faust Among Equals
Odds and Gods
Djinn Rummy
My Hero
Paint Your Dragon
Open Sesame
Wish You Were Here
Only Human
Snow White and the
Seven Samurai
Valhalla
Nothing But Blue Skies
Falling Sideways
Little People
The Portable Door

In Your Dreams
Earth, Air, Fire
and Custard
You Don't Have to Be
Evil to Work Here,
But It Helps
Someone Like Me
Barking
The Better Mousetrap
May Contain
Traces of Magic
Blonde Bombshell
Life, Liberty, and the
Pursuit of Sausages
Doughnut
When It's A Jar
The Outsorcerer's
Apprentice
The Good, the Bad
and the Smug
The Management Style
of the Supreme Beings
An Orc on the Wild Side

Dead Funny: Omnibus 1
Mightier Than the
Sword: Omnibus 2
The Divine
Comedies: Omnibus 3
For Two Nights
Only: Omnibus 4
Tall Stories: Omnibus 5
Saints and
Sinners: Omnibus 6
Fishy Wishes:
Omnibus 7

The Walled Orchard
Alexander at the
World's End
Olympiad
A Song for Nero
Meadowland

I, Margaret

Lucia in Wartime
Lucia Triumphant

SAEVUS CORAX GETS AWAY WITH MURDER

The Corax Trilogy: Book 3

K. J. PARKER

orbit

orbitbooks.net

Copyright © 2023 by One Reluctant Lemming Company Ltd.
Excerpt from *The Eight Reindeer of the Apocalypse* copyright © 2023 by One Reluctant Lemming Company Ltd.
Excerpt from *Sixteen Ways to Defend a Walled City* copyright © 2019 by One Reluctant Lemming Company Ltd.

Cover design by Lisa Marie Pompilio
Cover illustrations by Shutterstock
Cover copyright © 2023 by Hachette Book Group, Inc.

Orbit
Hachette Book Group
1290 Avenue of the Americas
New York, NY 10104
orbitbooks.net

First Edition: December 2023
Simultaneously published in Great Britain by Orbit

Orbit is an imprint of Hachette Book Group.
The Orbit name and logo are trademarks of Little, Brown Book Group Limited.

The publisher is not responsible for websites (or their content) that are not owned by the publisher.

The Hachette Speakers Bureau provides a wide range of authors for speaking events. To find out more, go to hachettespeakersbureau.com or email HachetteSpeakers@hbgusa.com.

Orbit books may be purchased in bulk for business, educational, or promotional use. For information, please contact your local bookseller or the Hachette Book Group Special Markets Department at special.markets@hbgusa.com.

Library of Congress Control Number: 2023941501

ISBNs: 9780316669047 (trade paperback), 9780316668989 (ebook)

Printed in the United States of America

LSC-C

Printing 1, 2023

For my friends;
Given what's coming, our only hope
is to have no hope at all.

1

Isn't it nice, I remember thinking as I tried to yank an arrow out of a dead soldier's eye, when things unexpectedly turn out just right? And then the arrow came away in my hand, but the eyeball was firmly stuck on the arrowhead. I glared at it. A standard hunting broadhead, with barbs, which was why it had dragged the eye out of its socket. I could cut it away with a knife, but could I really be bothered, for an arrow worth five trachy?

Everything about this job (apart from the flies, the mosquitos, the swamp and the quite appalling smell) had been roses all the way. For a start, Count Theudebert had paid *me*, rather than the other way around. In my business – I clear up after battles – you have to pay the providers, meaning the two opposing armies, for the privilege of burying their dead, in return for what you can strip off the bodies. Since we're a relatively small concern and the big boys (mostly the Asvogel brothers) outbid us for pretty well every job worth having, we tend to get contracts with wafer-thin margins, and our profits are generally more a state of mind rather than anything you can write down on a balance sheet, let alone spend. But the Count had written to me offering me a flat-rate fee for clearing up the mess he intended to make in the Leerwald forest, plus anything I found that I might possibly want to keep. That sort of deal doesn't come along every day, believe me.

I could see where the Count was coming from. Five thousand or so of his tenants, living in a clearing in the vast expanse of the Leerwald, had decided not to pay their rent and had killed the men he'd sent to help them reconsider their decision; accordingly, he had no choice but to march in there, slaughter everything that moved and find or buy new tenants to replace the dead. The tenants didn't own anything worth having, so no reputable battlefield clearance contractor would want the job on the usual terms. Either the Count would have to do his own clean-up, or he'd have to hire someone.

He wasn't exactly offering a fortune, but times were hard and we needed the work. Also, as my good friend and junior partner Gombryas pointed out, chances were that the Count's archers would probably do a fair amount of the slaughtering, which would mean arrows ... Nothing but the best for Theudebert of Draha, so they'd be bound to be using good-quality hard-steel bodkins on ash shafts with goose fletchings – again, not exactly a fortune but worth picking up, and if what people were saying was true, about a big war brewing in the east, the price of high-class once-used arrows could only go up. Also, he added, according to the Count's letter there'd be dead civilians as well, and even peasant women tend to have some jewellery, even if it's just whittled bone on a bit of string. And shoes, he added cheerfully: everybody wears shoes. At a gulden six per barrelful, it all adds up ...

Gombryas had been right about one thing. There were plenty of arrows. But they turned out to be practically worthless, which was wonderful—

"Over here," Gombryas yelled. "I found him!"

I chucked the arrow with the eyeball on it and shoved my way through the briars to where Gombryas was standing, at the foot of a large beech tree. Its canopy overshadowed an area of about twenty square yards, forming a welcome clearing. Nailed to the trunk of the tree was a man's body. He'd been ripped open, his ribcage prised apart and his guts wound out round a stick. Piled at his feet were his clothes and armour: gorgeous clothes and luxury armour. Nothing but the best for Theudebert of Draha.

"Charming," I said.

Gombryas grinned at me. "I guess they didn't like him much," he said. "Can't say I blame them."

He had a pair of clippers in his hand, the sort you use for shearing sheep or pruning vines. I could see he was torn with indecision. Gombryas collects relics of dead military heroes; relics as in body parts. His collection is the ruling passion of his life. Mostly he buys them for ridiculous sums of money from dealers and other collectors, and he's not a rich man, so he finances his collection by harvesting and selling bits and pieces whenever we come across a dead hero in the usual course of our business. Theudebert was definitely in the highly sought-after category. Hence the agonising decision: which bits to sell and which bits to keep for himself?

The point being, Theudebert had lost. He'd led his army into the Leerwald, knowing that his tenants were forbidden to own weapons and therefore expecting, reasonably enough, not to have to do any actual fighting, just killing. What he'd overlooked was the tendency of forests to contain trees, which any fool with a few basic hand tools can turn into a functional bow in the course of an afternoon ... Tracing the sequence of events by means of the position of the bodies, I figured out that Theudebert was only about half a mile from the first of the villages when he walked into the first ambush. About a third of his men were shot down in what could only have been a matter of a minute or so. Understandably he decided to turn back, figuring that the tenants had made their point. He was wrong about that. There were further ambushes, about a dozen of them, strung out over about five miles of forest trail. Finally, Theudebert had turned off the road and tried to get away through the dense thickets of briars, holly and withies which had grown up where his late father had cleared a broad swath of the forest for charcoal-burning. The beech tree was, I assumed, the place where the tenants had finally caught up with him and his few surviving guards.

"Will you look at the quality of this stuff?" Olybrius said, waving a bloodstained shirt under my nose. "That's best imported linen."

"It's got a hole in it," I said.

Olybrius gave me a look. "Funny man," he said. "And you should see the boots. Double-seamed, and hardly a mark on them."

I should've been as delighted as he was, but somehow I wasn't. I wasn't unhappy, either. We'd lucked into a substantial windfall, at a time when we badly needed one, and for once the work wouldn't be particularly arduous (except for the flies, the mosquitos, the swamp and the truly horrible smell) – and, God only knows, my heart wasn't inclined to bleed for Count Theudebert, even though he was a sort of relation of mine, second cousin three times removed or something like that. Quite the opposite; when you've spent your life either imposing authority or having it imposed upon you, the sight of a head of state nailed to a tree with his guts dangling out can't fail to restore your faith in the basic rightness of things. Just occasionally, you can reassure yourself, the bullies get what's coming to them, so everything's fine.

I decided that whatever was bothering me couldn't be terribly important, and got on with the work I was supposed to be doing. Since I'm nominally the boss of the outfit, it's more or less inevitable that I get the lousiest job, which in our line of business is collecting up the bodies, once they've been stripped of armour and clothing and thoroughly gone over for small items of value, and disposing of them. Usually we burn them, but in a dense forest packed with underbrush it struck me that that mightn't be a very good idea. That meant digging a series of large holes, a chore that my colleagues and I detest.

Especially in a forest. It's the nature of things that forests grow on thin, stony soil; if there was good soil under there, you can bet someone would've been along to cut down the trees and plough it up a thousand years ago. Typically there's about a foot of leaf mould, really hard to dig into because of the network of holly, ground elder and bramble roots. Under that you find about ten inches of crumbly black soil, along with a lot of stones. Then you're down into clay, if you're lucky, or your actual rock if you aren't. On this occasion Fortune smiled on us and we found clay, thick and grey and sort of oily, which we laboriously chopped out with pickaxes. Two feet down into the clay, of course, we struck the water table, which turned our carefully dug graves into miniature wells in no time flat.

Still, we were only burying dead soldiers, so who cares? Let them get wet.

Gombryas and Olybrius had finished stripping the bodies and loading the proceeds on to carts long before we got our pits done, so they and their crews gathered round to give us moral support while we dug. I was up to my waist in filthy water, I remember, with Gombryas perched on the edge of the grave explaining to me the finer points of relic collecting. For instance: singletons – organs of which there are only one, such as the nose, the heart and the penis – are obviously more valuable than multiples (fingers, toes, ears, testicles), but complete sets of fingers, toes, ears &c are more valuable still. But you can make a real killing if a rich collector has got nine of so-and-so's fingers and you've got the missing one, which he needs to make up the set. Accordingly, after much deliberation, Gombryas had decided to keep Count Theudebert's heart and liver (preserved in honey) and one finger; the rest of the internals and extremities would probably be alluring enough as swapsies to net him either the complete left hand of Carnufex the Irrigator – with most of the skin still on, he told me breathlessly, which is practically unheard of for a Warring States-era relic – or the left ear of Prince Phraates; he already had the right ear, but the First Social War wasn't really his period, so the plan was to swap both ears for the pelvis of Calojan the Great, which he knew for a fact was likely to come up at some point in the next year or so, because the man who owned it had a nasty disease and wasn't expected to live . . .

"Gombryas," I interrupted. "How much is your collection worth?"

He stopped and looked at me. "No idea," he said.

"At a rough guess."

He thought for a while, during which time he didn't speak, which was nice. "Fifty thousand," he said eventually. "Well, maybe closer to sixty. Depends on what the market's doing at the time. Why?"

I was mildly stunned. "Fifty thousand staurata," I said. "And you're still here, doing this shit."

He was shocked, and offended. "I'd never sell my collection," he said. "It's taken me a lifetime—"

"Seriously," I said. "All those bits of desiccated soldiers are worth more to you than a life of security and ease. Fifty thousand—"

"Keep your voice down," he hissed at me.

"Sorry," I said. I straightened my back and rested for a moment, leaning on the handle of my shovel. "But for crying out loud, Gombryas, that's serious money. You could buy two ships and still have enough left for a vineyard."

"It's not about money." This from a man who regularly went through the ashes of our cremation pyres with a rake, to retrieve arrowheads left inside the bodies. "It's about, I don't know, heritage—"

"Talking of which," I said. "You've got no family. When you die, who gets all the stuff?"

He shrugged. "I don't know, do I? None of my business when I'm dead."

"Maybe," I suggested, "your fellow collectors will cut you up and share you out. Wouldn't that be nice?"

He scowled at me. "Funny man," he said.

I gave him a warm smile and started digging. Quite by accident, I made a big splash in the muddy water with the blade of my shovel, and Gombryas's legs got drenched. He called me something or other and went away.

Six feet deep is the industry standard, but I decided I'd exercise my professional discretion and make do with four. I called a halt, we scrambled up out of the graves and started tipping the bodies. They rolled off the tailgates of the carts and went splash into the water, displacing most of it in accordance with Saloninus's Third Law, and then we filled in, making an eighteen-inch allowance for settlement. Not that it mattered a damn in the middle of a forest, and we'd been paid in advance by a man who was now exceptionally dead, but there's a right way and a wrong way of doing things, and I hate it when Chusro Asvogel goes around making snide remarks about the quality of our work.

So that was that. We loaded our tools on to the carts and made our way back to the forest road. It was blocked with fallen trees.

Not so much fallen, I noted after a cursory examination, as chopped down. I started shouting the usual stuff about shunting the carts into a square, horses and people in the middle, but nobody seemed to be paying attention. That, I soon gathered, was because they were looking at the archers who'd suddenly appeared out of the trees, and were standing there looking at us.

Nuts, I thought. But I put a trustworthy look on my face and walked towards the treeline. "Can I help you gentlemen?" I said.

A man came forward. He was being helped by two others, and his left leg dangled, the way they do when they're broken. "Who the hell are you?" he said.

I explained. He looked at me. "Seriously?"

"It's what we do for a living." I paused. These, presumably, were the people who'd just shot to death a famous general and six thousand trained soldiers. "Morally," I said, "I guess the stuff belongs to you, but we've just done a hell of a lot of work, so—"

"We don't want any of that," the man said.

I can't say I warmed to him straight away. I guess he looked the way you'd expect a man to look when he's just miraculously won a battle he really didn't want to fight. I'd put him a few years either side of sixty, but men age quickly when they're tenants of someone like Theudebert; a short man, slight, bald, with a wispy white beard. "Are you sure?" I said.

"I just said so, didn't I? You keep it. Sell it. Just go away."

Which was exactly what I wanted to hear; more, I guess, than I deserved. "How about the weapons?" I said. "There's spears, shields, helmets, some body armour."

"Are you deaf?"

"For when they come back," I explained. "You'll need weapons then."

He frowned. "They won't come back," he said.

"Want to bet?" Shut up, my inner voice yelled at me, sounding remarkably like my mother. "You killed the Count and six thousand men—"

"No." He looked at me. "That many?"

"Six thousand, one hundred and fourteen," I said. "Of course they'll be back. You've got to be punished. Otherwise, the whole doctrine of the monopoly of force falls apart."

"The what?"

I may be many things, but I'm not an educator. I have better things to do than spread enlightenment. "At the very least," I said, "keep the bows. They're standard Aelian issue, top of the line, about the best you can get unless you upgrade to composite. Keep them and practise with them, and when the bastards come back, wearing proper armour instead of just skirmishing kit, at least you'll be able to make a fight of it. Your homebrew bows simply don't have the cast to shoot through plate armour, or lamellar."

He had no idea what I was talking about. "I told you," he said. "We don't want their garbage. And we don't want you. Go away."

"Fine," I said. "And thank you. But trust me, they will be back." I wasn't getting through to him. Besides, it wasn't any of my business. "Make yourselves stronger bows," I told him. "Practise."

"Get lost."

None of my business, after all. I smiled and walked away. "Well?" Gombryas said in my ear, in a whisper they could've heard in Boc Bohec.

"It's fine," I told him. "They don't want the stuff."

"Really?"

"Really," I told him. "Let's get out of here before they change their minds."

So we did that, and pretty soon we were out of the forest and back into the light, which made me nervous. I didn't know if the Count's people had heard the news yet; probably not. As soon as they found out what had happened, they'd be busy. Also, most likely, they'd want their weapons and armour back. "For all we know," I told Gombryas and Olybrius, as we rattled along the main road to the sea, "that was history in the making. You can tell your grandchildren you were there."

"Tell them what?"

Indeed. The Count would be back, a new man with a new army, more soldiers, better weapons; they'd have a strategy this time, and they'd win. The tenants would be slaughtered and replaced, the rule of law would be upheld, future generations would grow up secure in the thoroughly reinforced knowledge that you can't fight City Hall. Definitely none of my business.

(Oh, did I mention I'm the son of a duke? Not that it's ever done me any good, since I left home under something of a cloud when I was fifteen, and shortly after that my father put a price on my head, forty thousand staurata dead or alive – which sounds impressive, but it's rather less than my sister and brother-in-law are offering, on the same terms; of course, my brother-in-law is the Elector, so he can afford to pay top dollar. But heredity definitely ought to put me on the side of the landlord against the tenant, capital against labour, divine right against malcontents and Bolsheviks; and I've seen the mess that tenantry, labour and Bolshevism have made of things when they've been given the chance, every bit as bad as the mess they rebelled against. Accordingly I tend not to think in terms of monolithic blocs, idealisms and ethical systems. The world makes more sense, I find, if you interpret it in terms of idiots and bastards. And if you ask me which category I fall into, I freely admit: both. My father, by the way, is a much less amenable landlord than cousin Theudebert was. I kid myself that I'm liberal and enlightened but I don't suppose I'd be significantly better, in the incredibly unlikely event that I get the chance to find out.)

We sold the stuff at Holdeshar for rather more than I'd anticipated. We got the going rate for the clothes, a very good price for the boots, shields and helmets and silly money for the bows and arrows. Dealers I'd known for years suddenly gave me big smiles for the first time ever, and asked if there was any more where that came from. Needless to say I said yes, though I was lying. How soon can you deliver? they asked. That made me feel uncomfortable. Maybe there really was going to be a war, after all.

There's always a war: it goes without saying. Every day of every year since the Invincible Sun moulded the first man out of river mud and propped him against a tree to dry, there's been a war somewhere – little wars, silly little wars, scraps over boundaries and trade, cattle raids and state-sponsored piracy, scalp hunts, punitive expeditions, reprisals for reprisals for reprisals, pre-emptive reprisals for diplomatic snubs that haven't even happened yet . . . Little wars keep me fed and clothed and busy, and being busy is good because it doesn't leave me any time to brood on how badly I've screwed up my life. But big wars – the major empires and federations up on their hind legs ripping out each other's throats – are mercifully rare: once in a generation, which is why there are still human beings, and why the entire surface of the earth isn't covered in briars and withies. About the only thing I can say for myself is that I've stopped two big wars from happening, the Sashan Empire against the West; me, with my two grubby hands and my poor overworked brain, even though strictly speaking it was none of my business. I guess I don't approve of war. Burning and burying bodies and tracking my next job of work by a trail of burned farmhouses has led me to certain conclusions. I won't attempt to defend them, since there are all sorts of good arguments for war, devised by some of our species' finest minds, and I wouldn't presume to contradict them. I always come back to Saloninus's definition of a sword – a piece of metal with a slave on both ends.

There are worse places than Holdeshar, at least a dozen of them. We chose the back bar of the Humility Exalted for the shareout. The drill is, I find the buyers and do the selling, deduct the overheads and the running costs and divide up the balance between the heads of department according to the established ratio: 10 per cent for me; 10 per cent for each department. It was nice to have something tangible to hand out for a change. For the last three jobs we'd done, they'd had to make do with fine words and promises.

I left the rest of them in the Humility and crossed the road to the Temple. The local branch of the Knights of Equity have an office there, in a small room behind the high altar. Before they were a bank, the Knights were crusaders, fighting to free the holy places from the Sashan and the Antecyrenaeans. In the end their army was slaughtered to the last man, but their fundraising arm somehow neglected to show up for the final battle, and they were left orphaned, without a reason for existing but with a very great deal of other people's money, which they were naturally reluctant to hand back. So they reinvented themselves as a general charitable fund, although for various reasons they never got around to distributing anything. Now they're the biggest bank in the West, slightly ahead of the Poor Sisters. They've tried to have me murdered more than once but I still bank with them, mostly because the only alternative would be the Sisters, who don't like me one bit. Most of the other banks went belly-up during the financial crisis, which I caused by encouraging the Sashan to annex the fabulously wealthy island of Sirupat; I was king of Sirupat at the time (don't ask: it's complicated). Anyway, these days there are only two real players in the money game, both of them shadows of their former pre-crisis selves, but definitely still going and about as trustworthy as a scorpion. Which isn't a bad thing; you can always trust a scorpion to sting you, if you provoke it.

The chief clerk of the Knights in Holdeshar is an old friend of mine. She looked up as I walked in. "Get out," she said.

"Don't be like that," I said. "I'm paying in."

"Get out," she repeated, "before I call the guards."

"They're in the Humility," I told her. "My boys are buying them drinks. Come on, Lessa, be nice. Bearing grudges doesn't suit you."

"Piss off and die," said my friend, then she shrugged. "Paying in?"

"One thousand staurata, cash money."

I wouldn't say she actually softened, but she reached for her ledger and opened it. She's a tall, thin woman, maybe just this side of sixty, sharp as a knife; she used to be a Sister until she had to quit the order under a bit of a cloud, something about a certain sum of money not being where it should have been. The Knights were glad to have her because of her comprehensive knowledge of where the Sisters had buried various bodies. Ending up in Holdeshar was a matter of choice rather than rotten luck or prejudice; she claims to value the simple, quiet life, which I guess I can understand.

She ruled a line across the page, then looked at me. "Go on, then," she said. "Let's see it."

I had the money in a satchel under my coat, which I took off and hung on a hook behind the door. I dumped the satchel on the desk and opened it. She wrinkled her nose. "It smells," she said.

"That's the bag," I explained. I'd taken it from round the neck of one of Theudebert's adjutants. Waste not, want not.

"Why is everything to do with you always so horrible?"

I shrugged. "Beats me," I said, and emptied the bag on to the desk. She scrabbled the coins towards her and started to count.

You don't dare talk to Lessa while she's counting. When she'd finished and reluctantly conceded that it was all there, I said, "You know all about politics and stuff. Is there going to be a war?"

She thought for a moment. "Not sure," she said.

"Not sure yes or not sure no?"

"Not sure," she said. "The Aelians want one, but the Sashan don't. At least, they don't want one now, not with all the problems they've got at home—"

"What problems?"

"But on the other hand, if they have a war now they'll almost certainly win, but if they wait six months or a year the Aelians stand a much better chance of at least making a fight of it. Which is why I'm not sure, like I told you."

"What problems?"

She grinned at me. "Oh, it's all just rumour and speculation. Besides, it's restricted information, favoured customers only. Sorry."

"I've just paid in a thousand staurata."

"Yes, but I don't like you. Here's your receipt. I'll have the letter of credit sent to your branch at Auxentia. Goodbye."

I went back to the Humility. Olybrius and Carrhasio were working up to one of their usual drunken shouting matches. Polybius had ordered the house special, which was something grey with bits in it. Gombryas was talking intensely to a fat man who was almost certainly a fellow collector; next to his elbow on the bar was an ominous looking clay pot, sealed with resin. I considered asking the landlord to bring me a pot of green-leaf tea, but decided I couldn't be bothered. Then the man I'd arranged to meet came in, and we sat down in the quiet corner, furthest away from the door.

"Twelve thousand staurata," he said. "Take it or leave it."

It was a modest little war, more of a police action, in Cheuda, which is a nice enough place if you like that sort of thing: flat, which is good from the haulage point of view, but inland, which isn't. He was representing the rebels, who were quietly confident of victory; tomorrow I'd be meeting the government, who were equally confident but likely to be more noisy. "Ten," I said.

"I've got a firm offer of eleven from the Asvogel brothers."

"Take it," I said. "They're a good firm, very reliable. And they can afford to work on wafer-thin margins. We can't."

He looked at me. I knew for a fact that Chusro Asvogel had offered him nine fifty, because Chusro told me so himself. "We prefer to work with smaller operators," he said. "Match the Asvogels' eleven thousand and the job's yours."

"I'll match their nine fifty, with pleasure. That's actually less than I offered you a moment ago, but that's fine by me."

I think he'd made up his mind that he didn't like me. "Ten thousand staurata."

"Nine seven-five," I said, "and that's my final offer."

"You said ten a moment ago."

"Times change." I waited three seconds, then grinned at him. "All right, ten," I said. "After all, that's what the job's actually worth to me. Does that sound fair to you?"

He sighed. "I hate bargaining," he said.

"You're not very good at it," I told him. "But then, why should you be? You're an idealist."

That made him grin. He still didn't like me very much. "Damn right," he said. "When you're building the Great Society, every compromise is a betrayal."

"Of course it is," I said. "Have a drink."

He had several, and then he signed a contract and walked unsteadily away, leaving me to pay the tab.

The government man, who I met the next day, was easier to take. "His Majesty has authorised me to accept nine thousand staurata," he said.

"Eight."

"Nine," he said. "You've already signed an agreement with the rebels, so you're in no position to haggle."

"True," I said. "In that case, why not ask for ten?"

He shrugged. "Not my money," he said. "Besides, if we asked for ten thousand you wouldn't make a profit, and then you'd be out of business and we couldn't use you in the future. We like working with people we know. It makes life easier."

He bought the drinks. He had red wine; I had peach tea. "Do you think there's going to be a war?" I asked him.

"I should think so," he said. "Otherwise I've just taken your money under false pretences."

"I mean a real one. Aelia versus the Sashan."

Everyone I'd asked that question had stopped and thought before answering. So did he. "On balance," he said, "yes. But not quite yet."

"Really?"

He nodded. "The Aelians want to strike now, because of the internal politics inside the Sashan Empire. So they're looking to provoke the Empire, but the Empire's perfectly capable of keeping its temper until it's ready. That's the advantage of being a monarchy. It's harder for other people to bounce you into doing things you don't want to do. Of course," he added, "that's only true if the monarchy is stable."

I gazed at him for a moment. "And the Empire isn't?"

He gave me a you-know-better-than-that look. "Not for me to say," he said. "I'm just a political officer, not a diplomat. My job is to run errands."

None of my business, I decided. A really big war, between the Sashan and the Aelians, would be way out of my league. The only firms big enough to handle it would be the Asvogels and the Resurrectionists, and I doubted very much whether they'd end up making any money. It's no good collecting huge quantities of the stuff if nobody wants to buy it, and when there's a big war there are only two potential buyers, both of them inclined to be brutal in their approach to negotiation. Here's what we're prepared to pay, they say, take it or leave it; and the price they offer is 30 per cent of what it'd cost them to make the stuff new in their ordnance factories, which is generally about how much it costs Chusro Asvogel and his pared-to-the-bone-efficient operation to collect it off the battlefield. Furthermore, if you offer the stuff to one side and they don't like the price you're asking, they take a dim view of it when you set off to sell the stuff to the enemy. You're likely to find yourself arrested and your stock impounded, on a charge of supplying aid and comfort to the enemy. If you do manage to make a sale, it's a safe bet they'll pay you in scrip, not actual cash, which you'll end up having to discount at forty gulden in the stauraton, always assuming the Knights or the Sisters will touch it at all. So; if a big war happened, our best bet would be to go north to Permia or south to Blemya and stay there until it was all over, and wait and see if there was anything left to come back to.

All the more reason, then, to get as much of our sort of work as we could, as quickly as possible, and build up a nice reserve in the bank in Auxentia City to tide us over until it was safe to come out. But it's too hot and dry in Blemya and in Permia it rains all the damn time.

I went back to the Humility, where Gombryas was eating

a late breakfast: salt pork and fermented cabbage. He was in a good mood. "I managed to unload Theudebert's spine on my pal the bonemeal merchant," he said. "I got three hundred for it."

"His *spine?*" I don't know why I was surprised. "Well done," I said.

"He's going to have it mounted on a plain mahogany panel," Gombryas said with his mouth full. "Anyway, that's good, because now I can get the Symmachus kneecap and still have enough left to put something down on the Temrai scapular."

"I thought you said it's a fake."

He shrugged. "If it is, it's a good one. The point is to get good stuff for swapsies before the prices all go up."

"That's likely, is it?"

"Bound to be, if there's going to be a war."

"But if there's a war," I said, "heroes on both sides are certain to die, increasing supply at the expense of demand, driving prices down, so what you ought to be doing is selling now, at the top of the market, with a view to repurchasing once prices start to fall—"

"Oh, shut up," he said. "You don't know what you're talking about."

It's ten days from Holdeshar to Cheuda by road (up the Grand Military, then west on the New Trunk until it crosses the Southern Post, follow your nose and you're there) as opposed to four if you sail up the coast to Acris and head inland from there. But that would mean three days on a ship, and I loathe sea travel. So I put it to the heads of department and we voted on it: five to one in favour of going by sea. But it's my company, so we went by road.

At that time there weren't quite as many of us as there used to be. Daresh Asvogel had lured away some of my best men about a year earlier – I don't blame them; he was offering silly money – and we lost thirty to mountain fever during a spectacularly ill-judged operation in south-eastern Blemya. We were down from five hundred to about four hundred and twenty, and the sort of work we were doing and were likely to get didn't justify replacing the losses, as far as I could see. I made the decision, but it wasn't universally popular. Polycrates, who functions as my loyal opposition, reckoned that by downsizing we were putting ourselves out of the running for all the worthwhile contracts, and Lenseric, whose department (boots) had been more or less cut in half, complained that it was no longer possible for him to do his job . . . One good thing, though, was that it made moving about slightly easier. Four hundred and twenty men take up less space, on ships or on the road. As regards productivity and being able to get the work done in the time available, I hadn't actually noticed much difference, which shocked me, I must confess. Artax Asvogel always made fun of me for carrying passengers. Hateful to think he might have been right all along.

We were two days from the Cheuda border when we were practically run off the road by a column of horsemen, riding way too fast for the conditions. They slowed down just long enough to tell me that they were all that was left of the late king's army; the rebels had pulled off a spectacular pre-emptive attack, slaughtered the infantry in a riverbed, captured and executed the king and the entire government; the cavalry had managed to cut their way through, though it cost them 40 per cent losses, and they had absolutely no idea what they were going to do next, except that they'd be doing it somewhere else, a long way away, because the rebels had promised faithfully to crucify every regular soldier they managed to catch . . .

I felt sorry for the man who told me all this, but first things first. "What about my battlefield?" I said.

"Wouldn't if I were you," he replied. "Those bastards are out of control. They'll probably eat you."

"We've got a contract," I said. "I paid good money."

He looked at me. "Suit yourself," he said. "I wouldn't go back there for a million staurata."

That's not the sort of thing you want to hear. I reckoned I knew what he was talking about. You get it in some wars; rebellions, mostly, and civil wars, but it can break out anywhere. It's when the two sides are so thoroughly mad at each other that they forget they're human and kill everything that moves. I've seen it first-hand more than once, and it's a horrible thing.

Gombryas and Polycrates had seen it, too, so they knew what I was talking about. "Well," Polycrates said, "that's that, then. All that money wasted. We might as well go home."

"Are you kidding?" Olybrius said. "We can't afford to lose nineteen thousand; it'd break us. No, we hang about, wait till those lunatics have gone—"

"Really?" Polycrates was in one of his dialectic moods. "Wait where? For how long? Eating and drinking what? We're in the middle of fucking nowhere."

"So are they," I pointed out. "The rebels, I mean. Someone give me a map." Someone obliged. "All right," I said. "That cavalryman said something about a slaughter in a riverbed." I scanned the map, trying to think like a soldier. I've never been one, but I read a book about it once. "There," I said, pointing. "See these hills here, and then the river runs down into this valley? That'll be it. I'm guessing the king drew his line across here, which should've worked but for some reason they panicked and ran, and the only place for them to go would've been here, funnelled down into the river, no way out, and the rebels outflanked them here and here and—" I shrugged. "There you go," I said. "And the cavalry would've been out here on the flank waiting to encircle the rebels, and when everything started going wrong they'd have smashed through here, and then straight on down to the road."

I think Polycrates was impressed in spite of himself. "So what?" he said.

"So," I said, "in order to get in position to do all that without being seen, the rebels must've come over the mountains here or here. Which means they travelled light, three days' rations at the very most. True, if they wiped out the king's infantry they'll have inherited their supplies, but they're still a long way from home. They'll have been relying on capturing the baggage train in order to have something to eat on the way home. Long story short, they're in no position to hang about. Do the job, mutilate a few noble corpses, then straight back on the road again, that's all they'll have had time for. Also, they've just killed the king and his army. They'll want to get to the city as soon as possible and slaughter the bourgeoisie. You don't spend your wedding night in the cider house playing skittles with the boys."

Someone laughed at that, and I'd won the debate, though naturally Polycrates sulked and told everyone I was leading us into disaster. I told them we'd wait a day, which we could afford; if I was right about where the battle had taken place it would take us another day to get there, and I pointed out a ridge we could hide behind until we were sure the crazy rebels had gone. "It'll be fine," I told them. I even believed it myself, God help me.

*

A note in passing about war and killing.

Generally speaking, most people don't like to kill. I remember the first time I killed anything. It was a rabbit. My father and my brother and I were out hawking, and our second-best buzzard had caught a rabbit but neglected to kill it. My father took it away from him and handed it to me to pull its neck. I'd seen it done a few times; no big deal. Take the back legs in your left hand; right thumb under the chin, right forefinger on the back of the skull; pull with your left hand and push with your right until you feel something give; job done. So I did it, and I did it well. But I can't say I took to it. Almost an act of betrayal; there's life on one side and death on the other, and I was doing death's work for him, in spite of the fact that relatively soon he'd be coming for me, and I wouldn't like that at all – it didn't feel right, somehow, converting a living thing into inanimate matter, as though I'd been handed a bottle of fifty-year-old claret, opened it and poured it away. Mind you, we roasted the rabbit on a spit in camp that evening and it tasted better than any rabbit I'd eaten before or since, and I guess that was because we'd provided it for ourselves, by skill, patience and teamwork. I don't know; even now, every time I kill something or somebody I feel that sense of betrayal. But treachery has been a fundamental part of my life ever since I left home, so I'm starting to get used to it, the way a fish gets used to water. Anyway; Saloninus once said that the man who's tired of killing is tired of life, but it's something I could probably learn to live without, thanks all the same. And I think I can safely say that most people would agree with me.

Which is a problem for generals and commanders of armies. A few hundred years ago Carnufex the Irrigator commissioned some research. He had his spies go round the camp, buying the men drinks and helping them drink them, and they questioned the battle-hardened veterans who made up Carnufex's elite corps of archers, the backbone of his army, and found out that only one man in five ever made any attempt to aim at the enemy. The other 80 per cent simply loosed off their arrows in the general direction of the other side. Why? asked the spies. You're all cracking good shots or you'd never have made it into the corps. And it's a battle, for crying out loud. If you don't kill those bastards, they're going to kill you and your mates. Because, the archers replied, if we aimed we might hurt somebody.

By and large, in my experience, that proportion sounds about right. One man in five is sufficiently scared to want to get them before they get him, or has a personal reason for wanting to get even, or just likes cutting into people. Four men in five are normal, like you and me. They really don't want to be there, they don't want to hurt anyone; they just want it to be over. If they're trained soldiers they know their best chance is to stick together, which means doing what the officer tells them. They're happy to exercise skill and energy in the use of their shields. They'll block an attack against them or one of their pals, quick and fluent as lightning. Actually killing someone, though: very much the last resort, not something you do unless you're unlucky enough to find yourself toe-to-toe with one of the 20 per cent and there's nowhere to run. Which probably explains why there are survivors after battles, and the human race is still going after all these years.

But from time to time you get bad situations, and suddenly everything's different. Something happens and people get angry, and the proportions are reversed. Now it's 80 per cent who want to kill someone. That's a very different dynamic. I've

seen it a few times and I can't say I care for it very much. It's
not something you can predict, let alone orchestrate. Horrible
sad sights don't usually do it. I've often seen armies march into
one of their own villages after it's been torched by raiders and
all the people shot or cut down in the street; and all they do is
bitch about having to work burial detail, or nose about among
the ashes looking for food and items of value. And I've seen a
regiment of grown, rational men reduced to slavering fury at
the sight of a dead cat with an arrow in its neck. It's complicated, unpredictable, more or less impossible to understand,
but it happens, and if you're in my line of work you have to
be able to recognise it and allow for it. That's part of my job.
Usually I'm quite good at it.

I'd read the map perfectly, and everything had happened the
way I'd said it had. We found the dead infantry in the riverbed,
about seven thousand of them. I'd say about a third of them
drowned; the rest were slaughtered trying to get out of the
water. There were a few rebels among the dead, easily recognised on account of their cheap, trashy equipment, but it had
clearly been an unusually one-sided fight. I'm guessing (and
this is only a guess) that that was when the bad stuff set in. It
helps the berserk fury if killing people is easy, and relatively
safe. By the looks of it, the king's infantry were mostly stuck
in the deep, clinging mud on either side of the river. The rebel
archers had dry standing about ten yards away, and that was
when about half of the soldiers died. Then the survivors managed to drag themselves free and make a run for it. They didn't
get far, and they didn't put up much of a fight. The whole thing
was probably over in the time it takes to heat up a pot of soup.

Massacres in rivers and riverbeds are an unmitigated

nuisance. The men who'd been slaughtered running away were no bother, but the ones in the river were hard, exhausting, mucky work. We hauled them out with ropes, which meant that some poor fool who believed in leading by example had to wade out and attach the ropes, and by the time he got back on solid ground he was so tired he could barely stand. Then we had a choice: we could stack the corpses on the carts, mud-caked and stinking, and take them away for cleaning, processing and burial, or we could use this convenient river for washing off the muck, and risk the bad guys coming back.

If I hadn't been so horribly tired I'd have done the sensible thing. But I was worn out and filthier than I'd ever been in my entire life, so I said, the hell with it, wash them off here and have done with it; and while we're at it, let's get a fire going and burn the dry ones, before it starts raining again. That led to a certain level of complaints, which I dealt with by shouting, which I never do. Then we all set to work; stripping the bodies, washing off the clothes and armour and footwear, trying to think how we were going to pack all the wet stuff so it wouldn't go mouldy in transit—

They were on us before we knew it. Looking back, I think what we'd done wrong was light the fires. Some people have strong views about cremation. I'd assumed the king was going to win easily so I hadn't bothered checking to see if the rebels had cultural taboos. I still don't know if that was the reason, and I don't honestly give a damn. Maybe they were just so thoroughly worked up that they didn't need a reason, or even an excuse.

I was stacking bodies ready for stripping with a man called Habanek. I can't say I knew him very well. He was one of Gombryas's crew originally, but he and Gombryas didn't get on so he transferred to my department, corpse management as some joker decided to call it and the name stuck. I was working with him because I needed someone to grab the feet while I lifted the head, and he was nearest. I remember, we'd just lifted a body and suddenly he dropped his end. I looked at him and he had this funny expression on his face, as though he'd just remembered something. Then he fell over, on top of the corpse, and I saw an arrow between his shoulder blades.

Then there was a lot of yelling, and I looked round and saw three or four of our boys down, and I thought, oh. If I'd been trained as a soldier, which was always the idea before the unfortunate thing with my brother, I imagine I'd have known what to do and coped rather better than I did. But instead I stood there for a good four seconds, trying to figure out what was happening; and then an arrow came unpleasantly close, so near I heard it as well as saw it, and that was enough to be going on with. I was still holding some poor dead bastard's head. I dropped it and ran, with a vague idea of getting back to the carts. But then I saw the carts and there seemed to be some sort of battle going on over there, men fighting each other, and only an idiot runs *towards* the fighting. At which point it dawned on me that we were surrounded, and it said in the book I read that once you've been surrounded it's all over.

Then I felt like someone had rabbit-punched me, but there wasn't anyone there. I realised I'd been struck by an arrow; not head-on, an arrow that had hit something else and been deflected or bounced off. For some reason, that had the effect of waking me up out of my head-full-of-fog stupidity. I remembered that I was in charge, God help me, and I had to do something about this mess before every friend I had on earth got killed.

Do something. What, for crying out loud? I looked round again and I'd more or less decided to run to the carts and see what was going on over there when this man suddenly appeared – I caught a glimpse of him at the very edge of my vision and swung round to face him, and he lashed out at me with a billhook.

A few notes on the billhook as a weapon. In the right circumstances, it's very effective. It's one of the few hand-held weapons that can cut through plate armour, if you're standing just right and have the time and the room for a full-blooded two-hand swing. But we live in an imperfect world, crowded and noisy and jostling. Billhooks were designed for cutting branches and saplings, which tend to hold still, something that people rarely do. If you're looking for a single key word to sum up the billhook as an instrument of mayhem, I think I'd have to go for *slow*.

Which doesn't mean that the head of this particular example wasn't travelling at a hell of a lick. But it also had a long way to go – a wide arc, its radius (is that the word I want?) being the length of its eight-foot shaft – and that gave me time to step into the swing. That meant I got the shaft on the ball of my shoulder; it hurt like fun but it didn't break anything, and it meant I was a good three feet away from the sharp bit, and the man who was operating the hook had all the principles of leverage against him. I grabbed the shaft of the hook in both hands, brought my knee up between his legs and took the hook away from him as he wasted precious seconds dealing with the pain. While he was preoccupied I poked him in the mouth with the butt end, hard enough to smash his teeth. If he's still alive I imagine he's thinking hard thoughts about me, on account of only being able to eat porridge and sops in milk, but that's unjust. It would have been almost as quick and easy and safe for me to reverse the hook and slit his throat on the draw-stroke, but for some reason I didn't. Probably it was because killing him would've taken me a whole second longer and a certain degree of effort, but I like to think it's because I was the better man, more enlightened and humane.

Anyway, I left him sprawling on the ground hurting and legged it, back towards the carts. My shoulder wasn't right where I'd been hit, I realised, and that was a nuisance. In a fight, you need to be 100 per cent, in full command of your faculties, or else your options can be fatally limited. But I wasn't planning on doing any more fighting if I could help it. Old Carrhasio, who looks after jewellery, gold teeth and small items of value, always reckons that fighting is the best fun you can have, bar nothing. I don't think so. I've done a lot of it over the years, and as far as I'm concerned, you can have it.

There was indeed a fight going on at the carts; amazingly, it looked like we were winning it. I saw Olybrius, a fat man who'd led a relatively sheltered life, standing on a cart apparently yelling orders with a sword in his hand, while his crew and Gombryas's arrows-and-armour boys were having a brisk set-to with a bunch of men in muddy, ragged clothes. There were weapons involved, swords and spears for our lads, axes and hooks for the opposition; that worked for us, because the fight was a squash in between the carts, great for stabbing, not so good for swinging; also, the bad guys' hearts didn't seem to be in it any more, as though the urge to kill someone was on the wane and they'd woken up and realised they were in a horrible mess with nothing to gain from it. My boys, by contrast, were scared stiff, at that point in the terror cycle where the only thing that makes you feel safe is the other man being too dead to hurt you.

Splendid, I thought. Then Gombryas popped his head up and saw me and yelled my name. I ran towards him, tripped over a dead man, got up, recognised him as one of ours, felt terrible and scrambled as far as the cart Gombryas had just cleared of hostiles.

"Arseholes," Gombryas said, though whether he was describing the enemy or using the term as a mere exclamation I couldn't judge. "We're all right," he added. "We're fine."

One way of looking at it, I suppose. I turned back and looked at what was going on behind me. I couldn't see the archers who'd shot Habanek, but there were a few hundred men with hooks and spears between us and the river. They didn't seem to be doing anything, just standing there. I looked back the other way, at the carts, and there didn't seem to be anyone there I didn't know by sight, so I guessed we'd won and the enemy were either dead or running away. Then Polycrates joined us, followed by Olybrius. "They got Papinian," he said.

That didn't make sense. "They took him?"

"No, he's dead."

Oh, I thought; and at that point it dawned on me that this was one of those times when a lot of things change, and you can't go back to how it was before. I hate those moments. You'd think that after a while you get used to stuff like that, but it always messes me up.

"Why are they just standing there?" Polycrates said.

Good question. "With any luck they've had enough," I said. "Let's get behind the carts and try and look like we're more bother than we're worth."

So we did that, and I guess it must've worked. The enemy – for want of a better word – stood and glared at us for a bit, then turned round and trudged away, like labourers at knocking-off time who don't think they're getting paid enough. We waited till they'd splashed across the river ands were out of sight. Then we set about the dismal job of counting each other.

As I think I mentioned just now, my side of the business is corpse management. I do it because nobody else wants to, and it's got to be done, and I'm the boss. Hauling dead bodies around is, therefore, my daily grind, my day at the office, my bread and butter. I can't say I relish the work. Dead men are heavy, for one thing, and I suspect I'm laying the foundations of an old age racked with back trouble, except my chances of having an old age are negligible. Also, corpses aren't that easy to manipulate; they don't come with handles or carrying straps, and the centre of gravity of the dead human body is in a confoundedly awkward place. When I'm working with a partner who knows his business, I can get into a rhythm, but if the man on the other end is clumsy or having a bad day, I can guarantee pulled muscles by sunset, and this is a business where you don't get time off to heal. Whenever I try and shove corpse management off on to someone else, they tell me I should keep at it because I'm so good at it, and this actually happens to be true. Even so.

When it's your friends you're hauling about, it's different. No, that's not quite accurate. It's the same, but with heartache as well as backache. You turn a body over and see the face, someone you recognise, someone you know, but suddenly and wantonly changed from a person into a thing. For instance, I found my pal Bemel curled up in a ball with his head sliced into. Bemel and I worked really well together; no need for one-two-three-lift, we read each other's minds, and he was stronger than me and knew how to shift the weight so it was equitably shared, from each according to his ability. He was one of those slow-but-sure men, calm, smart, never tired, never frayed or bad-tempered. It took him a long time to get a joke, so you'd say something and he'd laugh five minutes later, but his default expression was a sort of whimsical grin, laughing at you and with you all the time. When we picked him up, the man I was working with dropped him, and his poor abused head flopped and hit a stone, and the way he didn't react made my heart stop for a moment. I don't think it's right that dead people should look just like living ones. They ought to shatter like pottery or deflate like a shirt taken off and dropped on the floor. It's needlessly hurtful to remind the rest of us of what's just been lost for ever, and if ever I come into the presence of the living God, I've half a mind to register a formal complaint.

We stacked them and counted them: eighty-six.

"I don't like saying this," said Gombryas, "but – well, you know. They wouldn't mind. If you asked them they'd say, go on, help yourselves."

It took me a moment to figure out what he meant. "No," I said.

"No offence, but that's just being stupid," Gombryas said. "They were in the trade. They'd understand."

He had a point. Eighty-six pairs of boots, eighty-six shirts, coats, pairs of trousers; not to mention rings, earrings, cash money, penknives, belt buckles, good-luck-charms – waste not, want not, and after all, it's what we do. "Fine," I said. "But be quick about it, for God's sake. I really don't want to be caught here if those lunatics decide to come back."

So we robbed our dead friends and threw their boots and socks in with what we'd salvaged from the dead strangers; then we built the usual pyre and lit the usual bonfire, which stank like nothing else on earth, the way they do. I was leaning against the tailgate of a cart, too tired to think, when Polycrates came up and stood next to me, too close as always. He has no inkling whatsoever of the concept of personal space.

"Not your fault," he said.

"Yes it was," I said. "I said we should strip them here rather than take them somewhere else."

"If we'd done that they'd most likely have hit us on the road," Polycrates said. "Which would've been worse."

I hadn't thought of that. And Polycrates doesn't even like me. "Thanks," I said.

"That's all right. You're not to blame. It just happened."

We buried Papinian. He was Echmen, and they're funny about cremation. He was our doctor, and he saved my life several times, stitching me up when I'd got myself cut, pulling me round from a bad dose of fever. He didn't like me very much. We put his surgical kit and his medicine chest in the grave with him, so he'd have them in the next world. I have no idea whether he believed in all that stuff, but most Echmen do, so we decided to play it safe. If he wasn't a believer he'd have been insulted that we mistook him for one. You never could win with Papinian.

Once we were on the road, that usually blissful hiatus when there's no more heavy lifting to do for a while and you can just sit on the cart box and enjoy having your spine jolted up into your brain, I thought about my work, my life's work and my life. The conclusions I reached were not pleasant. On the other hand, I argued, what else is there I can do? Besides, I had responsibilities. That, of course, was my customary line of argument; I'm responsible for all of them, my fellow lost sheep. Without me, they'd starve or get killed. But I'd just been responsible – the repetition is intentional – for eighty-six of them getting killed, for no reason, to nobody's benefit, so maybe that line of reasoning was starting to fray at the cuffs. I'd always assumed that as soon as something went badly wrong (such as nearly a quarter of us getting slaughtered because of my error of judgement) Polycrates or Papinian or one of the other perennial pains-in-the-arse would blame me for it, whip up their colleagues into a froth of resentful hatred and have me chucked out – the decision made for me, which is what's always happened in my life. Parting is so much easier when you're asked to leave. But that hadn't happened. Not my fault, Polycrates (of all people) assured me, on the one occasion when it really was my fault. I'm not to blame. It just happened. The hell with Polycrates, who only exists to make my life as awkward as possible. Even so.

Still, he wasn't the only one. While we were clearing up the mess, nobody had yelled at me or even scowled hatefully at me. Instead, they'd asked me what needed doing, and got on and done it. They'd turned a disaster into the usual routine, right down to peeling off dead men's trousers and slinging them in the back of the appropriate cart. Somehow, without knowing it, I'd created a way of life for these people, rather like the Invincible Sun creating heaven and earth and the birds of the air and the beasts of the field, and then us to manage it all. Bizarre thought. Like those hills in Antecyrene; they stand up out of a flat plain and you can see them for miles, and it's only when you start digging that you discover they aren't hills at all, they're cities – the sites of cities, and every time some bastard comes along and burns them to the ground, the survivors build a new city on top of the old one, until the mound is big enough to be mistaken for a hill; until the last time, when there's nobody left to rebuild, and then a thousand years goes by and nobody remembers there was ever anything there at all.

Like I said, miserable thoughts and depressing conclusions, briefly summarised as: it's a stupid way to live, but you're stuck with it.

We decided to take the short way back: the Eastern Extension as far as the coast, then get on horrible ships as far as Beloisa or Boc Bohec, where we could sell what little we'd managed to get and mitigate our losses to some small degree. After that—

"All depends," Olybrius said, leaning on the rail and gazing at the loathsome sea, "on whether there's going to be a war." He was still nursing a few souvenirs of the fight, a broken rib and a sliced-open thigh, and no Papinian to bind and sew him back together. "If it all blows up, we want to be a long way away. If not, we need to make some money fast. How are the finances looking, by the way?"

I'd already done the sums. "Not wonderful," I said. "I figure we'll have made a ten thousand loss on the job, which more or less wipes out what we made in the Leerwald. So if we want to take on another job any time soon, we're going to have to borrow the stake money."

"Who's going to lend us anything, if there's a war coming?" asked Lenseric.

"Quite," I said. "Actually, I was thinking of asking Sersy Asvogel."

"You're kidding," Gombryas said. "That arsehole."

"I was thinking," I said, "about asking if he'd like to buy us out."

That didn't go down well. "Are you out of your mind?" Polycrates said. "Us work for that bastard? Never in a million years."

"I didn't say work for him," I replied. "I said, buy us out. Meaning, he takes over the men and the kit and the goodwill, and each of us gets cash in hand and walks away. Meaning, goes off and does something else."

"What goodwill?" Polycrates said. "Everybody hates us."

"It's worth money to the Asvogel boys to stop us undercutting them on lucrative contracts," I said. "For years they've been waiting for us to go bust and somehow we've never quite managed it. Sersy Asvogel isn't the most patient man in the world. I reckon I could gouge him for a modest stake each."

"You're mad," Olybrius said. "First, the Asvogels wouldn't piss on us if we were on fire. Second, if there's a war coming, they won't be looking to expand. They'll have to ride it out and hope, same as everybody else."

"I said I was thinking about it," I said. "It was just an idea, that's all."

"Fuck your stupid ideas," Polycrates said firmly. "We stick together."

I didn't smile, and there was nobody to congratulate me on how clever I'd been, but at least I'd got the result I'd been looking for. I find that if I suggest to people the thing they want to do, they'll refuse to do it, because it's me making the suggestion. "If you say so," I said. "I don't reckon we've been particularly good for each other lately, but maybe I'm wrong. So, do we look for another war before the big one starts?"

"Of course we do," Polycrates said. "We've got a living to earn."

2

I don't believe in an afterlife, but if I did it would probably be horribly like Simocat in summer. If you know Simocat, that ought to tell you how wicked I've been and how guilty I feel about it.

It's one of those places where people run aground. You arrive there with something to sell, you end up selling it at a loss and find you haven't got enough money to get out of town. Or you arrive there as merchandise; after Auxentia City, Simocat is the biggest slave market in the West. Only they don't call it that. Simocat is nominally a Mezentine protectorate and slavery is strictly illegal in Mezentia, because it disadvantages the free worker. So Simocat is the regional centre of the indentures market, which is a completely different thing, except in practice.

Gombryas doesn't like going there, because he was indentured once. He was only a kid at the time. His father couldn't pay the rent on their miserable six acres of rock and mud, so he sold Gombryas for a seven-year stretch. The seven years quickly turned into fourteen by the subtle alchemy of the indenture system – the small print gives the master the right to charge the servant for board, lodging, clothing and tools, which can easily be made to add up to more than the servant's services are worth; the longer you serve, the more you owe your master, and the only way you can pay off the debt is by longer service – until Gombryas, being Gombryas, smashed his master's face in with a rake and ran away, and look what a success he's made of his life ever since. Anyway, that's why Gombryas doesn't care all that much for Simocat. I, by contrast, don't like it because it's a dump. Just because we both arrive at the same conclusion from different angles doesn't mean we can't both be right.

I'd brought us to Simocat rather than Scona or Boc precisely because it's Mezentine turf. If a war did break out, there was a 60 per cent chance the Mezentines would stay neutral, at least until the Sashan started winning major battles, so the risk of three dozen Sashan warships suddenly rearing up out of the morning mist was acceptably low. Albeit for the wrong reason, I'd chosen well. There were buyers in town when we got there, and they were paying silly money. I asked around and it turned out that they were Sashan agents, their mission being to scoop up all available military materiel on the open market, not because the Sashan wanted it but to stop anyone else getting it. So we sold out in no time flat and actually ended up making a profit.

"See?" Polycrates crowed at me, after I'd taken the buyers' letters of credit to the Knights and cashed them. "And you were all for giving up and running away."

"I was wrong," I conceded nobly. "Maybe we should stay in this business after all."

"At this rate we'd be mad not to," he said. "You want to get out there and start bidding on a few jobs. There's no knowing how long prices are going to stay this good."

That's another thing they do in Simocat: they broker wars. It's a new development, and one I'm not exactly wild about, but I suspect it's the direction the industry is going in. The idea is that instead of going to the governments direct and pitching for the rights to their latest spot of unpleasantness, you do all your bidding through an agent, entrusted by both parties with arranging all that sort of thing. It sounds crazy but it's catching on. The advantage to the government is that the agent pays them a fixed sum up front, and there's nothing like cash in hand when you're planning and financing a military adventure. It's not so great for us contractors, since naturally the agent slaps on his percentage, which comes out of our pockets. The only good thing about it from our point of view is that we're dealing with one guy, a professional, as opposed to two civil servants. That removes the horrible risk of only buying one end of a war, which is of course worse than useless. Anyhow, most of the leading agents resolved to set up shop in Simocat, which gives you an idea of what sort of place it is, among other things.

Another chunk of proof that Simocat is horrible: my pal Erriman lives there, by choice.

Erriman and I go way back. He was the third son of my father's steward, and we more or less grew up together. Then, when I was fourteen, Erriman's dad got found out. My father had him tortured for a week, trying to get him to say what he'd done with all the money he'd stolen, but the interrogator (a freelance: he came with excellent references) made a pig's ear of the job and Erriman's dad died on the rack before the interrogator had got round to asking him any pertinent questions. It turned out that Erriman's two elder brothers had squirrelled the money away in a Mezentine bank, where we couldn't touch it; neither, after our lawyers had worked their magic, could they, and for all I know it's still there. Erriman and his brothers, meanwhile, had legged it to Sueck, where my second cousin once removed the Margrave took them in, on account of some blazing row he'd had with my father. They did well for themselves in Sueck until Erriman fell out with his brothers over some trifling sum that couldn't be accounted for and left town in a hurry. After a few adventures he settled in Simocat, where he has a talon in a number of pies: indentures, commodities, shipping. He's probably not the saintliest man who ever drew breath, but we've always got on quite well, and over the years he's done me a few valuable favours at practically cost.

"For fuck's sake," he said, as his doorkeeper showed me in. "You again."

I smiled and sat down without being asked. Erriman scowled at me and poured me a drink. "All right," he said. "What do you want this time?"

I shrugged. "Nothing much," I said. "How's business?"

He handed me the drink and sat down. "Terrible," he said. "You do realise there's going to be a war."

"Maybe," I said. "Maybe not."

"There's going to be a war," Erriman said, "and I'm going to get wiped out. Everything I've worked so hard for all these years, gone, just like that."

"Surely not," I said. "You're way too smart to let yourself get burned by something as trifling as a war."

He glowered at me. "Don't you believe it," he said. "Anyhow, what are you doing in Simocat? You hate the place."

"Business."

The drink, incidentally, was Echmen peach wine. A bottle of it costs slightly more than a five-man fishing boat, complete with mast, rigging and nets. I don't like it much myself, but my father thought it was wonderful. That made me wonder if Erriman had been expecting me.

"You must be laughing right now," he said. "What with the Sashan paying crazy prices."

I nodded. "We actually made some money the other day," I said. "A strange experience. It's left me feeling rather light-headed."

He frowned. All his gestures and expressions are on a large scale, as if he was making sure they could see him in the gallery. "Tell you what," he said. "How much do you want for that outfit of yours? Cash in hand."

"Seriously?"

"Seriously."

"Not for sale," I told him. "Besides, I wouldn't sell it to you. We're pals. You never did me any harm."

"I'll give you forty thousand for it."

A curious feeling, like being punched in the solar plexus when you're almost too drunk to stand. "Forty thousand staurata?"

"No, forty thousand toenail clippings. Well?"

I was trying to do the mental arithmetic, to see where that figure had come from, but my mind slipped off the numbers like your feet off ice. "Don't be silly," I said. "There's a war coming, remember? It's going to put all of us out of business."

"Every disaster is an opportunity in disguise," Erriman said. "What'll happen is, all the competition will go bust and I'll end up with a monopoly. Forty grand. Think about it."

"I'll have a stab at it," I said. "Though that sort of figure's a bit big for my imagination."

"Push harder." He grinned. "Hey, this is a bit of a turn-up, isn't it? Me offering you money. Wasn't that way when we were kids."

Erriman always did know how to get at me. When we were kids, he had a whole armoury of pinches and armlocks and Echmen burns, which he was happy to teach me by example. He's six months older than me, and he's always been taller and stronger. When I was seven, I paid him three gulden to be my friend. On balance it was a good investment, but he's never let me forget it.

"Times change," I said. "I guess the better man won."

That made him laugh. "I guess," he said. "So, what was it you wanted? You did want something, didn't you?"

"Just to say hello."

He looked at me for a moment, then decided I was a puzzle that wasn't worth solving. "Forty thousand staurata," he said. "And I'll undertake not to fire any of your pals for at least eighteen months." He smiled at me. "You're not going to get a better offer."

"No," I said. "Probably not."

I was reminded, as I walked back to the Perfect Grace in Sheep Street, of a story I once heard, about a man who lost all his money gambling and ended up owing a fortune to a loan shark. To pay off the debt – he was an honourable man – he sold his body to his worst enemy, with a delivery date set a month ahead. Then he took the money and gambled with it and won a small fortune, but when he tried to buy himself back, his enemy refused. I can't remember what happened in the end, but what sticks in my mind is the poor devil's dilemma – more money than he's ever had in his life, and his death ineluctably scheduled in a few weeks' time. Forty thousand staurata. That, I told myself, is a great deal of money.

But not quite as much as I had put by in the Knights in Auxentia City. Put the two pots together, however, and suddenly the arithmetic comes alive – the big score, the mathematical definition of *enough*, all my dreams come true and all my troubles over. And it wouldn't be betrayal as such. Erriman was a reasonably honourable man, according to his lights; if he said he'd keep my pals on, he'd do it. It made sense, after all. He'd need men who knew the business. And maybe he'd be sensible enough not to put them in a situation where they were in danger of being slaughtered like fatstock in autumn.

The Perfect Grace is a dump, but I rather like it. Before it was an inn it was a temple, a very long time ago (it's a very old building) and nobody knows which religion built it or who was worshipped there. There's still the base of a high altar in what's now the buttery, and what used to be the nave has a small but rather lovely dome. These days it's black with smoke, but if you crane your neck till it hurts, you can still make out flights of mosaic angels adoring some god or other who was knocked through to make a skylight about three hundred years ago. The chancel is now the public bar, and my favourite room is in the south transept, with a view over the cloisters, which are now stables. It's a nice place to stay provided you don't eat the food, drink the beer or sleep in the beds. I bribed one of the cooks to make me a pot of green tea and sat in one of the semi-derelict side chapels, trying very hard not to think about Erriman's offer.

Erriman, of course, knows who I really am. Not many people do. That knowledge is worth a great deal of money, and

Erriman could've sold me to my father or my sister at any point over the last twenty years, but so far he hasn't, which says a lot about him. I assume it's because nobody's ever offered him the right price or tickled the soles of his feet with a red-hot iron; or maybe he's saving me up as a sort of pension or rainy-day fund, I don't know. In his position, I'd have cashed me in years ago, but the interesting fact remains, he hasn't, not yet. I've tried and failed to account for it many times, and all I can come up with is the fact that, a long time ago, I paid him three gulden to be my pal. It's either that or my having killed my brother and broken my father's heart. Erriman doesn't like my family very much. Neither do I. It's the main thing we have in common.

I was drinking my tea (the bowl was dirty and there was grease floating on the top) when Polycrates came in. "I've been looking for you," he said.

"Tea?"

He looked at me as though I'd offered to pee in his ear. "Someone brought this for you," he said.

This proved to be a letter. A tiny letter. Someone had taken the flyleaf of a very expensive book, written on it, then folded it up very small into a parcel and sealed it with a very expensive Mezentine intaglio seal. I looked at it, and felt like someone had pushed his arm down my throat.

"Who brought this, did you say?"

"No idea. Some kid."

Why would he lie? "Thanks," I said.

"Aren't you going to read it?"

"Yes," I said. "As soon as you've gone."

He scowled at me. "Who did you go and see?"

"An old friend."

"You haven't got any friends."

"An old acquaintance."

"Business?"

Forty thousand staurata. "No," I said.

"Oh, right. Some doll."

"No. Yes. Look, will you please go away? I want to read my letter."

He gave me his extra-special scowl and left. I waited, listening to his footsteps in the corridor. Then I broke the seal.

Hello, Florian. Bet you weren't expecting to hear from me.

Many years ago, when I was a kid, my brother and I were out riding in the forest. Let's race, he said. Too dangerous, I said. He laughed and charged off, so naturally I followed, and I'd just pulled ahead of him, flying like a bird, when I rode into a low branch. One moment I was absolutely concentrated on the job in hand and the path ahead; the next moment I was lying on my back, and everything hurt so much I couldn't breathe.

A bit like that.

Hello, Florian, the letter said. *Bet you weren't expecting to hear from me.*

The thing is, I'm in a hell of a mess. It's all my own fault, needless to say. I wanted to be happy so I tried to be clever. Silly me.

I know we haven't exactly seen eye to eye for a while. To be perfectly honest, I wouldn't turn to you if there was anyone else. But there isn't.

Help me and we'll call it quits; how does that sound? I can't ever forgive you. I don't suppose you can ever forgive yourself. But you wanted to go on living after – well, that stuff – and I found out yesterday that I want to go on living too, after the stupid thing I did. Actually, for the first time I think I understood you. We both did a bad thing. But letting justice take its course or falling on your sword; no, not yet. What's that line from

Saloninus? The beating of the heart, the action of the lungs are a useful prevarication, keeping all options open.

Help me, Florian. Please.

The man who's carrying this letter knows all the details. Come quickly.

Fan.

My name isn't Florian. It hasn't been for a long time.

Fan, however, is short for Phantis, my sister, who married the Archduke-Elector Sighvat IV of Stachel-Nagelfest two years after I left home. It was a dynastic marriage, needless to say, but also by all accounts a love match. Fan was sixteen, Sighvat was twenty-one; they'd met at the wedding of Gotprand of Entzwei, a distant cousin of both of them, the year before. By all accounts they fell in love, and just for once love and politics coincided perfectly. It was Fan who persuaded Sighvat (who I never met) to put a seventy-thousand staurata bounty on my head, dead or alive – ten thousand more than my father was offering, which tells you something about how Dad and Fan got on. By all accounts, he gave it to her as a birthday present, and she was thrilled. Everything I've ever heard about Sighvat suggests that he was an unusually competent and enlightened ruler; he didn't start wars or waste money on building pyramids, and by and large people liked him. It's common knowledge that he was devoted to my sister, and they'd recently had their first kid. How old would he be, now? About six months—

Fan was a nice kid when we were growing up, and everybody adored her, me included. She had a bit of a temper, but only when she didn't get her own way; and her own way and what everyone else wanted seemed to twine together perfectly, like the plies of a rope, so that was all right. There was only one real incident, when Fan was nine, and we never found out the truth of it. The nursemaid claimed that Fan had been impossibly rude to her, for which she'd got a smack; so Fan deliberately poured lamp oil on the maid's hair and set light to it. But it turned out that the maid was a bit soft in the head and in the habit of cutting herself and talking to angels, and Fan said it had been an accident and everything the maid said about her was just lies, and under those circumstances, who would you believe? Anyway, Fan was devoted to my brother Scynthius, the one I killed, and he doted on her. All one big happy family, apart from me.

I realised something was missing, and went looking for Polycrates. I found him in the outhouse in the stable yard, squatting on the privy.

"Who brought that letter?" I asked him.

"Piss off, Saevus," he yelled at me, tugging his pants up to his knees, which was as far as they'd go in that position. "What the fuck do you think you're—?"

"The letter," I said. "The one you gave me just now. Who brought it?"

"What?"

"The letter." I realised I had my hands round his throat. Not sure how they got there. I removed them. Polycrates stared at me. "What's the matter with you?" he said.

"I need to know who brought that letter."

He made an effort and dragged his mind back to the point at issue. "I don't know," he said. "Some kid."

"What kid?"

"A kid." He paused and tried to think. "This kid came into the inn and asked for the landlord. He was busy, so one of the tapsters came and the kid gave him the letter. I was in the parlour, and the tapster called me and said something like, this is for your boss. And I thought it might be important, so I looked for you and found you. That's it. Look, do you mind not standing over me like that when I'm—?"

"Did you see him? The child."

"Yes, out of the corner of my eye. I wasn't paying attention."

"Boy or girl? How old?"

"Boy. Twelvish."

"Which tapster?"

"I don't know, do I?"

I realised that, on balance, strangling Polycrates wasn't going to help much, so I left him and ran into the inn. There was somebody, a woman, fooling about doing something. "I want the tapster who got given a letter," I said.

She looked at me. "What?" she said.

It was like when you wake up out of a dream, and you lie there helplessly as the dream fades away and you lose it all, irrecoverable for ever. "One of the tapsters was in here earlier, and some boy came in and gave him a letter to give to me. I need to talk to him."

She shrugged. "I don't know anything about that."

There are times when I wonder why the Invincible Sun put it into our heads to invent money. It's caused a lot of trouble over the years and the most you can say about it is that it's a mixed blessing. But there are times when it comes in very handy. "If you find me the tapster who got handed the letter," I said, "I'll give you five gulden."

"Wait there," she said, and vanished. I sat down on a bench next to the door, trying not to think about how far the boy might have gone. Some time later, the woman came back with a man. She held out her hand and I put a five-gulden piece in it. She made herself scarce. "The boy," I said.

"What about him?" said the tapster.

"I need to find him."

The tapster frowned. "Never seen him before in my life."

I took a stauraton out of my pocket and put it on the table. "Like I said," I told him, "I need to find him."

The tapster looked at the coin. It'd take him six months to earn that, including tips and stealing from the pantry. "Really?"

"Really."

He pursed his lips. I guess he felt like a goatherd out in the wilderness who meets God, and suddenly he's not a goatherd any more: he's a prophet, whether he likes it or not. "I'll find him for you."

"You can do that?"

"No sweat." He took another look at the coin, then charged out into the sunlight.

I sat and read the letter, over and over again. Her handwriting had hardly changed at all. She'd always written like that, quite beautifully, almost like calligraphy. She was proud of it, because it was something she could do really well, even though she didn't have to. When you looked at a line she'd written you couldn't help smiling, no matter what the words actually said. That's Fan for you. Charm and grace swarm all around her, like crows.

The stupid thing I did. Justice taking its course. Another thing about Fan that everybody loved; when she broke the rules, which wasn't often, she came straight out with it, no lies, no excuses. I broke a window. I saw a honeycake in the pantry and I ate it. I spilled ink on the carpet in the library. No lies; no guilt. The thing has been done, so let's deal with it and move on. I can't remember her ever trying to cover up or pretend or shift the blame on to someone else, or ever getting punished, because she'd been honest and owned up. You don't feel guilty if you know you can do no wrong.

The stupid thing I did – what, for crying out loud? I had to stay put, because if I wandered off, the tapster wouldn't know where to find me when he came back with the messenger, if he came back with the messenger. Therefore, at a moment when my life was burning down all around me, I was stuck in a small room in the Perfect Grace like a prisoner locked in his cell during an earthquake.

Gombryas came to find me. "Where the hell have you been? I've been looking for you."

"Why?"

"Didn't know where you were." He peered at me. "What?"

"Nothing to do with you or anyone else," I told him. "Look, I'm waiting for somebody, all right?"

"Suit yourself," he said, and left.

A lot of time passed, and I felt every second of it, and then the tapster came back with a boy. Money changed hands, and the boy told me he'd been paid to deliver the letter. Who by? This man, he said, but he wasn't allowed to say who. That's all right, I told him, the letter was for me, I'm giving you permission. That didn't work, but ten gulden did. He's hurt bad, the boy said, but I can take you to him.

I think Papinian could have saved him; the messenger, I mean. Echmen doctors know so much more than we do about infected wounds, and in this case the damage wasn't all that bad. The arrow had gone straight through, an ordinary military bodkin by the look of it, no blades or cutting edges to carve a big hole and bleed you out. It was the infection that was killing him, and like I said, the Echmen can do wonders. But Papinian was dead. Shame about that.

He was a big man, fat, balding; he told me he was my sister's hairdresser. He'd been with her for years, ever since she first came to Stachel-Nagelfest; she'd come to trust him, he told me, and of course he'd do anything for her, anything at all. So when she told him to take the letter he'd said yes, of course, and though he didn't know it'd mean getting shot at, he didn't regret it one bit – then he grabbed my hand. "Am I going to die?" he asked me.

He was lying on a heap of straw in a livery yard. I don't imagine he was supposed to be there, but it was the sort of place where nobody seems to mind. "I'm not a doctor," I said. "But I've sent for one. He'll be here any moment now."

"She told me to tell you," he said. "You've got to help her. She's in deadly danger."

"What has she done?"

My sister, the hairdresser told me, had murdered her husband, so that she and her lover could seize the throne. The idea was that she would be regent for her baby son and her lover would marry her and be her prince-consort, and true love would overcome all obstacles and everything would be fine. But it hadn't worked out at all well. A bunch of stuffy old noblemen on the Council had been very negative about the whole thing, and some cousin of her late husband had stirred up the city mob, and there had been riots and one thing and another, and she'd had to barricade herself in the palace; then her lover had betrayed her and gone to the Council, telling them he'd had nothing to do with it and accusing her of all sorts of dreadful things; she and a few of her servants had managed to slip out the back way, leaving the baby behind, and make a run for it; and now she was all alone with those horrible people looking everywhere for her—

"Where?"

He grabbed my sleeve and pulled me close, like a drunk pawing at a barmaid. "The Pearl monastery at Cure Hardy," he whispered in my ear. "Do you know where that is?"

"I can find it."

"You've got to be quick," he said. "There's men looking for her. One of them recognised me; that's how I got hurt. You've got to help her. There's nobody else."

I removed him gently from my ear and tried to keep him calm till the doctor came. Nothing anyone can do, the doctor told me, and charged me half a gulden.

Simocat is that sort of town. If you're careless enough to leave your stable door unlocked, you can't expect any sympathy if strangers crawl in and die all over your straw. I left him and went back to the Perfect Grace. Polycrates and Gombryas were in the parlour, playing knucklebones.

"Where's the Pearl monastery?" I asked.

Gombryas shrugged, but Polycrates said, "Crossroads of the Eastern Extension and the Great Southern, about twelve miles from here. Why?"

"No reason," I told him. "Look, can either of you lend me ten staurata? I need some walking-around money and I've spent all mine."

Gombryas gave me a startled look and turned out his pockets: two staurata, thirty gulden. Under normal circumstances, Polycrates wouldn't lend money to God, not without a mortgage. "I've only got six," he said.

"That'll do. Thanks."

I bought a horse for fifty gulden, which is the sort of price my father pays for a good hunter. As it turned out, I got a bargain. Second-best horse I ever rode, and that's saying something. It got me to the Pearl in less than three hours; decent roads all the way, admittedly, but even so, not bad at all.

I'd worried about finding the place; silly me. The Pearl is fairly conspicuous. Trust my sister to hide somewhere that glows in the dark.

Really, it does. At some point, someone with rather more money than taste faced the front elevation with those stones they have in Permia, speckled like a hen's egg, that soak up sunlight during the day and look like iron in the forge at night. Presumably it was an act of piety and he reckoned he'd be let off his sins as a result, though I'd be inclined to doubt it. If there really is an Invincible Sun, I don't suppose he cares for show-offs. The most you can say for the result is that it makes the place easy to find, though since it's right next to a busy military road, I don't think there was a problem to start with.

It took a long time for the porter to appear. He opened a panel and scowled at me. "Don't kick the door," he said.

"Sorry," I said. "Look, I need to see my sister."

"Come to the wrong place, then, haven't you? This is a monastery."

"My sister's staying here. She's a guest."

He looked at me. "What's your name?"

"Saevus Corax." I hesitated. "Florian met' Einai."

"That's two names." He sighed. "Wait there."

I waited. A groom came out from the stables and took the horse. I sat on a bench in the porch, wishing I'd brought something to read.

I was miles away when the door opened. A monk came out. "Saevus Corax," he said.

"That's me."

"This way."

While I was waiting, I'd occupied my mind with questions to which I had no answers; among which was, why would Fan come here, and why would they let her in? I figured the first part had something to do with the Great Southern Road, which runs in a more or less straight line from Permia, across the isthmus and down the west coast of the Friendly Sea as far as Boc Bohec. If you were running away from Stachel, and you reckoned you could outrun the people chasing you because you had really good horses, the obvious thing to do would be to take the Imperial Post road, which would bring you out on the Great Southern at Spaher. Nine days, riding flat out; you'd need to change horses, of course, but there are way stations every fifteen miles on the Great Southern, and if you were fast enough you'd outrun the news of what you'd done, so your credentials would still be good. In that case, why stop at the Pearl? Why not keep right on to Boc, where you could get a ship to Scona, and from there across the sea to Sashan or Antecyrene and all points east? Pointless speculation; I realised, after I'd figured it all out, that I hadn't come up with anything informative or useful. That's just me, though. I prefer to run, but when I can't do that I think instead.

"Hell of a place you've got here," I said to the monk, as he led me through a cloister garden past a fountain in the middle of a carp pond.

He smiled at me. "We like it," he said.

He led me up a few steps into a colonnaded portico. There was a big bronze double door, about twelve feet high; beyond that, a high-roofed lobby with black and white marble tiles and niches in the walls for statues. Impressive if you like that sort of thing. "Wait here," the monk said. "I'll let them know you've arrived."

So many times over the years I've owed my life to my ear for pronouns. Them. There wasn't anything to sit on, so I stood, occupying my mind with valuation and inventory. You could make a fortune plundering this place, but only if you had cranes and really big, sturdy carts. My guess was that it had been built within the last thirty years, very recent for a monastery, and nobody had got around to cluttering it with the small, portable items of value that you generally find in such establishments.

A side door opened and a man came out; tall man, lean, soldier written all over him. He was wearing a velvet gambeson (that's the padded vest that goes under armour); it looked expensive but there were creases and rust stains. He stopped and looked at me. "You're Florian," he said.

"That's right."

"I'm going to search you for weapons."

I'd left in a hurry so I didn't have any, apart from my last-chance knife, which of course he didn't find. "Is it true?" I asked him, while he had his hand between my buttocks. "Did she really murder the Elector?"

"Yes," he said. "All right, you're clean. Put your trousers back on and follow me."

That was Fan all right. She'd send a letter begging me for help, but she wouldn't let me get close to her until I'd been thoroughly frisked. I followed him through a door, which opened into a panelled corridor which led to a small formal herb garden, with a fountain in the middle and a stone bench beside it. On the bench there was a woman, with her back to me. Facing me were two of the biggest men I'd ever seen in my life. They were bald and so densely tattooed they were practically illuminated, which made them Hus, from far away across the Friendly Sea. Practically nobody in the West speaks Hus, but I'm given to understand that if you can read the tattoos they tell you everything you need to know about the wearer – where he was born, what family he belongs to, whether he prefers his eggs poached or scrambled. As soon as I came through the doorway they sprang forward, grabbed my arms and lifted me off my feet: an original approach, but effective.

"Put him down," Fan said. "He's my brother." They put me down. "Out, all of you," she said. They left.

She turned round. "Hello, Florian," she said.

I looked at her. I hadn't seen her for eighteen years.

People – various aunts, friends of the family – always reckoned that Fan and I took after our mother, whereas my brothers, Scaphio and Scynthius, were just like Dad. I never saw it myself. For a start, Fan was a pretty child: round-faced, snub-nosed, great big eyes. Lots of pretty children grow up ordinary or downright plain, like me, but Fan had improved with age, in the same way that the Bohec starts as a dribble between two rocks and grows into a river a mile wide.

(A few notes on the subject of beauty. I'm not sure I approve of it. Mostly, I guess, because it offends my notions of justice. Beauty is probably the most unfair advantage you can have, after all. It amazes me that the idealists who crucify people in the name of social justice have never declared war on beauty, which is totally and irredeemably unjust. Wealth and power can be acquired, theoretically by anybody given the right circumstances. Beauty, on the other hand, is something you can't attain to, no matter how hard you try. Instead, it's broadcast recklessly by hopelessly irresponsible angels; a bit like turning

up at the door of an asylum for the criminally deranged and
handing out weapons. Worse than that; the lunatics in the
asylum were already unbalanced when they arrived. Beauty,
on the other hand, grows with you, distorting you from childhood, as though you'd been born possessed by a demon. And if
I sound like I'm being a bit negative about beauty, it's probably
because I grew up with my sister, and was able to see at first
hand what it can do to a person. There's that story, isn't there,
about the foxes who stole a baby princess and replaced her with
a fox cub, enchanted to look human; and only the little blind
page boy knew the princess was a fox, because he couldn't see
but he could smell.)

"Hello, Fan," I said. "My, how you've grown. Did you really
kill your husband?"

"Don't be nasty to me, Florian. I couldn't bear it."

I caught myself doing the geometry. One long stride forward, left hand to her chin, right hand to the back of her skull,
a quick, sharp lift and twist. I've never actually done one of
those, but I've seen it done maybe half a dozen times, and as
far as I can tell there's nothing to it. Eighteen years of perse-
cution, resolved with one simple intervention. Papinian could
pop back a dislocated arm or shoulder in the blink of an eye,
and all that pain and helplessness was suddenly over, leaving
you wondering what all the fuss had been about.

"Answer the question," I said. "Did you kill him or
didn't you?"

"Yes," she said. "Did you kill Scynthius?"

"Yes," I said. "But that was an accident."

"Was it?"

I looked at her, and she looked at me. There's all sorts of
legends about truth. In Echmen they'll tell you about magic

mirrors that reflect what people really are, not what they pretend to be. In Permia they reckon that if you taste the blood of a dragon, you hear the truth when people tell you lies. In Aelia somewhere there's supposed to be this building within whose walls it's physically impossible to tell a lie. "Yes," I said. "He wanted to fence. I was tired out, but he kept on and on at me and I gave in. His stupid coach had told him it wasn't proper training unless he fenced against sharps, so he had a foil and I had a real sword. He was trying out some new move he'd been learning and he got it slightly wrong. If I hadn't been so tired, maybe I could've pulled the lunge, but it all happened so quickly, I don't know. And then he was lying there dead and I was standing over him with a bloody sword in my hand, and this voice in my head said, Dad's not going to believe you. So I ran. That's it. That's the truth."

"But you did kill him."

"Yes. No. It was an accident. Accident killed him. I'm no more to blame than the sword."

She looked at me. Great big beautiful eyes that didn't like me much. "Dad says you did it on purpose," she said.

"He wasn't there. I was."

"I wish I could believe you." Great big beautiful eyes filled with sadness. "You can't imagine what it was like, Florian. Scynthius dead and you gone, and Dad in floods of tears. I'd never seen him cry before, did you know that? It was horrible. Noise and shouting and dogs barking and men crashing round the house looking for you, under the beds and in the cupboards. I get this recurring dream about it, only it's not you they're searching for, it's me, and when they find me they drag me out by my hair, and I keep telling them, it wasn't me, I didn't do it, and they don't believe me."

"It was an accident," I told her.

"Yes, well, you would say that, wouldn't you?"

"Because it's true."

"Let's not talk about it any more, all right?" She screwed her eyes tight shut, then opened them again. "I want to believe you, really I do, but it's not as simple as that, is it? You can't make yourself believe, if you don't really."

"And you don't want to."

"I don't know what I want," she said, turning away as though looking at me was like walking through cobwebs and getting gossamer caught in her hair. "I want it never to have happened, and then my life wouldn't be all screwed up, and everything would be the way it should've been. But I can't have that, can I? You know what, Florian? Just seeing you makes my skin crawl."

"Fine," I said. "I'll go."

"No." That made me turn my head and look at her. In some country the far side of Echmen there are monks who spend their entire lives training to draw a sword as fast as it can possibly be done. The moment they perceive a threat, the sword flies from the scabbard, and the draw is itself a cut. There's no time to think, it's pure trained reaction. "No, you can't leave me like this. I'm scared, Florian. They're hunting me. If they catch me, I'll be killed."

Fan never told lies when she was a kid. She never had to. "Why the hell should I help you?" I said. "All my adult life you've been persecuting me. If they kill you, I'll be rid of you at last. You have no idea how wonderful that would be."

"You don't mean that. You wouldn't have come here if you meant it."

"No," I said, "I don't suppose I would. You know me, Fan, always kidding around."

She threw her arms around me and hugged me. She always was stronger than she looked. When she was twelve she punched one of the footmen in the stomach – he'd accidentally spilt apple sauce on her party frock – and he went down like a felled tree. I could feel the muscles of her arms tighten against me as she applied pressure. There are snakes in Blemya that kill their prey by wrapping themselves around it and squeezing. "You won't let them hurt me, Florian. Promise."

"Of course," I said. I wanted her to let go, but she didn't. She smelled of jasmine and lamp oil scented with rosewater. Boxers have this trick: if you're getting beaten to a pulp by the other guy, grab hold of him and hug him until you've got your breath back. "I'll do anything I can to help. I promise."

She let go. "I knew you would," she said. "You always protected me, when we were kids."

I couldn't remember anything like that, but I was prepared to take her word for it, so long as she stopped touching me. "You're my sister," I said. "All right, let's get down to business. Why here?"

She sat down on the bench, hands demurely folded in her lap. "We're patrons of the abbey, Siggy and me," she said. Sighvat was her late husband. "We gave them a lot of money. They don't know about Siggy yet."

"Ah. So you don't plan on staying here."

"No, of course not. As soon as they hear about what happened, they'll betray me. I can't trust anybody but you; that's why you've got to help me."

"What about Dad? Surely—"

"He won't help me." So much pain in four monosyllables. "He says I'm not his daughter any more."

See what I mean about my family? "Screw him, then," I

said. "There are plenty of places we can go," I said. "I'm good at not being found. I've had the practice."

"We need to go now," she said. "You were ever such a long time getting here, I was worried sick. There are men looking for me. Not soldiers. Hired thugs."

"Bounty hunters."

"Is that what they're called?" She gave me a sad smile. "I don't know about that sort of thing. Siggy always dealt with it, when we were looking for you."

"Bounty hunters," I said. "How do you know?"

Clearly she didn't like talking about it, and I felt bad for making her uncomfortable. "They nearly caught us," she said, "at Lescoval. So my maid Altzi and three of the servants dashed off in the carriage, pretending to be me, while the rest of us hid in a cellar. The only one who managed to get away and come back was poor Euchryas. My hairdresser. You met him."

I nodded. "And he could tell they were bounty hunters and not soldiers."

"That's what he said. They weren't wearing uniforms; they all looked different. They did horrible things to poor Altzi and the men, trying to make them say where I was, but they wouldn't."

I shrugged. "It doesn't actually make a great deal of difference," I said. "Soldiers are better trained but the privateers try harder. The key thing is to keep moving and look like you're somebody else. That's always worked for me."

"I knew you'd know what to do," she said, and I swatted away the buzzing thoughts of irony. "How soon can we leave? I don't want to stay here a moment longer than I absolutely have to. Florian, I'm scared. They'll take me back and I'll be crucified."

"Just a minute," I said. "I need to think. It may be that you'd be better off waiting here while I go and get my friends. I don't want us to get caught out on the road with just me and your three bruisers. At least here there's places to hide, and presumably the abbot wouldn't just hand you over to a bunch of goons—"

"No," she said quickly. "Don't leave me. I couldn't bear it."

"Fine," I said. "In that case, leave your people here and you come with me. So long as we don't hang about, we can get to Simocat in three hours. Don't tell them where we're going. What you don't know can't be beaten out of you. Are you all right with that?"

"Anything you say," she said.

Half of me wanted to wrap her in velvet, the other half of me wanted to stamp on her. I don't know if it's family or women or just people I've abused who've abused me; or maybe I simply lack basic social skills that everybody else takes for granted, I don't know. To be honest, I've never had the luxury of sticking around in one place long enough to find out. "Fine," I said. "I've got a fast horse; you can have that. Have you got anything decent I can ride?"

She thought for a moment. "Not really," she said. "We were in the carriage, but we lost that. There's a chestnut mare that Aristaeus usually rides. He's my chamberlain. You met him just now."

"It'll be fine," I said. "If we get separated, just head for Simocat and find an inn called the Perfect Grace. Ask for a man called Gombryas and tell him who you are. He'll look after you."

"Gombryas," she repeated. "All right. I'll need a few minutes to get ready."

"Are you kidding? I thought you wanted to go right now."

She scowled at me. "Fine," I said. "I'll wait for you outside the gate."

A monk told me how to find the stables. There was nobody about, so I saddled up my expensive grey and a huge brown monster with staring eyes which I took to be the chamberlain's mare. She headbutted me three times before I could get the bit in her mouth. Then a groom came up and asked me what the hell I thought I was doing, and I was just about to explain with my fist when Fan appeared. "Why are you taking so long?" she demanded. "I've been waiting for you for hours."

She was wearing a blood-red riding cape, velvet, with seed pearls at the cuffs and a hood. The hood would make her invisible. Mind you, I don't suppose the Archduchess of Stachel-Nagelfest is allowed to have any scruffy old clothes, by law. In her hand was a bag, also velvet but an incongruous blue. It looked heavy for its size, and I figured I didn't need to ask what was in it.

The groom had made himself scarce as soon as she showed up. "Let's go if we're going," I said.

Fan always was a good horsewoman. When we were kids she had a skewbald gelding, Bunny or some such name, to which she was devoted. One day Scynthius, Fan and I were out riding and Scynthius decided he wanted to race (he always wanted to race; it gave him an opportunity to win). We were up on top of the hill, where it's flat. I wasn't really in the mood, so when the other two pulled ahead I didn't make a great effort to catch them up, but Fan was determined, and she managed to sneak in front and stay ahead, which drove Scynthius wild. The hilltop road is about two miles long, and then you go zigzagging down through the woods. Fan was still just about in front when they reached the end of the road, and she reckoned she'd won, but as she eased up Scynthius darted past her and went hell for leather down the forest track. Fan wasn't having that; she hurtled after him, trying to force past him. The track was really the bed of a stream, stony and rutted and twisting backwards and forwards, not the sort of surface you want to go fast on. Scynthius didn't give a damn. He was a superb rider and he knew it, and Dad would tease him for days if he let his sister beat him. I saw them charge off out of sight into the trees and slowed to a walk. Kids, I thought to myself.

A third of the way down the track, I found Fan. She was trapped under the horse, which had broken its leg. I yelled for Scynthius, but by that point he was long gone, making sure of his victory; he wouldn't stop till he reached the stable yard. I managed to drag Fan out from under the horse, with her yelling at me the whole time not to hurt Bunny. I don't think she realised she'd broken her ankle until I told her. I got her up on my horse and we walked back. She kept on and on at me; Bunny will be all right, won't he? I knew precisely what my father would say. Scynthius and I would be to blame, for letting her race. You're men, you should've known better, how could you have been so stupid, and that's a perfectly good horse you two have cost me. Then Scynthius would be forgiven, because he'd done it in the name of Victory, and in a day or so it'd all be my fault. Yes, I told her, Bunny will be just fine, because if I'd told her the truth she'd have had hysterics, and I had to get her safely home.

My father sent a couple of men up the hill to kill the horse and bring it back on a cart. A few days later, my father and I were both taken ill. We had violent stomach cramps and couldn't stop vomiting. Scynthius and Scaphio were fine. Whatever it was, it passed in a day or so, and when I was allowed out of bed I went and found Fan.

"What was it?" I said. "Mushrooms?"

"I don't know what you're talking about."

"I bet it was mushrooms," I said. "I remember when we were out in Long Meadow playing rovers, and you asked me what those mushrooms were, and I told you, they're dangerous, don't touch them. So you went back and picked some."

"You're mad," she said. "Why would I do a horrid thing like that?"

"Good question," I said. "I can see why you wanted to kill Dad, because he had your stupid horse put down. But why me? All I did was pull you out and take you home."

"You lied to me," she said. "You told me he'd be fine, and you knew it wasn't true."

"I told you what you wanted to hear," I said. "That's what I always do."

Anyone who knows me will be aware of my need to have the last word. It's pathetic, but it's practically a point of honour. With Fan, though, you might as well not bother. You can have the last word till you're blue in the face, but you'll still lose. She just looks at you, and you know she's won. Anyway, the point of the story is, she's a very good horsewoman and she likes to go fast.

Fine by me. We made it to Simocat in no time flat and got there with her fresh as a daisy, me feeling like I'd just been threshed. When we got to the Perfect Grace, it was on fire.

Simocat is one of those places where fires are very bad news. The streets are narrow, the buildings are high and all the roofs are thatched. Luckily, the owner of the house opposite had plenty of manpower, being in the indentures business; he'd ordered out his entire stock in trade, and they were scrambling about with ladders and long hooks, pulling the thatch off all the roofs in the street. I guess if you live somewhere like that, you know what to do and have all the necessary kit stockpiled where you can get at it in a hurry. I grabbed a man with a bucket and made him hold still. "What happened?"

He shook his head. "Don't ask me," he said. "These men showed up, with knives and swords, looking for someone. Then some of the people staying at the inn started fighting back, so they ran for it. I think they set it on fire to keep from being followed."

I had that cold feeling. "Anybody hurt?"

"Don't know, I didn't see it."

I let him go, then got Fan down off her horse. "They've been here looking for you," I said.

She gave me a horrified look. "Don't let them get me," she said. "You promised."

Why is it that I keep getting forced to think when my head's spinning? I grabbed the reins out of her hand and tied them to a rail. "This way," I said.

3

I don't have many friends in Simocat, and Rudingaria isn't one
of them. But a few years back I did her a good turn, something
she's resented ever since. She keeps a cathouse in Joinery Row.
Anybody in that line of business in Simocat needs to have very
good security. Rudingaria called me all the names under the
sun but I said it wouldn't be for long. "And don't offer her a
job," I said.

"Why not? Actually, she's not bad."

"She's my sister."

Fan wasn't at all happy about being left but I couldn't help
that. I sprinted back to the Perfect Grace just in time to see
the roof cave in.

Gombryas was standing outside, watching with a tragic
expression on his face. I didn't need to ask. His tin chest had
been in his room, with all his latest acquisitions in it. "What
happened?" I asked him.

"They were looking for you," he said. "They got hold
of Polycrates and started smacking him around. Then

Olybrius and I came running when we heard him yell, and Carrhasio, and there was a bit of a scrap. I think Carrhasio killed one of them; you know what he's like. Then more of the lads showed up and they knew they were outnumbered, so they smashed a lamp on the floor and the whole place went up. They darted out the back way and we legged it into the yard."

"Any of our lot hurt?"

He shook his head.

"It's a steel box," I told him. "It'll be fine."

He didn't believe me, but I think he was grateful to me for trying to cheer him up.

Eventually, he managed to pull his box out of the rubble with one of the long hooks, and I left him tenderly checking its contents. Polycrates had a split lip and two swollen eyes, for which he blamed me. Olybrius said, "What the fuck have you got us into this time?"

"That's what friends are for," I told him, which didn't impress him terribly much. But killing somebody had put Carrhasio in a thumping good mood, so I asked him to take charge of getting the lads together. "What's going on?" he wanted to know. "Who were those goons?"

"People who want to hurt my sister," I said.

"You haven't got a sister. Have you?"

"Yes and no," I said. "Well, don't just stand there."

It didn't take us very long to get back on the road. "Where are we going?" Polycrates wanted to know. "I didn't know we'd got another job."

"We haven't," I said. "And we're going to Beniel to see an old friend of mine."

"Why?"

"Because I say so," I said, and left him hating the back of my head.

Fan was where I'd left her, hooded and mysterious and as inconspicuous as a volcano, sitting on a barrel holding the reins of the horses. "This is very bad," I said. "Apparently the bounty hunters know I'm your brother. Nobody knows that."

"We need to get out of here," she said. "They'll come back. We've got to go *now*."

"You're right. Why didn't I think of that?"

That got me a scowl. "Florian—"

"Please don't call me that," I said, "not where anyone can hear you. Which reminds me. How long have you known that Saevus Corax is me?"

"What? Oh, not long. Look, we can't just stand around here; we've got to *go*."

"We're going," I said, "trust me. So, apart from you, who else knows?"

"Oh, Siggy, naturally. I imagine he told the men he paid to find you. No, wait," she added, frowning. "No, I don't think so. I think he died before he got round to doing that."

"Not Siggy, then. Who else?"

"Don't keep on at me. I can't think." She closed her eyes, the way kids do. "Well, the woman who told me, obviously. And anyone else who was in the room at the time."

"Such as?"

"I don't know, do I? My maids, courtiers, the Mezentine ambassador, anybody at all. That's what it's like at home, there's always loads of people standing around."

"What woman?"

"I don't know. Some woman." She summoned up every ounce of determination and ransacked her memory. "A thin woman," she said. "Tall and thin-faced woman in a creased red dress. There was mud on the hem. Siggy gave her a thousand staurata."

Hopeless. "Fine," I said. "In other words, we have no idea who we're up against. But that's all right. How much money have you got?"

She looked at me. "Me? Nothing."

"The big squashy bag?"

"That's my personal stuff."

"Valuable personal stuff."

"Everything I own is *valuable*," she said. "Naturally. But right now it's all I've got in the whole world, and you're not going to steal it."

No, I thought, not immediately. "Then we'll have to manage without, I suppose," I said. "Right, I'd better introduce you to my people. Try and be polite if you possibly can."

"Don't tell them who I am," she said. "If they know, they'll betray me to the thugs. You haven't told them, have you?"

It was that how-could-you-be-so-stupid voice I knew so well from my childhood. "No," I said. "But I'm going to."

"You *can't*. Florian—"

"Saevus," I said. "We talked about that, remember?"

When we got back to what was left of the Grace, Carrhasio was in model-of-military-efficiency mode, pointing in various directions and shouting at people. I bypassed him and looked round for Gombryas, who was busy with his tin box. The fire had burned through the straps, so he was having to do the best he could with string. "This," I said, "is a very important person. We're taking her to a safe place. Got that?"

He looked at me. "You what?" he said.

"She's going to pay us a lot of money."

"Fair enough." Then he grinned. "Polycrates is all right with that, is he?"

"He'll be fine," I said.

"You haven't told him yet, then."

"He'll be fine," I said. "When you see Carrhasio, tell him she'll be riding in the third wagon with me, and I'll want him and three others. Tell him they should be prepared to fight to the death, if needs be."

Gombryas nodded. "He'll like that. How much money did you say we're getting?"

"Lots."

"Ah."

I think that deep down, under all the bluster and attitude, Polycrates is basically shy. Particularly with women, or at least women he isn't paying by the hour for the pleasure of their company. "How much will you bet me," I said to him, "that I haven't got a sister?"

He looked at Fan. All that was visible under the hood was her nose. "This her?"

"Yup. We're taking her somewhere safe."

"Says who? If it's going to be dangerous—"

"There'll be money," I said.

"How much?"

"Forty thousand staurata."

It wasn't a figure I'd just plucked out of the air. But I realised I'd made the decision, having given it careful thought for at least twenty seconds. Not a hard decision to make. If I was going to get Fan safe, it followed that I'd have to do something about my people as well. If they were Erriman's men, not mine, nobody would have any reason to hurt them. As it turned out, forty thousand was a good figure. Polycrates evidently thought so, anyway.

"Fair enough," he said. "Where are we going?"

"Somewhere," I told him. "Be a pal and tell Olybrius and the others, will you?"

You may have gathered by now that I like to keep on top of things. My whole life is basically driving wolves to market; everything not doing exactly what I tell it is a threat, and I daren't take my eye off anything for a second. I managed to find time to scribble a note to Erriman; I accepted his offer, but I needed the boys for one last thing, so he'd have to wait a short while for delivery. I gave the note and a gulder to one of the potboys, and off he ran, taking ten years of my life with him. It's not every day you sell your friends, but I couldn't spare the time to mark the significant moment. I ticked it off my mental to-do list and put it out of my mind.

Or tried to. As the wagons rattled out of the North Gate – I reckoned we'd take the Northern Ancillary as far as Deudabec, then head off cross-country – I couldn't help reflecting on what my life as Saevus Corax had come to. Eighty thousand staurata in the Knights in Auxentia City; that was something. Two major wars averted; but now there was definitely going to be a war, everybody said so, which took all the fun out of that. Five hundred men fed, clothed and provided with gainful employment; no, I wasn't buying that. Without me, who knows what they might have achieved: happy homes, families, useful and profitable lives in other fields of endeavour. Quite probably they'd remember the day I sold them to Erriman as the turning point, when things finally started to get better. Be honest, I told myself; what you've achieved over the last ten years is still being alive ten years later, plus eighty thousand staurata in a bank. Bearing in mind what you were up against, not so dusty, after all.

She sat next to me in the cart, frozen stiff with distaste, only the very tip of her nose showing under the red velvet hood. "Where are we going?" she said.

"A place I know," I said. "You won't have heard of it, and you don't know where it is."

"Where are we going, Florian?"

I sighed. "Dis Hexapaton," I said.

"Thank you. Why there?"

"A friend of mine owes me a favour."

"What happens when we get there?"

"If we're lucky, nothing."

She made that disapproving noise she was so good at when we were kids. "Just for once, give me a proper answer. You think you're being clever but really you're just being tiresome."

I forgave her for that. Years of being the pampered darling of an archduke had clearly left her under the misapprehension that information is something you just give away, like tossing handfuls of pennies to the mob. Straight answers to direct questions; some people don't know they're born. "If we're very lucky," I said, "we'll be able to stay with my friend until I've had a chance to figure out who's after you and how much they know about me. If I know that, I can decide where's the safest place for you to go."

"I don't follow."

I found a tiny scrap of patience I didn't know I had, tucked inside the lining of my soul. "I've got a few things put aside for emergencies," I said. "Places I can go, people who are under an obligation to help me, stuff like that. Some people who know me know where some of these things are. So the idea is, I catch hold of whoever's chasing you and hit him in the same place over and over again with a shovel handle until he tells me everything he knows about me. Which is, by extension, everything his bosses know about me. Then I'll have some idea of what's safe and what isn't. For various technical reasons," I went on, "this is a course of action best undertaken at Dis Hexapaton. That's why we're going there."

I couldn't see her face because of the hood but I knew exactly which expression she was favouring me with. "That's how you live your life, is it? That's pathetic."

"What can I say? I'm a victim of circumstances."

She sighed. "Was it worth it?" she said. "Really? It seems to me that ever since you killed Scynthius, you haven't really had a life. All you've done is run away and hide. Where's the point in that? You haven't had any benefit out of being alive; you've just existed, like a hunted animal. And think of all the people you've hurt along the way. People have died, Florian. And for what? Really, what's the point?"

I allowed myself a few seconds before I answered. "It's obvious, surely. I knew I had to keep going, because one day my sister the fairy princess would need me, to save her from the consequences of her actions."

"Now you're just being spiteful," she said. "That's sad."

Sometimes the last word isn't worth having.

Dis Hexapaton isn't the sort of place anybody goes to on purpose. People go past it on the way to somewhere else, or find themselves stuck there because a wheel comes off or a horse dies, or the rain finally stops and the mist clears, and the small huddle of buildings you'd headed for because there was nowhere else to go turns out to be Dis Hexapaton. How my old pal Cynisca ended up there I have no idea, but I don't imagine it was active choice.

I first met Cynisca in a bar, many years ago. She'd just been stabbed in the neck by a temporary friend, a disagreement about the fee for services rendered. There was this woman lying on the floor squirting blood, and nobody seemed inclined to do anything about it. For some reason I dropped to my knees and clapped my hand over the hole, and kept it there until someone fetched Gombryas, who fetched Papinian. It turned out that the man who'd stabbed her was the local boss of everything, and saving the woman's life might be construed as a criticism of his behaviour. He took it that way, certainly, and things were rather fraught for a while, until Carrhasio split his head like a log. We left town under something of a cloud, taking Cynisca with us. She got better thanks to Papinian, and on a whim I gave her five staurata. Three years later I ran across her in Shau Bohec, running the biggest brothel in town and married to the mayor. I got my money back and we parted on good terms. Later I heard that the mayor had been executed for corruption and Cynisca had sold up and moved to some place in the middle of nowhere called Dis Hexapaton. I found it eventually on a very old map, and memorised the location for future reference, and now there we were.

"What the hell is this place?" Fan said loudly. "There's nothing here."

Not strictly true. There was a short street of about a dozen houses on either side of a rutted track. The ruts told me that heavy carts went up and down there regularly. Heavy carts meant bulk transport; not agricultural produce, because the Hexa valley is marginal sheep country. The red mud rang a bell. Clever old Cynisca, I said to myself, and I jumped off the cart and went exploring.

An iron mine isn't a hard thing to find. First you stumble on a fast-flowing stream the colour of blood; you follow it upstream until you find a cluster of buildings and a fifteen-foot-high waterwheel, and there you are. I saw half a dozen men, filthy dirty, sprawling on the grass eating bread and cheese. "Where is she?" I asked.

One of the men pointed to one of the buildings. "Watch yourself," he said. "She's in a mood."

That told me I'd come to the right place. I headed for the building, which looked just like all the others, and banged on the door. A voice I recognised invited me to piss off, so I pushed the door open and went in.

"Oh, for fuck's sake," she said.

"Hello."

"You arsehole," Cynisca said. "You've got a nerve. Where's my money?"

I took that as a reference to the hundred staurata I'd borrowed from her the last time we'd met, which I guess I'd neglected to pay back. "Right here," I said. "Sorry it's been so long. You're looking great. How's business?"

"What do you want?"

"To give you your money, of course. Nice place you've got here."

"Interest," she said. "Eight years at five per cent."

"Of course," I said. "I make it a hundred and forty-nine staurata, six gulden."

She scowled at me, then shrugged. "Take your word for it," she said. "Hello, Saevus. Where is it, then?"

"In the cart," I said, "down in the street. I'll go back and fetch it, and then we can talk. How's that?"

"You want something."

"Yes," I said. "Back in a tick."

We had a whip-round back at the carts, which didn't make me very popular. "What the hell are we doing here?" Olybrius wanted to know.

"We're not stopping long," I told him. "You remember Cynisca, don't you?"

"That mad bitch. She's not here, is she?"

"She's mellowed," I told him. "These days, she's a pussycat."

Once I'd given Cynisca the money and she'd counted it, she thawed a bit. "I've been hearing things about you," she said. "Drink?"

"Why not? Nice things, I hope."

She poured something red and thick into a clay cup and handed it to me. "People are looking for you," she said. "Not a very nice class of person."

"Oh."

She shook her head. "One good thing about running a mine," she said, "there's always plenty of muscle about. They didn't like the look of my boys, and I told them I hadn't heard from you in years, and then they left."

"When was this?"

"Four days ago, maybe. One day's pretty much like another round here. Let's see, it was the day after we had the flood in Number Three shaft. I had most of the boys up here working the pump, which was just as well. Soon as they showed up, I thought, here comes trouble." She counted on her fingers. "Five days ago, because we got Number Three open again yesterday, and it was five days out of commission."

"Did they say why they wanted me?"

She shook her head. "No. Just, have you seen him; have you heard from him lately. There was about a dozen of them that I saw, but the lads reckoned there was more of them hanging back up in the lane."

Splendid, I thought. "Out of interest," I said, "why an iron mine? It's a bit out there for someone with your background."

She gave me that look. "I inherited it," she said. "Fair and square, from my husband."

"The mayor?"

"After him. Three years. Decent enough man in his way. He knew what he wanted and so did I. Then he got mountain fever, and I thought, the hell with it, if he could run this place, so can I." She shrugged. "It's better than work, at any rate. It's a good seam, and we can ship down the river on barges to Simocat. I reckon I'll stick it out another ten years and then go back to Beloisa. There's worse ways to live, trust me." She stopped, and gazed at me. "You didn't say what it was you wanted."

"A small favour," I said.

"No."

"A very small favour. I just need somewhere to park my sister for a day or so."

"Your *sister.*" Her eyebrows shot up. "Since when did you have a—?"

"Oh, I've had her for ages. Look, I'm in a bit of a hole and I need for her to be safe. Like you said, you've got the muscle. She's not the sweetest woman who ever lived but she doesn't eat much and if she annoys you, you can hit her. And you owe me."

She had a scarf round her neck, even though that fashion died out years ago. "Is this anything to do with nasty rough men looking for you?"

"Quite possibly."

She thought for a moment. "You've got more men than me," she said. "Why don't you look after her?"

"I need to be somewhere else. Only for a day or two."

"You're up to something."

"Me? God, no. Just trying to keep a step ahead of the wolves, same as usual."

"A week," she said. "And that's all. And she can sleep in one of the charcoal sheds."

"That'll be fun for her," I said. "I don't suppose she's ever slept in a charcoal shed before."

Fan wasn't happy. "You're leaving me here," she said. "In a mine."

"You don't have to go underground," I told her. "They're getting the guest quarters ready for you right now."

"But I don't know these people from a hole in the hedge," she said. "You can't just go waltzing off and dump me on a load of perfect strangers. How do you know I can trust them? The moment your back's turned, they'll sell me to the hired killers."

"Cynisca is one of my oldest and dearest friends," I said. "You'll like her, she's a doll."

For a moment I thought she was going to burst into tears. "Don't leave me here, Florian," she said. "I'm scared. You're all I've got left."

Just as well, I didn't say, that your bounty hunters never caught me. "Don't worry," I said. "I'll be back very soon and then everything'll be fine. Promise."

My fault. If you must have the last word, *promise* is a comprehensively stupid last word to choose. Force of habit, I guess.

I'm not a soldier, but I know soldiers the way maggots know sheep. Chances were that the people I was thinking very hard about weren't soldiers either, though some of them may have been, at some point.

Being a predator is all about empathy. A really good predator understands the mind, nature, motivations and mental processes of its prey. Now I've been prey for my entire adult life, thanks to Fan, and my dad, and I guess the reason why I'm still alive is that none of my hunters has ever been able to, or bothered to, get right inside my head and understand me, like a parent or a sibling or a lover. That's the main reason; a small but important subsidiary factor is that, when I have to, I can be a pretty good predator myself. After all, I've learned from the best, and hundreds of lives and thousands of staurata have been expended on my education.

The point being, apart from my colleagues and employees, nobody knew about Cynisca and me; not unless you went way back and interviewed the survivors at the village where I'd first met her. But someone – a predator – knew about her, and had sent goons. Really rather depressing, when you thought about it; the information must have come from one of my people. My friends, for want of a better word.

Still, not to worry about that, for now. Needless to say, nobody had a map. I don't suppose such a thing exists, for the same reason nobody's ever written a biography of the crazy old woman who sells wilted lavender at the stage door of the Gallery of Illustration. But I'd had a good look at the landscape, if you could call it that, on the way in, and I'd seen what I needed. So, presumably, had the goons. Oh well.

There was a gulley you had to go through on the way to the mine, unless you were prepared to take a three-mile detour and cross the blood-red river. The Invincible Sun crafted that gulley specifically so that one day it'd be the perfect place for an ambush. He narrowed one end so it could be blocked with a few big rocks or a fallen tree (and He caused a massive oak to grow in just the right spot, bless Him), and scattered the sides of the gully with boulders to hide behind, and scooped out a sort of hollow where you could hide two dozen men to charge out at the critical moment – He thought of everything, which I guess is no big deal if you're omniscient, and there it was, just lying around waiting to be used. I'm surprised they don't run out excursions from the military academy so the cadets can see what a really high-class ambush looks like.

We didn't set up there, naturally. Instead, we spent a cramped night huddling in a small clump of withies and brambles about a mile further on. There was no way to close the road, so we'd have to rely on perfect timing, and there was a very real risk that if we had archers on either side of the road we'd end up shooting each other, so we left the bows and arrows behind and made do with basic hand tools. Carrhasio was so angry with me, I'm surprised he didn't hit me.

"You're mad," he said. "A mile up the road, there's the perfect spot."

"Calm down," I told him. "Try and breathe."

"Yes, but—"

I looked at him and suddenly he got it. "Oh," he said. "Right. They've been this way once, so they'll be expecting—"

"Yup."

"And then when we don't hit them there, they'll figure there isn't going to be an ambush, so—"

"Yes."

He scowled. "I still think we should hit them back there. It's fucking perfect."

Carrhasio was a soldier for most of his life. I think it was twenty years before he made sergeant.

They walked into our trap about an hour before daybreak, when the sky was still dark blue and the rabbits were still skittering about on the verges. I stood up and we all yelled at once at the tops of our voices, and that was it. They knew they'd been had, and we didn't have to kill anybody at all. The clatter of falling weapons was music to my ears, like heavy rain after a six-week drought. I jumped up, glowing with the fierce joy of having been right for once, and waved my forces forward to take possession of our prey.

"Oh, for crying out loud," somebody said. "Saevus, you clown."

I knew that voice.

Most people judge by appearances, and look where it gets them. I tend to form my lightning-quick first impressions from how people sound. It's a stupid way to carry on, but at least voices convey some elements of useful information, which physical beauty or the lack thereof generally doesn't. From a person's voice you can get some sort of idea of where they're from, the circumstances of their upbringing and the basic elements of their personality. You'd be wrong, of course. For instance, this voice would lead you to believe that it belonged to an actress. The accent was upper class, but the purity of the diction had been carefully studied and acquired. It sounded younger than it actually was: an attractive voice, with a wide range of expression, but it put you on your guard. The presumption would be against believing a word it said.

"Stauracia?" I roared. "What the hell are you doing here?"

She and I go way back. We tend to blunder into each other at inconvenient moments, and convenient ones by appointment. She used to run a gang doing more or less what I do, only posing as poor friars devoted to the relief of suffering – properly speaking, she's Sister Stauracia, though if she ever took vows of poverty, chastity and obedience, they lasted slightly less time than it takes to fry an egg. She and her crew would go to the kings and generals I'd bought salvage rights from and ask for permission to tend the wounded and the dying; in practice, that meant looting everything worth having off battlefields I'd paid good money for, and if I objected she'd burst into tears and the king or general would have me and my boys run off with extreme prejudice for interfering with the angels of mercy. Thanks to various run-ins she's had with me, she discovered a natural talent for strategy and tactics and now mostly works as a commander of small units of special forces; I believe the technical term is condottiere, though I prefer the more colloquial word goon. Anyhow, she's about five years younger than me, and if I thought I could trust her not to sell my severed head to the highest bidder I'd be in love with her, but I'm not. She's probably the smartest human being I've ever met and I enjoy her company, even though it usually means circumstances of violence, betrayal, loss, pain and death. Still, you can't have everything.

I hadn't noticed her until she spoke because she was flanked by three enormous men in armour. She was wearing a simple grey nun's habit with a hood, which she now threw back. "You moron," she said. "People could've been hurt."

I grabbed her elbow and towed her away into the trees. "Let me guess," I said. "You're here for the archduchess."

"Yup." She glared at me. "Your sister. You know, the one who put the price on your head. The one who'll pay really big money to have you killed. The one who's made your life a misery ever since I've known you."

"Oh, that one." I scowled at her, but it was all bullshit. "Don't tell me, that's why you took the job."

Actually, that made complete sense. Stauracia's had several opportunities to turn me in to my loathsome relatives for ridiculous sums of money, and for some unaccountable reason she never has. Unaccountable as in there's no accounting for. "Yup," she said. "I thought I was doing you a favour. Actually, I am doing you a favour, but you're too stupid to realise."

"She's my sister."

She gave me a look in which compassion and contempt were perfectly alloyed, making (like copper and tin combined to make bronze) a substance entirely different from its components. "You fuckwit," she said.

"Yes."

She sighed. "Understood," she said. "Trouble is, I paid a lot of my own money to hire these idiots, and if I don't bring her in I'm going to be out five thousand staurata."

"Awkward," I said. "On the other hand, all I have to do is give the word and my boys will slaughter them like sheep."

"No they won't."

"No, I don't suppose they will. All right, here's the deal. My sister will hire you and your colleagues to protect her against the bad guys. How about that?"

"Don't be stupid. She hasn't got any money."

"A hundred thousand in jewellery. I'm guessing, but I don't imagine I'm far out."

She shook her head. "Here's my counter-offer. I'll break my word to my employers and take the loss on the five thousand and help you save your poisonous sister for free. Well?"

I made a show of thinking about it. "I could live with that," I said. "Thanks."

"Drop dead."

"No, really," I said. "Thanks."

She looked at me. That same unique alloy. Twice in the past we nearly made a go of it, but somehow it never happened. My fault. In spite of ferocious competition for the job, I'm still my own worst enemy.

Imagine if you will the first ever meeting between the two people you (for want of a better word) love most in the whole world. Naturally you'd want them to be friends, but clearly that wasn't going to happen. "I know her," Fan shrieked, as soon as she saw Stauracia. "Why isn't she chained up?"

Stauracia rolled her eyes. "Fine," she said. "I'm leaving."

Fan jumped up and stood behind me. "She came to see Siggy," she said, pointing. "Siggy didn't send for her, she asked to see him. She said she could deliver you, dead or alive, for three hundred thousand staurata."

I have to confess I found that mildly disturbing. "Bullshit," I said.

"It's true. Go on, ask her."

Stauracia gave me a scowl, her it's-all-your-fault special. "It wasn't like that."

"Really?" I said. "You went to see the archduke?"

I could see Stauracia was upset, but it was too late to unask the question. "I was broke," she said. "It was after the Sirupat thing. Obviously I didn't mean it."

"She meant it," Fan hissed over my shoulder. "The only reason we didn't take her up on it was that Siggy didn't have three hundred thousand at the time, and she wouldn't take less."

"All I wanted was a stake," Stauracia said, "to get myself set up again. I lost everything, because of you. So I thought, I'll gouge the archduke for fifty thousand down. Obviously I never intended to deliver." She looked straight at me, like an arrowhead on the string. "You do believe me, don't you?"

"Water under the bridge," I heard myself say. "Everything's changed since then. Now we're all on the same side."

"You arsehole," Stauracia said. "You don't believe me. After everything I've done for you."

"She never said anything about fifty thousand down," Fan said. "Just three hundred thousand, dead or alive."

"I was negotiating, you silly bitch. Obviously you don't lead off with your actual offer."

"Take it or leave it, she said. Siggy tried really hard to raise the money, but after Sirupat we were terribly hard up. Otherwise—"

"It doesn't matter," announced my raised voice. "And, yes, I believe both of you. You, naturally," (to Stauracia), "because I trust you with my life, and you because it's just the sort of thing she'd do if she needed money quickly. Really, it's no big deal. Really."

Things went downhill from there. I'm one of those people who'd far rather have a blazing row that clears the air than a fortnight of sulks and point scoring, which is probably why I'd never make a good general. Stauracia, by contrast, understands the value of the long game, and she's good at it. Give her guerrilla warfare over a pitched battle any time, and ninety-nine out of a hundred professors of strategy would agree with her. Fan, of course, recognised that she was in an almost unassailable defensive position and settled down happily for an indefinite siege, something she was always very good at, even as a kid.

"That woman," she said to me, "is evil. She murders people for money."

"No she doesn't."

"She was hired to kill me. You think you can trust her because you're in love with her, but you can't. The moment you lower your guard—"

"Shut up, Fan. You're wrong on all counts." She was making my teeth hurt. "She was hired to catch you, not kill you. I trust her more than anyone else I know. And I'm not in love with her."

She gave me that look. "You think you're so clever and you understand people, but really, you haven't got a clue. Well, that's fine when it's just you, but it's not, is it? Really, Florian, I don't see why I should have to die just because of your appallingly bad judgement."

Sometimes I remind myself of the sea. Every day it tries to climb the beach; every day it crawls just so far and then it gets dragged back. But does it ever stop trying? Stupid sea. "Listen," I said. "She's had a dozen opportunities to turn me in over the years. She could've made more money than you can imagine. And guess what, every time she's let me go. Damn it, she's rescued me. I'd have died in one of Siggy's dungeons years ago if it wasn't for her. And if anyone's in love around here, it's her with me. God only knows why, but it's the only possible explanation for what she's done for me. So if she says she's going to help you, she's going to help you. Whether you like it or not."

"You're an idiot, Florian. You make me so angry I could scream."

I left her to it and went outside. In the yard I passed her maid – that's right, Fan had insisted on having a maid, to get her dressed and fold her clothes and brush the iron-ore slurry off her shoes, so Cynisca had got some woman from the nearest village. I was paying her a small fortune, though if you ask me she was working harder to earn it than I ever had, stacking corpses. Cynisca was furious about the whole thing and was barely talking to me. One less critic to listen to, so fair enough.

"You must be out of your tiny mind."

I hadn't seen Polycrates coming, so I guess he was lurking in a shed doorway, with a view to ambushing me and telling me things about myself, probably things I already knew. "Not now," I said. "I'm having a bad day. Maybe tomorrow."

"Fuck you, Saevus. We need to deal with this, right now."

Which I could've done, quite easily: a feint to the chin with my left followed by a short right to the solar plexus with all my body weight behind it. That's what my father would have done, and quite probably my poor dead brother as well. My father's a duke, he knows when to talk and when to punch, and it always seems to have worked well for him. "Nothing to deal with," I said. "Leave me alone."

"No." He stepped out in front of me, barring my way. He'd positioned himself perfectly for getting-hit purposes; mind you, he's been doing that his whole life. "I've had enough of you and your lies and your stupid family. I'm not your fucking servant. You can't order me about like I'm one of your father's serfs."

"Money," I said. "A hundred thousand in gemstones."

"You what?"

"That's what's in it for you. We get my sister safe, there's a hundred thousand staurata. Naturally, you'll get your share. That's a much better proposition than the battlefield salvage business right now, what with a war brewing and everything. Guaranteed money. Enough to ride out the war somewhere safe and not come out till it's all over. Or have you got a better idea?"

He looked at me as if I was a narrow bridge over a ravine, leading to a cave full of money. "Bullshit," he said. "You expect me to believe you're doing this for the cash."

"No, of course not. I'm doing this for my sister. You're doing it for the money."

Polycrates has a complex relationship with the truth. He believes that bad people are always wrong, and good people are always right. Facts tend to disrupt his view of the world, like rocks just under the surface of the water, but somehow he manages to rise above them and carry on believing. "You're a moron, Saevus, and you're going to get us all killed. If I had the sense I was born with, I'd walk away right now."

"Fine. You do that. Just out of interest, where would you go?"

"Fuck you," he said, and stalked off. The last word, but not one of his better efforts.

But he was right, of course. Objectively speaking, what I was doing wasn't exactly sensible, and I was putting a lot of lives at risk. The sooner the situation was resolved, the better for all of us. I needed advice, so I went to the person best qualified to give it.

"Slit her throat" was what I got. "Or if you don't fancy the idea, let me do it. Happy to oblige. I'm not usually into cold-blooded murder, but for her I'll make an exception."

"No," I said. "Think of something else."

Stauracia has a beautiful frown. It draws your attention to her eyebrows and her mouth. "Trouble is," she said, "the whole world's about to go to hell, which complicates things. All the safe places I can think of are likely to be slap bang on the front line, any minute now. Aelia's out, and so's all of northern Blemya. And you can forget about the Olbian delta, or any of the Sisters' houses east of Choris. You really couldn't have picked a worse time."

"Awkward," I said. "Come on, you must know somewhere."

"Shut up and let me think." She thought. "I suppose there's always Ogiv."

"Brilliant. What's Ogiv?"

"A convent," she said. "Daughter house of the Iron Rose. It's away to hell and gone the far side of Ancola, out in the sticks. It just so happens I know the prioress."

Ancola. Too hot in summer, too cold in winter, shifting effortlessly from drought to flood and back again with no perceptible in-between, and the locals put fennel in everything, even porridge. We had a war up there once and it was the rainy season. We all swore a terrible oath that nothing on earth would ever induce us to go back there. "Fine," I said. "Ideal. How in God's name are we supposed to get there?"

"Ship. Oh, come on, don't be such a girl."

The art of navigation is one of the many things I know very little about, but I do know, from hard experience, that messing about in boats at the top end of the Friendly Sea at any time between the end of the grape harvest and spring sowing is an exceptionally stupid thing to do, which is why the people who live up there don't do it. "Talk sense. Who's going to sail us north of Drepanon when the northern trades are blowing?"

"I may know somebody." She gave me her very best scowl. "Look, I'm trying to be helpful. You said, where can we go where we'll be safe and nobody's going to come after us? To which the answer is, Ogiv, because it's a godforsaken shithole where nobody goes and you can't get there at this time of year because sailing is incredibly dangerous. Why is it," she added, looking straight at me, "that every time we talk about something, it turns into an argument?"

No answer to that, so I didn't bother trying to think of one. "Your people," I said. "Will they be all right about going to Ancola?"

"They will if I tell them to. How about your lot?"

"Not sure. I think they've had about as much of me lately as they can take."

"Oh, you'll handle them, you always do. Poor bastards," she added, with feeling. "It must be a shitty life, working for you."

Quite. But it's amazing what people will put up with if they think they have absolutely no choice.

I went looking for Polycrates and found him playing knucklebones with Gombryas and Olybrius in a derelict wheelhouse. Three birds, one stone. "I've been thinking," I said.

They looked up at me. Polycrates was holding the bones, about to throw, and there were over five staurata in the pot. If I'd known they had that much money I'd have borrowed it from them. "Oh fuck," he said. "Now what?"

I squatted down on the ground next to him. "It's entirely unreasonable of me to expect you boys to risk your lives and lose money just to help me out with my family problems. Especially if we're going to Ancola."

"Who said anything about Ancola?"

"That's where I'm headed," I said.

"But we agreed, after the last time," Olybrius said. "Never again."

"Exactly. So I'm not going to ask you to go there. Instead, I want you three to take the lads and go and bid on that frontier war Daresh Asvogel was talking about, down in Framea. From what Daresh said it's a quick in-and-out job, no messing, and since the duke's lot are bound to win, you needn't bother paying both sides, so we can afford it, just about. It should get us around twelve per cent return on capital, which isn't much, I know, but since I'm not going to be there, obviously I'll waive my share, so it'll be worth your while. Then, when I've got my sister settled and you've finished in Framea, we'll meet up somewhere and figure out what we're going to do next. How about it?"

They looked at me. "Sounds good," Gombryas said cautiously. "Sure, why not?"

Polycrates was trying to peer inside my head, but my face was in the way. "I thought the idea was," he said, "that we need you, because we're too stupid to be let out on our own. Isn't that what you've always told us?"

"Not in so many words." I gave him my earnest look. "Come on," I said. "Naturally, under normal circumstances I wouldn't split us up, because this is what I do: it's my living. But right now I've got to take care of this business with my sister, and there's no reason why you should put your necks on the line when you could be in Framea earning money. I'm trying to be nice, for crying out loud. Why do you always have to make difficulties?"

Now Olybrius was looking thoughtful as well. "Usually when you're in the shit you drag us along with you," he said.

"Admitted," I replied. "And you've always stuck by me, which is wonderful and don't think I don't appreciate it. But not this time. I haven't got the right to treat you like you're my private army. So, go to Framea. It's a piece of cake; you don't need me."

Gombryas was staring at me as though I'd suddenly started talking in Dejauzi. Polycrates was way ahead of him, albeit in the wrong direction. "Just a minute," he said. "Couple of days ago, you were talking about a hundred thousand in jewellery. Now it's why don't you boys piss off to Framea and leave me here with the ice and that tart Stauracia." He curled his lip, something I've never seen anybody else do, though you read about it in books. "You must think we're stupid."

"Oh, for crying out loud," I said, almost like I meant it. "Yes, as it so happens, I do, because you are. I'm trying to fix it so you don't have to risk your lives for my sake, *again*, and you think I'm trying to screw you out of money. That's disappointing, it really is. It'd be different if you were saying, it's all right, Saevus, we're with you, come what may, thick and thin. But you'd never say that in a million years, and I don't blame you: that's absolutely fine. But turning on me when I try and do the decent thing because you think I'm planning to cheat you. That's sad."

"What's all this about a hundred thousand?" Olybrius said.

Polycrates gave him a look that should've stopped his heart. "His sister's jewels," he said. "At least a hundred thousand, probably more. That's what he'll get for helping her escape. The idea was, we were all going to get a share, but apparently he's been having second thoughts about that."

"You didn't tell me—"

"Well, I'm telling you now," Polycrates snapped. "And I'm telling you, this stinks. He's stitching us up."

"You're an idiot, Polycrates," I said. "Come on, you two, you don't want to take any notice of him. What about it?"

Olybrius was doing owl impressions. "I don't know," he said. "I don't think we should split up."

"It's hardly splitting up, is it?" I said. "Look, you've all been saying it for years when my back's turned: you don't need me to do a simple job. One of you can handle it perfectly well."

"That's another thing," Gombryas interrupted. "Which one of us?"

"Sort it out among yourselves," I said airily. "The point is—"

"I'm not taking order from *him*."

That made Polycrates snarl like a dog. "Well, I'm not," Gombryas said. "He's got no more idea of running things than my mother's cat."

"Fine," I said. "You do it."

"Fuck that," Polycrates said, which nearly got him a mouth full of knuckles, except that I got Gombryas's arm behind his back before he was in distance. Gombryas sat down again. "There you go," Olybrius said. "My point exactly. We need you, even if it's only to keep the peace."

"Hardly," I said. "You just need to get a grip, that's all. Anyway, I've said all I'm going to say. You think it over, talk to the lads and tell me what you want to do. And for God's sake try and act like grown-ups. I've got enough on my plate as it is without you clowns scratching each other's eyes out."

I left them scowling at each other and went to find my sister. She was sitting by the window of what had once been a well-house, but which was now her private apartment-come-audience chamber. She'd bullied a couple of Cynisca's men into cleaning it from top to bottom and giving it three coats of lime wash, and Cynisca had lent her a chair and a table. Her maid was combing her hair. "What do you want?" she said.

"Good news," I said. "I've found a safe place."

"About time, too. I can't stand it here a moment longer. Everything's filthy dirty, the people are pigs and the smell makes me sick. Have you got rid of that woman yet?"

"No," I said. "She's coming with us."

"No she isn't. I don't trust her."

"She's coming, because it's her friend who's going to take you in."

"In that case I'm not going."

"Fine," I said. "If you ask nicely, maybe Cynisca will give

you a job washing miners' shirts. But I wouldn't count on it, after the way you've behaved."

She told the maid to get lost with a tiny movement of her head. "How can you be so stupid?" she said. "That woman was hired to capture me. If we go with her, I might as well slash my wrists right now."

"Think about it," I said. "Do you trust me?"

She looked at me. "Yes," she said, after an insulting pause. "Yes, I do. I don't have any choice. You've done some really bad things, Florian, but I guess I do. I mean, you didn't stab me the moment you saw me, so—"

"Fine," I said. "No, you listen. Stauracia hates you, and I can't say I blame her. She hates you because all my adult life you've been hounding me. Left to herself, she'd cut your head off and stick it up on a pole for the magpies. But she understands that you're my sister, and the most important thing to me right now is saving you from the consequences of your actions, so she's prepared to do whatever it takes to get you safe. In return, you're going to give her a hundred thousand stauratas' worth of jewellery, out of the stash you brought with you."

"Go to hell."

"In due course," I said, "but not right now. I've told her that's what your little nest egg is worth. I lied, of course: it's at least three times that. I had a good look at it while you were having your bath yesterday afternoon. You get to keep the rest. I don't want any of it."

"You've told that woman about my jewels. Oh, that's wonderful. Why didn't you just stick a knife in my throat and be done with it?"

"Stauracia's not in it for the money. But she's going to get a hundred thousand, because she'll have earned it. Which is more than you ever did. I thought you loved him, for crying out loud."

She frowned. "Oh, you mean Siggy. Yes, I did."

"You have an unconventional way of showing it."

"I loved him and he loved me. But then Bryennius came along, and I knew in an instant that we were meant for each other. And he had such wonderful plans, for what he was going to do when he was Archduke. He was going to help all the poor people; he really cared about them. And don't you dare criticise me, not after what you did. You have absolutely no right to pass judgement, you know that."

"You murdered him."

"He was standing between me and true happiness," she spat at me. "For God's sake, Florian. I had a chance to be happy. I deserved it, God knows, after you screwed up my life for me."

"So it's my fault."

"Yes. Everything is your fault."

I took a deep breath. "True," I said. "All right, let's not talk about it any more. You're still going to give Stauracia a hundred thousand for helping you escape."

"Like hell I will."

"Then you can pack up your stuff in a sack and start walking," I said. "Because Stauracia's not going to help you unless you pay her, and I can't save you on my own, and if you stay here, sooner or later Cynisca will strangle you, even if you pay her a thousand a week. Your choice, Fan. Think it over and let me know what you want to do."

The last word and a good exit line, solving nothing. I could feel her hating the back of my neck as I walked away.

*

"Look after yourself," Cynisca said, as we were getting ready to move out. "Look, are you all right for money?"

I try and anticipate every contingency, but I hadn't expected that. "No," I said.

She handed me a cloth bag about the size of a large cooking apple. "Six hundred," she said. "Pay me back when you can."

"No," I said. "But it's a sweet thought."

"Halfwit."

"That's probably an overestimate. Thanks, Cynisca."

"Get stuffed. And for God's sake take the money."

I took the money.

It's never exactly fun getting from Dis Exapaton to the coast. Cynisca floats her iron down the blood-red river on barges as far as Astoch, so we hitched a ride; after that it was carts on really bad roads, with knee-deep ruts down to the underlying limestone. It had been Cynisca's idea. Her convoys made the trip once a month, regular as the phases of the Moon, so we were marginally less conspicuous than if we'd set out on our own, and we had the carters as additional muscle. At the coast, the idea was to buy passage on an ore freighter heading for Scona, but jump ship at Patrocleia or one of those something-and-nothing places on the south-east coast, then catch an empty lumber barge going north to load up at Olbia. We'd get off before it got there, naturally, and either charter or buy something to take us up the Ostar as far as Leva Savotz, then walk from there – short cut through the forest and join the Northern Military at Errima or somewhere like that. It seemed perfectly reasonable on a map, which means precisely nothing.

Looking back, I would have to say that the happiest time in my life was the five or so years I spent earning a precarious living writing plays – farces and burlesques – for the Gallery of Illustration in Beal Regard. If you'd told me back then that that was as good as it was going to get, I'd have slashed my throat with the nearest sharp edge; but you didn't, so here I still am, thank you ever so much.

During that halcyon period in my life, one day was pretty much like all the others. I'd wake up with a headache and a queasy stomach, roll off the bed on to the floor and count my money – never a time-consuming job, and it served to spur me on to new heights of creativity. I spent the morning scribbling rhyming couplets, liberally seasoned with laboured jokes, mostly puns. An hour or so before noon, I'd copy out the individual parts and take them down to the theatre, where the actors snatched them out of my hands and swore at me because I was hopelessly behind schedule, as usual. In the afternoon we'd rehearse next week's piece, with the carpenters and scene painters sawing and hammering all around us and everybody miserable as sin. In the evening I'd go home just as the punters started to arrive. I never once saw anything I wrote in the evening, all the way through; nor did I wish to. Instead I went trawling round the bars and taverns where the Profession drank when it wasn't on stage, angling and begging for work – a curtain-raiser for the Standard, a cart-wreck of a script to fix for Andronica at the Academy, three comic songs and something for the performing dogs at the Amphitheatre. I worked for practically nothing, which was what my stuff was worth. I knew everybody to smile and nod to. I was a small but important cog in a huge and complex machine for extracting coppers from apprentices, stevedores and clerks; one step up from cockfighting, ferret-racing and the shell game, and slightly more legal than organised prostitution.

I enjoyed the buzz, the companionship and the feeling of being useful, but the thing about those days that makes me look back on them with dewy-eyed nostalgia was the relative absence of issues of life and death. They weren't entirely lacking, of course. They never are. There was always the prospect of starving to death, a very real possibility in the lower echelons of the Profession (I knew half a dozen actors who did just that, when the interval between walking-on jobs turned out to be a little bit longer than flesh and blood could stand) and of course there were drunken fights and jealous-rage stabbings, and the Drama tends to live in neighbourhoods where they'll cheerfully cut your throat for the shoes on your feet, especially if you're one of the more popular sizes. But stuff like that is just forces of Nature, like drought and sandstorms and plagues of locusts. You didn't have to spend your days trying to figure out how to kill people, or keep people from killing you. I rather liked that aspect of it, I have to confess.

My sister put paid to all that. She found out that the hack playwright at the Gallery was actually me, and she sent unpleasant men to find me, which they very nearly did, and that's how Saevus Corax was born. He was supposed to be a new leaf, a fresh start, a brave new world and my ticket to the big score, after which all my troubles would be over. He's been a disappointment to me, just as I was to my father. Runs in the family, I guess. My biggest fear, one of my biggest fears, is that one day I'll wake up and find that he's become the real me, something I can't run from, peel away or scrub off with a wire brush. Maybe that's already happened. I don't know any more. Anyhow, my problem, so of no interest to anybody else.

I suspect, however, that the playwright of the Gallery of Illustration would've reacted rather differently to finding a beautiful woman in floods of tears. He would've been sympathetic, or helpful, or guilty. But probably not angry.

"For God's sake," I said. "What are you whining about now?"

She looked at me through shining wet eyes. I bet Siggy was used to that look. "Go to hell," she said. "Leave me alone."

We were three days out of Dis Exapaton, and by my standards we'd done pretty well. Nobody had died, we didn't seem to be being followed, we had food, the wagons were moving and everybody was still on speaking terms, more or less. We'd found a ruined priory to spend the night in, and there was even a well with clean water. "What's the matter?"

"You don't give a damn."

"Probably not. What's the matter?"

She gave me two seconds of big wet eyes. "Everything's horrible, Florian," she said. "I'm dirty and hungry and I've worn the same clothes three days in a row and I smell, and it's too hot and every time the stupid cart goes over a pothole my head feels like it's going to split open. I don't want to go on living if it's going to be like this. I'd rather be dead."

It occurred to me that she'd been crying with no audience, so she might be sincere. I guess misery is like love: blind. A lot of really unprepossessing people manage to get loved, and a lot of circumstances with which I don't have a problem are a living hell for other more sensitive souls. "Tough," I said. "There's absolutely nothing I can do about it."

She gave me a furious glare. "You could feel sorry for me."

Yes, I thought, I could, but I didn't. "Come on, Fan," I said, "it's not that bad. And it's not like it's going to last for ever. It won't be all that long before we get to Ogiv, and then you'll be safe and you can start making things the way you want them to be. It'll be all right, you'll see."

"Like hell it will," she snapped. "Assuming we get there without being murdered, I'm going to have to spend the rest of my life in poverty and squalor."

"Define poverty and—"

"Because you'll have given all my money to that woman."

Fine, I thought. "Bullshit," I said, as kindly as I could manage. "A hundred thousand. That'll still leave you a quarter of a million. Have you any idea what a quarter of a million staurata actually means?"

There were tears rolling down her cheeks. "Siggy bought me the jewels," she said, "so that if anything bad happened and I lost everything and had nowhere to go, at least I'd be provided for. I wouldn't have to starve to death or beg in the street. So long as you've got them, he told me, you'll be all right. And now you want to steal them from me and give them to your—" She stopped; the word was too vulgar to cross the lips of an Archduchess. "Your *friend*. I don't know how you can be so cruel. But, then, I suppose someone who spends his life pulling rings off dead men's fingers is used to that sort of thing. Still, your own sister—"

"Is that what you were crying about?"

"Go to hell. Why don't you just kill me and steal the stupid things and have done with it?"

I never actually met my brother-in-law in the flesh, but I have a pretty shrewd idea of what he would have been like; the job description says it all, really. Even so. A man more sinned against than sinning, probably, on balance. "All right," I said. "So far we've been doing it my way, but if you like we can do it your way instead. What would you like me to do? Just give me one constructive suggestion and we'll try it. Just so long as you stop snivelling."

That set her off crying again. There was a play at the Standard, *The Tyranny of Tears*, with Andronica as a manipulative wife. I never got to see it, but I bet she was brilliant. The only actress I ever saw who'd be capable of playing my sister.

"Fine," I said. "Have a good cry, and when you've done that, maybe we can talk about it like rational human beings. I'm sorry, but I don't negotiate with terrorists."

I walked away and went looking for Stauracia. She was sitting in the shade with her back to a wagon wheel, eating a pear. "Presumably that's your sister making that appalling noise," she said.

"Yup."

"What she needs is a good smack," she said. "Just say the word."

"Don't tempt me."

"You really are an arse, Saevus," she said, through a mouthful of pear. "I don't suppose it's occurred to you to see things through her eyes for a change."

I was tired. I sat down next to her. "Why would I want to do that?"

She sighed. "Understanding," she said. "Actually, you surprise me. I always reckoned that was what gave you your edge."

"Excuse me?"

"Understanding," she said. "You think about people, you understand them, and that's how you can outsmart them and make them do what you want. It's the one useful thing I've learned from you, only I'm not as good at it as you are. But when it comes to your own flesh and blood, you can't be arsed to do it."

I shrugged. "Maybe I don't want to understand her," I said.

"It's not about wanting. It's about gaining a tactical advantage."

"Maybe she's too completely twisted for me to unravel."

"Oh, come on, it's not difficult." She munched the last mouthful and threw away the core. "I know exactly how the stupid bitch is feeling."

"Really?"

"Of course. For one thing, she's terrified. Scared stiff. She's not used to physical danger like you and me. She doesn't know how to fight, or the technicalities of being on the run. That kind of stuff is second nature to people like us, but she's different. Refined." She scowled. "Entitled. Same goes for discomfort. She has no experience with pain. She's never been dirty before. She can smell her own sweat on her clothes and she hates it, and she can't just change into something clean because she hasn't got anything to change into. For someone like her, that must be hell on earth."

"My heart bleeds."

"These things are relative," she said. "For her, it's torture. And probably she's feeling really angry with herself for screwing everything up the way she did, plus there's being dumped by her lover the moment things started to go wrong: that wouldn't help. Also, she'll be missing her husband. You told me, they were really fond of each other."

"She killed him."

"I don't suppose that makes any difference. She'll still be missing him, like any widow. He was part of her life for years and years, and now suddenly he's not there any more. I imagine it's pretty devastating."

I shrugged. "I expect you're right."

"I know I am. But you know what the worst of it is? She's a hundred per cent dependent on the man she's spent all her life hating and blaming for everything that ever went wrong for her. Just try and imagine what that'd be like."

I tried. "Can't. Sorry."

"Well, there you go. No wonder she's snotty and miserable. In her shoes, I'd probably give up. Mind you, she's the most self-centred person I've ever met in my entire life. That probably helps her keep going. I don't suppose it's crossed her mind for one moment that if she died right now, the sun would still come up tomorrow."

I nodded. "And you think giving her a good smack would solve all that?"

"No. But it'd make me feel a lot better."

I like Stauracia. Sometimes I can almost bring myself to believe she's on my side. "Right," I said, "now I understand her. Does it help? Let's see. No, it doesn't. I ought to let you turn her in for the bounty. She's no good for anything."

"Neither are you, for that matter."

"Never said I was."

She nodded. "That does make you slightly better than her," she said. "Slightly."

I stood up. "Thanks," I said.

"You're welcome. If I were you, I'd get a hold of that jewellery. She's so feckless, she could easily lose it."

"You think so?"

"And then come back for it later, after we're all dead."

"That sort of feckless, right. I'll think about it."

"Think hard. If you've got it, she can't kill you. She still hates you, you know that."

"Were you always like this, or are you getting more like me?"

"Wash your mouth out with ashes and water."

4

The next day, we were in a part of the country I'd never been to. A few times over the years, I'd been on that road but always turned off where it meets the old Grand Trunk, headed for Phaenomai Einai and what passes for civilisation in those parts.

South of the junction, the country changed. We were on the North Downs. I read a book once that said it's all chalk's fault. The Downs are chalk, which is why the grass doesn't grow properly and there are no trees to speak of, not even withies or elder. It's not like the steppe or the moor. It goes up and down all the time in a series of little steep hills, and the sky is enormous. Nothing lives there except wild sheep, descended from flocks that belonged to people who got wiped out in the war before the war before last; from time to time, we saw the ruins of their houses, small and far apart, easy to make out because nothing grows vigorously enough to overwhelm them. It's great country for seeing if anyone's following you, but lousy for being inconspicuous. Luckily, we appeared to have it all to ourselves.

Cynisca's carters knew all about it, of course, so that was all right. We didn't need to worry, they told me, because there was nowhere between the crossroads and the old abandoned fort at Guron where anybody could stage an ambush. If there was anybody about they'd be kicking up a dust cloud, just like we were, and in case I was fretting about somebody following us by night, I could forget about that, because just look at the state of the road. If you tried blundering about on that by moonlight, you'd break your legs before you got half a mile. Wonderful, I said. Nothing to worry about.

Which meant that, when they came, I was ready for them. I'd split us up into four, with me, Gombryas, Polycrates and Olybrius leading; I didn't want to involve Stauracia's people, just in case she'd overestimated their devotion to her. In the event I needn't have worried. At the first sign of trouble they ran like hares, but they didn't change sides or turn on us, so that was fine.

Even though I was prepared and I'd figured it all out in advance, down to the last detail, it was a horribly close-run thing. For a start there were more of them than I'd anticipated, so we were actually outnumbered. Also, they were superbly equipped in Type 7 scale armour, which meant my archers were wasting their time at anything except close range. Most of all, they were proper soldiers, which of course we aren't. They understood that the way to survive an encounter like that one was to get to where they were supposed to be as quickly as possible, rather than stopping dead in their tracks as soon as the arrows started pitching. In the end we had to slug it out hand-to-hand, which ought to have been the end of us, except that my boys managed to get themselves completely out of position and ended up backed against the carts with nowhere to run; at which point Stauracia turned up out of the blue with fifty or so men who hadn't legged it, attacked the bastards in flank and rear and got them jammed up so close that they could barely move. Even then they managed to turn and face her, and if Carrhasio hadn't killed their commander it could have turned out very bad indeed.

Actually it did. Thirty-nine of Stauracia's fifty were killed when the bad guys turned, and all of Cynisca's carters; we lost eighty-seven, including Olybrius. Carrhasio and Polycrates got cut up pretty badly, and of course we had no exceptionally brilliant Echmen surgeon to stitch us back together. We killed three hundred and seven of the bad guys, for what that was worth, which was nothing at all.

"This is a fucking godawful mess," Stauracia said, as I bandaged her arm. "It's a disaster. We're screwed."

"We won," I said. "The enemy were wiped out to the last man."

"So bloody what?"

So bloody what indeed. The best you can say about victory is that it's better than defeat, most of the time. "Here's an interesting thing," I said. "Their kit. I recognise it."

"What are you drivelling on about now?"

"It's a consignment we stripped off Prince Luitprand's men about three years ago, up in Kurmach. I sold it at Schanz Fair; we got silly money from an Auxentine dealer who had a customer waiting. I tried to find out who, but of course the dealer wasn't telling."

"What's that got to do with anything?"

I shrugged. "How's that?"

"The bandage is too tight. Do you want to cut off all the blood in my arm?"

Some things are true and important but don't need to be

said; quite the opposite. Yes, it was bad. It would have been worse if we'd lost, but not all that much. Stauracia's contingent was down from over a hundred to eleven. I'd lost eighty-seven – what? Colleagues, employees, friends, pairs of hands: words can be hopelessly inadequate sometimes. Eighty-seven components of my life; a bit long-winded, but maybe it helps you get a bit closer. And there's another stupid, useless word: lose, for crying out loud. I've lost my hat. I've lost the key to the charcoal shed. I lent you my shovel and you've gone and lost it. She's lost her husband. I've lost my friends. Loss is a term we use when something that was there isn't there any more. A bit like using the palm of your hand to drive in a nail.

They were, of course, mad as hell at me. I let them call me names for a while, then I held up my hand for silence. "I agree," I said. "You're right. It's my fault."

"Fuck you," Polycrates said. "You can't just apologise and then everything's all right."

"Of course I can't," I said. "You know your trouble? You never could take yes for an answer."

In the battle, if you can call it that, Polycrates had fought like a tiger. If it hadn't been for him, we'd probably all have died. He'd come out of it with deep slashes to his face, shoulders and arms, and a puncture wound clean through his thigh that only just missed an artery. He got that standing over Carrhasio when he went down, shielding him with his arms because he had nothing else to fend the cuts off with. "Don't you dare make jokes, Saevus. This is it. We've had enough. We're through."

I nodded. "I think that's the sensible decision," I said. "I wouldn't stick with me, not after this. I wish I had some money to give you, but I haven't. Sorry."

He was so weak from loss of blood that I could've floored

him with a modest left jab. "Fuck that," he said. "We want your sister's jewels."

"Not mine to give," I said. "Of course, you could simply take them anyway. If you can find them."

Polycrates let out a long, sad sigh. "You can't help it, can you? No matter what happens, you just keep on twisting and screwing and cheating. Nothing gets through to you, does it?"

I shrugged. "Not something I'm proud of," I said. "Actually, I don't think I'm proud of anything. Certainly not how I've treated you boys. If I had a conscience it'd be giving me hell right now."

"You know what?" Polycrates said. "Screw your sister's fucking money. We're just going to walk away and leave you to it. How does that sound?"

"Eminently reasonable. Actually, it'll be a weight off my mind. At least I'll know you won't be in harm's way any more."

I think he'd have taken a swing at me if he'd had one good arm to hit with. "How about you?" I said, turning to Gombryas. "Going or staying?"

"Staying." He grinned. "The way I figure it, we've killed all the goons so we don't have to worry about them any more. And the fewer of us there are, the bigger the shares of the pot will be." He turned to Polycrates and smiled. "I've done all the work, so why shouldn't I hang around for payday?"

"If you live to see it. Don't bank on it."

Gombryas laughed. "You always were thick as a brick, Polycrates. Don't you get it? He wouldn't be trying to get rid of you if there was any more danger."

Polycrates closed his eyes and shook his head. "I don't care," he said. "Keep the stupid money. I can't stand him a moment longer."

I'd brought something with me to the meeting. "Yours," I

said, handing Polycrates the bag of money Cynisca had given me. "Six hundred staurata you didn't know I'd got. Keep it for yourself or share it with your boys. At the very least it'll get you to the coast and on a ship."

He looked at me as though I'd just handed him his own liver. "That's supposed to make everything all right, is it?"

"No, of course not. After all we've been through together, it's positively insulting. But as it happens it's all I've got."

He reached out and took the money, like someone being forced to dig his own grave. "You're an arsehole, Saevus. We could've sold you to your enemies for good money."

"Go back to Simocat and find a man called Erriman," I said. "When we were there last he offered to buy me out. Top dollar. Tell him I'm dead and you're the new boss. You won't get as much as he offered me, but it'll be enough to see you right. Erriman's a smart man; he'll make a better fist of running things than I ever did. You won't get killed by bounty hunters and you might even make a living."

Polycrates gazed at me as if I was the sea. "You're serious."

"Yes. This is it. I'm officially retiring from the business and handing it over to you. You may not be the sharpest knife in the drawer, Polycrates, but you couldn't possibly make a worse hash of it than I have. Tell the lads, will you? I haven't got the guts to face them."

I walked away and looked round for something to do. The bodies of the goons we'd killed were still lying where they'd fallen, so I decided I'd make a start on them, even though it wasn't my business any more. I was stacking boots when Gombryas found me. "You're serious, aren't you?" he said.

I nodded. "This time it was just too much to bear," I said. "I decided I don't want to do it any more."

"Do what?"

"Lead men. Lead them to their deaths. Why the hell should I, for crying out loud? Let some other bugger do it for a change. I quit."

He sighed and sat down next to me. "They had a vote," he said "About two hundred are going with Polycrates, and the rest are sticking with you and me."

"Oh, for God's sake."

"They don't trust him. Can't say I blame them. He's an idiot."

"That's stupid," I said. "Two hundred's not enough to handle our sort of job. Erriman won't want them, so they won't get the money I went to all that trouble to arrange. Why the hell won't people ever do as they're told?"

"I know," Gombryas said. "It's like herding geese. Still, what can you do?" He was whittling a stick. Actually, that's a hopelessly inadequate description. Gombryas doesn't whittle; he checkers. You know that beautiful and extremely useful diamond pattern they put on the handles of fancy knives and tools, to give them a grip so they don't slide out of your sweaty hand and do someone a mischief? Gombryas is an expert at it. He can do it without even looking down at the work, by feel and instinct, but all the rows are parallel and all the little diamonds exactly the same size. When he doesn't have a knife or a tool to checker, he checkers sticks and then throws them away. "Could be worse, though."

"Really?"

"Oh yes. They could all have stayed. As it is, I expect you'll find a way of pissing off the loyalists. Something you're good at, when you've a mind to."

"I never managed to piss you off."

"You never tried." He was holding the stick between his thumb and little finger, so he could draw the hook of his knife all the way down in one continuous line. "That's what you're doing, isn't it? Getting rid of us."

"Trying to."

"You'll manage. And then there'll just be you and your sister and that tart Stauracia and all that money."

I sighed. "That's not the reason."

"You don't like getting the lads killed. Fair enough. Some of them are going to stick to you like dogshit. If you want shot of them, you'll have to run away or something."

"How about you?"

He laughed. "I figure I'm not just one of the lads. Well? Tell me I'm wrong."

"You're wrong."

"Liar."

"If you're right," I said, "and I'm not saying you are, not by a country mile, but let's just suppose. That'd be more of a reason than ever to get rid of you."

He examined the stick, which was now a work of art, and threw it away. "I think there's money at the end of all this," he said. "So if it's all right with you, I'll hang around."

"Suit yourself," I said. "And if you ever call Stauracia a tart again, I'll break your arm."

That made him grin. "You're weird, Saevus, you know that? She's actually not bad looking at all, and God knows she's up for it, you can practically smell it. Still, I guess it wouldn't do if we were all alike."

"All right, Gombryas," I said. "What's the deal?"

He shifted his weight and leaned forward. "Simple," he said. "First things first, we get your sister safe and settled so you don't have to worry any more. Then you and me and the lads, and your lady friend, we do one more job. Then we pack it in, go our separate ways, and they all live happily ever after. How about it?"

Something about the way he said it made my skin crawl. "Just any old job, or have you got something specific in mind?"

"Oh, I expect something'll turn up. Something with no risk and good money." He smirked at me. "I have faith."

"There's a war coming," I said. "A big one. It'll be a storm, and either we find somewhere to snuggle down and ride it out, or we'll get washed away. You do realise that, don't you?"

"War's just another word for opportunity. I'm not bothered about any of that."

Polycrates and his boys took all the carts except one, and three-quarters of the food, and Cynisca's iron ore, even though I pointed out that it didn't belong to them. Polycrates reckoned he could get good money for it at Falcata, where the lumber barges unload, and then look around for a cargo for the journey home. The proceeds would stake them for a small war somewhere, if Erriman wasn't interested in buying the business in its reduced state. For once, Polycrates had come up with a viable idea, though I can't say I approved of stealing.

"Well, so long," I said to him, when they were ready to leave. "I know we've had our differences, but I want you to know—"

"Piss off," he said. "You're an arsehole, Saevus. I wish to God I'd never set eyes on you."

"Fair enough," I said. "Go carefully. Be safe."

"Drop dead."

The last word; I let him have it, though if you ask me he squandered a glorious opportunity. I watched them go until they were out of sight, and all that remained was the cloud of dust kicked up by the horses and the cartwheels. Properly speaking, I should've stood there gawping until that faded out of sight as well, but I couldn't spare the time.

"You don't want to bother yourself about him," Gombryas assured me, as we trudged north on the South-East Trunk. "Or any of them. Bunch of arseholes. But you shouldn't have let them have all the carts."

I don't like walking at the best of times. Horses do it so much better than we do, having more feet to do it with. "Oh, I don't know," I said. "Think about it for a moment."

He pulled a face, like a cow trying to calve a baby elephant. "Think about what?"

"Dust."

He nodded. "You reckon we're still being followed," he said. "And they're holding back so we won't see them, but they're keeping track of us—"

"By the cloud of dust we're kicking up. Except now we aren't: Polycrates is. True, it'll look like we just doubled back on ourselves, but there's plenty of ways to explain that, like we suddenly changed our minds, or the boys went on strike or something. In any case, if someone's following us, they'll be led off in the one-eighty-degrees wrong direction, which can't be bad, can it?"

That earned me a grin. "He was right about you," he said. "Everything you do, there's a twist in it. Can't say it's done you much good over the years, but you're a smart bugger."

The one cart I'd kept back was, of course, for Fan to ride in. I couldn't imagine her walking, though it didn't take much imagination to think of the sort of things she'd say, step by step, all the way to Ogiv. They would probably be true but I didn't want to hear them. Stauracia volunteered to drive the cart, which was noble of her.

"Does she talk much?" I asked her, on the third day.

"No, thank God," Stauracia replied. "Mostly she just sits there muffled up in a scarf against the dust. She sort of radiates suffering."

"She's always been good at that," I said. " I remember when she was six, she slipped and skinned her knee. She was brave at us for a fortnight. Not a word of complaint, just those big eyes glowing with patient endurance."

She nodded. "It makes me wonder how you'd have turned out," she said. "If you hadn't left home."

"Badly," I said. "But in a different way."

"You'd have been happier."

"I doubt it," I said. "Nobody in our family's ever been happy, except possibly my great-great-great-uncle Arach."

"What did he—?"

"Firmly believed he was a chicken," I said. "I imagine chickens are happy. More so than members of my family, at any rate."

She sighed. "Funny man," she said. "Still, I'm inclined to believe you. I never particularly noticed that rich bastards are happier than normal people. They're just miserable about different things."

"My sister's never been happy. People have died trying to make her happy, but it's a waste of time. It can't be done."

"Tell you what," she said. "You can drive the cart and I'll walk. How about it?"

"Absolutely not."

Four more days after that, and then we came to the edge of the downs. Below us the country fell away steeply, until it levelled out into the coastal plain which stretches from Cepso to Hervida Bay. Most of the plain is reclaimed moorland. Some clown bought it from the Diocese about two hundred years ago, figuring he could drain the bogs and stop the soil erosion by building banks, digging ditches and drains and planting trees. He shipped in about twenty thousand families from Auxentia to do the work, and when he ran out of money they were stuck there. A lot of them died but some of them didn't, and their descendants are still living the dream, yeomen farmers, each with clear title to two hundred acres of couch grass, gorse and bog cotton, and the few sheep the wolves haven't got around to eating yet. About the only thing worth having on Cepso Moor is the ponies, descended from fifty or so Sashan-Durman crosses the rich clown brought in to pull carts in his iron mines, which turned out to be unviable. They roam about in enormous herds, and every third year the locals round them up, kill them, salt the meat and sell it to Auxentine slave dealers to feed the stock in trade. Needless to say the ponies would be worth five times as much alive in Olbia or Scheria, but first you'd have to get them there, and there are plenty of other ways to lose money with far less effort and stress.

"If someone is following us," Gombryas said, as we followed the river north-west, "and if they were smart, they'd have taken a short cut across the top of the downs and be waiting for us at Cepso Cross. They'd figure we'd figured we'd lost them on the downs, so we wouldn't be expecting trouble."

"Who said anything about going near Cepso Cross?" I said. "My idea is, follow the river as far as that bridge, can't remember what it's called, and then straight over the hog's back to Hervida."

"Can't take the cart over the hog's back."

"Omelettes and eggs. It'll save us three days and we won't

have to go anywhere near any towns or villages. And if my sister kicks up a fuss about having to walk, tough."

Fan solved the problem of having to walk by turning her ankle over so comprehensively that it swelled up like a log, meaning she had to be carried. We rigged up a sort of sedan chair out of spearshafts roped together, and I insisted on being one of the four bearers, because that's what leadership is all about, not asking someone else to do the things you dread most. It says a lot about the life I've led that crossing the hog's back holding up one corner of a chair with my sister in it doesn't even make the top ten of my worst ever experiences. Even so, I was relieved when we finished scrambling down the steep shale escarpment and came out into the watercress meadows at the bottom. You can't eat the watercress, needless to say, it's a poisonous variety that turns your kidneys to pulp, and the only living things for miles around are insects. But at least it's flat, and it was almost pleasant to be squelching in mud after ten days of dust and rock.

"I don't think I can take much more of this," Fan told me. "It's not worth it. I think I'd rather die."

"Cheer up," I said. "We're nearly there."

"It's horrible. Everything is horrible, from the moment I wake up till the moment I go to sleep. What on earth is the good of being alive if it makes you feel like that?"

"Ask Siggy's tenants. I imagine there must be a reason, or they wouldn't keep doing it."

"Why do you have to be horrible, too? Everything you say is meant to make me feel bad. If you hate me that much, why don't you just cut my throat?"

She always had the knack of asking difficult questions. "I don't hate you," I said. "I just wish you'd shut up occasionally."

I thought a lot over the next couple of days about what Stauracia had said: put yourself in her place; try and imagine how she feels; what it must be like for her. Maybe I wasn't doing it right, but it didn't seem to make any difference. With an effort I could see inside her mind, and what I found there didn't make me any more inclined to love and pity her. For a start, we were so much alike – forged on the same anvil under the same hammer out of the same rusty and imperfect stock; both of us eventually ending up in the same place, which was somehow inevitable from the outset. Which of us was the other's fault I wouldn't like to hazard a guess. At least it explained why I hadn't bashed her head in or tied her to a tree and walked away. It'd be like trying to scrape off my own shadow with a blunt knife.

One morning, early before the mist came down, I walked on ahead up the slope until I reached the top, and there, exactly where I'd hoped it would be, was the sea. If you've been paying attention you'll have gathered that I have an ambiguous relationship with large quantities of salt water. I hate sailing and being on boats, but I frequently need to travel large distances quickly, and the sea is handy for that. A ship from Hervida Bay could take us all the way to the mouth of the Ostar, and then a barge would carry us upstream to Sticklepath, and you can practically see Ogiv from there. A fortnight with nothing to do but sit still and feel sick. Almost a holiday.

"There's a man I want to see," Gombryas said.

"In Hervida?"

"A collector," he said. "Someone told me he's got a genuine Antipater finger."

"I thought you'd already got one."

"I have. But if I had a spare, I could trade one of them and my Supilumas fibula for something really good."

Hervida Bay didn't strike me as the sort of place where you'd find rich eccentrics with morbid hobbies. It's mostly built out of bits of broken ship, washed up from wrecks off the Five Claws. Sensible enough, but it means the buildings have odd-looking curved walls, and everything stinks of tar. The whole point of Hervida is that you can stop there and unload without having to brave the Claws or go out far enough to avoid them, which means risking getting snatched up by the current and driven out into the open sea. The downside is that anything landed at Hervida has to go inland up the road we'd avoided by crossing the hog's back. There are worse roads, but it's enough to make a sensible man stop and think, and probably decide to go trading somewhere else. But they do a modest business in herring and salt cod, so there's always a few ships coming and going, and it's worth the Knights' while to have an office there. Gombryas's pal turned out to be the Knights' factor, which was handy, since he knew all the ships that called regularly and agreed to find us one going in the right direction. I asked him if he'd heard of anybody snooping round asking questions about us. He looked puzzled and asked if we were anybody special. Absolutely not, I assured him. We're so insignificant we barely exist.

In any event, we got our ship and Gombryas got his finger, though I have an idea he had to pay rather more for it than he'd hoped. It came in a little tin box about the size of my hand, with a brass catch. Would you like to see it, Gombryas asked me. No, I said. He looked at me as if I was mad and said, fair enough. "Got something else you might like to see," he added.

"No, thank you."

He pulled a small bundle wrapped in sacking out of the front of his shirt. "Careful with it," he said. "It's not mine; it's on loan."

"Put it away, for God's sake."

"It's not a body part. Go on, you've got to see it."

Sometimes it's easier just to agree. He handed it to me. It was small, about the size of a grapefruit, but heavy. Too heavy for a bone or a kid's skull. I unwrapped it. "Cute," I said.

"Solid gold."

I didn't doubt it. "That's old," I said.

He grinned. "Yup."

It was a couter. You don't know what a couter is, and why the hell should you? A couter is the piece of a suit of articulated plate armour that covers the point of the elbow. If this one had been made of steel, it'd have been well over five hundred years old, probably older, since articulated plate went out with the old Empire, and nobody really knows how to make it any more, and nobody these days can afford to dress their soldiers up like steel lobsters. But this one wasn't steel. It was pure yellow gold, with a faint reddish tinge.

"Some fool trusted you with that," I said.

That got me a scowl. "Collectors don't rip off collectors," he said, bending the truth like a smith making a horseshoe. "I got first refusal on it. I said I needed to get it assayed, but that was just an excuse."

"It must be worth—"

"Fuck what it's worth. I'm not planning on buying it. I need you to see it, that's all."

I smiled at him and handed it back. "Come on, Gombryas," I said. "You know better than that. It's a scam. This chum of yours is trying to play you."

"It's genuine."

"Bullshit," I said. "It doesn't exist. It's a myth."

At which moment Stauracia came up behind us. Gombryas had his back to her, and she's got this habit of walking very quietly. "What's that?" she said.

Gombryas jumped up like he'd been bitten. He tried to stuff the couter back down his shirt but Stauracia grabbed his wrist and did that thing she does, which she selfishly refuses to teach me. "Fuck, that hurts," Gombryas yelled. "Get her off me, will you?"

Stauracia took the couter out of his hand and let him go. "He's right," she said. "It's a myth. Someone's playing games with you." She was looking hard at the couter. "Good work, though. If I didn't know better, I'd say it was the real thing."

"But it isn't," I said. "There is no real thing."

"No, of course not." She turned it over to look at the inside, then handed it back to Gombryas. "You didn't pay money for that, did you?"

Gombryas wasn't talking to her. He hates being beaten up by girls. "It's genuine," he said to me.

"Gombryas—"

"My pal says it's a fake. He says it's worth its bullion value and that's all. But I know."

I sighed. "Of course he says that," I told him. "The whole essence of the scam is making the mark think you don't know what you've got. You know that as well as I do."

"Fuck you," Gombryas said. "You're an idiot, you know that? It's a once-in-a-lifetime chance, and you're pissing on it."

We all (except me) need to believe in something. Gombryas believes in the big score. So does Stauracia. I'm more of an agnostic. I acknowledge the possibility of the big score, but possible and real aren't necessarily the same thing.

The biggest big score is, of course, the gold armour of the First Emperor's bodyguard. And, yes, it's fairly well documented that the brigade of guards existed, and that His Imperial megalomaniac Majesty had a thousand suits of articulated plate armour made for them out of pure gold (almost pure: nine-ninety-two parts fine, which was as good as they could get it in those days. Nowadays we can just about manage nine-seventy-three, if we're lucky.). The emperor and his guard and the armour are facts, if anything in history can be called a fact. After that, you're into the realm of probabilities, possibilities and wishful thinking.

Reasonably enough. If (big if), when the First Emperor died, his loyal bodyguards volunteered to die with him so as to be able to guard him in the Afterlife against the hundreds of thousands of innocents he'd murdered during his life, and if (bigger if) they were buried in their gold armour, it stands to reason that whoever did the burying would have made absolutely certain sure that the location of the tomb was kept secret, for obvious reasons. Therefore all the accounts of the tomb, with their wealth of tantalisingly picturesque detail, must be lies: the caves in the mountainside, the seven gates, the seven hundred stairs going up and the fourteen hundred stairs going down, the colossal granite winged lions, the pool of sweet water and the fountain, the crystal sarcophagus, the whole nine yards. Nobody would have known about any of that, or not for very long.

I ask you, therefore: how can anybody be stupid enough to believe – especially now, a thousand years later, a thousand years during which every cave in every mountain in the known world has been probed by idiots and found to be empty? God only knows how many men and women have died looking for it. It hasn't been found. Therefore—

Gombryas sulked all the way across the Friendly Sea to Boc Ostar, which was probably no bad thing. Gombryas never gets seasick, and he treats his weaker brethren as though they're making a lot of fuss about nothing. Since he wasn't talking to me, he couldn't tell me to pull myself together and quit snivelling. One small blessing, in the midst of endless misery.

Once we were safely back on wonderful dry land, however, I needed him to do things for me, so I decided I'd better make my peace. "I'm sorry," I said. "I didn't mean to call you an idiot. It's just you were acting like one."

We were floating up the Ostar on a grain barge. They come downstream laden with wheat from the vast, fertile plains, and then get towed back upstream empty, unless someone pays the crew a trivial sum to give them a lift. Not dry land, strictly speaking, but it's not real sailing, so I don't mind, and it's ever so much better than walking. Even Fan couldn't find much to whine about, apart from the midges and the heat and the food and the bargemen's hairy armpits and the smell. "That's all right," Gombryas said. "But you're wrong. It was genuine."

There's nothing to do on a barge except listen to people. "What makes you say that?"

His eyes lit up. "For a start, I had it assayed. Nine-nine-two pure."

I sighed. "It's gold, Gombryas. Gold doesn't tarnish or corrode, so there's no patina to tell you if it's old or not. If you want to make something that looks like it's a thousand years old, all you've got to do is get hold of a fistful of Imperial coins and melt them down. The colour stays the same and the metal assays Imperial pure. Yes, the coins are rare, but people do keep finding hoards of them, in clay pots, out in Permia and places like that. You could get hold of them without too much bother, if you didn't mind paying silly money."

"The markings were right."

I nodded. The First Emperor's assay marks are a matter of public record; you can look them up in books in a good library. Which is the first thing a competent forger would do. "I bet they are."

"Not the assay stamps. The brigade numbers."

That made me frown. Collectors aren't like normal people. Their brains work in a different way. Take Gombryas, for example. For everyday purposes he's got just smart enough to walk and breathe at the same time. But when it comes to his hobby-obsession, he displays a level of erudition that would shame the monks of the Studium, along with a grasp of scientific method worthy of a Sashan professor. He knows all kinds of weird, abstruse shit; the minutiae of the lives of the great commanders, drawn from careful reading of obscure texts housed in remote libraries, which he chooses to visit whenever the opportunity arises, often in preference to some of the best and cheapest brothels in the known world. He told me once that he learned to read just so he could check out the dates of Carnufex the Irrigator in the original sources, to tell whether a shinbone he'd been sold was a dud or not. That's collectors for you.

So, if Gombryas was all excited about brigade numbers, whatever the hell they were, I was perfectly willing to believe that brigade numbers are a thing and relevant to issues of authenticity. "Go on," I said.

"The guy I borrowed it from," he said, "told me it had to

be no good because the brigade numbers are all wrong. But obviously he's going by the numbers in the Notitia."

"Obviously. What's the—?"

"And I happen to know, because I've been to Schanz and seen the actual manuscript, that all that stuff was added in later. It's in different handwriting and different colour ink. Everybody else goes by the copies, because they can't be arsed to make the trip, so they think—"

"Got you," I said. "And?"

"If you want to know the real brigade numbers," he went on, "you've got to piece them together from what it says in the campaign reports. Like, we know that before the First Emperor formed the household guard, they were the army on the north-eastern frontier, because it says so in Frontinus and he was there, for crying out loud. So you go back to Essian, which is where Urmhart copied it all out from, and Essian says the army that beat the Hus was the fourth and seventh brigade. Actually it doesn't say that in so many words, but it says they were Drasio's men, and we know Drasio commanded the fourth and the seventh at Stenachora because there's that gravestone on Sirupat. So obviously it follows, the emperor's guard was the old fourth and seventh."

"Absolutely," I said. "What about it?"

He gave me a sour look. "So when it says in the Notitia that the guards were listed as the fifth, sixth and ninth, that's obviously wrong. And that's what my pal was going by. And the brigade number on that couter was the fourth."

You really wouldn't think it to look at him, but Gombryas knows his stuff. "All it proves," I said, "is there's a forger who's as smart as you are when it comes to figuring things out from dusty old documents. That's all."

"No," he said, with rapidly evaporating patience. "Because if you were the buyer, you'd believe the numbers in the Notitia, like my chum did. So if you were the faker you'd use the Notitia numbers, even if you knew they were shit."

Imagine a dam, something like that huge thing they built in Sashan five hundred years ago, and it's still there, holding back the entire force of the Cavaben river. Now imagine one tiny crack in the wall, somewhere near the top. Let the dam be my disbelief, and Gombryas's argument the crack. "Not if you were really smart," I said. "I mean, I don't imagine the faker made that thing on spec. I imagine he had a buyer lined up, and he knew for a fact that this buyer had read all those books you've read, so he knew the truth. But for some reason the deal fell through, probably because there was something else wrong about it that the buyer picked up on but you didn't notice, so the faker was left with this thing on his hands, only worth the gold it's made from. That makes much more sense to me than it really being genuine."

I can imagine how Gombryas felt. It would be as if he'd just been granted a vision of the Invincible Sun, and everyone he mentioned it to told him not to be so silly. "Nobody else knows about the brigade numbers except me. If anyone else knew, I'd have heard about it. It's a big thing."

"Who else have you told, apart from me?"

"Well, nobody. I mean, it's a valuable secret." He paused. "I'd have heard about it," he said. "People in our line talk to each other. They like to show how smart they are."

Ten thousand years of scholarship summed up in eight words. "You could be right," I said. "But even if you are, so what? Maybe that thing's what you think it is. But you can't afford to buy it, even as scrap gold. I couldn't afford to lend you the money, even if I was inclined to, which I'm not. Your best bet—"

"I know where it came from."

Oh dear. We looked at each other.

"And the bad thing is," he went on, "that girlfriend of yours knows about it now, and she's not stupid, and I don't trust her as far as I can spit."

"Have you told her about these brigade numbers of yours?"

A look of pure contempt. "She's up in all sorts of stuff," he said. "If anybody knows what I know, it's the Sisters, and she was very thick with them a while back. And she knows I'm interested, so she'll be thinking, what if? She'd cut a man's head off for an earring."

A slight exaggeration. "She thinks it's a scam," I said. "She said so."

"You don't want to go believing everything she says." He was getting wound up, to the point where something was liable to snap. I'd seen him like it before, when there was a danger of something good slipping out of his grasp. Gombryas is like a sleepy old bull. You can push him so far with absolute confidence, but no further. "You're serious about this, aren't you?"

"Yes."

I nodded. "Well," I said. "Fair enough. I owe you one. And I did agree, after my sister's safe, one last caper. Presumably this is what you had in mind."

"It's the big score, Saevus. I can feel it in my balls."

The crack in the dam had just got a thousandth of a hair's breadth wider. "Fine," I said. "Where is this thing? Broadly speaking."

"Anticonessus."

Oh, for God's sake. "We can't go to Anticonessus, Gombryas. You know that as well as I do."

"Things are different now. There's a war coming. Nobody gives a shit any more."

"No."

"You owe me. You said."

I stood up. "I'll think about it."

"You *owe* me."

I walked away, about fifteen yards, which is as far as you can go on a barge, no matter how finely tuned your sense of melodrama. Stauracia stepped out from behind a stack of empty barrels. "What do you reckon?" she said.

"You were listening."

"It's a small boat. His voice carries. What do you reckon?"

I looked at her. "You're not serious, are you? The First Emperor's gold armour. What are you, twelve years old?"

She was serious. "That stuff about the brigade numbers," she said. "I thought I was the only person in the world who knew that."

It's disconcerting when someone you've always thought was smart turns out to be an idiot. "Not you as well," I said.

"Saevus—"

"Treasure hunters," I said. "God knows I've done a lot of stupid things in my time, but at least I've never been a treasure hunter. That's a fact I hug closely to myself every time the self-loathing starts to get too much to bear. Only morons believe in that stuff, Stauracia. Morons who die young and thereby make the world a better place."

"Finished?"

I nodded.

"Good," she said. "Because I happen to know for a fact that the First Emperor's tomb is in Anticonessus."

"You what?"

"I've known it for some time," she said calmly, as if mentioning in passing that the Invincible Sun does her nails for her. "Where in Anticonessus, not a clue, and it's a big country. But, yes, he's right about that. And if he's right about that—"

"He's a dreamer," I said, rather more loudly than I intended. "Just like the rest of you. Wasps' nest for brains. All that shit about Frontinus and Essian—"

"Happens to be true."

"It's all bullshit," I said. "It's a game idiots play, like Saloninus's plays were really written by Earl Gudbrand, or Jovian the Great was murdered by the Poor Sisters. It's a great big pot of piss soup with a few croutons of truth sprinkled on the top to give it flavour."

"You swore," she said. "You never swear." She was giving me that how-could-you-be-so-stupid look. "All right, nine hundred and ninety-nine times out of a thousand, it's all garbage. One time in a thousand, it's true. I think this could be that one time."

"Stauracia—"

"I think this could be Aeneas and the lemons."

I was so angry I could've hit her. Well, no, I couldn't; but if Aeneas Peregrinus had been there, I'd definitely have hit him, for noticing a basket of odd-shaped lemons in the market at Beloisa and going on to discover Essecuivo. Ever since then, whenever some deluded clown wants to destroy himself, he quotes Aeneas at you. Meanwhile, there are a thousand ships mouldering at the bottom of the sea because dreamers like Gombryas think they've figured out the location of Essecuivo. I tell myself it's a kind of natural selection, the method used by the Invincible Sun to weed out halfwits before they can breed.

But Stauracia – well. I guess it goes to show, nobody's perfect. "Fine," I said. "Now, if you were eavesdropping, you'll have heard where I said we can't go to Anticonessus. Or did you miss that bit?"

"Gombryas may have a point," she said. "Things are different now. The Patriarch and his mob are all dead, the Optimates and the Populists have more or less wiped each other out, most of the major cities are just heaps of ash: it's wide open. You can do what you like. There's nobody much left alive to care."

"It's still Anticonessus."

"I think we should go. Nobody in their right mind would ever think you'd go there. So it's a good place for you."

That shut me up, but only for a moment. "I've got my sister to think of. I can't go doing anything, no matter how stupid and suicidal, until she's safe."

"Fine. We take her to Ogiv, then we go to Anticonessus. I knew you'd come round to my way of thinking sooner or later."

The thing about a book is, it can last a hell of a long time. Hundreds of years; thousands, even. Doesn't matter if it's a bad book – look at Eucrinus's *Commentaries*, or *The Price of a Rose*. If garbage like that has managed to survive for a thousand years, it's not inconceivable that this stuff I'm writing now might somehow still be around long after I'm dead and gone, and nobody's left who understands the full significance of the name Anticonessus. So maybe I'd better explain, just to be on the safe side.

Anticonessus is a long, thin country stretching north-east from the Olbian Gates right up to the shores of the Golden Sea, which isn't a sea at all, just a very big lake at the foot of the Naxa Mountains. The only thing that grows in Anticonessus is violence, and since they produce more of it than even they can consume locally, they export it to their neighbours in bewildering quantities. The First Emperor tried to solve the problem by conquering Anticonessus, deporting the entire population to the far corners of the Empire and resettling it with docile people from the Mesoge. That worked fine for about a hundred years; then the Anticonessians broke loose and came home, with extreme prejudice. Florian the Great (after whom I was named, incidentally) took a more pragmatic approach. He hired practically the entire adult male population and unleashed them on the Sashan, hoping they'd wipe each other out and solve two problems. It didn't work out like that. The Anticonessians conquered three immense frontier provinces, turning them into deserts in the process, but then they reached the mountains, gave up and came home. Florian had died in the meantime, sensibly enough, so his poor unfortunate son had to deal with the aftermath, something he was intellectually and financially unequipped to do, and the consequence was the Second Anticonessian War, which ultimately led to the fall of the Empire. Moral: don't mess with these people. Sooner or later, they'll have you.

About twenty years ago, the Anticonessians got religion. It's something they're prone to doing, once every hundred years or so, and the result is usually bad news, for themselves and everybody else. This time around, the guilty party was a minor hill-country strongman who decided he was the Messiah – I think he genuinely believed it, at least to begin with – and set about redeeming humanity by killing as much of it as he could manage with the resources available to him. Two or three years later he sacked and burned the capital city, built a vast temple on the ashes and declared himself Patriarch. The good thing about that was his decision to close the borders, to keep out the infidel. Nobody was allowed into the country, but nobody could leave it, either. The rest of the world breathed a sigh of relief and turned its attention to other existential threats, like famine and plague. Nobody really knew what was going on inside Anticonessus after that, and nobody cared, but it's probably safe to assume that the Patriarch's version of the kingdom of God on earth wasn't unalloyed bliss, because not long ago – round about the time I was getting into mischief up in Sirupat – there was a revolution, the Patriarch ended up dangling from a rope, and the Anticonessians indulged themselves in a civil war which by all accounts was something else, even by their exacting standards. It was the kind of war to which the members of my profession were expressly not invited (even the Asvogel boys don't do business in Anticonessus) so it was of no interest to me. If they want to slaughter each other, let them. Senseless death on an industrial scale is, after all, part of the fabric of existence. Someone told me once that there are whales up in the Permian Sea that gobble up three tons of shrimps every day. Tragedy if you're a shrimp, but none of my business.

One thing that sort of made sense, and dislodged a few more crumbs of stone from the face of the dam, was the First Emperor's tomb being in Anticonessus. The Anticonessians believe that contact with the dead defiles you irreparably, so they don't rob graves, even ones stuffed with priceless artefacts. Against that, bear in mind that when he conquered the country, the first thing he did was empty it of Anticonessians, so their beliefs about the afterlife shouldn't have been relevant—

God help me, I thought, I'm starting to think like a treasure hunter. If I'd had the sense I was born with, I'd have slashed my wrists there and then.

*

"You're planning something," Fan said. "With the strange man and that whore. I've heard you talking."

Still two more days to go on the river. You can't hurry a barge. It goes as fast as ten horses can pull it. If you put on an extra pair of horses, it actually slows everything down. "Yes," I said.

"So you admit it."

"Why not? It's what we're going to do after we've got you safe. Nothing to do with you."

She burst into tears. I tried to remember what Stauracia had said, but the noise my sister makes when she's crying tends to blot out all forms of rational thought. "I promised you, didn't I? I said I'd get you safe, and that's exactly what I'm going to do."

"And then you're going to waltz off and leave me, and then those horrible men will find me and I'll be dead." She lifted her head and gave me the full benefit. "That's your idea of making things right, is it? A token gesture to ease your conscience, and then it's back to normal, killing and thieving with your evil friends. You know, that's exactly what I'd expect from you, so why am I surprised?"

It's odd, because I can stand up to most people and most things, when there's nowhere left to run. "You'll be fine," was all I could think to say. "It's a safe place. You'll have plenty of money. The people are good people. And you keep telling me, the sight of me makes you feel sick. Why would you want me to stick around?"

"I'd have thought it was the least you could do, after wrecking my entire life. But clearly you don't see it that way, so there's no point discussing it. You go off with that disgusting woman and forget about me, and when I'm dead you won't have to think about me any more. That's what you want, isn't it?"

I guess it was like fencing with a man in full armour, using only a foil. You can hit him as often as you like, but it makes no difference. But he only needs to land one or two good hits and you're on your knees. Inevitable, I guess, that anything to do with my sister made me think about fencing. I am, after all, living proof, reluctantly living proof, that in a fencing match the best man doesn't always win. "Whatever you say, " I said. "But we're going to the monastery, and you'll be safe there, and after that you can get on with your life and never have to see me again. That's got to be the best thing for both of us, surely."

"You murdered my brother. You ruined my life. What makes you think I can ever forget that?"

There's an old saying about the fox and the hedgehog. The fox knows many tricks, the hedgehog knows one good one. That's my sister and me. One good trick is all it takes. "Tell me what you want me to do and I'll do it," I said. "Only for God's sake stop beating up on me."

She looked at me. "Why?" she said.

I was glad when we got off the barge. It was raining hard, and we had six or so miles to walk, along a track that couldn't make up its mind if it wanted to be a road or a river. I hadn't been up that way for a long time, not since Prince Actaeon's ill-considered police action against the Avenging Hand. It was the same road that did for Actaeon, whose heavy cavalry churned it up so badly he couldn't bring up his supply train. I think I recognised some of the ruts.

We got there about an hour after the sun had set. We hung back while Stauracia went and hammered on the gate. Some old woman stuck her head out of a window and told her to go away. I didn't catch what Stauracia said but I guess it worked.

The gate opened and we went through, trailing so much mud we practically gave them an extra field. Someone held up a lantern, and I caught half a glimpse of a porter's lodge, with a flagstone floor and handsome granite stonework. "Wait there," the old woman said. "I'll send up to the abbess."

Much to my surprise, we weren't kept waiting for long. A woman appeared. She was about Stauracia's age, maybe a year or so younger. She was wearing a standard issue habit, which she'd clearly thrown on in a hurry, because out from under the hem and the cuffs peeped the hem and cuffs of a kingfisher-blue silk gown, fringed with enough seed pearls to fill an eggshell. Not just ordinary seed pearls; they were the freshwater sort, lumpy rather than spherical, and with that faint pink colour that you only get with the incredibly rare and expensive Echmen variety. I'm no expert, but I'd say uphill of four hundred staurata. Not, therefore, the sort of nightie you'd expect to see on a nun, even an abbess. The woman inside the clothes was equally improbable: flaming red hair and a face that would've secured her top billing at the Gallery, even if she was a deaf mute. All sorts of people get a true vocation to the contemplative life, but if she was one of them I'll cheerfully eat my boots. "Stauracia," she said. "I heard you were dead."

Stauracia grinned at her. "No," she said. "These are some friends of mine I'd like you to meet. This is Florian met' Einai, and this is his sister Phantis, Archduchess of—"

"I know who she is. What's she doing here?"

"Claiming sanctuary."

The abbess winced. "What about him?"

"He's not stopping."

"I thought she had a price out on his head."

"That was before she lost all her money. Bodvar sends his love, by the way."

The look on the abbess's face was pure terror, though she got rid of it quickly. "You want me to take her in."

"That's right."

"You do realise she's hotter than a stove."

"You'll manage. You're very good at keeping secrets. Just like me."

I'm not the most tender-hearted of people, but I don't enjoy watching someone suffer. "For God's sake, Stauracia—"

"Nobody knows she's here. It'll be fine."

I vaguely remembered Stauracia describing the abbess as a friend of hers. Curious use of the word. "All right," the abbess said. "But if anyone shows up here looking for her—"

"You'll defend her with your life's blood, naturally, it goes without saying. Thanks ever so much, Ingenua. I knew I could depend on you."

I gathered from the look in the abbess's eyes that Ingenua hadn't been her name for some time; and now I'd heard it, and so had my sister. Neatly done. "She'll have to bunk with the novices."

"I don't think she'd like that," Stauracia said. "You don't want to get on the wrong side of her, believe me. I think she'd be much happier in the guest suite. Oh, and you might want to find a couple of sisters who know about doing hair and dress-making and stuff like that. Two ought to be enough. She's got used to roughing it."

"All right," the abbess said. "Who are all those men outside the gate?"

"Oh, just some friends of ours. By the way, how's the redecorating coming along? I gather you're having the south cloister redone, after that flood."

Very neatly done. The abbess didn't answer, because it wasn't really a question, more a fairly unsubtle way of letting the abbess know that Stauracia had someone inside the abbey who told her what was going on; therefore poisoning my sister and chucking her down a well wasn't an option. "Wait there," the abbess said. "I'll tell the hospitaler to look after you."

She swept out, the hem of her silk gown scuffing up a little cloud of dust. When she'd gone, Stauracia let go a deep breath and wilted a little bit. "Thanks," I said.

"Piss off. That's a very dangerous woman, and now she wants my blood."

Not as dangerous as Stauracia, obviously, but then again, who is? "You trust her?"

"Don't be bloody stupid, of course I do or we wouldn't be here. Just, please bear in mind, I've used up one of my very best rainy-day resources for you. And her," she added, giving Fan a razor look. "This is the best I can do, both of you. If you don't like it, go suck an egg."

"Understood," I said. "By the way, who's Bodvar?"

Scowl. "Nobody you know. Now for God's sake try and behave. We're guests here, remember."

I didn't get to see much of the abbey. They wouldn't let us into the buildings proper, so we spent the night in the north cloister, where at least it was dry. I remember the amazing wall-paintings – relatively new, and usually I don't much care for modern stuff, but whoever they got to do them and however much they paid him, they did well. The whole of one wall was covered with a battle scene. Presumably it was an allegory of something or other – the battle between Orthodoxy and Heresy, or Purity of Body triumphant over Indigestion – but in places it was too real to be fun, if you know what I mean. My guess is, the painter had actually been in a real battle, once upon a time. He'd caught the way real bodies look, when they're all heaped up. It's not something you could figure out from first principles, if you'd never seen it for yourself. The nuns brought us something to eat: pork knuckles in a huge vat of fermented cabbage. I imagine it was what they were having, in which case the contemplative life is not for me.

"You can't leave me here," Fan said. "I don't trust these people. They'll kill me."

We were all ready to leave. "They're nuns," I said.

"She isn't. She doesn't look like any nun I ever saw."

"Nor me. But Stauracia says it's fine, so it's fine. Don't say a word," I added quickly. "Which reminds me. The money you owe her."

If Fan had had fur, it'd have risen on end. "I never agreed to that."

"Doesn't matter. You owe it to her, for saving your life."

"I'm not giving her anything."

I put my hand in my pocket and took out a large bag. "I thought you'd say that," I said. "So I've done it for you. Here's what's left."

"You *bastard*." She shrieked so loud, it put up two dozen rooks out of a nearby tree. "You stole from me. Give it back."

She made a grab for the bag. I let her take it, and she hugged it to her like a baby. "By my reckoning," I said, "what you've got there is worth closer to three hundred thousand than two-fifty. That's more than enough, even for you."

She'd opened the bag and was pawing through it. "You've taken my emeralds," she said, "and the ruby and diamond cluster, and the princess-cut solitaire Siggy gave me for our anniversary. You bastard, Florian. I want them back right now."

She made a grab for my coat, trying to get her hand in the pocket. "I haven't got them," I said. "I gave them to Stauracia. I wouldn't go mauling her about like that, she's liable to break your arm."

"You stole my present from Siggy to give to your—"

"Don't," I said, rather louder than I'd meant to. "Look, I don't give a damn about how you treat me, but Stauracia's put her life on the line for you. She doesn't care what you say about her, but I do."

"She's a thief and a whore and I hope she dies. I hope she sells you to the highest bidder. You deserve it. You deserve each other."

I took a deep breath. "Thank you," I said. "But I think she could do a whole lot better than me. Goodbye, Fan. Stay safe. Try not to piss the nuns off more than you can help."

"I want them back, Florian. Don't you dare walk away from me."

But you know what, I did. It nearly broke my heart to do it, but it was like putting down a heavy weight you've been carrying, or the first rain after a long, dry summer.

Stauracia's pal had given us a horse and cart, though I suspect it wasn't her idea. There was room for her and me on the box, and some barrels of flour and salt pork in the back to see us all as far as the coast. Stauracia had emptied the contents of another bag into her lap, and was looking it over with an educated eye.

"There's some good stuff here," she said. "Not worth what it'd have fetched twelve months ago, but not bad, even so."

"Put it away, for crying out loud," I said. "Before Gombryas or the lads see it."

She acknowledged the validity of that with a grunt, and stuffed the jewels back in the bag. "Well," she said. "We've got little miss sunshine safe, like I said we would. Now what?"

"You're sure your friend is all right?"

She grinned. "Like I said, she's a very dangerous woman. But that's good, because she'll do exactly what I tell her to. It's not like she's got a choice. Oh, come on," she added. "Don't look at me like that. You can't stand being in the same square mile with her, it's obvious. You should be skipping for joy."

"She's my sister," I said. "And she's right. I ruined her life, and everything she's ever done is my fault."

"You can believe that, if that's what it takes to soothe your precious conscience. Personally I think she's a long warm drink of piss."

"I don't think that changes anything," I said. "And like I said, she's that way because of me."

"Bullshit. Let's not talk about her any more. Let's talk about what we do next."

There are times when I can imagine what it's like being a piece of steel in a smithy. There are intervals when you're not being heated up to just short of melting point, but then you get bashed on with a hammer. "You mean this lunatic thing of Gombryas's. The treasure hunt."

"I think he's on to something."

"Absolutely not. Only idiots and losers believe in buried treasure. Only complete idiots and total losers go to Anticonessus. What's the matter with you, anyway? You've got a hundred thousand staurata in choice stones in your sticky little hands; you don't need to bother with this nonsense any more."

"Gombryas will make you go there. So I'm coming, too."

Oh, I thought; like that, is it? I hoped the moment would go away, but it didn't.

"Come on, Saevus, for crying out loud. Say something."

I had nothing to say that was fit for anyone with a shred of human feeling to hear. I don't know. Maybe it's the life I've led, being chased by bounty hunters and earning my living stealing from the dead. Maybe it's me. To this day – I know what happened all those years ago, when my brother insisted on fencing when we were both tired, and he misjudged a lunge and I didn't move my hand away fast enough. I remember it clearly. The memory is like steel. It's hard and sharp and when you try and bend it, it springs back. But a thought keeps nagging me. What if, after years of prodding and poking and probing, like when you've got a pip or a shred of meat stuck in a gap between your teeth, what if I've somehow managed to bend the memory just a tiny bit out of shape? It happens with even the finest steel, if you abuse it long enough and hard enough, fifty times a day, every day for twenty years. Maybe what I remember isn't what actually happened. Maybe I simply don't know the truth any more.

And because I don't know, there's a part of me that's frozen, suspended, like a man waiting for the result of a long-drawn-out lawsuit, or the final report of a committee. One of the consequences of this – breakdown, you could call it, or maybe it's more like a bottleneck or a gridlock; one of the consequences was that after the first time Stauracia saved my neck, during that business on Sirupat, there was a moment when we could have—

Excuse me. I'm not the most squeamish of people. The Soracii don't have pockets in their clothes, so they keep their small change in their mouths, generally tucked into their cheeks. So, when we clean up a battlefield with Soracian mercenaries, it's always worth prising their mouths open and having a feel about with your fingertip; you'll only get thirty or forty trachy per head, but it soon mounts up, and you come away with the price of a pair of boots or a side of bacon. And that doesn't bother me, that level of intimacy. But there are some things I can't even picture myself doing, not with that doubt hanging over me. There's a story in my family. A great-great-aunt or something like that came across her daughter in the stables, blowing one of the grooms. She looked at her and said, "Leave it alone, you don't know where it's been." Good story. The thing is, I know where I've been. Or at least I have a pretty good idea, but I can't quite trust myself about certain details.

Stauracia knows this about me. Part of it I've told her, the rest she's smart enough to have figured out. She knows she's wasting her time, but she still does it. I pretend to myself that I don't trust her, because there were those times when she tried to sell me to the bad guys, but that's just me kidding myself. And that's quite enough about me to be going on with.

"Fine," I said. "If that's what you want to do."

You can't get rid of Stauracia that easily. "There we are, then. All settled. We're going to Anticonessus."

That night we camped in a gully. I generally like to sleep close to the fire, so that if I wake up in the night I've got light to read by. While we were at Ogiv, a copy of Rutilian's *Images of the City of God* had somehow found its way into my coat pocket. I'd had a bad dream and woken up shivering. If anything could put me back to sleep, it'd be Rutilian's explanation of the dual procession of the Divine Essence. I found the book. It fell open about halfway through, because there was a sheet of parchment shoved in between the pages.

I recognised the handwriting. As I think I mentioned, Fan writes better than most professional scribes.

Florian—

I was there the night you killed him. I was up in the gallery. I wanted to watch Scynthius fencing, because he was always so graceful. I saw what happened. He overreached and lost his balance, like you said. But there was a moment when you could've turned your hand, and you didn't. I saw you. I saw your face. You did it on purpose. You had the chance, to make it look like an accident, and you took it. It was deliberate.

I never told Daddy, or Siggy. I couldn't bear to tell anyone, because you're my brother and I loved you so much. Listening to you, I think you've managed to talk yourself into thinking that it really was an accident. I couldn't tell you to your face, but you really do need to know. You need to know who you are, and what you've done.

Thank you for saving my life. I don't know if it's worth saving. I ask myself, would I have killed Siggy if I hadn't seen you do what you did? We'll never know, will we? You saved my life, but that doesn't change anything, not really. All you saved was the creature you turned me into.

Your sister,

Phantis.

Swell, I thought. Then I folded the letter and put it back in the book.

5

Anticonessus is called that because it's on the opposite side of the Conessus river. Opposite to what? To us, of course; us in this context being the Robur Empire. The Robur, bless them, saw the whole world in those terms: us, and savages. One of the consequences of that mindset is that, if you want to see one of the great Robur cities, like Auga or Civitas, you need to take a sharp hook with you to chop away the brambles.

Certainly, living next to the Robur was one of the things that made the Anticonessians turn out like they did. The Conessus is a big river most of the time, but it's fed by torrential rains in the Epsa Mountains, and once in a lifetime the rains don't fall, and you can cross the Conessus relatively easily at one of a dozen points. This the Robur did, every chance they had, and what they got up to doesn't bear thinking about, even for someone in my profession. The idea was to teach the savages a pre-emptive lesson they wouldn't forget in a hurry. On one level, sound thinking: what's the use of a punitive expedition, after all? You can slaughter a quarter of a million savages and burn their houses and their crops, and drag away the relatively few you don't kill to work your slate quarries, but that's not going to bring back the poor devils the savages scalped and murdered. No, the sensible thing is to do it to them first. "Let them hate so long as they fear" is one of the few genuine Robur quotes everybody knows, and you can see where they were coming from. And where it got them, in the end – provided, as I said, you bring a hook.

Moral: getting into Anticonessus is a drag, except when it doesn't rain in the mountains. You can't just wait till it's dark and slip across the border, because the border is a roaring river a quarter of a mile wide – except, of course, at Ennea Crunoe, where it's squeezed between two mountains into a nightmare of foam and violence, tumbling vertically down the world's biggest waterfall. At Ennea, the river is only three hundred yards wide. Piece of cake.

But there's always the tunnel. Amazingly, the Anticonessians dug it themselves, thousands of years ago, using antler picks and stone hammers to chip away the sandstone, and they've kept it clear and open ever since, except while the Robur were around. They did it because they believe that Ennea is the gateway between the real world and the land of the dead, so when you die you go through the tunnel, after which you're reborn as a – there's no simple translation for the Anticonessian word. It means foreigner, ghost, revenant, monster. You can see why the Robur blockade stressed them out so much. When the Robur closed off their end of the tunnel with massive blocks of stone, it meant that the dead (malevolent, by definition) were prevented from leaving Anticonessus for four hundred years. You can also see why the Anticonessians take a dim view of anyone coming up the tunnel the other way.

Accordingly, there are guards at their end. The task devolves on an order of monks, chosen in infancy and trained all their lives in religious orthodoxy and hand-to-hand combat. Even the First Emperor and the Robur were reluctant to mess with the Gatekeepers.

However—

It's an expression, isn't it? News from Anticonessus; or else you can say cold fire, dry water or rocking-horse shit. There is no news from Anticonessus. But the news from Anticonessus was that during the late unpleasantness, the Gatekeepers (for the first time in history) were kidded into taking sides in a civil war; and they picked the wrong side. Silver medallists in an Anticonessian civil war tend to cease to exist. Therefore (if the news was accurate) there were no more Gatekeepers and the tunnel was wide open. You could just stroll on through and there'd be nobody to hinder you.

Provided, of course, that the news was accurate. "It's true, I keep telling you," Gombryas said. "I had it from a bloke who's been there. He walked all the way through the tunnel and came out the other side, and all he saw was bats."

"Sure," I said. "I believe that that's what he told you."

"I've heard the same thing," Stauracia said. "It was in an intelligence report from the Sisters' station in Gordula. One of their agents—"

"Gordula's a thousand miles from Ennea Crunoe. What the hell would they know about anything?"

"The agent wasn't from Gordula. It was a round-robin to all heads of station. If the Sisters say the tunnel's open, the tunnel's open. You can take that to the bank."

"It may have been open then," I objected. "Doesn't mean it still is. How long ago was this report?"

"My man went through three months ago," Gombryas said. "How long?"

Stauracia shrugged. "Six months," she said, "something like that. It was a few months after the end of the civil war."

"Fine," I said. "Look, these people are lunatics. They think that unless there's someone minding the door, the dead are going to come swarming back in and start eating them. Therefore, just because the gate may have been open six months ago—"

"Three months," Gombryas said.

"Six months ago, we can't assume it's still clear now. And since we know the Anticonessian definition of someone walking *up* the tunnel—"

"We'll go there," Stauracia said, "and take a look. Carefully. If the tunnel's guarded, we'll turn round and come back. If it isn't, we'll go on. Now I can't say fairer than that, can I?"

I waited till Gombryas went for a shit, then turned on her. "You've got to stop encouraging him," I said. "On his own, I can handle him. With you egging him on—"

"Think about it," she said. "The First Emperor's gold armour."

"Don't say it. Please."

"The big score." She looked at me. "Just think about it, that's all I'm saying."

"You've already had your big score, you stupid bitch," I yelled at her. "One hundred thousand staurata. Silly money. You can't possibly want more than that. Not even you."

"Yes, but you haven't." She was looking at me as if I was the storm and she was the eye. "I know you, Saevus. You need to find somewhere safe. The only safe place in this world is a large amount of money. And don't forget, there's a war coming.

Everything's going to be different after that. I don't think a hundred thousand's necessarily going to be enough. But in Sashan or Echmen, with the First Emperor's gold armour—"

It's the way her mind works. And that mind has a proven track record as an inspired tactician; just ask the Sisters and the Knights, who don't hire just anybody. "You're crazy," I said.

"No, you are. You're crazy if you think everything's just going to chug along the way it always has, because the war really is coming this time, and when it gets here—" She was actually scared. "You've stopped it twice now, dead in its tracks, but you know what they say, third time's the charm. The simple fact is, the Sashan and the West *want* to rip each other to pieces, and you darting in between them and snatching away their latest flashpoint doesn't actually solve anything. And you know what happens if you try and stop two dogs fighting. They both bite you. It's serious, Florian."

"Please don't call me that."

"She does. It happens to be your name." She was giving me that big sister look of hers. "The big smash is coming, so we need to get out of the way, fast as we can. And like I just said, the only safe place to hide in the whole world is behind a huge amount of money, so much money that we can be a couple of Westerners living deep inside Sashan or Echmen, and nobody will bother us. You've got to understand that, while there's still time."

The big smash, the big score. A lot of people genuinely think in those terms. Me, I've been to a lot of places and seen a ludicrously huge amount of suffering and misery, the result of too many people trying to make the small score and avoid the small smash – wars over borders and trade routes and access to water, wars over who gets to be king, duke, chief, bishop, wars over relatively small amounts of money, wars over matters of principle, for crying out loud. Chusro Asvogel says that the human race needs a continual succession of small wars, because if we had peace for more than fifteen years, the upshot would be a really big war and none of us would survive. I think he's probably right, but I deny the assumption behind it, not because I don't think it's true but because for all my faults I'm human, and I don't want to believe that kind of truth about a species I belong to. But did Stauracia think that way – big scores, big wars, the world and all the people changing for ever? Or was she trying to kid me into something? And on that question hung all the law and the prophets, and I wasn't sure I knew the answer.

"Look at me," I said. "And tell me you think going to Anticonessus is a good idea."

She rolled her eyes. "Of course it's not," she said. "It's incredibly dangerous and stupid. But I think the gold exists, and the civil war means we've got an opportunity. And, yes, I think we *need* that money, or we'll be screwed."

There was always, of course, the possibility that she knew stuff I didn't. A woman who'd worked for the Sisters *and* the Knights, with a habit of reading documents carelessly left lying around in locked strongboxes; a woman who liked to keep her best cards up her sleeve. The latter is a deplorable habit, of which I'm guilty every time I've got anything remotely resembling a good card. If I knew something really hot in this situation, would I tell her?

"You know the gold is there, don't you? You knew before Gombryas talked to his horrible friend."

I knew she'd only look at me, and she did.

"Fine," I said. "Let's all go to Antifuckingconessus."

*

Easier said, of course, than done. It's a long way, even if you go by sea, and we were coming up to the time of year when the wind does something technical and only lunatics sail east of the Pillars of Gratian; if we went by land, we'd have a hideously long trudge on vile roads and then we'd reach Sashan territory, a neck of which we'd have to cross, and for various reasons to do with the stuff that happened on Sirupat, setting foot on Sashan turf isn't a good idea for me. There was also the small issue of money—

"Not a problem," she said. "I've got lots of it, remember?"

"Yes, but that's yours." I looked at her. "You're offering to finance this bloody stupid trip, out of your nest egg?"

"Don't be an idiot, Saevus. If we succeed, we're all so rich that nothing matters. If we don't succeed, we'll be dead. I think I can run to five hundred staurata."

Which wasn't like her at all. "Fine," I said. "Thanks."

And I meant it, too. It's nice to be coerced into a suicide mission at someone else's expense for a change, instead of having to foot all the bills myself.

So we headed for the coast and wound up at Port Sancres. Don't know if you've been there; you've probably forgotten it if you have. It's one long, narrow street running down a steep hill to a smallish bay. Nothing much happens there unless the weather turns bad, at which point ships on the Beloisa–Auxentia run make for it to ride out the storm. The Invincible Sun's sense of humour means that there are often nasty bits of weather at that end of the Friendly Sea shortly after the harvest and the vintage, around the time when the big freighters are carrying their bulkiest loads; as I said just now, Sancres is a small harbour, so it's a matter of luck whether there's room when you get there. If there isn't, you have to stay outside and get smashed into matchwood on the rocks, along with all the food you're carrying to the hungry folks back home. The rest of the year, there's nothing in Sancres apart from a few lobster boats, something you might like to consider next time you give thanks to your omnipotent, loving God.

We were in luck (good luck or bad luck: depends on your perspective, I guess). There was a small fleet of Denyen barges in the harbour, talking Scona marble to Antolbia, where they would load up with lumber for the return journey. Great big barges have to hug the coast and they move pretty slowly, so they make a habit of stopping at all the little out-of-the-way places, where the crew can sell and buy stuff on their own account. It's a recognised perk of barge work, to make up for the boredom, the length of time you're away and the murderous hard work loading and unloading at either end. There's always room for casual passengers on a stone barge, and they'll happily give you a ride so long as you're prepared to pay them silly money for it.

I know several members of the business community in Sancres, since we're in basically the same line of work. I pick up leftovers from battlefields; they scavenge the coves and beaches for flotsam every time a big ship comes for sanctuary in the bay and finds there's no room. Since it's seasonal work, some of my associates aren't above helping ships find the rocks even when there isn't a storm, by lighting beacons and signal fires at the wrong times in the wrong places. If you ask me, this is unethical, but they've been doing it for a long time in Sancres, so there can't be anything really bad in it.

Which is how I came to be knocking on the door of my old friend Catapygaena. She looked at me and scowled, like my friends usually do, and told me to go away. Just kidding, naturally.

"I was wondering," I said, "if you'd like to buy some stuff."

That was different. "What stuff?"

"Everything we've got, basically. Stock from our last job, picks, shovels, sacks, weapons, gloves, baskets—"

Catapygaena can smell a buyer's market the way sharks smell blood. "Come in and have a drink. What's all this about, then?"

"Going-out-of-business sale," I said. "And there's a slight but real chance that some of my lads might be interested in leaving me and joining your organisation. In which case, I'd be sorry to see them go, but I wouldn't want to stand in the way of them improving themselves. Sensible prices," I said. "No reasonable offer refused."

She studied me for a moment, trying to see the trap for which I was the bait. "Bollocks," she said. "Everybody knows, you're the great survivor. Other grave robbers come and go but you go on for ever. So what's really—?"

I shook my head. "Not this time," I said. "Long story short, I got the lads into a bit of bother, and Polycrates and some of the others decided they'd had enough and quit on me. Now there's not enough of us left to do the job, and I can't be bothered to start all over again. So I'm selling up."

"And?"

I shrugged. "Haven't made my mind up yet. I'm torn between mercenary soldiering and joining a monastery."

"So there really is going to be a war. What've you heard?"

"I didn't say that. Would you like to see an inventory, or just make up a figure out of your head?"

We discussed numbers for a while, and then I went down to the harbour and spoke to the lads. Catapygaena, I told them, had jobs for anyone who wanted them; decent wages, paid regularly, plus a modest but acceptable signing-on bonus. I'd had to fight like a cornered wolf to get them that, but I got it, which made me feel quite proud. It showed that Catapygaena acknowledged that anyone who'd worked for me had been trained, starved and battered into a superior category of worker.

"Does this mean you're breaking up the company?" one of them asked: Brocian, been with me for years, one of the best bent-sword-straighteners in the trade.

"No," I said. "But you've probably heard by now, we're headed for Anticonessus. You'd have to be out of your mind to go there. So I thought it'd be nice if I found you an alternative."

No, they hadn't heard anything about Anticonessus. When the yelling died down enough for me to make myself heard, I repeated Catapygaena's offer. Then they told me some things about myself which I already knew. This went on for a while, and I admit I was surprised by the warmth of their feelings – how could I do something like that, turning them loose after everything we'd been through together, didn't any of that mean anything, and so forth. Some of them were actually in tears. Rather a shock. I genuinely didn't know they cared. I wouldn't have, in their shoes.

"It's all right," I told them, "you can still be together; the only thing missing will be me, so that's all right. Oh, and Gombryas: he's quitting, too. And Catapygaena's a much better boss than me, she hardly ever gets her people killed, and you get to stay in the same place instead of all the travelling around. Sorry, but my mind's made up."

"Fuck you," said Sigister, one of the boot patchers; been with us six years or so. I never really liked him much. "Gombryas said we were going for the big score. You're doing this to cheat us out of our rightful share."

"In Anticonessus," I said. "Ask him if you don't believe me. And if you want to come along, you're more than welcome."

"Bullshit. Nobody chooses to go to Anticonessus. That's just lies to get rid of us."

"Ask the skipper of the barge. He'll tell you Gombryas and me are booked as far as Lachsar. What happens at Lachsar, anyone?"

No answer; because the answer is, at Lachsar, the Conessus river reaches the sea, and that's all.

"Like I said," I told them, "it's entirely up to you, but the offer's open. Come with me if you like, stay here, whatever. But make your minds up quickly, because—"

"What are you going to Anticonessus for?"

"Gombryas reckons he's on to some bones. He thinks they may be worth money. I promised him I'd go with him, soon as my sister was safe." Big shrug. "Who knows, he might be right and there's a small fortune in relics. Or maybe not. In any case, I'm honour-bound to go. You aren't."

"Here," someone called out. "Come and look at this."

I didn't recognise the voice, but there was a special sort of urgency in it that was hard to ignore. The lads began scrambling up the stairs that led to the top of the sea wall. I followed.

The sea was full of ships. I've never seen anything like it, except once. Big ships, all more or less identical; long, low in the water, I believe the technical term is galleass, though everybody calls them runners. They have five banks of oars and three masts; they can make eight knots under sail and six under oars, with a ramming speed of ten knots – I have no idea what that means, but apparently it's better than the Sashan quinqueremes can manage, and that was all that mattered when they were designing the things. They were black with new tar,

and heading from west to east. I counted a hundred and six.
Nobody said a word. I don't know about such things. I do know
that the standard crew of a runner is three hundred men, plus
fifty or so marines to do the actual fighting once the ships have
grappled to the enemy, assuming the enemy hasn't rammed
and sunk them first – thirty-five thousand men were on those
ships, a cityful, a number too huge to have any sort of meaning.

We don't get that sort of job, but Daresh Asvogel told me
once about the time he and his brothers cleared up after the
battle of Duain Cerauno. It nearly put them out of business, he
said, because the numbers, the scale was so impossibly huge,
twenty-eight thousand dead bodies, and the penalty clause in
the contract was savage. They were camped out on the battlefield for three weeks, lugging, shucking and shovelling, and
the stink and the flies were something else; after the first week
they stopped stripping and looting the dead and simply dug big
pits to shovel them into; a total dead loss, from a business point
of view, but all they wanted was for the job to be over so they
could get out of there, and even then it took them fifteen days
to move all that earth and shift all that rotting meat. Complete
and utter waste of fucking time, was how Daresh put it, and
he solemnly urged me never to undertake a battle with more
than eight thousand dead. More than that, he said, and it'll end
up costing you money, and where the hell's the point in that?

"That's not enough," Stauracia said. I hadn't seen her come
up on to the wall.

"A hundred and six," I said.

"Not enough. The Sashan galleys are smaller, but last I
heard the Sashan fleet was over three hundred. Presumably
the plan is to smash through by sheer weight, but that's not
going to work. You see, those things have too much draught;

they need deep water. The Sashan galleys are shallower, so they can go closer inshore, get in round the sides, outflank, encircle. Fuck it," she went on. "They must have realised that. If I can figure it out, so can they. But they carried on building runners nevertheless. Why would you do that, when you know you're going to lose?"

I decided if she didn't know the answer to that, there was no point telling her. "Who says that's the whole fleet?" I said. "For all we know, that's just the advance guard."

She didn't bother to contradict me. "You're looking at thirty-five thousand dead men," she said. "Pity about that. Still, the sea war isn't everything. They'll still have to slug it out on land; that's what these grand strategists never seem to realise. It all depends on what the Sashan want to achieve, I guess."

Achieve struck me as a funny word to use, in the context. Mostly, what war achieves is carrion. "Has it occurred to you," I said, "that those ships are going in the same direction as us?"

She shrugged. "It's a big sea. And a runner's a hell of a lot faster than a barge."

Which was, of course, true. A while back I had to listen to some bore in a bar explaining to me precisely why the runner was going to be the finest, most perfect war machine ever built. Always assuming, he added at the end, that it's used properly, because in the wrong place at the wrong time it's just a floating coffin. "Ah, well," I said. "Not our problem. Are we still going to Anticonessus?"

"Why not? I don't really see how that changes anything."

"We've decided," Sigister told me, about an hour later. "We're staying here."

"I think that's the right decision," I said. "Well, good luck, and I hope things work out. Like I said, Catapygaena's a doll once you get to know her. Better than working for me, anyhow."

"Fuck you," Sigister said. "You've screwed up all our lives, and now you're dumping us. I hope you can sleep nights, after what you've done to us."

I nodded. "But at least I'm not going to get you all killed," I said. "That's got to count for something."

I hadn't expected it to feel like that, sailing out of Sancres Bay and leaving them all behind, knowing I'd probably never see any of them again. It was like I'd been carrying twice my own weight on my back uphill for as long as I could remember, and now it wasn't there any more, and I could breathe. "What are you sighing about?" she asked me, joining me at the rail. "Come on, Saevus. Admit it, you were never any good at the salvage business."

"I buried a lot of bodies."

"Never made any money, though."

"True." I walked away from the rail and sat down on a barrel. "You know about sea stuff," I said. "Aren't they taking a hell of a risk, sending the fleet out at this time of year? I thought it was getting to the time when it's too dangerous—"

"Warships are different," she said. "It's about weight distribution and keel-to-beam ratios. Basically they don't flip over as easily as tubs like this. And going late in the season can be a tactical advantage. You're sort of daring the enemy to come out and do a bloody stupid thing. Either he risks his fleet getting blown on the rocks and smashed up, or you're going to come along and burn it down to the waterline before it's even left the dock." She frowned. "Fact is, they've got to be imaginative if they want to stand any chance of winning, because of the horrible disadvantage they're starting with. Like I told you. Not enough ships."

I don't like being on boats. You're floating on the surface of certain death, and everything is out of your control. "How much longer before we get there?"

"We're making about four knots. That's good. Two days, maybe three."

Three more days on a boat. Every time I set foot on one of those things, I make myself a promise: never again. "You were right," I said. "There's going to be a war."

"Not necessarily." She was looking out to sea. There was nothing out there except grey water. "The fleet may have been a show of strength at exactly the right time. Could be, someone in intelligence has heard something about, oh, I don't know, divisions in the Sashan court, with a war party and an anti-war party, and maybe they've timed sending the fleet out just right, and the anti-war party will win. Or it could be a disastrous mistake and just the excuse the hawks need. Without knowing what's really going on, you're always just guessing. You have to trust the people in power to do the right thing at the right time. Or you need to get your hands on a stupid amount of money and buy yourself an island." She turned and looked at me. "Three guesses which choice I'd make."

Thirty-five thousand men going to their deaths, or maybe they'd already got there. I could see her point. It would take an astounding amount of money to insulate yourself against people who do things like that. "What are you going to do with your hundred thousand?" I asked, mostly to make conversation.

"Already done it," she said. "There's an agent for the Golden Hand in Sancres, so I opened an account. I was just in time: he was packing up to leave."

The Golden Hand is the third biggest bank in the Sashan Empire, with its headquarters in the wonderful city of Suda, where the streets are paved with lapis lazuli, and even the beggars have slaves to trim their toenails for them. "Not a bad idea. Remind me," I said. "Can you speak Sashan?"

She nodded. "Not so bad," she said. "I have trouble remembering when to use the subjunctive. I know you're fluent. I've heard you."

"I once met a Sashan I really liked," I said. "I have no idea if the rest of them are like him."

She frowned at me. The man I was talking about was the Great King, in exile. Presumably, if things were happening and war was now feasible politically, he was dead. I felt sorry about that. "They're just people," she said. "Some of them are saints, a lot of them are bastards, and then there's about a million shades of grey in between. If you're worried about fitting in once we go and live there, I don't really think it's going to matter."

We, she'd said. I felt sorry for her. Years ago when I was in Choris, this dog followed me home. I kept trying to shoo it away, but it just barked at me. When I shut the door in its face, it howled. I tried to tell it, following me is a really bad idea, but I guess it didn't believe me.

Welcome to Lachsar. The Conessus flows out into a lagoon, all mud banks and sandbars; the way in is marked with a row of piles driven into the seabed, and God help you if you drift off line, because nobody else will. But the barge crew were anxious to go there, because they'd bought lemons and dried coriander to sell in the market, or, better still, trade for tortoiseshell and amber. They can't get lemons or coriander in Lachsar, but if you carry on thirty miles up the coast to Pellora, they're as cheap as apples in autumn; but the tides are against you, so sailing from Pellora to Lachsar is certain death, except for six weeks in spring. Tortoiseshell and amber are practically worthless in Lachsar. You can just wander down to the beach with a basket and help yourself, provided you're a resident. Try it if you're a foreigner and they'll hang you.

The crew, therefore, were more than happy to risk their lives tracing their way through the lagoon channels; in fact, if we'd objected, they'd have thrown us over the side. We landed just as the sun was going down. Half an hour later and we'd have had to ride out the night in the channels, a stupid thing to do because there's nothing for an anchor to bite into.

"The rest of the way we can walk," Gombryas said, as we trailed up the muddy beach. "Happy now?"

"Yes."

Gombryas and Stauracia had had some kind of falling-out on the ship. Neither of them was prepared to tell me what it was about. It wasn't quite at the tell-your-friend stage, but it wasn't far off it. Precisely what I needed most before setting out to penetrate Anticonessus.

"We'll need a cart," I said, "and supplies, and spare clothes, and I imagine you two will want weapons, though where we're going I reckon they'd cause more problems than they'd solve. How much money have we got?"

"Plenty," she said. "And too bloody right we need weapons. The absolute minimum would be swords, shields, bows—"

"What we want is a good knife each," Gombryas said. "Sort of thing you can tuck in the back of your waistband, so it's not obvious but you can get at it in a hurry. Anything else is just extra weight to carry. Like this."

He produced a big knife out of nowhere. I think I was supposed to admire it. "And new boots," I said. "This pair I'm
wearing came off an artilleryman in Antecyrene, and they're
starting to let in water. Let's be wild and reckless just for once
in our lives and buy something nobody's died in."

"I get my footwear from the Stenea brothers in Beloisa," she
said. "Ninety gulden, but it lasts. And I don't have to look like
I've just escaped from the slate quarries."

I resisted the urge to look at her feet, which was suddenly
very strong. "Fine," I said. "When we get to Lachsar, we'll
each of us do our own shopping. But we will need a cart, and a
couple of mules. I'll see to it."

"I'll do it," she said. "You'll just buy the first thing you see."

Stauracia bought the cart. She chose well and bargained
ruthlessly. Gombryas sat in the back, with the flour barrel
and the sacks of dried fruit, muttering something about giving
us love birds some space. It was probably just as well that
Stauracia had decided she couldn't hear anything he said.

"It's twelve miles up the road," Stauracia was saying.
"Then you reach a crossroads, and you take the left-hand
turn, then follow the road for a day until you hit a cattle-drove
going north—"

"What you want to do," Gombryas said behind me, "is keep
on the road out of town, past the crossroads, till you come to
a lake. There's a ferry, and you keep on for about six hours,
and then you come out on the old Imperial road which goes
straight to Ennea Crunoe. Otherwise you're going all round
the houses."

I stopped listening to them and amused myself with the
thought that I was in a cart with the only two people I had left
in the world, the only two people who cared about me and I

cared about. I'd have jumped out and made a run for it, only I didn't have the faintest idea where we were.

Thanks to all the expert navigational advice I was getting, we ended up following the Conessus river for two days as it snaked around through a big slab of couch-grass-and-thorn-sapling wilderness. We were on one side; on the other side was Anticonessus, the forbidden country. As far as I could tell, both sides of the river were identical and equally deserted, which was a blessing.

"Something nobody's given any thought to," I said to nobody in particular, "is how we're going to transport ten thousand suits of gold armour across this lot, and then get it on a ship to Auxentia or Scona. It's a bit late, I know, but I suggest we treat this as a reconnaissance mission. We go there, we find out there's no armour and it's all been a waste of time, and we come back. Or, in the incredibly unlikely event that there actually is something there—"

"A barge," she interrupted. "We load it on a barge and float it down the river to the sea. Obviously."

I'd been about to suggest that, honest. "Of course," I said. "Presumably you've got one of those handy-dandy collaps-ible barges that fold away in your pocket when not in use. Alternatively, we're going to need at least two dozen wagons, plus oxen, plus drivers. Have you the faintest idea of what ten thousand suits of gold armour are likely to weigh?"

"Six hundred tons," Gombryas said immediately. "So what we'll need is a really big raft. We could build it ourselves, but I figure we'd be better off getting it made for us. There's logging camps in the mountains over there somewhere." He made a vague gesture on our side of the river. "They must float lumber down the river all the time. Course, we don't tell 'em what we want it for, or they'd cut our throats."

"Make that six dozen wagons," I said. "Which means hiring a hundred and forty strangers, on the Anticonessus border. If only either of you had stopped to think this thing out just a little bit before dragging me out here into the armpit of the universe—"

"Coal barges," Stauracia said. "Two of them ought to do it. We charter them from the charcoal burners at Philargyron. While we were in Lachsar I took the trouble to ask around, and I got the name of the man who handles organising the barges at the Philargyron end. For three hundred staurata, we can have two barges waiting for us at Ennea Crunoe, and a hundred of his men, though we'll have to pay them separately. The big problem will be finding something to crate the stuff up in, so the handlers won't realise what they're shifting. I admit I haven't figured that out yet, but you would insist on rushing into this job without giving me time to think."

If I'd had a hat I'd have taken it off to her. "That's a hell of a lot of crates," I said. "And just the three of us to shift six hundred tons of heavy metal. It's just as well there won't be anything there, because if there had been, we'd have killed ourselves trying to move it."

And so on and so forth for two days, with the Conessus river roaring and crashing so loud over on our left that we had to shout to make ourselves heard. Looking back, two of the happiest days of my life. Or at least, two of the least unhappy, which isn't quite the same thing.

Nothing in your life, or even mine, could prepare you for Ennea Crunoe. You plod up a very long, flat rise, where you don't realise you're going uphill until you look back and see that the sky is somehow below you; and then you go over the top of the crest and look down, and there's a steep slope, and, at the bottom of it, Ennea Crunoe.

I guess it started out as gently sloping moorland, down which water trickled. These days it's a deep and unexpected ravine. The Conessus, about a quarter of a mile wide, falls off the edge, like a drunk walking along the top of a wall, into a rocky trench at right angles to the flow of the river, then storms its way round a hairpin bend and carries on downstream as though nothing had happened. The wall it falls off is about as high as the river is wide, so call it a quarter-mile, give or take. I'm trying to describe it as prosaically as I can, because if I started using words like stunning and breathtaking, you'd assume it was just a traveller's tale and I'd never been there. But the biggest things about it were the noise and the smell. The smell was just water, like when it rains after a long, dry spell. The noise was – I guess it was like being deaf, because you couldn't hear anything else, not people talking or the creak of the cartwheels or the crunch of your boots when you jumped down off the box. It was a bit like when your leg goes to sleep, and you move it with your hand but you can't feel anything.

No point trying to have a conversation, that's for sure. Gombryas grabbed my arm and pointed at something. He's got amazing long-distance eyesight. His mouth was moving so presumably he was telling me what he'd seen. I hoped it was the gateway to the tunnel, and followed him.

And that was precisely what it was. When we got closer, it wasn't hard to spot at all. Someone had gone to the trouble of building a magnificent classical gatehouse, with a colonnade, architrave and triangular pediment, and thirty granite steps leading up to it. Someone showing off – and a hiding to nothing, because compared to the falls it was tiny and ludicrous, but presumably it was only public money, so who gave a damn? Up close I could see that there had once been a long inscription, in elegant foot-high Robur capitals. Completely illegible now, of course.

If anything, it was louder inside the building than outside. I was starting to get a bit sick of having my head crushed in, so I stuffed my ears with some scraps of sheep's wool I'd picked off a thorn bush a few days earlier. It helped, a little: still deaf, but not so painful.

At least finding what we were looking for wasn't difficult. You go through the doorway in the magnificent façade and you find yourself in a square stone box. It would've been as dark as a bag in there if the roof hadn't fallen in at some point. In the middle of the floor of the box was a grand staircase, going down. It was wide enough for a platoon of soldiers to march down in battle formation; probably that was the original idea. Of course, nobody had seen fit to bring a lantern.

It was like some sort of horrible negotiation with death. In return for the noise abating just enough that we could hear each other shout, we had to give up light, and being able to see where the hell we were going. After half an hour of being deafened, it was a deal I felt I could live with. We found a wall, which was smooth, with grooves at regular intervals, so presumably built out of dressed stone blocks, and felt our way along it. The floor under our feet was smooth, with maybe an inch of water. For some reason all I could think about was that line from the catechism they made me learn when I was a kid: on the third day, He descended into hell. Quite, except that I don't suppose He had to walk, unless someone like me was handling the travel arrangements.

A bit like death, though, which is presumably why the Anticonessians think the way they do; doesn't seem quite so silly when you've actually been there and walked through it. For one thing you're blind, deaf and dumb, heading away from everything familiar into the unknown; assuming you come out the other side, you must be changed in some way, or else what's the point of all the overpowering stage effects and the melodrama? No, it's not unreasonable, in context. Imagine you're the first man to see it, ever. You say to yourself, there's got to be a reason for all that, and you set yourself to trying to figure out what the reason can be. Then the penny drops, and it's obvious. Well, it was obvious to me, groping my way along a carefully finished wall in the pitch dark and the deafening noise, going away from my sister and my old life towards a promise of unlimited wealth and a new beginning; and since you'd be hard put to find anyone more mundane and unimaginative than me, imagine the effect on a sensitive person, with ordinary decent human feelings.

I came to the end of the wall. At right angles to it, there was a blinding light. So I'd always gathered, from people who've nearly died and then come back; but this light came from a door, nearly closed but not quite, and the dazzling beam that hurt my eyes turned out to be nothing more than the boring old everyday Invincible Sun. A silhouette that reminded me of Gombryas gave the door a shove and I saw the world outside, bubbling with fiery gold like the runoff from a volcano. Welcome to Anticonessus.

We didn't hang around to admire the monastery buildings, though they looked amazing. Instead we got as far away from them as we could as quickly as we could go, until eventually we could hear ourselves think.

"Lunatics" was Stauracia's verdict. "Imagine being a monk, and spending your entire life getting hammered by that fuck-ing *noise*. Though I don't suppose it lasted very long. Pretty soon you'd be stone deaf and there'd be nothing to notice."

Stauracia was angry more than anything, as if the whole thing had been a studied insult to her personally. Gombryas looked as though he'd been beaten up by experts, who'd pulped his soul without leaving a mark on his body. Odd, because I'd never imagined Gombryas with a soul before.

"You do realise," I said. "We left all our stuff behind."

Gombryas gave me a sad stare. "Don't blame me," Stauracia said. "One minute we were poking about exploring, and then we were in the tunnel and all I could think of was keeping going and getting to the end. It's that damn noise, you can't think." She paused. "I suppose we could go back and get the stuff, now we know it's safe."

I looked back down the slope, to the gatehouse of the mon-astery: four hundred yards, if that. A stroll. "You can go back if you like," I said. "Besides, we'd never get the cart down those steps."

Gombryas looked at me. "It's ninety miles to where we need to get to," he said. "What are we going to eat, for crying out loud?"

It struck me as a stupid question, almost childish. Dead people don't need to eat, everyone knows that. "Go on, then," I said. "I'll wait for you here."

He glared at me. "I'm getting sick of you," he said. "You've done nothing but try and screw this job up from the get-go. You send away all the lads, so we've got nobody to haul the stuff—"

"That wasn't me. They decided they'd had enough."

"Bullshit. But you figured we wouldn't need them because

you don't think there's anything there. And now it's just you and me, and *her*, so what I'm asking myself is, what do I need you for anyhow? You don't think it's there, and one extra pair of hands isn't going to make shit difference. Why don't you just piss off back down the tunnel and leave me alone?"

"Because I'm your friend, Gombryas," I said. "Also, I'm not going back down there again, not for anything. At least, not until I've had plenty of time to get my head back together."

"Excuse me." Stauracia was using her ice-cold voice. "I'm here, too, remember? And, I believe, I'm just as much use as he is. More so. Can we please stop fighting and get a grip?"

The upshot of which was that Gombryas and Stauracia went back down the tunnel to fetch as much of the gear as they could manage, leaving me behind to keep guard and, if needs be, hold off the entire Anticonessian nation until they got back. To be fair, they spent a long time making torches out of dry reeds twisted and plaited thickly together, but with no oil to drench them with I don't suppose they burned worth a damn, assuming they ever managed to get them lit in the first place. I didn't ask, and they didn't tell. But there was a perfectly good lantern in the cart, so their return journey was no bother at all.

"What I heard about the Anticonessian civil war," Gombryas said, as we came down the far side of the slope, leaving Ennea Crunoe behind us in the dip, as though it had never existed, "was that nobody actually won; they just ran out of people to do the fighting."

So far, Anticonessus looked exactly like the country on the other side of the river: bleak, useless, above all empty. In fact, emptier. On the other side, at least there had been a few sheep scattered about in the far distance. This side, nothing but larks that got up from right under your feet and rocketed away shrieking, a few buzzards circling a mile away, and one snake, which Stauracia discovered by nearly sitting on it. Stauracia doesn't care much for snakes.

"Another thing," I said. "Assuming we get there, assuming there really is a First Emperor's tomb. It's not going to be standing proudly in the middle of neatly tended parkland, with a well-oiled front door and signs saying, 'This Way to the Mausoleum'. I imagine there's going to be digging involved, and there's only the three of us, and I notice that neither of you two saw fit to bring a shovel."

Stauracia wasn't talking to me at that particular moment. "We'll get there," Gombryas said, "and we'll see what we'll see. One step at a time, all right?"

Walking all day with two people who tend to sulk, you have time to think. The trouble is, you don't necessarily think about the right things. Essentially it's a variant form of Saloninus's Third Law (any human being is capable of doing any amount of work, always provided it's not the work he's supposed to be doing). I should have been thinking about the mess I'd got myself into, how I came to be there and what I could do about it. Instead I thought about my sister, and that horrible letter. I kept taking it out and reading it when the other two weren't looking; just in case I'd misunderstood it, I guess, and really it was about something quite other.

Fan was perfectly capable of writing a load of lies out of pure spite, hoping to plant a tiny seed of doubt in my mind that would eventually drive me mad. She'd do that because I'd made her give Stauracia some of her jewels, or because I'd ditched her in her hour of need, or just because she didn't like me very much. Or it could be true, which would explain why

Fan hated me so much. No matter how cunningly I wove the strands of reasoning or how tirelessly I traced and retraced them, it all came back to what I could actually remember about the quarter of a second between Scynthius making his ill-judged lunge and the point of my sword piercing his skin. I was there. I saw it. I ought to be able to remember. I remembered, you bet. But what was I remembering, the truth or a construct?

Truth is the consensus of all the reliable witnesses. There were no reliable witnesses to my brother's death. Therefore there could be no truth.

The hell with it. They taught me logic when I was a kid, including syllogisms, of which the above is an imperfect example. The fallacy lies in the conclusion, which should be: therefore there is no way of ascertaining the truth. But I like my version better, flawed or not. It wasn't that the truth was irrecoverably hidden: there simply wasn't one. What happened that night was an event which could only exist subjectively, depending on whose side you're on. I murdered him or it was an accident. There being no truth, I *choose* it to have been an accident, and my opinion is as valid as anybody else's – more so, in fact, because I was there. And because I've paid for that moment every second of my life, and what you pay for, you own.

There are far too many irrevocable moments in human life, and it's high time something was done about them; from the moment when your father realises it's too late to pull out, to the moment when you look down at the hole in your body and it comes home to you that you're not going to get away with it this time, and a million others in between. If my life, with its traumas and its capers and its many unintended consequences affecting a lot of other people – if it stands for anything, it's

fending off the irrevocable moment – not permanently, naturally, but at least long enough for me and a few others to get
away free and clear, until the next time. I fended off the war,
twice. Now it was back, and this time there was absolutely
nothing I could do about it. The fleet was at sea, and had
already passed Lachsar. Out of my hands, therefore not my
fault; but it meant that the acts on which I based my appeal for
redemption had been futile and achieved absolutely nothing.
Pity about that. I heard once about a scholar, a mathematician
who spent forty years formulating a theorem, and everybody
loved it to bits and they made him professor of this and that;
and then one of his students found the flaw in it, and his entire
life suddenly died. They let him go on being a professor,
because he still knew more about the private life of numbers
than any man living, but from that moment onwards he would
only ever be the man who was wrong about whatever-it-was.
In his shoes, I think I'd have hanged myself, but I gather he
had more moral fibre than me, because he stuck it out to the
bitter end, three years later. An irrevocable moment; a line in
a page of mathematical notations; a failure to move the point
of a sword four inches to the left.

Moral: don't go for long walks with nobody to talk to, or
you'll end up filling your brain with garbage. Instead, I told
myself, why not dwell on the sunny side of things? Namely:
your sister is now many miles away and you don't have to see
her ever again; you no longer have to take responsibility for the
lives of five hundred men; a war is coming, and the nice thing
about the worst happening is that nothing quite as bad is likely
to happen thereafter; and if we somehow manage to get out of
this alive, the rest of your life is your own.

Fallacy in the last line, it was getting to be a habit; even so.

It was three days before we saw another human being. On the fourth day, we came to a burned-out village, the first settlement we'd seen since we crossed the river. I know a thing or two about how you burn villages, including the technical term for it, which is chevauchée. Whoever had done it was no amateur. He'd known that you light thatch from the eaves, not the apex, and how to bar a door so that the people inside can't get out, no matter how hard they try. He'd known about all the places people run and hide: root cellars and cisterns and turnip clamps, where the fire burns itself out over your head and then you come out unscathed. He'd been round afterwards pulling out his valuable arrows so they wouldn't go to waste, and he'd killed all the livestock he didn't need to feed his men and chucked them down the well. Clearly a capable officer who could be trusted to carry out his orders, no matter how distasteful. And where would we all be without people like that? I left Gombryas ferreting about in the ashes – force of habit, I guess – and went looking for some clean water. Thanks to our friend the conscientious young lieutenant I had to go a long way, up a hill and down into a little combe where there was a spring without a dead sheep in it. I filled up the jug I'd brought with me, and I was just walking back the way I'd come when someone jumped out at me from behind a bush and took a swing at me with some kind of farm tool.

I dropped the jug, caught hold of the hoe or mattock or whatever it was and twisted it out of his grip; and then he tried to kick me, so I tripped him up and put my foot on his windpipe. "Calm down," I said, in Sashan. "I'm not the enemy. Can you understand what I'm saying?"

"Murdering arsehole," he replied, in Sashan but with a strong accent. "Go on, then. Do it."

"No thanks," I said. "Is there another village round here? Only my friends and I need to buy some food."

"Piss off, you murderer."

I kept my foot where it was. "Piss off you murderer yes, or piss off you murderer no? Only we do need to eat, and living off the land doesn't look like it's an option around here. No offence," I added, in case he was patriotic. He was about forty, I guess, though he looked older: thin and starting to go bald on top, skinny arms and big hands and an Adam's apple the size of my fist. Probably an honest man and a good neighbour once you got to know him, but I didn't have time. "Please," I added. "I can pay you a lot of money, if that would be any help."

The penny had dropped: I wasn't Anticonessian. His eyes widened, and a look of abject terror covered his face. He started mumbling something very quickly, under his breath; his version of the catechism, presumably. Bother, I thought, or words to that effect.

"Fine," I said. "Now I'm going to take my foot off your neck, but please don't bother trying to kill me, because I can't be killed. I'm dead already, and I don't want to hurt you if I don't have to. On three, then. One, two, three. There," I added, as he lay there perfectly still. "That wasn't so bad, was it?"

He stared at me. That made me feel rather foolish.

"Out of interest," I said, "you didn't happen to notice which direction the men who burned your village went, did you? Me and my friends, we can slaughter the lot of them for you, if you'd like us to."

He shook his head; he knew, but he wasn't telling. I guess even the enemy didn't deserve that.

There was no point giving him food; he wouldn't eat it. "Fair enough," I said. "Well, so long. Nice meeting you." I picked up my jug, which was now empty, of course, and headed back up the slope.

"Where the hell did you get to?" Gombryas asked. "Did you find any?"

"No," I said. He shovelled some things off the ground into his pocket and stood up. "We'd better be going," I said. "No point sticking around here, and for all I know, these people's friends might be on their way. Or the enemy might come back."

He didn't seem too worried. "I don't think there's anybody much left around here," he said. "Which is peachy for us. Still, you're right, we might as well move on. Sooner we get there the better."

We carried on walking, in what we hoped was the right direction. Gombryas kept pointing to a distant range of mountains, though I was fairly sure they weren't what he thought they were. Stauracia was having problems with her boots, which I tried to fix with the needle and thread I'd thoughtfully brought with me, but failed. I kept thinking about the man I'd seen at the village: was he all right, had he found something to eat, had anyone turned up to rescue him or had the enemy come back and got him? None of my business, I tried to tell myself, but apparently I wasn't listening.

We came across two more burned-out villages – no survivors in either of them – and a third which wasn't burned, just abandoned. They'd taken everything with them, all the food and the clothes and the boots (much to Stauracia's disgust), and they'd put a dead dog down the well. And this wasn't even *the* war, just some trifling local dispute in a faraway place of which we knew little. Soon, all the places I knew, Scona and Beloisa and Choris and Auxentia City, Olbia and Mezentia and Sirupat, they'd be like this, just as quiet and peaceful and safe to walk about in. The Sashan aren't colonists; they have enough trouble populating their own turf, which is vast and empty because of the wars they had to fight to get it, so they wouldn't be filling up the gaps with their tired, their poor, their huddled masses yearning to breathe free. No, what the Sashan like is a cordon sanitaire of empty desert, or its temperate-climate equivalent, where the only substantial communities are anthills. In ten years' time, say, a man could go there and clear away the brush and chop down the thorn trees to build a modest cabin and live like a king, or at least the monarch of all he chose to survey. Provided, of course, that he had the energy and the optimism, which more or less ruled me out. There it is; one man's graveyard is another man's brave new world, and all it takes to make it tolerable is a comprehensive ignorance of history.

"You could try packing it out with a bit of the lining of your coat," Gombryas suggested, which made Stauracia turn and stare at him. It was the first civil or constructive thing he'd said to her since Lachsar, even if it was patently impractical. "Then at least it wouldn't chafe your toe."

"Nothing left to pack," she said, looking down at her boot. "God, I hate this place. That last village we came to – no, I tell a lie, it was the one before that – there was a wagon with its wheels staved in and nine horses in a stable with their throats cut. What a stupid fucking waste. We could be riding instead of walking. We'd probably be there by now."

"Talking of which," I said, "do we have any idea of how much further it is? All I know is, it's something to do with those mountains you keep looking at. Assuming they're the right mountains."

Gombryas gave me a superior grin. "Nothing at all to do with it," he said. "I'm navigating by the stars."

"It's daylight."

"I look at the stars at night, and then I remember the direction, and in the morning I look for landmarks. Where we're headed is a straight line through that hill over there with the three pine trees, then keep on till we reach the river."

"What river?"

"Don't think it's got a name, but there's a river. It was on a map. I know exactly where we are, I promise."

"Oh, for God's sake," Stauracia said, sinking to her knees for the maximum effect. "We're going to die out here, all because of him."

"You be quiet," I said. "Gombryas is a born navigator. We'll be fine."

I gave some serious thought to waiting till they were both asleep, then taking my share of the food and heading back the way we'd come; but I hadn't really been paying attention, so I was just as likely to get lost and die in the wilderness without them as with them. Also, I told myself, there was the remote possibility that Gombryas knew what he was doing and we'd get there. After all, geese and swallows find their way across vast distances, and Gombryas isn't that much stupider than a goose.

On the ninth day, another trashed village; but this one had been fought over rather than burned or abandoned, and nobody had been round to clear up, so there were bodies to loot. Stauracia's shriek of joy when she found an intact left boot was enough to warm the hardest heart, and I found a dead man with a string of sausages packed in the hollow of his shield. It's a pity we're not birds and can't eat flies. There were plenty of those, enough for a banquet.

"This is good," Gombryas solemnly assured me, when he emerged from some shack or other, cherishing the end of a mouldy loaf. "This village was on the map. I was expecting it to be here. We're definitely on the right road."

There was, of course, no road. "Splendid," I said. "In that case, now you've got your bearings, how much further?"

"About two days," he said. "Over there, see that big, flat hill with the trees? Other side of that."

I stared at him. "Really?"

"Really. What're you looking at me like that for? I told you I know exactly where we are."

"Yes, but I didn't—" I shrugged. "Fine," I said. "Well done, you. I never doubted you for a second."

"Arsehole. Yup, we carry on in a straight line from here, down into that dip, up the other side, through those trees there and it's down in a valley. There's a lake, call it a lake, it's a big pond, with a sort of island in the middle. About two miles on from that, there you are."

He was giving me a headache. "You're amazing, Gombryas, you know that? You did all that just looking at the stars. That's brilliant."

That got me a scowl. "Piss off, Saevus. It's not exactly catapult science, walking in a straight line. And I saw a map."

Stauracia was standing behind him. I could see the look on her face. She was as stunned as I was. "Fine," I said. "Nearly there, then. Didn't I say you're a born navigator?"

Gombryas stomped off to sulk and poke around among the dead bodies. Stauracia came and sat down beside me. "He actually got us there, then," she said.

"I don't know about that. He could be wrong, or making it up."

"He seemed pretty definite about it. I believe him." She paused. "He's going to be terribly disappointed."

That didn't sound right. "I thought you believed."

"In the First Emperor's gold armour? Give me some credit."

"But you made me—"

"I didn't make you do anything," she said. "Except let me tag along." She took off her new boot, turned it over and examined the sole. "I think there's a nail sticking up through," she said, "but damned if I can find it. Funny, isn't it, how something so small you can't see it can give you such hell."

I took the boot away from her. "What are you playing at?" I said.

"Give it back." She took it before I could stop her. "And I'm not playing at anything. I knew you had to do this because you promised him you would. So I came along to keep you safe. I do a lot of that, only you never seem to notice."

I looked at her, trying to make-believe it would ever be possible for me to see her as she really is. "Thanks," I said. "But I don't need looking after."

"The hell you don't." She suddenly looked very tired, as if whether or not she won didn't matter any more. "These days I'm a woman of independent means," she said. "I can do what the fuck I like. If that's traipsing around after you, what of it? You always were a stupid, ungrateful arse, Saevus. Saevus," she repeated, "not Florian. I really can't see you as a Florian. A stupid, ungrateful arse who wanders through life pissing on people and feeling superior. And one of these days you'll get yourself killed and I'll be free of you, but I don't suppose it'll do me much good. Meanwhile, you're this really bad habit I can't seem to shake off, and sooner or later you're going to ruin my health, but I can't do a thing about it.

But you know what, I just keep on and on, doing it to myself, until I'm so tired I could cry. Too late to do anything about it now, of course. It's just a matter of keeping on going until it all plays itself out."

She stood up, realised she was only wearing one boot, put the other one on and walked away.

It didn't take two days; it took three and a half. We went through the trees on top of the hill, out the other side and down into a valley, where there was a lake (more of a large pond, really) with an island in the middle. On the north shore of the lake was a burned-out village, a substantial one in its time, but its vicissitudes had no bearing on our navigation, no pun intended, so we didn't bother to stop.

"See that hill over there?" Gombryas said, pointing. He knows his eyesight is about a million times better than mine. "You can just make out a building there, on the western slope."

"No I can't. You know I can't."

"Well, it's there. That's where we're headed. Told you I knew where it was."

Stauracia was peering, too. "I can see it," she said.

I doubted that, but she hates to be left out of anything. "Right," Gombryas said. "I say we stop here for the night and press on in the morning."

"Really? I'd have thought you'd have wanted—"

"It's been there a thousand years," Gombryas said sagely, "it'll still be there tomorrow. And it's further away than it looks, and we don't want to be stomping about in that heather in the dark. It'd be bloody stupid to come this far and then bust a leg at the last minute."

Fair enough, and maybe the closeness of the big score was

making Gombryas use his brain, for once in his life. "What is that building?" I asked.

"Temple," he said. "Something like that. My man told me, the entrance to the tomb is directly under it. The locals won't go near it because they think it's haunted or bewitched or something."

As soon as the sun set, the temperature dropped. Stauracia feels the cold. "We should light a fire," she said. "There was a dead thorn tree back there. There's nobody alive except us; it won't be a problem."

"The hell with that," I said, but Gombryas agreed with her, though I suspect he was just trying to get on her good side. "Oh, come on," she said. "It's not exactly like we've been making ourselves inconspicuous the last ten days, and nobody's come near us. And if I freeze to death, I won't be any use to anybody."

"Fine," I said. "You're the expert tactician. Excuse me if I lie awake all night listening out for the slightest noise. I won't mean it as a criticism."

I didn't, though. I slept right through till dawn, at which point Gombryas nudged me awake with his boot. "Come on," he said. "Today's the big day."

It nearly broke my heart to see how happy and excited he was, because of course there wasn't going to be any buried treasure, and then he'd be depressed and miserable. But then we could leave Anticonessus, so that was all right. "Yes, fine," I snapped at him. (I'd woken up with a headache.) "Only for crying out loud, try not to be so bouncy. Next thing, you'll be bringing me sticks to throw for you."

Stauracia was sleepy, too, which wasn't like her. "You know what," she said, as we started off up the slope, "I'm actually starting to wonder if there might not be something there after all. I mean, this building's turned out to be exactly where he said it'd be. Maybe he really is on to something after all."

"Don't you start," I said. "Listen to me. The very most we can hope to find is an empty cellar. If there ever was a First Emperor's golden army, it'll have been looted by the locals years ago. But there wasn't, because it's all just a stupid myth: it always is."

"In which case," she went on, "we really do have a problem, because how in God's name are we going to shift all that heavy metal back the way we've just come without hiring a small army, who'll undoubtedly turn on us and cut our throats the moment they see what we've got? We might just have pulled it off if you'd still got your old crew, but you had to be all noble and send them away for their own good. I guess we'll just have to find them all again and get them back. And it would have to be in Antibloodyconessus of all places. That's going to be a real turnoff if we have to start recruiting." She sighed. "Probably the sensible thing to do would be to bring the Sisters in on it. We'd have to settle for a percentage, like a finder's fee, but I guess ten per cent of more money than you ever thought possible is better than nothing. He won't see it that way, of course, idiots never do, so we may have to deal with him—"

"Stauracia," I said, "shut up. There's nothing there. We're wasting our time."

"On second thoughts, the Knights rather than the Sisters, because I know the station chief at Chasarene, and he's got discretion for up to two hundred men and fifteen ships purely on his say-so. Maybe we could do a deal with him personally without bringing the Order in per se. He's a greedy son of a bitch, but I know a few things about him he wouldn't want his bosses to hear, so I'm pretty sure I can handle him. Of course, soon as he hears the word Anticonessus he's going to stick his fingers in his ears and start humming very loudly, so we may have to fix things so he doesn't have any choice but to help us, if you catch my drift."

When she's like that, it's generally easier to let her run on till she stops. So I did.

A temple, Gombryas had said, but it clearly wasn't. It was a blockhouse, that unambiguous statement of early Imperial policy; let them hate, and so forth.

You can't fault the reasoning. Blockhouses are big, square and absolutely identical wherever you go, thereby demonstrating that the bastards who now run your country have infinite power and endless resources. Instead of building a castle out of the local stone, they ship in a special sort of magic grey dust from somewhere inconceivably far away, and cast the whole thing like it was a brooch or a lampstand. That strikes you as an incredibly difficult way of doing it, but you know they must have their reasons, and their reasons are far too deep and complicated for a yokel like you to understand – resistance, therefore, is futile, and bashing your head against a wall isn't likely to hurt the wall one bit. And there the blockhouse is, on top of a hill where everybody can look on it and despair, and you see it every day until it sinks deep into your mind, like a barbed arrowhead. They built the horrible things so well that most of them are still there. They're too tough to be broken up by the neighbouring farmers to build barns with, and there was something in the mixture they cast them out of which poisons the ground they stand on so comprehensively that nothing ever seems to grow there ever again.

Which set me thinking: if I was an Anticonessian, knowing for a fact that foreigners built that thing and all foreigners are actually dead people with an irreconcilable grudge against the living, and I saw it standing there, without even a bramble daring to poke its head up out of the ground, would I want to go poking around inside in case there was something nice in there, or would I stay well away? And if I was the First Emperor, anxious for a degree of peace and quiet to spend eternity in, wouldn't I figure that under a blockhouse in Anticonessus might just be what I'm looking for?

"Stands to reason," Gombryas was saying, "that someone's already found a way inside, because someone fished out that couter my pal showed me. So there's got to be a way in, and all we've got to do is find it."

I let him burble on. It seemed to make him happy. I was having mixed feelings myself. There was an Imperial block-house on my father's land when I was growing up. My father used it as a vast wine cooler – he had a vast amount of wine – and servants were in and out of it all the time, fetching bottles and laying down new acquisitions, making sure the tempera-ture was just right, changing the straw and turning every single bottle through forty-five degrees eight times a year. The cellar underneath, which the Imperials used to store supplies, was our ice house. In winter, the entire staff turned out to smash the ice in our lake into big chunks, which were then carted up the hill and dumped in the cellar; the temperature never changed down there, so in the heat of midsummer my father had ice water to shave with and little cubes of ice to put in his mint juleps. For some reason I hated the place and never went near it if I could help it, but Scynthius and Fan made me go there to play pirates and Pellion-and-Eudocia. I was always the captain of the guard, so I had to stomp about in corridors making growling noises, until Scynthius got around to jumping out on me and killing me. I died lots of times in the cellars of that blockhouse, though I always came to life again afterwards, since I was needed for the game. But you're a lot more resilient when you're a kid, and maybe the game didn't need me any more. In any event, I had a pretty fair idea of the layout of a blockhouse, and like I said just now, they're all identical wherever you are. In which case, I knew more or less where to look for a passageway going straight down, if there was one, which there wouldn't be.

"There'll be a door at the end of this corridor," I told them. "It'll be a bronze door, and if it's still there we'll know that the locals truly believe in spooks, because that's the only possible reason for not smashing it up years ago and melting it down into ingots. If it's there and it's locked, we're screwed, of course."

But it was there, a huge green slab, embossed with Imperial lions, and it was ajar, just enough for a man to slip past if he didn't mind leaving some skin behind. Lying next to it was a wooden beam, which some enthusiast had used as a lever to prise it open on its seized hinges. Just the thought of it made me feel tired. "Someone's been here," I said, rather redundantly. "Don't get your hopes up."

I think my constant negativity was starting to get on Gombryas's nerves. "It's there," he said. "Stop whining and let's find the way in. It can't be far now."

This time we'd brought a lantern. Gombryas had found it, snuffling about in dead people's houses. "I'll go first," he said, and I wasn't inclined to argue. There was no truth in all the old stories about the emperor's tomb being riddled with devilish booby-traps, because the tomb was supposed to be the emperor's palace for all eternity, and who wants to be for ever tripping over tripwires and getting squashed by massive stone blocks when you're groping your way to the toilet in the middle of the night? Even so. "You should be standing in a room about thirty foot square," I called out after him. "At the far end, there'll be an archway. Got that?"

"Come and see this," he called back. "You really want to see this."

So Stauracia and I squished ourselves past the bronze door, and it was as dark as a bag; odd, because, like I just said, Gombryas had a lantern. "Gombryas?" I called out, and then something bashed the back of my head, and I went to sleep.

6

"You fucking watch him," someone was saying. "He's dangerous."

I opened my eyes. There was light in the room, which was just like the one at my dad's house, only without the racks of wine. I could see a dozen men lining the wall opposite me. The voice was coming from behind me. It sounded familiar.

"He's awake, look. For fuck's sake, keep your eye on him."

It sounded a bit like Gombryas. I tried to say something to him, but my mouth was full of linen. It tasted of sweat.

"Stop worrying," someone else said. "He'll be fine."

"Fuck that," Gombryas said. He sounded terrified. "I've seen him in action. You think he's trussed up safe, and two seconds later he's on his feet and slitting your throat. What you've got there is the most dangerous man who ever lived."

"Sure," said the other man. "He doesn't look too dangerous to me right now."

"You're an idiot," Gombryas said. "I know him. You should've cut his head off like I told you to."

I was tied up with rope, hands behind my back, feet together. "The hell with that," someone said. "The punter wants him alive. If he's dead, we don't get paid. Stop moaning, he's not going anywhere."

Oh, I thought, and various things that had been bugging me made sense. The campfire, and me going fast asleep and waking up with a headache. The fire was to let them know we'd arrived. The headache was something Gombryas had put in our drinking water, so he could go ahead and make arrangements. I really wanted to know where Stauracia was, but I couldn't see her and I couldn't move.

"He doesn't look all that dangerous to me," someone said.

"Don't say that, you'll set him off again."

"You're all stupid, the lot of you," Gombryas said. "Here, you, check the ropes again. Bet you he's already got the knots loose."

One of the men on the wall straightened up, sauntered over, peered down at me and gave me a kick in the ribs. "They're fine," he said. "Come and look for yourself."

"I'm not going near him."

The man laughed. "Suit yourself," he said, and I saw him walk away. "Obviously he did something to you sometime: that's why you're so shit scared of him."

Gombryas didn't reply to that. "Come on," said someone else I couldn't see, "let's get him shifted and out of here. I don't like this place, it's too boxed in."

"Be careful, for God's sake," Gombryas said. "He'll wait for just the right moment, and then he'll make his move and you won't know what hit you. He's got it all planned out in his head, you bet your life. He calls it doing the geometry."

Gombryas, I was thinking; I really hadn't seen that coming.

Maybe you did, but that's because you don't know him the way I thought I did. I really wanted to know where Stauracia was; had they killed her, or was she in on it, too, or was she trussed up in the other corner of the room where I couldn't see her?

They put a bag over my head before they lifted me up off the ground. Gombryas insisted on that. So I didn't get a chance to look for Stauracia. "Skinny little bloke, isn't he?" someone said, as I felt myself being carried lengthwise. "Mind his head on the door. Ah well, not to worry."

Having nothing better to do, I kept myself entertained figuring it out. Anticonessus: because it was a sure way of getting rid of the last remaining loyalists in our crew, the ones who'd stick with me through thick and thin, except if it meant going to Anticonessus. And here because there was a block-house, with its massive walls, few doors and fewer windows; a perfect killing bottle, for someone determined not to take any chances. Even so, it seemed like a lot of trouble to go to. Was I really that scary? The most dangerous man who ever lived. I thought about that, and maybe it wasn't so far off the mark, at that. I'd never ever thought about myself in those terms, after a lifetime as a hunted fugitive, but Gombryas was plainly terrified of me, of what I might do when cornered, and he doesn't frighten easily. Over the years I've killed a lot of people because I was as terrified as a hunted fawn and there was no other way to get round them. I guess some people would be flattered to be called the most dangerous man in the world. I just found it depressing.

I listened as carefully as I could, but nobody said anything about bringing the woman or being careful not to bump her head on the doorpost. That probably meant she was dead. That would make sense. Gombryas knew what Stauracia was capable of, and if they didn't need her for anything, why take the risk of keeping her alive? And if she was one of them, she'd have said something by now. She'd be the one giving the orders, you could be sure of that.

And if she was dead, nothing mattered anyway. And the sooner I was dead, too, the better. But if she wasn't—

The beating of the heart, Saloninus says in one of his tiresome *Eclogues*, the action of the lungs, are a useful prevarication, leaving all options open. I needed to stay alive until I knew what had happened to Stauracia, and everything after that depended on the answer to that question. But the punter wanted me alive, so that was all right. And, yes, I'd been doing the geometry ever since I opened my eyes, but as yet I couldn't make it work. Sometimes it does and sometimes it doesn't, and it's because sometimes it doesn't that we need things like graves and cemeteries.

After a bit, I could feel daylight permeating the bag over my head, and the air didn't smell of blockhouse. A nasty bump to the back of my head suggested I'd been put in a cart. "Watch him, for fuck's sake," from Gombryas, and a bored sigh from someone who could no longer be bothered to tell him to piss off. No second bump on the cart floor, no references to the other piece of cargo. Nothing conclusive as yet, but it was starting to look (on the balance of probabilities) that my life was now over.

After that, a lot of time went by during which nothing much changed. It was dark and I couldn't move, the cart bumped over rocks and potholes, breaking my concentration into tiny bits the size of gravel as I tried to figure out all the possible sequences of events, from the moment I stepped into that horrible room. They'd grabbed her, or they'd tried to and she got away. Unlikely that she'd got away, because I'd heard no references to chasing after her, catching her, not catching her, searching the place till they found her because, after me, she was the most dangerous human in the world – leave the possibility open, but assume for now that they'd grabbed her – then what? Gombryas didn't like Stauracia, so when he slipped out the night before to make the final arrangements, he'd have said: soon as you've got him, cut her throat, she's a fucking menace. That was almost certainly the sort of thing he'd say; I know him, and he has a robust attitude to problems and dangers, nail them before they nail you. They'd go with his suggestion, because they had no pressing reason not to.

Or had she ever walked into the horrible room? Maybe not. She was behind me when I walked in. Maybe she stopped short on the threshold, by prior agreement. I'd slept the previous night like a log, dosed with Gombryas's sleeping draught. Maybe she hadn't. Maybe she was the one who put it in my drink.

Gombryas and Stauracia, allies to betray me? I couldn't see it myself, but, then again, I'm really stupid a lot of the time. Stauracia had been uncharacteristically eager to come on the trip, and the love stuff had struck me at the time as harder to swallow than a square apple. On the other hand, why bother? She could've sewn me up at any point since I ambushed her in the woods, and no need to share the payoff with Gombryas or anyone else. Unless Gombryas only suggested the deal to her relatively late – after we'd brought Fan to Ogiv, maybe. Getting rid of my crew first made sense, but after that she wouldn't need Gombryas. I could see Gombryas needing to set up this perfect killing bottle, if he was that scared of me. But Stauracia could've handed me over to the bad people anytime and anywhere. Also, Gombryas could do with the money, but Stauracia had already made her big score, in the form of Fan's jewels. On the balance of probabilities, therefore—

The hell with the balance of probabilities, because in that case, if she hadn't sold me down the river and betrayed me to my enemies, she was most likely dead, and I couldn't bear that. It's no good, I decided, I really need to know: facts, not conjectures. And I wasn't going to get any facts with a gag in my mouth and a bag over my head. Therefore the gag and the bag had to go. Simple as that.

What was the only lever I had against these people? They needed me alive, or they wouldn't get paid. Big lever.

The simplest and most convincing way, I've always found, is just to breathe out and not breathe in again. I said simple, not easy. Not breathing until you're a hair's breadth away from dying isn't easy, but it's uncomplicated, you don't need specialist training or equipment. You don't need to understand how to do the frantic kicks and jerks, they come naturally, no previous knowledge required; and if you genuinely empty your lungs, instead of faking it, you can't help but be convincing.

"He's having a fit," someone said.

"No he's not, he's doing it on purpose," Gombryas yelled. "Don't touch him. Leave him."

"Stop the cart." Then they were fumbling with knots, and the bag came off my head, and the gag came out of my mouth.

I was in no fit state, but that couldn't be helped. I dragged air into my poor abused lungs, made my best guess at where Gombryas was, because I couldn't see worth a damn, my vision was all blurry, and used the convulsions in my stomach and legs to throw myself in what I hoped was the right direction. I connected with someone, got an elbow round his neck under his chin, and groped at his waist for a knife in a sheath. Gombryas always has one, unless the authorities take it away from him, and I know without having to look where it'll be.

There was a knife where a knife should have been. Therefore the man I was strangling was Gombryas. Fine. I allowed myself the luxury of another deep, deep breath, which felt like swallowing a porcupine, and touched the knife to his throat. Just a touch. I didn't dare press any harder, because my hands and arms still weren't under proper control.

Nobody seemed to be doing anything, which was probably just as well. I couldn't speak, needless to say. All I could do was cling desperately to my old pal and only hostage, hoping I didn't accidentally crush his windpipe or pierce his jugular vein, until gradually my eyes came back into focus and the roaring in my ears faded enough to allow me to think.

"Where is she?" I said.

Gombryas, of course, couldn't reply, because I was strangling him. But someone else had the presence of mind to answer for him. "She's dead," he said.

That was all I wanted to know. I let go of Gombryas and dropped the knife. No point in anything now.

"Break his arms and legs," Gombryas was saying, as they tied me back up again. "Even he can't do much with two broken arms and two broken legs, and he'll still be alive."

Sound advice, and probably what I'd have done, but they ignored him. My guess is, they'd had about as much of Gombryas as they could take. I don't blame them. He's an acquired taste.

I don't remember much about the rest of the cart ride. From time to time the cart stopped and they unwrapped me and stuffed food in my mouth – much to Gombryas's disgust; he doesn't need feeding, he tried to tell them, he can go days without food, he's unnatural – and then they tied me back up again, replaced the gag and the hood, double-checked the knots ... If I'd been capable of giving a damn, I'd have told them they didn't need to worry. I wasn't going anywhere. Why bother?

There was one tiny point on which I was still slightly curious. So, about the tenth or eleventh time they fed me, I asked, "Who's the punter? My dad?" The man feeding me nodded. I'd guessed as much, but it was nice to have it confirmed. Once that was settled, that was it as far as I was concerned. Even the pain of being cramped and trussed stopped bothering me, and I barely noticed it. No further interest in the proceedings. None of my business.

They had to dump the cart and carry me to get through the tunnel. Gombryas was absolutely terrified. "This is when he'll make his move," I heard him tell them. "He'll have been planning it for days; he's got it all worked out." Someone told him to shut the fuck up, which made me smile around the gag. "Watch out for his feet," Gombryas went on. "For God's sake don't get where he can kick you."

I'd been trying to scare myself with the thought of what my father would do to me; a bit like sticking pins in your leg when you've lost all sensation in it. Agonising pain would be blissful, because it'd mean the leg was still alive. But it wasn't. I dreamed up the most sadistic tortures I could imagine, but the thought had no effect on me whatsoever, apart from a vague feeling of bring it on. The sooner it was over and done with, the better. Not looking forward to it exactly, but anticipating the relief of not having to be alive any more; not to mention not being trussed up, or having to shit in my trousers, or the sheer boredom of lying in the dark with nobody to talk to and nothing to read.

They'd got another cart at the end of the tunnel. It had slightly worse suspension than the other one.

"Been thinking," someone said, as I woke up out of a rather unpleasant dream. "While we're at it, we could pick up the sister. We're practically passing the door."

"What's the point in that?" someone else said.

"Bet you the old duke would pay money to get his little girl back safe. And, if not, there's bound to be somebody who'll want to buy her. But we're headed for the duke anyhow, so it's worth a shot."

"Fuck that," I heard Gombryas say. "You need to get him delivered soon as possible. I keep telling you, he's dangerous. You've seen what he's like."

"I don't know," someone else said. "I don't like working on spec. There's always the risk of pissing someone off, for one thing."

"It won't be any bother," said one of the earlier speakers. "We just scoop her up while we're passing. Then we say to the old man, we've got your daughter, if you want to see her alive again, it'll cost you so much. Put it like that, he'll come across all right, you bet."

"I heard she's worth money," someone else said.

"Good money," said yet another voice. "And nobody seems to know where she is apart from sunshine here. It's worth thinking about."

"How much are we talking about?"

Pause. "Got to be worth seventy, eighty thousand. I just thought, since we're going that way anyway, it'd be dumb not to, if you get my drift. Two birds with one stone."

"Well?"

That must have been addressed to Gombryas, because after a minute he replied, "She's got money, too. Lots of it. On her. Jewellery. But first things first. If you want to go after the sister, you'll have to break his legs, at the very least."

"How much jewellery?"

"Loads," Gombryas said. "But break his legs first. Or cut off his hands."

"If there's loads of money, how come you never said anything about it?" Somebody laughed; a question not needing to be answered. "Don't worry, sounds like there'll be plenty enough for all of us. Of course, we could knock you on the head soon as you've shown us where the sister is. Specially if you keep on nagging."

"You've got no fucking idea who you're dealing with," Gombryas said. "Otherwise you'd have broken his legs *and* cut his hands off. So don't go blaming me if you all end up dead."

They talked it over, slowly and calmly, for the next two days, then took a vote. As far as I could gather, Gombryas didn't have a vote. They decided in favour of grabbing Fan as well. It would mean a detour, and possibly some violence at the convent but nothing serious, just a door or two to smash in and a few women. One of them took the view that it would be like finding money in the street.

I didn't have a vote either, but if they'd offered me one I'd have abstained. None of my business, not any more.

*

"Somebody needs to clean him up," somebody said. "He stinks to high heaven."

"You do it, if you're so bothered," someone else replied. "Don't you start," he added, no guesses who he was talking to. "Yes, all right. You, sit on his head while you change his trousers."

I was gradually piecing together a few facts about the voices, more from force of habit than any actual will to do anything with the information. There were three leaders, I couldn't quite figure out the power structure between them, and maybe a dozen others who did as they were told. I knew which ones talked a lot, which ones only spoke when they had something useful to contribute, the smart ones and the ones who were tolerated because they were occasionally useful. I also kept track of the deterioration of their relationship with Gombryas, who was gradually transforming from a joke into a pain in the arse. If I'd still been capable of any feeling, I'd have been worried about Gombryas. He wasn't making any friends, and now he'd told them the name of the convent and the fact that Fan had a stash of valuable jewellery, they really didn't need him any more. I'd have warned him if I wasn't gagged and hooded, but there: if wishes were horses, and all that.

I think I made myself listen and take an interest, because it was something, a thing. Otherwise I'd have had nothing to occupy myself with except the fact that Stauracia was dead.

Had I seen that coming? Obviously not. Before I got Fan's letter, there we were in Count Theudebert's country, quietly going about our business, not a care in the world. Then the Fan business, finding her, getting over the shock and the unpleasantness. And then suddenly there Stauracia was, involved, back in my life and filling all the available space in my head, though I honestly believe I didn't realise it at the time. Fair enough. You don't notice the moment you catch the plague; it's only later that you know you've got it, when the symptoms start to show. Maybe it was Fan suddenly showing up again; the resolution of unfinished business, maybe, or the way she stuck around even though there was nothing in it for her. Correction: no money to be made out of it. My guess is, the idea of me being in love was so wildly implausible that it never crossed my mind until it had happened, and I only really found out about it in that room in the blockhouse, when it dawned on me that she was probably dead.

Love, for crying out loud. It was something I hadn't given a thought to since I was a kid, before Scynthius and the accident. I'm not saying I didn't believe in it. By the same token I believe there's such a place as Essecuivo, where the lemons come from, a million million miles away across the deep blue sea; but I've never been there and I can't really imagine myself ever going there, and I couldn't care less. Maybe it's because of all the stupid things stupid people say about love: it's the sweetest thing; it makes the world go round; love is all you need. You get the idea that it's like honey or silk or those sweets the Sashan make out of eggwhite and rosewater, and of course it isn't.

Love is actually the cruellest thing, because it can cause more pain than anything else. The worst thing you can do to someone is have them love you, and then you die. Or you can kill someone who someone loves, that's a really dirty trick. Or you can love someone and then they stab you in the back, or sell you to your father's hired goons. If Fan hadn't loved Scynthius, she wouldn't have hated me as much as she does. If my father hadn't loved me, he wouldn't have put a price on my head when I killed his other son, who he loved even more. If I hadn't loved my father and my brothers and my sister, running away would just have been a detail of geography. And if I hadn't loved Stauracia, I expect I'd have made some sort of effort to stay alive, instead of lying peacefully in a cart in trousers bulging with my own shit. Now then: tell me that love isn't the cruellest thing, and try and keep a straight face. Love is crueller than what the Echmen do to prisoners, or famine or plague or even war. Love makes things matter, and for that I can never bring myself to forgive it.

"Stop whining," someone said. "We've got a ship. It's tied up at the dock at Sunelonti. It'll be fine."

Gombryas had been fretting about what was going to happen when we got there, wherever there was. Now at least I knew that. Sunelonti Eipein, a fishing town on the west coast of the Friendly Sea, formerly a significant port but sadly come down in the world; a bit like me. Ideal for the purpose, because at that time of year you could sail south-east across the sea to somewhere like Axen or Vestris (they'd want to avoid a big place like Beloisa, just in case), and then hike fifty miles or so inland to my father's country, with only one fairly straightforward river to cross. Clearly I was in the hands of intelligent, sensible people.

If we were heading for Sunelonti, and we'd been on the road for – what? Fourteen days or was it fifteen? – at thirty miles a day. I cared just enough to do the arithmetic. We were nearly there.

I tried to be scared, but I couldn't. There'd be a boat trip (I hate boats) and then two days on a cart, then a fraught interview with my father and presumably my brother Scaphio, and then a great deal of pain, and then I'd be free and clear, unless

I'd been wrong about the Invincible Sun all along, in which case my troubles were just about to start, but I didn't think so. No, hang on a minute, we were stopping off on the way to collect Fan from Ogiv, weren't we? Actually, I didn't know. The issue had been decided, but not where I could hear it. People can be so thoughtless.

Maybe where I've gone wrong all my life is being impatient, proactive, bustling about doing stuff instead of lying on my back in my own shit waiting for stuff to come to me. Because the question was solved, without me having to lift a finger, around the middle of the next morning. The cart stopped, someone told someone else to wait there, keep an eye on him for fuck's sake. Then we waited for a very long time, and then I heard Fan's voice, swearing and arguing and very, very angry. Among the many things she said was, You give that back, it's mine, how dare you, my father will do this and that when I tell him. Then the sound of the flat of a hand being applied to a face, then a short pause in the flow of passionate speech, and then a lot of stuff about how someone or other was a dead man; then, eventually, a declaration that she wasn't getting in *there*, with *him*.

Well, at least I knew where I was. From Ogiv to Sunelonti, three days.

Three days, but with a cabaret. I don't think Fan drew breath the whole way. Why they didn't stick a gag in her mouth I really don't know. Maybe her threats had got to them, or maybe they got a kick out of listening to the pampered kitten yowling – not something you get to hear every day, in the social circles in which they moved, and I guess if you played it as comedy, it could go down well, especially at the Lyric or the Arcade; not at the Gallery, but we were always strictly a burlesque house. Maybe it was just that with Fan at full volume, they couldn't hear Gombryas drivelling on about how if they let me blow my nose I'd kill them all. In which case, fair enough.

I wasn't really inclined to play it as comedy. I remembered what Stauracia had said: try and understand her, get inside her mind. And what she'd said, in the letter. Ideally I'd have liked to talk to her about it, but it wasn't possible, so that was that. So, instead I used my imagination. I tried to imagine what it would be like for Fan meeting my father again, after what she'd done. He'd disowned her, she'd told me; never wanted to see her again, in this world or the next. It'd take a great deal of anger to make my father say that to his daughter, of whom he'd always been so fond and proud. I'd go as far as to say that he was fonder and prouder of her than of his deer park, or the folly he'd had built on top of the hill overlooking the house, and that's really saying something, if you knew Dad.

No, really. He'd grown up in that house, needless to say, and practically every day of his life he used to wake up and look out of his window and see that hill, and think to himself: all it'd take to make this house the most perfect house in the world would be a folly on top of that hill. He'd nagged my grandfather to death about it, but the old man was adamant. No, because it'd mean cutting a bloody great clearing in the woods, and that'd scare off the deer and the boar, which would fuck up the last drive of the day, and then the people that really matter won't want to come here to hunt any more, and if that happened we might as well not exist. So, shut up about your stupid folly, it's not going to happen. Until at last the old man died; and my father was pretty cut up about that, but at least it meant an end to forty years of waiting, and a week later the architect arrived from Choris with enough drawings to cover the walls of a palace. And, five years later, it was finished; and as far as my father was concerned, the last and greatest imperfection in the way Creation was organised had finally been resolved, and everything was now for the best in the best of all possible worlds. And then, six months later, his stupid son murdered his clever son, and everything collapsed around him in a thunderstorm of shit and piss—

But at least he'd seen his clever, pretty daughter married to an archduke, and not just any old Archduke, an Elector as well. That would've been something to cling on to, on the dark days when even the view from the window wasn't cutting it any more. The power, the importance, the relevance, the knowledge that his blood would be pumping through the veins of the next Archduke Elector; something to show for a life that probably hadn't turned out quite the way he'd planned, in terms of honour and achievement and love. Then a day when a letter came; no, it'd have been a messenger, a very apprehensive messenger who'd spent three days in a fast coach on bad roads trying to figure out exactly how he was going to phrase it. Your daughter and her lover just murdered her husband, and now she's a wanted fugitive. I can see how even the perfect folly in precisely the right place wouldn't have been much of a consolation, in the circumstances.

And Fan, coming home to face all that. Women are red hot on multi-tasking, so my guess was that while she was yelling and moaning and making threats at the men in the cart, she was thinking about that meeting, planning her strategy, choosing her words carefully, and her gestures and facial expressions, trying to anticipate the areas in which she'd have to defend, and determining how best to exploit the areas in which she'd have scope to counter-attack. Doing the geometry, in other words, although my father always quoted that line from Saloninus, tuning your instrument at the door, which is actually much neater. Yes, the meeting promised to be a dialectic treat, and a small part of me was alive enough to hope that I'd be around to see it, or hear it at the very least, though I reckon you'd lose a lot of the subtext if you couldn't see the looks on their faces. Andronica at the Gallery was absolutely the best at that sort of thing. You could write her a page of tripe, and with a few glances and head movements and subtle adjustments of her shoulders and feet, she could turn it into the funniest thing you ever saw in your life.

Andronica always figured that comedy was much harder than tragedy. I'm not sure I agree. Both Fan and my father had always been pretty straightforward to play for comedy, as you will by now have appreciated. Doing them straight would call for a degree of genuine human insight and feeling that I don't think I possess, on account of having had my sensibilities stunted in adolescence. Andronica once told me that the funniest thing I ever wrote was *Charity*; funny, she called it, without being vulgar. It was, of course, my one and only attempt at genuine human drama.

The hell with it, I thought; not my problem, because it wasn't my fault, just a ridiculous freak accident brought about by my brother's reckless enthusiasm for playing with weapons. And who knows, the two of them might even now be able to reconcile and find common ground in the sight of me being slowly tortured to death; in which case, to be fair, my living would not have been entirely in vain.

Andronica kept me on the payroll because although I wrote tripe, I wrote the sort of tripe she knew she could turn into pure gold. Moral: I can't actually think of one, but that's probably because I'm too stupid.

You can smell the sea at Sunelonti, even through a miasma of your own bodily excretions. I think it's because the wind blows inland at just the right angle across the very wide, open beach, which is usually ankle-deep in decomposing seaweed. Anyway, you can smell it as soon as you go through the gap in the hills, about four miles from the coast. Nearly there, I told myself. Nearly over.

Except that I guess I was starting to heal, the way you do, the way you can't help doing even if you don't particularly want to. Possibly it was something to do with dwelling so much on the past, in the dark inside the bag over my head, with nothing but Fan to listen to. I wasn't scared of dying, or even the pain, but – to be honest with you, I really didn't want to see my father again, the look on his face, the disappointment, the hatred. That was something I wanted to skip.

So. I could escape. More realistically, I could try and escape and get killed. Happy – no, not happy, not in the least, but satisfied with either option. Just so long as I didn't have to go home.

Time to start doing some very belated geometry.

I'm no soldier, but I've pulled rings off the cold, pulpy fingers of enough soldiers to know that in a tactical situation there are tipping points, moments, fulcrums; this is the place where the application of a little pressure can achieve a result, here and only here. The key to the art of soldiering is figuring out a point where circumstances neutralise all the enemy's advantages and turn his strengths into weaknesses, his superiorities into vulnerabilities.

Numbers have a lot to do with it. The greatest victories in history have been where a smart guy, monstrously outnumbered, has turned the other man's bloated superiority in numbers into a liability, a killing bottle. Take one example of many: Carnufex the Irrigator at Fons Bandusiae, where a simple outflank and surround meant that the enemy's seventy thousand heavy infantry were pinned between a cavalry onslaught and a river in spate, with no room to manoeuvre, herded like cattle, panic, slaughter, 90 per cent of the casualties in that battle either drowned in the river or were trampled to death by their own side. And that's why Carnufex was a genius, and people like Gombryas wet themselves at the thought of getting their hands on a splinter of his jawbone.

Numbers, and a confined space, and if at all possible a natural hazard. Like, for example, the gangplank of a ship.

Think about it. A gangplank is a plank: narrow, insecure. People can only cross it in single file. Two of them are carrying a dead weight. On either side and directly below them, the most hostile natural hazard in the world, namely water.

Of course, I wouldn't risk it, in their shoes, not in a million years. I'd have me rowed out in a boat and hoisted on to the ship with a crane. But a boat's not so different from a plank. Talking of planks, I'd have me strapped to a board so I couldn't kick out with my feet. But there, I'd have done what Gombryas suggested and broken my arms and legs, and they'd neglected or wilfully refused to do that, so clearly they weren't nearly as smart or sensible as they thought they were. Neither was Carnufex's opponent at Fons, whose name escapes me, and nearly everybody else, because he was too dumb to deserve remembering.

The other thing a great tactician needs is flexibility. Focus on the moment, and the possibilities that it brings. Visualise the possible outcomes, as clearly as if you were sitting in the front row at the Gallery watching the show; see how they play out, eager to seize on any point at which you can insert the blade of a crowbar. Create a sequence of events in your mind, and test it to make sure it's feasible; once you've imagined it, it exists, it's a written script, and all you need to do then is act it out – simple job, piece of cake, even actors can do it and you know what they're like. Above all, do the geometry: distances, timings, at the precise moment when A is at point B, where will C be and will he be able to reach? I'm a lousy chess player, which surprises me, since I can do this sort of complicated time-and-space planning with comparative ease. A great deal depends on how much you know about the variables – mostly, the people involved. Either you know them personally, the way I know Gombryas, or you know the type (soldier, officer, hired goon, sentry, warder) well enough to figure out how they'll react, which vector they'll move on, how quickly, with what degree of experience, skill and confidence. Like fencing: you know that if you lunge, he'll take a step back and raise his hand into Fourth, so you anticipate that and turn your wrist over at a specified time (by which point your hand is in a specified place) so that your sword is pointing at his navel instead of his head; but he'll have anticipated that, so you need to use that knowledge to plan a refinement that he won't have considered . . . As I would do if, for example, I was fencing with a superior opponent who I happened to know very well, for the sake of argument my own brother, and I wanted to kill him and also – why does everything have to be so complicated? – make it look like an accident.

I really, really wished I could get a chance to talk to Fan about that, if only for a few minutes.

Maybe that was it. Perfectly happy to go to my death, but first I needed to ask her about a few things. But she wouldn't want to talk to me, even if the goons were to allow it. Therefore I had to escape, then make an opportunity for a private talk with my sister. After that – who gives a damn about after that? It's important to a tactician to look ahead, but not too far ahead, or you get lost and lose your way. Do one thing at a time and do it supremely well, I always say.

One thing at a time. A gangplank (or a small boat). Water on three sides. A kick and a wriggle. They drop me. I fall in the water.

They would have been thinking: he won't try anything on the gangplank, he's too smart for that, he'll realise that if we drop him he'll go splash in the sea, and he's trussed like a chicken so he won't be able to swim, he'll sink like a stone. Carnufex the Irrigator or Senza Belot, in my shoes, would therefore be concentrating on a way of not sinking like a stone the moment he hit the water. Tricky; but consider the career of Senza Belot, who won all those battles by doing the apparently impossible at precisely the right moment. And the impossible turned out to be possible because Senza had thought about it in advance. A simple conjuring trick.

Talking of which, I knew a conjurer once, only he called himself an illusionist. Andronica hired him for the Gallery, a half-hour spot between the farce and the burlesque, so I got to know him reasonably well, hanging around in the green room while the farce was grinding through its grimly inevitable per-mutations. His best trick was escaping. They'd truss him up like a chicken with ropes and chains and a bag over his head, and five minutes later he'd be free, not a mark on him, taking his bow while the audience talked to their neighbours or ate apples. Escaping being something of a hobby of mine, I asked him how he did it. Easy, he told me. When they tie you up, you tense certain muscles in a very specific way. Then, when you relax, the ropes will be loose and you can scriggle out of them. Here, he said, the eleventh or twelfth time I expressed scepticism, I'll show you.

The illusionist didn't last long at the Gallery. The audience chatted among themselves or ate apples during his act not because it wasn't spectacular – actually it was pretty amazing – but because they knew it was all a lie, and the only possible interest in it would be if one night he made a mess of it, which would be amusing. But he never did, he was flawless, you knew he'd be out of there in no time flat, so no point in watching, no fun. Fortunately, the only member of my audience who properly knew me was Gombryas, and he'd made such a nuisance of himself that nobody was interested. The more he warned, the less inclined they were to listen. The only question remaining, therefore, was whether I could hold my breath under water for three minutes twelve seconds.

No, probably not, but you can extend the time quite a lot by practising, like pearl divers and people like that. So, since I had nothing better to do, I spent the next day learning to hold my breath. When the time came for me to be fed and my trousers to be cleaned, I did the things the conjuror told me. Like me, he'd learned how to do the geometry, precisely and fluently, until it came as naturally as breathing. Or not breathing, as the case may be.

Inside my bag there was no day or night, but I could hear seagulls, smell rotting seaweed and feel the cart bouncing over cobbles. Welcome to Sunelonti Eipein.

"My father," Fan was saying, "is going to have you flayed alive and nailed up on a barn door for the crows to peck at. He did that once, to a man who raped one of the kitchen maids. Guess how long it took him to die. Go on, guess."

No reply, or the man was mumbling.

"Two days. Two days, with no skin. The crows pecked his eyes out. Just think what it'd be like, seeing the crow's beak coming straight at you, and then not being able to see anything any more. I thought he'd have passed out from the pain, but, no, he was awake all through. Made the most awful fuss. My brother pleaded with my father, put him out of his misery, it's upsetting the gardeners, but once my father's decided to do something, he does it. Of course," she went on, "you could give me my jewellery back and let me go, and then we'll say no more about it and pretend none of this happened."

She was telling the truth about the man who raped the kitchen maid. I was the brother who pleaded. I don't suppose it was a coincidence that she chose to remind me of it. I'd be pleading again soon enough, and to the same effect. Like I cared. Having my skin ripped off would be a bit like realising that Stauracia was dead, only not quite as bad. Nevertheless, I did need to have that conversation with my sister. I kept reminding myself about that, just in case I forgot.

"Shut your face," someone eventually said. "Before I shut it for you."

"You're going to wish you hadn't said that," Fan said. "You're going to wish it a lot."

The cart stopped. Geometry time.

I saw it clear as day, in spite of the bag. One of them gets down off the cart, wanders off to find the ship, talk to the captain – first he's got to find the captain, who's probably busy shouting at someone for buying the wrong grade of biscuits, or why the hell isn't that loaded yet, we'll miss the tide. He talks to the captain – we've got cargo to load, yes, fine, you don't need any help, do you? No, fine, no worries. He comes back. They lift me out of the cart, and then it's either the gangplank or the boat. Gombryas is nagging them about breaking at least one of my limbs while there's still time. They ignore him; he's turned into a buzzing mosquito, they don't bother listening any more. In any case, Fan is droning on about flayings and disembowellings, making it hard for them to think straight. I'll feel their boots on the plank, or the boat swaying gently under my weight as they load me on it. Then, showtime.

"Nobody move."

Everything changed. I knew that voice.

Someone said, "I thought you told me you'd—" and then stopped talking, abruptly, at exactly the same moment as something went *thump*. I knew that sound, too; an arrow, suddenly dumping all its terminal velocity into flesh. Then a scream – Fan: a world-class screamer since she was a wee tot. Then a lot of yelling and bashing, lasting fifteen seconds at most. Then dead silence.

Everything had changed. I'd know that voice anywhere.

"God, you stink," she said, and pulled the bag off my head.

I tried to say her name, but my voice wouldn't work. Two weeks or whatever it was, on your back with a gag in your mouth; also, I'd never expected to say that name ever again. "You two, over here. Gently, for fuck's sake. No, stuff it, leave him where he is, we'll take this cart. Move it, for God's sake, there'll be soldiers along any minute."

I was looking at her: Stauracia, alive.

Not that it mattered one tiny bit, but she wasn't looking her best. There was a scar, a big one, running diagonally from her hairline on the left, across her forehead but missing the eye socket, then down through the bridge of her nose across the right-hand corner of her mouth. Nobody had got around to stitching it up; probably too late for that now, through Doc Papinian might have been able to do something, if he'd had the decency to stay alive until he was needed. Still, you know what they say. More than just a pretty face; which was probably just as well.

"Leave them," she was yelling. "Yes, and leave her, we don't want her. Just leave everything and let's go."

Three hundred thousand staurata in finely wrought gemstones. Trouble was, I couldn't get my mouth to work, and there was still a gag in it. "Florian," I heard Fan squeal, "you're not going to let her leave me here, are you? For God's sake, Florian."

The cart was moving. All I could see was sky.

"Seventy-five staurata," Stauracia said. "For this bunch of inadequates. You get what you pay for, I always say. Still, they did the job."

They'd been all she could get, at short notice, in Sunelonti, bearing in mind she was paying with a draft on a Sashan bank rather than actual clinking money. Dock hands, mostly, and a couple of chuckers-out from the brothel. Angels of mercy, I told her, and worth every trachy.

"This isn't so bad," she said, tracing the scar with her fingertip. "Just a flesh wound, really, where your mate Gombryas slashed me. The hole in the gut was the nasty one. But I packed it with moss and spider's web and tried not to think about it, and here I am. I learned how to do that from that Echmen doctor of yours. No magic, he said, just clean moss, spider's web and a bit of stick to poke it in with. Then wait for it to mend, clean it out and cauterise it with a hot iron. That wasn't a lot of fun, actually. Did the job, though."

"Gombryas," I said. "Is he—?"

She nodded. "Arrow clean through his head and out the other side." She paused and grinned. "I wish there'd been time to harvest his fingers and a couple of toes, but I didn't want to hang about in case the law turned up."

"Shame," I said. "He'd have liked that."

Poor Gombryas, I thought: my pal, my friend. A good man in his way, and he only ever let me down once. Still, it didn't matter one little bit, because Stauracia was alive. "You do realise," I said. "Fan's jewels. The boss goon had them. You could've—"

She shrugged. "Knowing your sister, I don't suppose they were still there when the authorities turned up. Don't worry, there's no extradition in Sunelonti. She'll be fine."

The thought had crossed my mind, and it was kind of Stauracia to have checked, so she could set my mind at rest. Of course, she could have been lying. But that would be rather sweet, too.

She paid off the goons and drove the cart to a barn, out in the middle of nowhere, which she'd noticed on her way in; instinctive strategic thinking, typical. "I got lucky," she was explaining. "I found the cart we came out in, you remember, the one we left at that gatehouse, by the waterfall. Of course it was no fucking use for going fast, but I happened to come across a farm with actual living people in it, and I traded the cart and team for a horse. Well, a pony, actually, but what the hell, it got me to Sunelonti, and I was pretty sure that's where they'd be headed for. I felt as sick as shit gambling on that, so it was lucky I was right."

Not only had she hired two dozen killers, at an excessively high price; she'd also thought to buy provisions for two for six weeks, blankets, basic medical supplies, a change of clothes and footwear for me and a small portable stove. "There's a stream down there in the dip," she said. "For fuck's sake, go and wash."

That night, we made love on a heap of straw, black with mould and crawling with spiders, carefully, so as not to rip open her scars. It had been a long time since I'd done anything like that, and I made rather a hash of it, but she didn't seem to mind. It's the thought that counts, she told me.

"Auxentia City," I said firmly. "That's where my rainy-day money is."

"Fuck Auxentia City," she said. "Too dangerous." She gave me that how-can-you-be-so-stupid look. It was different with the scar; in fact, the effect was rather cute. "Look, we don't know how much Gombryas told your dad's people. It's quite possible he told them about your stash in Auxentia, because it'd mean you'd be likely to go there at some point. Very likely, in fact, if this scheme proved to be a washout. Think about it. It's exactly what you're contemplating doing, after all."

That didn't take very long to sink in. "Marvellous," I said. "That means my life savings—"

She shrugged. "It's only money," she said. "And guess what, I've got loads of money. We've got loads of money. Which is why we're going to Suda."

I knew I wasn't going to win the argument, but I felt obliged to try. Stauracia likes winning. It would be churlish to deprive her of even a small pleasure. "You must be out of your mind," I said. "There's a great big war about to start. You can't just hop to and fro across the border any more. We're the *enemy*."

She grinned. "You may be," she said. "I'm not. Little friend of all the world, I am. Besides, I can get us a couple of diplomatic passes. Genuine Sashan ones. I know a man in Toris: it's on our way."

I loved her for that, too. Beauty is only skin deep, but having a corrupt official in Toris at the precise moment you need one the most – that sort of true spiritual beauty is very rare. "In that case," I said, "it's a deal."

"Suda?"

"Suda," I said. "Never been there. What's it like?"

She smiled, and lay back on the bed. "Hot as buggery," she said. "Lots of old buildings, with carvings and stuff. The people stink of garlic. Far as I can remember I'm not wanted for anything there."

"It sounds like heaven," I said.

"Four hundred thousand staurata," she replied. "My stash, and your sister's contribution. What's four hundred thousand in darics?"

I did the maths. "Just shy of a million," I said. "Assuming you got the good exchange rate."

"It'll just have to do," she said.

So we turned around and went south until we reached Chambia, where the Northern Trunk crosses the old Military Express, where we turned east. The Express dates back to the last big war against the Sashan. It was built in a tearing hurry to get supplies to the fortified cities on the east coast, to stock them up in case they came under siege. In the event, all the cities surrendered as soon as the Sashan fleet rounded the Cape, but the road is still there, and it's held up remarkably well, all things considered. If you're one of those ungrateful people who ask, *what did war ever do for us*, there's your answer.

Two days on the Express. She found me sitting on the ground next to the cart. "What the hell are you doing?"

"What does it look like?"

"You're *crying*." She kneeled down beside me. "For fuck's sake," she said, "what's that in aid of?"

"Oh, nothing," I said. "Gombryas."

"You clown."

I nodded. "But he was my friend," I said. "And I never had a chance to tell him, no hard feelings. He'd have wanted to know that."

"No hard feelings? He *sold* you to—"

"Yes, all right. But no hard feelings. That's important."

She looked at me. "You know what, Saevus," she said, "you're the most fucked-up man I ever met in my life."

"No hard feelings," I said. "Except he cut up your face. I'd have had to pay him back for that." Then I couldn't say any more, because of the stupid blubbering. She put her arms around me and called me a moron, and I remember thinking: maybe I was wrong about love. Maybe it is all you need, after all.

7

There used to be inns and roadhouses all along the last hundred miles of the Military Express, but most of them have gone now, apart from the Poverty & Compassion at Spets. The Poverty survives because it's the last change of horses for the government mail before the coast. They know me there, so I wasn't too keen about stopping. "The hell with it," she said. "By the time they've sent word to anybody, we'll be over the sea in Sashan. That's the nice thing about a war. It screws up communications."

Fair enough; so we had a proper room with a bed instead of sleeping under the cart, and Stauracia managed to kid the landlord into taking her note of hand on the Sisters in Coram for seven staurata, truly an achievement worthy to be enshrined in song and story. "Why didn't you tell me you had money in the Sisters?" I asked her. "We could've—"

"I haven't."

In which case, more remarkable still. Five staurata for a ship across the Friendly Sea; two for living a life of riotous dissipation between Spets and the coast, provided we could find anywhere to spend it. "Fuck it," she said, when we woke up next morning, "let's have bacon, and some proper wheat bread. I haven't had decent food for as long as I can remember."

But they didn't have any bacon or wheat bread, so we made do with porridge, which wasn't so bad after weeks of dry biscuit. I'd been doing a variant of the geometry in my head: how long would it take a message to reach my father from Sunelonti, then back again with instructions, and by the time the instructions came back, how far would we be from the coast, at the rate we were going? I allowed for exceptionally fast ships and fast horses, and it still worked out fine, even if the bad people were reporting to my father's steward on Scona rather than dragging all the way out to the house itself. Hooray for geography: for once in my life, it was turning out to be on my side.

"And that's assuming they can track us," she pointed out. "Which I can't see for one minute, because we've been sleeping rough, not stopping at inns, and the road's been nice and empty. I couldn't find us right now, and I'm bloody good."

Also – she didn't point it out, but she didn't need to – we were going to Toris to see her friend the corrupt official, not to any of the obvious ports which would be the logical places for us to make for, if we were taking the quickest way to the east. So even if my father had forked out for a fast yacht, and the winds were just right, the chances of there being anyone to meet us when we reached the coast were slender enough to allow me to sleep at night. Normally, getting a ship at Toris would be a serious problem, but not if we had Sashan passes. Toris is officially neutral, an independent mercantile republic, though in reality it's about as independent as your hand is from your brain. "About bribing your pal," I said. "What are we going to use for money?"

She gave me a sweet smile. "We won't need any money," she said.

Nor we did. He took one look at her and sagged, as though some joker had stolen his spine. "It's all right," she told him, "really. This time I'm going away and I'm never coming back."

Two passes, coming right up. He looked up at me as he wrote. "Do I know you?" he said.

"Not if you've got any sense."

He looked past me, at her. "Does he—?"

"He's not coming back either," she said. "Stop worrying, you'll give yourself crow's feet."

He finished writing out the passes. She examined them carefully, then gave them to me to check. I nodded. Good as the real thing, because they were the real thing. "What happened to your face?" he asked her.

"Walked into a door," she said.

"It's a shame," he said. "You used to be really pretty."

She still is, I told him, but not where you can see. He ignored me. He wasn't the sort of man who pays attention to sidekicks.

According to the passes, we were Umbyses and Gordoula, deacon and deaconess of the Eternal Flame at Suda, returning from a goodwill mission to the Invincible Sun at His temple at Auge. I wasn't exactly keen about anything identifying me with the Sashan priesthood after the business on Sirupat, but it wasn't as though I had any say in the matter. Take it or leave it. We took it.

"You look Sashan," she said, as we walked along the seafront. "Or at least you can if you try. I don't."

"No big deal," I said. "Your family was originally from

somewhere up in the Olbian delta. When the Sashan invaded, your lot got deported wholesale to Colmessus, on the Echmen border. Thanks to your exceptional piety and purity of spirit, you've worked your way up through the church hierarchy and transcended your lowly origins. That accounts for the way you look and your dreadful accent. But I wouldn't worry about it. In the habit you're practically invisible."

She nodded; a concession, actually that's not bad. I felt rather pleased with myself. "Is the Sashan clergy celibate?"

"Nominally. In practice—"

"Fine." Then she frowned. "Do you mind?" she asked. "About the scar."

"What scar?"

Not in the way she meant; but I could see it being a problem, because once seen, never forgotten, and the last thing I wanted was for us to be memorable. I know a bit about makeup, because of my time in the profession, but it was far beyond anything even Andronica could have fixed. When it healed, it lifted the corner of her mouth, so she looked like she was grinning all the time. I didn't actually mind that. It made her look like she was happy. That took some getting used to, but I rather liked it. "And are you?" I asked her.

"Piss off."

Me, too, I didn't add. At least, I assumed that was what it was, rather than a bad cold or the symptoms of some rare disease. I wouldn't know, not having been in that state for a long time.

My state of happiness (if that's what it was) lasted about an hour into our sea journey. Then it fizzled away like the water you pour round the edges of the forge fire to keep it in shape.

"For God's sake stop making that ridiculous noise," she said. "People are looking at you."

My reply took the form of groans. She rolled her eyes at me and went for a walk on deck. When she came back, she had a thoughtful look. "Dead yet?"

"Yes."

"Mphm. I was talking to a couple of men," she went on, sitting beside me with her back to a barrel. "One of them's a factor for a big outfit shipping bulk fruit—"

"Don't," I told her, "mention any kind of foodstuff."

"Bulk fruit," she repeated, "and he's heading back home, because of the war and stuff, and he's been hearing things from his home office." She paused. "Interesting stuff."

I swallowed a mouthful of volcanic lava. "Let me guess," I croaked. "The Sashan are winning. Poised for complete victory. Any minute now, the Great King will grind his enemies to dust under his heel. They always say that."

"No," she said, "and that's what's interesting. That's not what he said at all."

Interesting, to put it mildly; interesting enough to make me forget about the apocalypse going on in my colon. Apparently, the fruit man had heard from his people at home that the enemy fleet had won a battle, sunk a great many Sashan ships and hadn't been sent gurgling to the bottom. In fact, it was still very much in existence, which was more than could be said for the Sashan navy, and when last heard of was cruising along the south coast, possibly looking for somewhere to land and disembark troops.

"A Sashan told you that."

The Sashan are remarkable people. They can believe two contradictory things at once – the evidence of their own eyes, and what the king tells them, mutually exclusive but equally valid. One of the reasons why Sashan can justly pride itself on the outstanding excellence of its intelligence and communications is that everybody knows what the news will be, long before the exhausted despatch rider tumbles off his horse and collapses on the paved yard of the way station. We won. The enemy were slaughtered to a man and have ceased to exist. And, if you know the news, why not post it up on the gate and have it shouted in the street without bothering to wait for the actual messenger? There may be slight discrepancies of detail, but they can be sorted out later, or quietly forgotten about. The important thing is the truth, or at least the gist of it. Over the centuries, the Sashan have figured out all manner of ways of adjusting the past where it doesn't quite fit the present, the way you work the heels of a new pair of shoes with a broom handle. Once adjusted, the result is the truth; and, because Sashan bureaucrats were compiling lists of everything from the names of kings to the number of horseshoe nails in the reserve stock at Way Station 4,886 back when my ancestors were still skinning gazelle with scraps of flint, for most of human history the Sashan truth is all there is – and it works just fine, it makes sense, it forms a coherent narrative, and you get into the habit of assuming, if the Sashan say a thing, it must be true.

So, if they see a battlefield covered in dead Sashan soldiers and one of their cities wreathed in smoke and flames, and the king tells them that the battle was won and the city was saved, they interpret what they've seen in the light of what they've heard, and thereby arrive at the truth. The battle was hard fought, but the king personally led his bodyguard in a ferocious charge, cut his way through the enemy ranks and killed the enemy general with his own hand. Meanwhile an unfortunate fire swept through a couple of city blocks (probably started by traitors; more news on that story when we have it) but was quickly put out by the garrison. Afterwards, the king devised a cunning strategy where he could lure the enemy into a trap by pretending to abandon the city, thereby sealing their fate and setting up a final glorious victory, after which the savages would no longer exist as a nation.

It helps, of course, that the Sashan really do win nine-tenths of their wars, and have a superbly organised system of logistics that prevents food shortages when there's a bad harvest, and libraries and a tradition of education and scholarship that makes us look like children, and an average level of prosperity that we can only dream of. Which is why I used the word truth earlier; sooner or later, what the king says becomes true, even if it wasn't true at the precise moment he said it. Of course, they don't use the word Truth. They say *vrta*, because they talk Sashan, not Robur or Aelian, and the words we use to translate *vrta* are necessarily crude approximations to a term with wide and subtle penumbras of meaning. But a native Sashan speaker knows perfectly well what *vrta* means, and the world machine of which *vrta* is a key component works exceptionally well, so what could there possibly be to object to?

"I know," she said. "Scary, isn't it?" She frowned. "Saevus," she said, "do you think it's possible the Sashan might actually lose this war?"

I stopped and thought about it before answering. "No," I said. "No, that's not possible. They've got five times as many men, ten times the ships, and they know things about supply and infrastructure that would make your head spin. Also they've got infinitely more money, and a unified chain of command, and an unbreakable political will to win. The only reason they haven't conquered the world is because they've got more sense than to want to, and because we don't have anything they need. But I guess it's possible they could lose quite a few battles and get chased out of a fair bit of territory before they get mad enough to stop pulling their punches. Mostly it depends on the Great King. If he's—"

"What?"

Shut up a minute, I'm trying to think, because a thought had just struck me.

Did I ever mention that I met the Great King once? Not the man who sits on the throne, the real one – in the Sashan sense, naturally. He'd been deposed by a palace coup and escaped into exile, after which the truth quickly healed over, and it turned out that he wasn't the real king after all; but he was the king all right, I knew that the moment he spoke to me. When I met him, he was living in a palace in a desert surrounded by murderous spiritually minded cannibals, who had guaranteed his safety in return for various things I don't need to bother you with right now. He wasn't the real king so he didn't matter one bit; but while he was still alive, there would always be a remote possibility that the truth would change, or evolve, or emerge shining from the shadows, and he'd be back where he started from, Father of his People, Brother of the Sun and Moon; the old truth, same as the new truth apart from the subtle differences. But if he was dead – really *dead* dead – the result could easily be a sudden hole right in the middle of the web, the point where all the strands reach out from. And until new strands were woven and the replacement truth was resolved and hardened off ready for use, it was just remotely possible that the great and invincible Sashan Empire was momentarily paralysed—

It was a moment of brilliant insight, though I do say so myself, but all I could think about was the man I'd met, in the desert, when I was dying of thirst and he saved me. I'd gone there to kill him and steal his wife, but (being the king) he didn't hold that against me. I liked him, a lot. If he was dead, that was a bad thing and a reason to be sad. While I was explaining my flash of intuition to Stauracia, I kept remembering his voice and the sparkle in his eyes. A considerate, kind-hearted man who forgave his enemies. The nicest man I ever met, though of course that's not really saying a great deal, given the company I've always kept.

"You know what," she said, after a long pause. "You could be right."

I hadn't wanted her to say that. I wanted her to point out the flaw in my reasoning, which would mean he was still alive. "Maybe," I said. "But if the Sashan really did lose a battle, it'd be because something's wrong in the centre. You know how they work. Don't move until you can be certain of bringing overwhelming force to bear on the enemy. If they lost the battle, it's because either they hadn't got all their ducks in a row, or else we've suddenly come up with a new Carnufex and nobody thought fit to mention it. And you and I are in the trade; we'd have heard about it."

She gave me a look. "Don't say *we*," she said. "We're good Sashan now, remember?"

"Sorry," I said. "Force of habit. It's just, the Sashan have been *them* for as long as I can remember. You should've heard what my dad had to say about them."

"You told me you like them."

"I do." I shrugged. "Anyhow," I said, "to answer your question, yes, it's possible that *we* may have lost a battle, and your pal the fruit factor may be telling the truth. I don't see how it affects us particularly."

"An enemy fleet cruising up and down the south coast, and you think it's none of our business."

"Oh, come on," I said. "You're talking about Suda. We may have lost one battle, but *Suda*. It's the most heavily fortified city on earth."

She considered that. "You're right," she said, "I'm just being silly. Probably something to do with having a million darics in a bank there. Makes me antsy."

The world, according to the Prophet, is in haste and rushes to its end. I can see where he's coming from, but I can't say I've ever let it bother me too much. Clearing up battlefields for a living has taught me one thing. There's always a war, and the war is never over. Even when the great lions are lying down with the great sabre-toothed lambs and you can flit to and fro across the Friendly Sea with nothing to worry about apart from death by drowning, there's still a war going on somewhere. And for the people caught up in that war, it's just as bad as Aelia and the Sashan with their teeth locked in each other's throats. I guess I've grown used to it, like all the other things I live with daily but you don't have to, and that makes me – what? Insensitive, I guess, or you may choose to call it something else. After all, I don't know you from a hole in the ground, and the way your mind works is probably a total mystery to me.

Still, the Sashan were now at war with a loose coalition of the main Western powers, and an Aelian fleet was operating off the south coast, where we were headed. Awkward, to say the least.

"We get off the ship at Nouris," she said, "and we head north, up as far as Sangra, somewhere up there. Then we work our way down. The passes will be good enough for that, we could just as easily be going home via the west coast. We take it nice and easy, keeping our ears open. We'll be fine."

She was thinking aloud. She's got a knack of making an option she hasn't made her mind up about yet sound like a commandment from out of a burning bush, so you agree with her and she snaps at you for being stupid: why would anyone want to do a dumb thing like that? "Whatever you decide," I said. "I'll be guided by you."

"If you don't like it, say so. Or you might just possibly consider contributing something, instead of picking holes in every damn thing I say."

We didn't get off at Nouris. Instead, we were still on board the ship when it made an unscheduled stop at Pasanda, in the mouth of the Gulf. I asked the first mate what was going on.

"We're stopping here, Father," he said, and it was a split second before I remembered that I was some kind of priest. "Sorry. You'll have to make your own way."

"Why are we stopping?"

He pointed to some flags flying from the harbourmaster's tower. Oh, I thought.

The Sashan – did I mention that they're a marvellous people? – have a language of flags. Such a simple idea, odd nobody else ever thought of it. For example, a yellow flag means *plague; go away*. A blue flag means *help!* while green and white vertical stripes mean *stand by to be boarded for customs inspection*, while blue and yellow horizontal stripes are just there to let you know which direction the wind is blowing in.

A red flag, of course, means *mortal peril ahead; go no further.*
There were three flags on the harbour tower, all red.

"We'll find out once we get ashore," I told her. "We can't stay
on the boat. I don't think the crew know any more than we do."

She was extremely reluctant to get off the ship, but we didn't
really have a choice. "We could steal a lifeboat," she said. "We
could row out until we hit the current, and then it'll take us all
the way to the point."

"In full view of everybody on the dock," I said. "Not sure
what that's designed to achieve."

She scowled at me, as though I was the one who'd made the
idiotic suggestion. "I have a very strong feeling," she said, in
that explaining-to-idiots-and-children voice of hers, "that the
reason they're stopping all the ships is us. Probably you. I think
that if we go ashore, there'll be steelnecks waiting for us. And
you know what, I'm not in the mood for all that right now."

She gets these flashes of intuition, which prove to be valid
some of the time. She says about two-thirds; in my experience,
about a third. Intuition, of course, is just a patronising way of
saying she picks up on little strands of evidence without realising she's doing it. "No," I said, "the geometry's all wrong. If we
want a lifeboat we'll have to beat some people up to get it, and
that's probably the best way of making ourselves conspicuous
I can think of. Forget it," I said. "My father hasn't got the clout
to have all the shipping stopped east of the Gulf."

"Fine." I think she'd taken my point about the geometry,
an area in which she recognises my expertise. "On your head
be it, then."

"We can handle a few soldiers," I said. "Probably much
better geometry on the quay."

So we scrambled aboard the tender, which took us to the

dock, where there were no soldiers to be seen, only a lot of very confused and angry people. "What we need," she said, "is the place where the locals drink."

My thought exactly. Not hard to find. It went dead quiet when a priest and a nun walked in, but when they realised we weren't there to confiscate their souls they forgave us and carried on. Stauracia's ears are sharper than mine, so I let her do the eavesdropping.

"We want to get out of here," she said. "There's going to be a fight in a minute."

Good call. A fight would be inevitable in the circumstances; half the clientele insisting that what they'd heard was true, the other half knowing for a fact that it couldn't be, because the king always wins, the enemy always lose, and Suda is the most strongly fortified city in the world—

"It's just a rumour," I tried to tell her. "You know what people are like in wartime. It's probably just the usual garbage."

She looked at me. She was terrified. "We need to find out," she said. "Right now."

Two minds with but a single thought, two hearts that beat as one. I thought about it for a moment. "We're priests, right?"

"Yes. I think so. What are we again, exactly?"

Not like her to lose focus, especially when things turn sour. "We're a deacon and deaconess of the Eternal Flame at Suda, returning from a diplomatic jolly in the West. In practice, we're spies, so that means we're something quite high up in intelligence and can have people's wives and children taken away if they give us any trouble. We're big enough and ugly enough to hear the truth, and in situations like this we're part of the procedure for deciding what the truth is."

She looked mildly stunned. "Really?"

I nodded. "Your man did us proud," I said. "I thought you knew that."

"No, not really. He must be really scared of me," she added, with a slight frown. "That's—"

"Useful," I told her. "But he's not nearly as scared of you as the precentor of the local fire temple will be, when we come banging on his door and show him the passes. Cheer up," I said. "Thanks to your pal, we're two very scary people. What more could you ask for?"

Very scary indeed. At least, the precentor thought so, as soon as he saw what was written on the little clay tablets. "How can I help you?" he said.

I'd told her to leave the talking to me. "We need to know what's really going on," she said.

The precentor closed his eyes for a moment. He was a big man with a high voice and short white hair. My guess was that he'd got his job because he could be relied on to do nothing and do it exquisitely well. "The reports are, of course, uncon-firmed," he said.

"Of course," I said.

"Suda has definitely fallen," he went on. "The enemy fleet that sank our ships turns out to be one of two. The other fleet suddenly appeared out of nowhere, off Cape Ongyle. Nobody can offer any explanation of how it got there, it's simply impossible—" He screwed up his eyes again. "Since there was nobody to oppose them, they were able to land a large army, with artillery and siege towers. The garrison at Suda was taken completely by surprise. And, of course, there are rumours of treachery."

Of course. If the Sashan lose a city, it's always treachery. "Go on," I said.

He really didn't want to. "They broke into the city in the middle of the night," he said. "The witnesses say it was unbelievably savage. Essentially, they closed all the gates so nobody could get out, then burned it to the ground."

Nobody said anything for a while. "And?" I said.

"General Alyattes and twenty thousand men arrived too late to save the city," he went on, "but he immediately engaged the enemy. He was outnumbered two to one. He allowed himself to be encircled. As far as we know, there were only a handful of survivors." He paused, then went on: "The nearest army is Marshal Bardiya's, with eighteen thousand men, at the Orrhynthian Gates. But it would be suicide to try and engage the enemy with a such a disparity in numbers in what is now hostile territory. His lines of supply would be hopelessly overextended. I'm not a soldier, but I don't think you have to be to see how bad it is. Effectively, the enemy now control half of the south coast and inland as far as the Conessus river, as well as the lower half of the Friendly Sea."

She was staring at him, which was rather inconsiderate. He saw the look on her face and I could see the sudden wave of fear sweep over him. He'd just made a disloyal report. Worse still, he'd stated a load of facts that couldn't possibly be true.

"Thank you," I said. "That's most reassuring."

He turned and gazed at me. "Father?"

"Naturally I can't tell you anything," I said. "But you can rest assured, the king's plan is going well. The enemy have taken the bait, the sacrifice won't have been in vain. Suda—" I left the name hanging and gave him a brave smile.

"A quarter of a million people," he said. "My sister."

"We know who the traitors are," I said. "It's a tragedy we

had to pay so much for the information, but the king knows what he's doing. It was necessary."

He nodded, and I got the impression that I'd just done the kindest thing I'd ever done in my life.

"Now then," she said. "We'll need your help with a few things."

"Fuck," she said.

A suitable epitaph for a quarter of a million people. "Yes," I said.

"All that money." She took a deep breath and let it go, blowing a million darics into the warm night air. "Fuck it," she said. "Still, I never wanted to live in Sashan anyway."

"I've still got eighty thousand in the bank in Auxentia City," I said. "Let's go there instead."

"And walk straight into the arms of your dad's goons." She forgave me, and went on, "No, it just means we're going to have to carry on earning our living, that's all. Pity, but there it is. After all, it's not like that money was honestly come by."

A marvellous woman, by any standards. Everything she'd worked and fought and murdered for, gone just like that, and she could let it go with a single sigh. "Now what?"

I thought about it. "We could stay here," I said.

"Don't be stupid."

"We could. We're deacons, it says so on the clay tablets. Being a deacon's not so bad. Better than work."

"We aren't really—"

"Yes," I said, "we are. Because the only documentation that could prove we aren't would have been in the archive at Suda, and Suda's gone for ever. Therefore we're deacons. Really and truly. Sashan truly, anyhow. Think about it. There's a war on, we could make out like bandits."

Her eyes widened a little. "Who would we report to?"

"Anybody we liked. Sashan logic," I told her. "When no evidence exists to disprove it, what you assert is genuinely the truth. We go north, a long way into safe territory, we show up at the first temple we come to and report for duty. They find us something to do, and we're in."

She thought about it for several seconds, which I found rather flattering. "No," she said. "Sorry, but the Sashan are the *enemy*. Being here makes my skin crawl."

"It didn't when you had a million darics."

"That was different." She looked at me. "You stay here if you like."

I shook my head. No words needed or conceivably suitable for purpose.

"Right," she said. "In that case—"

I think the truth is why I like the Sashan. Because, in Sashan logic, I didn't murder my brother. Not unless what Fan wrote in her letter was true.

Stauracia's bright idea was that we should head for Anticonessus. No, shut up for a moment and listen. We've been there, it's empty, not a living thing anywhere. So we go north to Anticonessus, then cross the river and we're back home. Then she would think about how we were going to get my money out of the bank in Auxentia City, or something else equally helpful. Anyway, that was what we were going to do.

I didn't really mind. The things you do for love don't have to be accounted for in the usual way.

*

If I'd known the difference being a deacon makes, I'd have gone into the church when I was twelve.

A deacon – a black deacon, duly accredited and attached to a serious order like the Holy Flame of Suda – doesn't need to worry about the trivialities of life. If he wants to go somewhere, nobody asks him why, or tells him you can't get there from here, or asks him for money. At a stroke, the vast and bramble-like complexity of Sashan bureaucracy is his friend, not his enemy. You want to go to Anticonessus? Fine. We can arrange a special mailcoach for you, or, if you'd rather ride, we can find you good horses, which you can exchange at way stations as soon as they get tired, and would you like a cavalry escort or would that just slow you down? If you don't want to bother with money, here's a warrant to requisition anything you feel you might need, better than money, actually, because the sight of it will terrify innkeepers and shopkeepers so much they won't dare to try and screw you. On balance, we recommend against the cavalry escort. You won't need it. Robbers will occasionally pull down soldiers if they're desperate enough, but one look at the black habit will send them scampering the hell out of your way, because they know what happens to anyone who messes with the clergy. Besides, there are no robbers in the king's country. Likewise the roads are always perfectly maintained, but if they aren't and you break an axle or a horse goes lame, the first passer-by will run, not walk, to fetch a blacksmith or fetch you his own horse so you won't be delayed. The only downside to being a deacon is the abject terror of everyone you meet. Of course, not everybody would consider that a disadvantage.

"Which is one of the reasons," I told her, "why I like the Sashan. Things are properly organised. It's an ordered society."

"Was an ordered society." She'd been looking out of the coach window. "I think it's all going to shit."

She had a point. We were on the North-Western Mail, a typical Sashan road: broad, level, metalled, running along embankments and through cuttings, straight as an arrow and nearly as fast, to make sure the king's word doesn't go cold between his mouth and the recipient's ear. But from time to time the coach had to slow down because of the long, straggling groups of people, walking or leading donkeys with a few sad bits and pieces precariously roped down; Sashan citizens, trying to put as much distance as they could between themselves and the latest phase of the king's infallible plan. They did their very best to get out of the way so as not to hinder the king's mail, but even the North-Western isn't wide enough for a coach to get past a thousand people without slowing down a little bit. They knew it was only a day or so on the road before they reached a way station, where there'd be food and shelter and someone to tell them what they had to do. But we passed the way stations, and some of them were deserted, others were already crowded out with refugees, and a couple of them had been burned to the ground. If I were a Sashan seeing all that, I reckon I might be forgiven for wondering if God had died and nobody had seen fit to tell me.

"What I've been trying to figure out," she said, "is how the hell we managed to get a second fleet into the South Sea without them even noticing."

"Oh, that," I said. "Well, you'd need a lunatic."

"What's that supposed to mean?"

"You'd need a lunatic," I said, "because it'd mean launching a fleet from somewhere in Blemya and sailing in a straight line across the open sea, a hundred miles out of sight of land, and trusting your own skill with a chart and a sextant to bring you out precisely where you needed to be to come in the other side of the Gulf so as to outflank the Sashan Royal Navy, at precisely the right time to win an impossible victory. You'd have to be barking to think you could do that."

"Or a military genius."

"Tautology," I pointed out. "If it didn't work, of course, and if your fleet with a third of your entire army on board got sunk in a storm out in the middle of the ocean, or overshot and ended up getting beached on the Caryoba peninsula, you'd have lost the war at a stroke and condemned your entire nation to a thousand years of slavery. But if you pull it off, you win. For the time being, at any rate. Purely temporary victory, needless to say, because you can't beat the Sashan."

"You really are starting to think like them," she said. "That's disturbing."

"It explains," I said, "why they chose now to start a war. They've found a lunatic, a second Calojan or Forza Belot." I shook my head. "They used to say Forza Belot was worth a hundred thousand men. Probably an underestimate. He still lost, eventually." I looked past her, out of the window, at a column of people walking slowly. "Gombryas really, really wanted a bit of Forza Belot," I said. "But there are only six authenticated specimens, so he never stood a chance."

The reference wasn't lost on her, naturally. Forza Belot only failed because he ran out of men, and that's why Simmagene is deserted to this day, to the point where nobody can say for sure where it used to be. "The bigger they are," she said, "the harder they fall. You can see for yourself. It's all too centralised. It only takes one reverse and the whole thing starts coming apart."

I didn't want to argue military strategy with her, because she knows far more about it, and she doesn't take prisoners. Besides, maybe she was right. A truly brilliant soldier can achieve the impossible – Astyanax, or come to that, Felix or Florian the Great. In which case, one day there could well be uninhabited desert as far as the eye could see on both sides of the Friendly Sea, not just the west. I wasn't sure I wanted to think about that. None of my business. "If those are the Sky Mountains over there," I said, "the Conessus ought to be somewhere over there, in that dip."

She gave me a look. "You've got a truly awful sense of direction," she said. "It's a miracle you can find your arse with both hands."

The Conessus wasn't anywhere near where I thought it was. I'd been looking for it out of the left-hand window, and it was on the right.

"So with you being in the trade," she was saying, "how come there's a military genius and you'd never heard of him?"

"It's your trade, too," I pointed out. "Why are we slowing down?"

Because the driver didn't want to miss the turning, which is quite hard to see, since nobody in their right mind ever goes to Anticonessus, so the road isn't used much. A narrower road than the Mail, not arrow-straight; well-maintained, like all Sashan roads, but nobody had bothered to clear the trees and briars and general vegetable rubbish from the verges, to forestall any possibility of an ambush by bandits (although there are, of course, no bandits in the king's country; they'd be stamped on straight away and, besides, you only get bandits where there's poverty; but they still clear the verges, presumably out of force of habit or respect for tradition). It slowed the coach up a little, but not significantly.

Until we came to a featureless place in the middle of nowhere. No, I tell a lie, there was a stone. Egg-shaped, about waist high, nothing written on it, or nothing that had survived the wind and the rain. The coach stopped. Why have we stopped? You're there.

I'd been expecting melodrama, like the other frontier we'd crossed, or at least a river. Where's the river? Down there in the dip. What dip? If you carry on a quarter of a mile there's a dip, so they tell me. Never been past here. But the king reckons there's a dip, or that's what he told the Mapmaker General, and that's the river.

She remembered that she was a deaconess. "Keep going," she said.

The driver looked at her. "Sorry, Mother," he said (he was old enough to be her father). "This is as far as I can go. Standing orders."

Sashan thinking. Anywhere there's a possibility of trouble, the king pitches his border a quarter-mile from the real border, and leaves a sort of geographical anomaly into which anyone without legitimate business is absolutely forbidden to go. You can afford to do things like that when you own a third of the known world. And standing orders come direct from the king. Even a deacon could get in real trouble if it got out that he'd questioned standing orders.

"Thanks," I said, "we'll walk from here. Come on," I said to her. "It's all downhill to the river."

Between us, Stauracia and I know a thing or two about walking a long way in godawful places. Being deacons, we'd had our choice of the very best stuff, even though there was a war on, so we had best quality boots that actually fitted, handy knapsacks with comfortable straps that didn't dig in or chafe, wool blankets, oilskins, water bottles and all the army biscuit we could carry. I'd never been so well prepared for a horrible journey in my entire life. "I don't know, do I?" she replied, when I asked her how she was planning to get across the river. "Presumably there's a bridge or a ford or something."

I explained that it was a closed border. "Bullshit," she said. "There's always a bridge or a ford. There's got to be some way for diplomats and trade attachés and people like that to go backwards and forwards. They just say it's a closed border to put people off going there."

"The Anticonessians think everybody this side of the river is some kind of zombie," I said. "I don't think there'll be a bridge."

"Or a ferry. Or maybe there's a boat discreetly tied up somewhere. There's got to be some way the Sashan and the savages talk to each other. There always is."

Not always. We sat on the riverbank and looked out across the vast river. No animals, no birds, precious few midges. "I'm guessing," she said, after a long silence, "that the road brings you here because this is where the river is nice and shallow and you can wade across."

We got five yards. Then we got very wet. "Fine," she said. "You can swim, can't you?"

I happen to know she's a superb swimmer. I'm not. "Not with all this gear," I said.

"Don't be such a girl. When I was a kid I used to swim in the Ossick, and that's easily as wide as this."

I sat down. Water gushed off me and pooled around my arse. "Quite a lot of cultures believe in a river dividing the land of the living from the land of the dead," I pointed out. "The idea being, it stops you from nipping backwards and forwards over the line when you feel like it. To get across the message that death is for ever, they chose the image of a river. You know, the ultimate boundary, the final frontier. If you think I'm going to try swimming in that, you need your head examined."

"Fine," she said. "You stay here."

Actually, it could have been worse. It stripped off our boots, emptied our pockets, filled our mouths and our eyes with water and bashed us against several large rocks, but eventually we crawled out and lay gasping on the shingle, a mile downstream from where we'd started. I nearly drowned, but she saved me. "The hell with you," I said, as soon as I was up to making words. "We nearly died, and now we're screwed."

She looked at me. "I'm sorry," she said.

"Forget it." I sat up. My chest hurt like broken ribs when I breathed in. "Now what?"

"Don't know," she said.

Me neither. No sign of life anywhere. My guess is, that part of Anticonessus was uninhabited waste even before the civil war. We had no food and no boots. If you doubt the truth of the old saying *you can't take it with you*, try swimming the Conessus. Between us, we owned about as much property as a newborn baby.

"It's not so bad," I said. "I wasn't much better off when I ran away from home. Mind you, that was farmland. This is—" I couldn't think of a word for what this was. "Doc Papinian told me once you can go three weeks without food, so long as you've got water. Twenty-one days at twenty miles a day, that's four hundred miles. There's got to be *something* within four hundred miles."

She called me a fuckwit. We started walking.

*

Time passes and things change, but books are for ever, unless the mice get at them or some fool burns down the library, so by the time you read this Anticonessus might be the homeland of a vigorous, thriving civilisation. For all I know, you might be reading this in an Anticonessian translation, presumably in the hope of gleaning a few insights into what the earthly paradise was like a thousand years ago. In which case, it was horrible. Sorry about that, but at least it proves how far you and your people have come, in a relatively short space of time.

The country south-west of the Sashan border is – there's a technical name for it which I ought to know; high up, thin soil, loads of hills and valleys but no actual mountains, no trees, nothing but miles and miles of that kind of coarse-bladed grass that not even sheep can eat. There's no cover, so when the wind blows all you can do is crouch down until it stops. If you're ill-advised enough to walk across it in bare feet, don't be surprised if the edges of the grass slice you up like knives. On the positive side, you don't need to worry about wolves, because apart from a few annoying birds that jump out just before you tread on them, there's nothing alive up there.

We hardly said a word to each other for two days, and then she saw something in the distance. She pointed it out to me. "No idea," I said.

"Fuck it," she said. "Let's take a look."

Not a house, or a cottage or a barn. That would be too much to hope for. For a long time as we walked towards it I thought it might be a blockhouse, but it wasn't, though it was an easy mistake to make. But much, much bigger than a blockhouse, when you got up close. It was only the perspective, in that huge empty country, that made it look small.

I think we both started thinking the same thing at about the same time, though neither of us wanted to say it for fear of sounding idiotic. But, I was thinking as it grew bigger with each step, it could be. Architecturally it had all the hallmarks of the early First Empire: straight lines, flat roof, complete absence of ornamentation. It obviously wasn't Sashan: they couldn't build anything so ugly if their lives depended on it, and no Anticonessian could have fitted any idea as massive as that into his tiny brain. I tried to remember what I knew about different types of stone and where they came from. This thing was basalt, for crying out loud. The nearest basalt was Olbia.

"It can't be," she said. "It just can't."

"Basalt," I said.

"Shit and fuck and piss." She looked at me. "You're right, it's basalt. Who the fucking hell—?"

We both knew the answer. Only one man, since the world began, would have had the power to organise thousands of tons of precision-cut basalt blocks, all the way from Olbia to here. And only one man would have wanted to.

"I really wish Gombryas was here," I said. "And we weren't."

She looked at me. "We could get out of the wind for five minutes," she said.

"We might as well, since we're passing," I said.

There had been a gate once, but even bronze corrodes eventually. The hinges were still there, and a few green wisps of foil, brittle as autumn leaves. We walked in. There was a tiny little lodge, or loggia or whatever it's called, then a sharp right-hand turn—

I expected it to be dark in there, but there were windows, high up, just under the eaves, cunningly placed so that the light could get in but the wind and rain couldn't. The light slanted in diagonally, if that makes any sense, and everything was a blaze of yellow gold.

"Will you look at that?" she said.

The legend was, of course, untrue. A pack of lies. The First Emperor hadn't been buried with his ten thousand loyal soldiers. Instead, he'd had one thousand lifesize statues carved, out of basalt, and the gold armour had been wired on, because gold is for ever but leather and fabric aren't.

She started to laugh. I let her. I didn't feel much like laughing myself.

Some time later, when she'd stopped laughing and then crying, we sat down on a big gold box, which I'm guessing was the First Emperor's coffin. "Well," she said, "we did it. The big score."

"Yup."

She took a deep breath and let it go. "Presumably," she said, "Gombryas was right and one of these statues is missing a cuisse. I can't be bothered to look, can you?"

"No," I said. "But I doubt it. I think Gombryas's thing was a fake. After all, we only had his word for any of it. It was just a ploy to trap me. This is—" I made a vague gesture "—a coincidence."

She thought about it for a moment. "Like it matters."

"You want my professional opinion?"

"Go on."

"You could mount an expedition," I said. "You'd have to hire a lot of men, five thousand minimum, plus carts, horses, supplies. You'd have to pay a lot of officials on the Sashan side. Oh, and you'd have to build a bridge over the river. It could be done. You might just break even if you're lucky, but my gut feeling is, it'd end up costing you money."

"The big score."

"Absolutely. The king might just be able to pull it off, in spite of the expense, if he wanted the prestige. But he doesn't need it, so why bother? That's why it's still here. More trouble than it's worth."

"I think we're the first people to come here for a thousand years." She was looking round. "I ought to be impressed," she said. "But it's just sad. So he managed to figure out a way to beat the thieves. So what?"

"I think he believed in life after death."

"I'm still having trouble coping with life before death," she said. "Probably not for much longer, though." She turned her head and looked at me. "I think this is probably it, Saevus. I'm sorry. I think this is as far as we go."

Well, I thought. If you've got to end up in a tomb, this was quite likely the top of the line, the cutting edge, even after a thousand years of progress. Our tomb now. Monarchs of all we surveyed. And my mother said I'd never amount to anything. "Bullshit," I said. "We keep going."

"Why?"

Because I've found you, and there's a reason for living. "Force of habit. What else is there?"

"My feet hurt," she said. "They hurt so much I can't think, And I'm hungry. All I can think about is food, and my feet."

I looked up. "I think we can do something about that," I said.

Ten thousand gold suits of armour meant ten thousand pairs of gold sabatons. That's the bit that completely covers your feet. Mine fitted remarkably well; my life hasn't been all sunshine and roses, but at least I'm blessed with average-size feet. We had to pack hers out with blades of grass.

As for food; that's what had made me look up, a bird startled out of its nest. We found a dozen of them, in the corners and crevices, and in each nest two or three eggs. Tough on the birds, but as far as I was concerned it was treasure beyond my wildest dreams, the stuff of legends, Essecuivo, King Florian's Mines, the once and future big score. Life itself. What can be more precious than that?

8

Two more days. She was complaining about the weight of her gold shoes. She had a point. "Over there," I said, "look."

She followed my finger. "Who the hell can that be?"

"Anticonessians," I said. "We're in Anticonessus, remember? They'll kill us as soon as look at us."

She thought for a moment. "We're Anticonessians," she said. "We lost our way and we've been wandering around in circles in the sun without hats on, our brains are fried and we can't remember who we are or where we came from."

"That's stupid."

"It's worth a try."

I looked at her. She was practically shrivelled. I could see she was human and, on the balance of probabilities, female; apart from that, she could be anyone from anywhere. "They talk Sashan, don't they?" she asked.

"I think so. I can't remember."

"Fuck it," she said. "Let's give it a go."

In the steppe, the geometry is slightly different, though

essentially the same. If we hid from them, whoever they were, the open space would kill us. If we went and said hello, there might well be useful lines and angles I could exploit. "Fine," I said.

As we drew closer, I started wondering: sunstroke, for real? I knew who these people were. "That's not who I think it is, is it?" she said. "It can't be. That's crazy."

"I think it is," I said.

I was right. A long, straggling column of carts, drawn by miserable-looking oxen. They use oxen because they're cheaper, though it's a false economy. But, then, the Asvogel boys are like that.

My old pal Daresh Asvogel was riding point, on a milk-white horse that presumably used to belong to some senior officer. He stared at me, thinking, once upon a time I knew someone who looked a bit like that.

I was too choked up to speak. I opened my mouth, but nothing came out.

"Hello, Saevus," he said. "What the hell have you got on your feet?"

"Everything's going to hell," said Daresh Asvogel, pouring us wine from a silver chalice. "Screwed, stuffed, fucked to buggery. You want mint with that?"

Dried mint, not fresh; from a little rosewood box. That, apparently, was how bad things had got. "The war," I prompted.

"Don't talk to me about the fucking war." Daresh scowled at it, as if it was in the coach with us. "It's a total disaster. Shit up to our armpits. Fucking Chusro's fault."

It may have occurred to you to wonder why I get on so

well with the Asvogel boys, given that they are, they were, my deadliest rivals and did everything they could to put me out of business. But I've never taken it personally; and for some reason, each of the brothers thinks that I'm on his side in the endless, unceasing strife and bickering between them. Accordingly I've spent more hours than I care to remember listening to Chusro bitching about Sersy, Daresh moaning about Chusro, Sersy white-hot with anger because Daresh and Arta were ganging up on him – I'm firmly convinced that they love each other more than life itself, which is probably why they're always at each other's throats. "What did Chusro—?"

"Only went and bought the whole fucking war from the king's man in Bomains." For a moment, he was too angry to speak. "I told him, you must be out of your fucking mind, and you know what? He just grinned at me. It'll be fine, he said, the lunatic. I said, you can't just buy one side of a war, what if they lose? The Sashan won't lose, he said, hold your fucking water."

"Calm down," I urged him. "Breathe."

He did as I suggested, though it cost him dearly. "I'm not going to tell you what that arsehole paid," he went on, "because you wouldn't believe it, not in fifty million years. But it's everything we've got, plus humungous loans from the Knights *and* the Sisters, only the stupid bastard didn't tell them we'd only got one side of the frigging war or they'd never have lent us a trachy. When they find out they'll have his head. Did he ask me, or the others? Like fuck he did. Just went ahead and did it. And now, guess what?"

"The Sashan are losing."

Daresh closed his eyes. "Big time," he said. "Arseholes sunk their fleet, and now there's been a shitting great big battle at the

Gates, and this pissing dickhead of a new general the Aelians have got made mincemeat of the Army of the West and the Royal pissing Household Cavalry. It was a massacre, Saevus. We stood and watched it from the hilltop; it was a joke. Sixty thousand dead Sashan, and no bloody use to us whatsoever. And we'd hired on two thousand extra hands, carts, supplies, barrels—" He had to stop; he couldn't go on. "Bloody Aelians didn't give a stuff, they just left it all lying, the shits. So Chusro says, well, if nobody wants it, we might as well stroll down and help ourselves."

"Chusro said that."

He nodded. "I told him, you do what you fucking well like. I'm not going down there; that's not our battlefield. Fuck you, he says, we're going, so off he goes, and what do you think happens? Fucking Aelian cavalry."

"Not good."

"Too fucking right not good. Bastard cavalry make straight for him, he legs it, they chase him up the mountain, you know, on the river side of the Gates?"

I nodded. Horrible place.

"Cavalry gets the carts and slices up about a thousand of the men, mostly the new hands, thankfully, but even so. I say, fuck it, let's get the hell out of here, so me and the lads, we're off out of it. We came here because we reckoned they wouldn't follow us; you know, Anticonessus – where Chusro is right now I couldn't begin to guess, but what the fuck. It's over, Saevus. We've had it. We're out of the business."

That got to me. "You're kidding," I said.

"Straight up," said Daresh. "I don't see how we can carry on, not after this. We've got no money, all that debt, and we can't work, because the Aelians are winning. Fucking

Chusro. For all I know, the stupid sod's dead in some river-bed somewhere. I'm only glad Dad's not around to see it. It'd break his heart."

"It's the war," I said. "It's changing everything."

"Too right," Daresh said. "Don't know who this Aelian arsehole is, but the way he's carrying on, makes no sense to me. I think he must be mad. Seriously crazy. Everywhere he goes, he's burning villages, trashing crops, poisoning wells, killing the locals right, left and centre. You heard about Suda."

"Sore topic," Stauracia said. "Yes, we heard."

"Fucking lunatic," Daresh said. "Roasted a quarter-million civilians, and all that *stuff*. There was enough stuff in that city to pay for the war for five years, and the arsehole just sets fire to it. I ask you, why would anyone do that?"

"To make a point, I guess," I said.

"Fuck making points," said Daresh, "it's *criminal*. Far as I can tell, he's planning on making the whole of Sashan into a desert. Total war. Where's the sense in that? All he's going to achieve is, he'll make the Sashan good and mad and then they'll come over the sea and do it to the West. How's anybody supposed to make a living when there's nothing fucking *left*?"

Stauracia looked at me, then asked, "Does anyone know anything about this man? He can't just have appeared out of nowhere."

Daresh shrugged. "He might as well have," he said. "According to some people I was talking to, his name's Tisander and he was colonel of some piss-arse supply corps in some poxy little war up north somewhere. Then his whole army got slaughtered, leaving just him and about three thousand auxiliaries, and he had to get them home somehow. Which he did, apparently, and suddenly everybody realised, he's the greatest military genius since fucking Felix, so of course some arsehole gets to thinking, let's get hold of this nutcase and turn him loose on the Sashan." He paused and sighed deeply. "Don't know if it's true or not, it's just what some people told me. I guess stuff like that happens from time to time, or they could just have been making it all up."

Nobody said anything for a long time.

"Anyhow," Daresh said eventually, "that's our news. How the fuck did you two get in such a state?"

I gave him a sheepish grin. "We've been treasure hunting."

"What, at your age? No, seriously, what've you been up to?"

I leaned forward and pulled a sabaton off my foot. "We've been treasure hunting," I said. "Tell me what you make of that."

He looked at it. All the colour drained from his face. "Fucking no way," he said.

"Out of interest, how many carts have you got?"

"You're serious." He looked at Stauracia. "Is he serious?"

"Deadly serious," I said. "We found it. It's real. And it's all still there."

"Fuck a weasel sideways." He turned the sabaton over in his hands, then gave it back. "Really?"

I smiled. "I think I can safely say all your troubles are over," I said. "And ours, too, unless you're a total prick."

"Oh, come on, Saevus, you know me, we're pals. I wouldn't screw you, not for a million darics—"

"It's worth rather more than that," I told him, and he took it like a blow to the head. "Just sitting there waiting. You can even back the carts up to the door for loading. You know what," I went on, "I'm glad we ran into you."

The look on his face. "I'll see you right," he said. "Both of you, I promise."

"Oh, don't say that," I said. "That means you'll cut our throats, the moment we've shown you where it is."

"No, really, I—" My heart bled for him. He knew there was nothing he could say that would make me trust him, because I knew him too well. He was like a man who's gone out to dinner and realised after he's finished eating that he's left all his money at home. "I wouldn't screw you, Saevus," he said. "I promise. On my brothers' lives."

"It's the big score, Daresh," I said. "And Stauracia and I know where it is, and you don't." I counted to three under my breath, because deep down I'm a horrible person and I like watching people suffer. "But that's fine. We'd be dead in the desert if it wasn't for you. Come on, I'll draw you a map."

"Out of interest," she asked, "how the hell did you get across the river?"

Silly question. "Over the bridge."

"What bridge?"

He gave her a look. "The bridge. Don't you read maps?"

She looked at me. "Not on any map I ever saw," I said.

He sighed, and pulled a map out of a sort of side pocket in the coach door. "There," he said. "Bridge."

About twenty miles from where we'd crossed the river, losing everything in the process. "That's not a Sashan map," I said.

"No, it's Vesani, I bought it in Ap'Escatoy about three years ago. What's the big deal?"

The king didn't know about the bridge. Fine. None of my business. "What sort of a bridge?" I asked him.

"Just a bridge," he said. "Stone, I guess it's old. Wide enough for two carts abreast. Quite a decent road on the Sashan side, and then it's just grassland. The savages don't go up there, so I guess they don't know about it."

Dear God, I thought. "And it's still there."

"I guess so, why? Oh, right. Getting the stuff out again once we've got it. Bad idea. We really don't want to go anywhere we'd be likely to run into those Aelians. You know how people get sometimes."

Actually, I was thinking: how can there be a bridge on a closed frontier and nobody knows about it? Apart from map-makers in the Vesani Republic, a thousand miles away. But nobody tells me anything. "Let me see that map," I said.

He gave it back. She snatched it before I could get my hands on it. "North," she said. "What's all this up here?"

I looked over her shoulder. "That's the Bullhead Mountains," I said.

"Piss. All right, what's this?"

Daresh took the map from her. "Oh, that," he said. "That's a pass through the Bullhead. Don't think it's got a name. Never been there, but Sersy went there once. It's no big deal, just a hole in the wall. You can get carts and stuff through, so Sersy reckons."

"What's that on the other side?" she said.

"Nothing," said Daresh. "Just grassland and garbage like that. Nobody lives there, just a few savages passing through twice a year with a load of sheep."

She was tracing the map with a fingertip. "That's, what, sixty miles? And then you reach this river here, which feeds into the Ostar."

I frowned. "You'd need barges."

"Break up the carts and build rafts," she said, as though it was the easiest thing in the world. "And the Ostar takes you straight to Olbia." She glared at me. "I thought you said it was a closed border."

"That's what I'd been told," I said.

"I wish you'd get your facts straight. Still," she said, "no harm done. We hike north, might be a bit tight on supplies but we'll just have to be careful, through the gap and then rafts all the way to Olbia. Piece of cake."

Daresh looked at her. "You're wasted on him," he said.

(True. Once, years ago, I came across a copy of Saloninus's *Ethics*, which had a bit in it that's missing from all the other copies, or else it's something that someone added later. Love came about, it said, because the gods grew jealous of mortal happiness, so they sliced them in two, right down the middle, and scattered the halves across the earth. Love is when one half finds the other again.

For years, I convinced myself that Saloninus could never have written anything as soppy as that, but it occurs to me now that I may have been too hasty. If it's a later addition, the forger caught Saloninus's style just right, which is very hard to do, and the rest of the book makes much more sense with the missing passage restored. Mind you, there are some very clever people about, and not all of them are scrupulously honest.

I imagine I'd have come to the same conclusion if she'd let me see the map instead of snatching it away from me, but what the hell. There's no point in the left hand competing with the right.)

"I make it fifty million darics," she was saying. "Each suit of armour, fifty thousand darics, bullion value. Fifty thousand times a thousand is fifty million."

Daresh was asleep, with his mouth open. I'd been looking out of the window. "Fine," I said. "That's a lot of money."

"Depends on what the war's doing to the gold price, of course," she went on. "Probably good, from our point of view. Gold's good in wartime because you need it to pay for bulk supplies, but silver goes up because that's what you pay the soldiers with. Now, if we can contrive some way to be paid for the gold in silver, we'd be laughing. Unless, of course—"

"What do you make of that?" I asked her.

She looked where I was pointing. Then she swore and poked Daresh in the ribs. "Stop the coach," she yelled at him.

"No, don't do that," I said. "We need to keep going."

Nobody listens to me. The coach stopped and Daresh jumped out, bellowing orders as soon as his feet hit the ground. Carts in a square, get your helmets, get your bows, you know the drill. They've got a drill, I thought; I'm impressed. We never had drills when I was running the show, we just ran about like headless chickens.

The first wave were horse-archers, shooting from the saddle with short horn-and-sinew bows. After them came the footsloggers, thin men in rags with hayforks and bean hooks. Daresh's boys killed about two dozen of the archers and ever so many of the infantry, and then they started pouring over the carts and that was more or less that.

Daresh, stupid bloody fool, had decided to be a strong leader. He was rallying his forces for a counter-attack when some man who looked like a walking skeleton came up behind him and took the back of his head off with an adze. I noticed it out of the corner of my eye, because I was giving all my attention to the geometry. Stauracia and I were under a cart, and I needed to see a gap in the human torrent big enough, in space and time, for us to dart through. I had my eye on three riderless horses, their saddles emptied by Daresh's archers at an early stage of the proceedings, but the angles and the flow weren't quite right—

"Fuck this," Stauracia said, and scrambled out past me. I yelled at her to stop, because her vector intersected the arcs of two men with bean hooks, but she wasn't listening. I followed her as if I was tied to her with a rope. My hands were empty, but I managed to grab a dungfork from a dead man without slowing down.

When I was a kid, morning exercises used to include throwing the javelin. We had a big straw target nailed to the traphouse door. Compared to Scynthius I was pretty hopeless, and a shitfork isn't like a craftsman-made, perfectly balanced hunting javelin. If I threw it, I'd be empty-handed when the second bastard intersected my line. If I didn't throw it, or I missed, no more Stauracia.

I hit the first bastard in the head; I'd been aiming for the midriff, goes without saying. The fork hit him, the tines flexed and the fork bounced off. No matter; while the poor fool was reeling, Stauracia whipped out her pet knife and stabbed him daintily through the heart. Meanwhile, his pal was swinging at me with his hook. But I knew all about that, from fencing lessons; a long step sideways and back, trace and traverse, the drill sergeant called it, and the attacker blunders past you, off-balance; you kick the inside of his knee and he's sprawling on the deck. The approved procedure at that point would have been to stamp on his ear, but I really couldn't see any point in that. None of my business whether he lived or died.

Stauracia had seen the three horses and was heading for them; like I keep telling you, she's smart. The geometry looked good in front; I glanced over my shoulder as I ran, but actually that's not best practice. You can't do much about what's going on behind you, so knowing about it only scares you, which slows you down.

Stauracia ran at the horses, so of course they spooked. She managed to grab the reins of one of them; it pulled her off her feet and dragged her a few yards, and then she had the sense to let go. She was screaming at them, white-hot anger; she'd have had all three of them flayed alive, if there'd been anybody about to take orders from her.

I grabbed her arm and pulled her up. "Fucking horses," she was yelling. I was pointing at two more horses about twenty-five yards away, but she wasn't paying me any attention. Fine. I let go of her, and walked, not ran, up to the horses, who were snuffling under the blades of the coarse grass, looking for something to eat. I got hold of the reins of one of them, then led it across to the other. Then I looked round, confidently expecting to see Stauracia lying on the ground with her head cut off.

No such thing, fortunately. She was rushing towards me. "No," I said, loudly without shouting. "Walk." Might as well have saved my breath. The horses shied, but I'd wrapped the reins twice round my wrist, so that was fine.

She put her toe in the stirrup and sort of floated up on to the horse's back. I don't know how she does that, and it's a joy to watch. Me, I'm strictly one hand on the pommel, one hand on the crupper, foot in the stirrup and *heave*, and I'm always mildly surprised when I make it. "Which way's north?" she yelled at me.

"I don't know, do I?"

"Oh, for God's sake," she said, and kicked her horse into a standing gallop.

*

A footnote on Anticonessian society. There would appear to be at least two social classes. One of them's dirt poor, wears rags and kills people with farm tools. The other can afford hand-crafted composite bows, exquisitely made saddlery and harness and superb thoroughbred horses. Nor do they stint themselves when it comes to eating and drinking, even when on the hoof. Our saddlebags (tooled and embossed leather, with silver buckles) were stuffed with rye bread, white goat's cheese and a rather fine dried sausage, seasoned with pepper, cumin and something else I couldn't identify, though Stauracia reckoned it was probably nutmeg. To wash it down with, two skins of a rather good white wine, with a delicate bouquet, like apples.

"Fucking piss," she said, when we stopped and looked back and were satisfied we had the world to ourselves once again. "That's just so unfair."

"That's the big score for you," I said. "You can touch it, but you never actually get your fingers round it. That's west, so that must be north over there."

"Fucking piss and *shit*." Her anger nearly broke my heart. "We could go back," she added. "Just close enough so we can see if they made it or not."

"They didn't make it," I told her. "It wasn't going well when we left. I imagine they were all dead by the time we got the horses."

"You can take your imagination and shove it right up." I could see the hope ebbing out her face, until there was none left. "Back where we bloody well started."

No, I didn't point out, because we had fast horses and supplies for ten days. I love her dearly, but she tends toward the glass-half-empty school. "I told you," I said, "treasure hunting's a mug's game. You're lucky if you break even. Which we just did, so let's be on our way."

She wasn't looking at me. "It could have been worse," she said. "We could've actually got the bloody stuff, and been on our way to Olbia, and then the bastards hit us."

"Better to have loved and lost, surely?"

"Oh shut up."

I look at things differently. Any sequence of events that I come out of riding a comfortable horse and with enough to eat I consider to be a victory. Of course, there was now another criterion to add to that. Any sequence of events that *we* come out of.

But we had, so no worries. She reluctantly agreed with my definition of north, and we went there. She sulked for the first two days, but after that she was fine. Eighty thousand in the bank in Auxentia, she pointed out; that's quite a lot of money. Then we set about considering how we could get there, and how we could get the money without being nabbed by my dad's goons, and before we knew it we were looking at some very impressive mountains, with a gap in them.

She, of course, had had the wit to steal Daresh's map out of the coach door. "We ride alongside this tributary river here," she said, "and then, when we reach the Ostar, there'll be ships and barges. We can probably trade one of these poncy saddles for a ride, or probably just cut off the buckles. Don't know if you've noticed, but they're solid silver."

"I saw that," I said. "Even my dad only ever had silver plate."

"Stupid," she said. "Silver's a rubbish metal, too brittle. We should sell the harness no matter what and get proper stuff. Nothing spoils your day like a busted girth buckle in the middle of nowhere."

I was considering the map. The Ostar is a long river; we say it's the longest in the world, but I bet there's something bigger in Sashan, the king would insist on it, even if it meant digging canals. It doesn't flow in a straight line, or anything like it. Instead there are long stretches where it loops and wiggles, and one of its meanderings comes quite close to the northern border of my father's country. Quite close; sixty miles, something like that. It used to bug him, because most of his friends had waterfronts on to the Ostar and he hadn't. At one point there was a scheme to marry my brother Scaphio to some girl with a view to getting access to the Ostar as part of her dowry, but it fell through, like a lot of my father's clever ideas.

She was looking over my shoulder. "Don't worry about it," she said. "We'll be on a boat in the middle of the river; nobody will know it's you."

"Even so," I said. "It's horribly like going home. The hell with it. I'm being stupid."

"Yes, you are. Hundreds of boats go up and down the Ostar every day. Also, the last place they'll think to look for you is on the doorstep."

There are times when she sees things much more clearly than I do. "Not a problem," I said. "Now all we've got to worry about is the war."

The pass through the mountains was terrifying and very boring. Terrifying because I was expecting armed men to jump out at us from every bend in the twisting road; boring because absolutely nothing happened, and there was nothing to see except cliffs. We'd saved the last quarter of one of the wineskins to celebrate reaching the river, and we drank it looking down on a silver ribbon winding through a dark green eternity. "I hate the fucking grasslands," she said. "I can't wait to see the back of them."

I was getting to like them, mostly because they were deserted. Deserted, and supposed to be that way. The next day, we rode out of Anticonessus. Technically, I pointed out, that meant we were leaving the land of the living and entering the realm of the dead. If that was the land of the living, she replied, they could have it. I gave her no argument on that score.

In the middle of the river, there was a boat.

I recognised the pattern. It was one of those big, square things – cogs, I think – that they use for carrying bulk cargoes on the Ostar. It shouldn't have been on the tributary, because it's too shallow. "What the hell do they think they're playing at?" she said. "It'll run aground or hit something and sink."

It was crowded; crammed with men and women, standing-room only. Not sailors or soldiers or anybody with a reason to be on a boat: you could tell that just by looking at them, even at that distance. "I'm guessing they're refugees from somewhere," I said.

"They're not going to get very far if they carry on like that."

They might as well have been on the moon, as far as we were concerned. There was just enough depth of water in the middle of the river to keep them afloat. If they tried to come over to the bank, they'd get stuck, or rip the bottom off. "Ours or theirs, do you think?" she said.

"No idea."

Nominally we were still in Sashan territory, and they were headed downstream, naturally. "Sashan, I guess," she said. "What's the war doing all the way up here?"

"A military genius being brilliantly unpredictable," I said. "They do that a lot."

I did the geography. It was possible. A northwards lightning strike with cavalry direct into the soft underbelly; Carnufex did it in Scheria, and it would have worked if it hadn't been for the unseasonably early snowfall. No snow in Sashan, of course. "It makes you wonder what the king is playing at," she said.

"I expect he knows what he's doing," I said. "So the military genius needs to keep him off balance. Brilliantly unpredictable."

The boat was dangerously low in the water, I could see that. But I don't suppose there was anybody with the authority to say, no, sorry, you people can't come on board, it's too risky. You'd need to be a total bastard to say that, unless you had a warrant and a uniform. "I don't suppose they've got a map," I said.

"Couldn't read it if they did." She was frowning. "If they got this far, it probably means nobody's chasing after them," she said. "Still, it wouldn't hurt to be careful. We've been a bit slack the last couple of days."

Ah, the war. Like wolves or malaria or snakes in your bed, something you've got to have in the back of your mind, all the time. Unless of course you're a licensed scavenger, in which case it tends to leave you alone, like the little birds which pick shreds of meat out of the teeth of crocodiles. But I was a civilian now, and even the Asvogel boys were probably out of business. Hard to imagine, that: a war so intense it melts the frame of the forge.

We saw eight more cogs loaded with refugees, and two big columns of carts and walkers, on the opposite bank, heading the other way. "That's dumb," Stauracia said, "they're walking straight into the war." Presumably they don't know that, I said.

We tried calling out to them, but they couldn't hear us or took no notice.

"Which means," she said, "that there must be war where we're headed, as well as where we've just come from. Fuck it." She thought about it for a while. "Maybe the king's finally pulled his finger out and counter-attacked."

"My guess is," I said, "he's launched an offensive against the West, in the hopes they'll pull their genius out of Sashan to defend the homeland. Only that'd be a hiding to nothing and the king's not that stupid. I met him once, remember."

"You said he'd died. I was talking about the new king."

"I guess I was wrong about that. This feels like what he'd do. The man I met. And somehow, I think I'd know if he was dead."

She gazed at me. "You worry me," she said. "You're starting to sound like you actually believe all that shit."

"I know him," I told her. "He saved my life in the wilderness. That's a bloody sight more than the Invincible Sun ever did. So, on the balance of probabilities—"

"Saevus." Full eye contact. "You don't, do you?"

"No, of course not, I'm just kidding. But if I could make myself believe in something, and if I could choose, I reckon there are worse gods. It's just a shame he's getting the stuffing kicked out of him, that's all."

"I'm glad I can't see inside your head," she said. "I can't abide a mess."

The tributary joins the Ostar through a gap between two tall, gradually sloping hills. So you hear it before you can see it: the great river, rising in the foothills of the mountains whose name I can never remember, slowly fattening like whey-fed pigs until it gushes out into the Friendly Sea. Five times in all of recorded history it's frozen over; apart from that, it just gets on with the job of shifting a great deal of water from one place to another.

The thing about the Ostar is, it's busy. There are always boats on it, big boats, little boats, sailing or drifting downstream, being towed upstream by big, slow horses. It's like a city where all the houses fall down and get rebuilt once a day. Wars have been fought over various aspects of it, but they don't bother it more than flies bother a cow; a whisk of the tail or a lick of the ears and they've gone. Kings and archdukes have built bridges over it, which have all ended up as flotsam a few miles downstream a week or so after the first heavy rain in the hills. It's too big and strong to mess with, so it doesn't care.

"Where are all the boats?" she asked.

It was the sort of question you don't answer. "How much food have we got left?" I asked.

"About a day's worth. But there's towns and villages." As she said the words, it occurred to her that maybe there weren't, not any more. "Oh, for God's sake," she said. Actually, it's rather charming, the way she takes everything so personally.

We rode on for about an hour. Then she said, "You remember Sirupat."

"Yes, oddly enough."

"There was going to be a war," she said. "This one. But you stopped it. At the time I remember thinking, that's a pretty neat thing to do, but I didn't – I never said thank you for it."

"Nobody did. Don't worry about it."

"Someone should've," she said.

"I was wasting my time," I said, "evidently. All that trouble and effort, and what happens? We get the war. A few years later, but so what?"

"It was a pretty amazing thing to do, even so. I don't know, I never really believed in it. You remember when we sat looking out of the window as the Sashan fleet sailed past?"

"All at the bottom of the sea now. Weird thought," I added. "They looked like nothing on earth could possibly be stronger. I thought I was so clever, fixing all that. It was like I'd diverted the Ostar and sent it crashing down where I wanted it to go. Fact is, I'm so stupid I shouldn't be allowed out."

"I keep wondering where those people were coming from," she said. "The ones who were going the wrong way."

I wasn't enjoying the conversation. "Maybe with our end of fifty million darics we could've found somewhere the war can't get into," I said. "But I doubt it, not this war."

"You never know, we could win. If this lunatic genius can get to the capital—"

"And burn it to the ground, and slaughter a million people." I shrugged. "Three-quarters of the Sashan live east of the capital. All this idiot is doing is making sure that, when the Sashan hit back, they hit back good and hard. Whether by that point there'll be anyone left alive—"

"Shut up, Saevus, that's not funny."

Forza Belot, I thought; he'd have won, only he ran out of people. The young men die, on the battlefield or heaving their guts out with dysentery. The women and the old men try and cope, but they can't. They leave, or die where they are. No food is grown in the countryside, so the cities starve. They set off to go somewhere else, but only a handful of them get there. All because Forza Belot had a genius for the form of chess known as strategy, so he kept winning battles in the face of overwhelming odds, until nobody was left. It's not defeat that does the real damage, it's victory. "Whoever this idiot is," I said, "I'm just glad Gombryas isn't here to see it. He'd have pined away from desire, yearning for a bit of his shin."

Different people burn down villages in different ways. The Molausi, for example, start at the edges and work inwards, while the Vesani always begin with the temple or the town hall or whatever passes for a civic centre. The Cure Doce flay livestock, leaving the heads on, and nail the hides to trees, whereas the Anticyrenaeans are punctilious about burying everybody they kill. The Aelians are upwind burners, which makes a lot of sense, unless the wind changes and suddenly you're scampering like hares to get out of the way. The Sashan, by contrast, are strictly sunwise. They always start in the east and burn west, regardless of wind or the layout of the village. I guess that's because fire is their idea of God, so torching houses is a sort of religious act.

"Sashan," I said. I'd been on my knees, crumbling cinders between finger and thumb.

She nodded. "Sunwise?"

"Yup. Which is good news for us," I added, "because they can be careless about leaving food behind. Aelians would've made sure of every last grain of flour."

The village had had a name once; Calcries, and the inn was the Glorious Redemption. I'd passed through it, many years ago, not long after I ran away from home. I stole a ham hock there, I remember. Now the house I robbed was gone, as though it had never been, which I guess let me off the hook. Undeserved absolution, the story of my life.

I didn't count the root cellar we eventually found as stealing, because the essence of theft is taking things from someone, and there was nobody left. It was Stauracia who noticed the charred timbers in the floor of a burned-out cottage. We found flour, hard cheese, dried ham and jars of fermented bloody cabbage. I protested like mad, but she insisted on taking a couple.

Six days along the south bank of the Ostar, heading west. We hadn't seen a single boat, not even a barge. Or a living soul on the towpath.

Plenty of dead people, though. Gombryas once told me I can read corpses like a book. He meant it as a compliment (he was trying to borrow money) and he was right, I can. I was able to reconstruct every burned village and desperate, futile skirmish between the local home guard and the Sashan army as though I'd been there and seen it happen. I could even hazard an educated guess at the orders the Sashan commander had given to his junior officers: take your time; do a thorough job; the object of the exercise is to send them a message they can't fail to understand.

"This isn't fair," I said. "I'm out of the business. I shouldn't be knee-deep in dead bodies any more."

"Do they bother you?"

"They used not to," I said.

"Can't say I'm exactly happy about them," she said. "But look at it this way. Dead people are a lot less hassle than living ones."

One of the aspects of dead bodies I'm red hot on is how long they've been dead. From the generous sample of data I'd been provided with, I reckoned the Sashan were about a week ahead of us. The last village we'd come to had been deserted when it was torched, and the last two clusters of corpses were old men and boys. "There ought to be a town up ahead," I told her. "Cultatep. It's where they drive sheep to be loaded on barges."

"Been there."

"Then you'll remember it's a walled town," I said. "If you put a garrison in there, you could make a fight of it. A couple of hundred men could hold it against three thousand, for at least six weeks. Longer if you could ship in supplies and reinforcements down the river."

She reined in and let her horse graze. "You're not as observant as I thought you were," she said. "The Sashan are using the river."

Of course they were, but I hadn't seen it. Idiot. Several thousand men, plus horses and wagons, would've torn up the towpath. We'd have seen thrown-away jars, worn-out boots, blackened circles where they'd lit fires, trampled and flattened areas where they'd grazed their horses. The air should have reeked of thousands of men's shit. "They're in barges."

She nodded. "My guess is, they're working both banks simultaneously. This isn't about killing the locals, it's to cut a major supply line."

Why the hell hadn't I seen that? "So there's probably ships," I said.

"Of course there are. A fleet of flat-bottom galleys in midstream, and teams of marines working both shores. Meaning," she went on, "they can only go as fast as a warship can row upstream. In which case, we're going to run into the bastards any day now."

Oh, I thought.

"You can forget about Cultatep," she went on. "Either it's ashes or there's a Sashan garrison, depending on how they've decided to play it." She paused to think. "If I know the Sashan," she went on, "their idea is to row two dozen galleys up as far as Sark Veloe, then scuttle them and walk back. Job done."

The thought made me shiver. The Ostar is shallow at Sark Veloe, where the river flows between two sheer cliffs. Two dozen hulks would block it completely, and it'd take a full regiment of engineers six months to get it clear. But the king wouldn't stop at that. The king thinks big. He'd set his men to undermine the cliffs, collapsing them into the river, blocking it and turning the Sark valley into a lake. But the Sark valley isn't big enough to hold all the water from the Ostar, not for very long. Beyond Sark, there's the lowlands, in the middle of which sit five large cities, and then it's downhill all the way to Choris. Now that, I had to concede, was an idea fit for the Great King.

"What?" she said. "Why are you pulling that face?"

I told her. She looked at me. "They couldn't," she said. "That's—"

"War," I said. "It's what Carnufex did, five hundred years ago; that's why they call him the Irrigator. He diverted four rivers and drowned a city. But the king's got to go one better, so he's going to drown Choris Anthropou." I shrugged. "Which will end the war, regardless of what the military genius gets up to in the heart of the Sashan homeland. Oh, I imagine they'll do their best," I went on. "They'll dig ditches and build embankments, and then the Sashan cavalry will come and knock them down again. But it can only end one way, because the king's made up his mind, and once that's happened – that's the Sashan for you. The king can't just win the war; he's got to win it in *style*. He needs a gesture, something people will talk about for ever and ever. The savages attacked us, and you know what the king did? He sent the mighty river to drown the whole world, and all that was left was one family in a boat, and two of every kind of animal."

She was looking at me. I made myself calm down.

"My guess is," I said, "that it's not just a few galleys and a few thousand men up ahead of us, it's a fleet of galleys and the whole Royal Engineers. And there's absolutely nothing anybody can do about it, because the entire army is in Sashan with the military genius, winning irrelevant victories."

She didn't say anything for a while. Then she nodded. "I think you're probably right," she said. "Still, we don't know it for a fact. You could be wrong."

That's human beings for you. We all know that sooner or later we're going to die, but we carry on as though it's only one of a number of possible outcomes. We scrabble about after happiness, comfort, love, the big score. Every day we look at the inevitable and do the geometry, with a view to escaping, or preventing the war. There comes a point where you either give up or start believing in something – God, or the greater good, or in my case the Great King. Usually the belief is conditional. We know that what we've chosen to believe in is actually a big lie, but the alternative is giving up, which is no alternative at all. As far as I was concerned, it made sense to back the winner, even though I wouldn't be there to collect my winnings. It's no coincidence that the portrait on the Sashan daric never changes, and doesn't look like anyone on earth. The individual kings come and go, here today and gone tomorrow, but the king is permanent, constant, in control; and unlike the Invincible Sun you can see him, touch him – well, you can't, but it's a known fact that there are people who can – and you can most definitely feel and experience his power and his governance, which is all around you in every detail of your daily life, controlling the price of the food you eat and the width of the road you walk along and the specifications of the boots his soldiers kick you with. The thing you believe in isn't necessarily good, but you know it's real, and in the long run that's all that matters.

So, in spite of all that, we stopped and figured out a new route to Auxentia City. It would mean leaving the river straight away and heading south, keeping the mountains on our right, bypassing Choris and eventually ending up at Beloisa or Boc Bohec, a short dash across the Middle Sea from Auxentia.

"Are you sure?" she said.

"Yes," I replied. "It's no big deal. Compared to the war, it's nothing."

Heading south would, of course, mean crossing my father's country; going home. But that was all right, I told her. I hadn't been there for a lifetime; nobody was likely to recognise me after all those years; it's the last place on earth anyone would expect me to be.

"It'll be fine," I told her. "We go to Auxentia, we get the money, then we go south into Blemya. It's a big country, not so bad if you don't mind the flies, and it'll be years and years before the war gets there. We could buy an olive grove. There's good money in olives."

Because olives don't grow in Sashan. "If you're sure," she said. "Your choice. If you don't want to go, we can think of something else."

"The hell with it," I said. "We'll go."

There's a lot to be said for growing up next to a range of mountains. For one thing, you always know where you are. If you can always see them, far away in the distance, you can navigate; you never get lost. True, they make you aware of limitations; there's only so far you can go in that direction and

then you come to the wall and you've got to stop. I think that
mentality has always been deeply rooted in the people of my
father's country. They look up and see the mountains to the
east and my father's house on the other side, and they know
they aren't going anywhere; if the mountains don't stop them,
he will. But that's fine, because my father's country is good,
deep soil, gentle hills, plenty of small rivers, reliable rain,
regular seasons. There's a lot of money to be made there, and
the good shepherd shears his sheep, he doesn't skin them. My
brother Scynthius was always daydreaming about what was
on the other side of the mountains, but I couldn't work up his
level of enthusiasm. As far as I was concerned, the mountains
were a fact of life, one I was happy to put up with. My father
accepted them, too, albeit with not quite so good a grace. If
he'd had the money he'd have had them knocked down and
rebuilt a few miles to the left, so as not to block his view, but
he couldn't afford it, so what the hell. I think he was kidding
when he told me that, but I'm not entirely sure.

"I haven't seen those for years," I said. She scowled at me.

"Don't start getting pathetic, Saevus," she said. "You used
to be a spoiled, pampered, entitled little brat, before you pulled
that silver spoon out of your mouth and tried to poke your eyes
out with it. Some of us had a hard time growing up that wasn't
our fault. I didn't have it easy when I was sixteen. So don't give
me any of that blue remembered hills shit."

I smiled at her. "It's fine," I said. "The last thing I'd ever
want to do is go home, trust me."

"That's all right, then," she said, and gave me a peck on the
cheek. When she does that, it's like when you're fencing and
the other guy sees an opening and nips in under your guard.
My instinct is always to traverse and shift into a high Third,

with a view to a demi-volte in half time. And isn't it curious how any sort of affection makes me think in fencing imagery?

We hit a trail. It wasn't hard to find. A lot of people and animals had been that way not so long ago. At first I assumed it was refugees, but the trail was straight, making a way through rather than following a road or a track, and the detritus was military, not civilian. All the king's horses and all the king's men.

"We should turn back," I said.

She thought about it. "Maybe not," she said. "If this is an active war zone, you never know what you'll run into if you start wandering about, and all these stupid hills mean you can't see worth shit what's coming. My guess is, following in their wake is probably the smartest move. They're not likely to turn round and go back the way they just came."

Quite right. I should have seen it that way, but being in sight of our mountains was jumbling my brains.

They weren't our mountains, of course. They were only ours up to an imaginary line from the peak of each mountain going down plum-line-straight to the centre of the earth; the far side belonged to our neighbour, the Cardinal, who we didn't like terribly much. They were no earthly use for anything needless to say, apart from being something to look at. We had a few hundred tenants grubbing a sort of living out of sheep on the lower slopes, though getting any rent out of them was generally more trouble than it was worth. Scynthius had a plan for improving the mountains: clear out the tenants, plant ten thousand acres of pine trees, thirty years later we'd have the makings of a lumber industry, logs shipped down the Ostar, or upstream to the shipyards at Olbia, undercutting their traditional suppliers. My father was deeply impressed, but I couldn't see ten thousand acres of three-parts-grown pine as we rode by, so presumably Scynthius's project died with him. My doing, therefore, that wilderness of heather and scrub; my fault. Well, of all the things I've been guilty of, that was pretty low on the list. Besides, it's too dry and windy for forestry on our side of the mountain.

A Sashan army in trash-and-burn mode tends to move in a straight line. Inevitably; everything the king does is a gesture. A straight line is the shortest distance between two points, so it's a metaphor for the king's wrath, swift, efficient, implacable, unstoppable. I did the geography and figured out where this particular straight line was headed. Nuts, I thought.

"I think I may be going home after all," I said. "Unless we leave the trail."

She didn't say anything. Neither did I.

We came across some dead bodies. It was a place I remembered. Fan had been given a falcon for her tenth birthday, and we all packed up and dragged out there in coaches so she could fly it for the first time, beside a certain stream where it was 98 per cent certain she'd get a heron. But as soon as she released it, the stupid bird flew up and roosted at the top of a very tall ash tree. We sat around for a long time, ate the picnic while Fan sobbed her eyes out. Then it was late and we had to start back again, so we left the falconer to catch the bird (don't bother coming back without it, my dad told him; he never did) and trooped off home.

I didn't recognise any of the faces, but my father had a lot of tenants, most of whom I'd never met. But I recognised some of the armour and weapons, because they'd hung on the walls; extremely valuable, some of them, collectors' items and overwhelming sentimental value. I counted up to six hundred, then stopped bothering. Most of them died of arrow wounds, and there weren't any Sashan among them. Old habits die hard, but I didn't take anything.

A mile further on, we came to a small stand of birch trees, new since my time. The trail passed straight through the middle. Nailed to the first trees of the stand, on either side of the track, were two halves of a dead body, split down the middle.

"Stauracia," I said. "I'd like you to meet my father."

It's a traditional Sashan statement. I think it goes all the way back to Bardiya III, who marched his army between the two halves of the king of Antecyrene. A bit clichéd these days, but the Sashan are red hot on tradition.

He'd changed, inevitably. His hair had gone white and wispy and thin, and time had softened his jaw and hollowed his cheeks. The crows had had his eyes, which spared me the ordeal of looking into them. They'd stripped him naked before they nailed him up, and being Sashan they'd split him with absolute precision, from the apex of his skull to the centre line of his dick. Part of me couldn't help thinking: all your life you've been afraid of *that*.

Stauracia offered to take him down and bury him but I said no, leave him. She looked at me like I was strange in the head, but it wasn't vindictiveness on my part, trust me. He'd died defending his home, his property and his people, the three things he loved above everything else in the world, after I'd taken his beloved son from him. They'll pass through over my dead body, he'd have said, and the Sashan had gone one better; so leave him there, his own monument, spectacular if a trifle melodramatic. Above all, he reminded me of the rat. Did I tell you about the rat? When my grandad was a kid, seven years old, he killed a rat in the stable yard with a home-made bow and arrow. His father honoured him by nailing the rat to a door; and eighty years later, there it still was, the last bit of home I remember seeing on the night I ran away. A bit shrivelled, and missing one leg and half its desiccated tail, but still there, its own monument. If a rat could last eighty years, why not a duke? I felt I owed it to him to try. And it would've appealed to his sense of humour, and tradition.

There was a bunch of heads hanging by their hair from a branch of another tree, like apples in autumn. They were all strangers, apart from my brother Scaphio.

Saloninus once said: when the last witness is finally dead, the truth becomes malleable, before setting hard. Memories, the past, are a territory with disputed sovereignty. But when the last witness dies, those memories are nobody's business but yours; you own them outright; they're yours to do what you like with.

One memory in particular, now the joint property of Fan and me.

"Well," Stauracia said, "at least that's one less thing to worry about."

I looked at her. She was quite right. No more goons hunting me. My father was dead and I'd fulfilled my obligations towards my sister, The end of the world was a small price to pay for that.

As we came out the other side of the birch wood, I caught sight of the mountains away in the distance. I started laughing and couldn't stop, and then broke down completely. Tears, for

God's sake. She got me down off my horse and made me sit with my back to a tree. "I understand," she kept saying. "He was your dad."

I shook my head and pointed. "My mountains now," I said.

My mountains; my hills and valleys and woods and streams, with a Sashan trail like a spear thrust straight through them. The hell with it.

"It's fine," I told her, after I'd pulled myself together. "You don't have to call me Your Grace or anything. Just plain old Saevus will do fine."

I don't think she thought that was very funny. She'd got a basinful of water and made me wash my face, like I was six years old. "No, but really," I insisted. "I'm a duke now. Monarch of all I fucking survey."

"Big deal," she said. "You were a king on Sirupat."

"True. Like you called me back there, entitled. Still, I can honestly say I never thought I'd live to see the day."

Early next morning we climbed the top of a hill I knew well and looked down on the house. The Sashan had trashed and burned it so that only a footprint was left. Now even the scene of the crime was gone, which would make reconstructing it impossible. Brambles grow quickly in ash. In five years' time, nobody would know it had ever been there.

"It means you're free," she said. "We're free. We can get away from here and go somewhere. Look at me when I'm talking to you. It's over. You survived."

I nodded. "The king did me a favour," I said. "You can see why I'm on his side."

"*Not* funny."

"I mean it," I said. "He's killed the last witness, he's

destroyed the evidence and he's made me a duke. And he doesn't even know me from a hole in the ground."

More to the point, the king had given me a road to walk down; make straight in the desert a highway for His Grace. Straight being the operative word, but that's the Sashan for you.

"I'm guessing," she said, "that this is one of several expeditionary forces, and the idea is that they all meet up just outside Choris in time to stop people leaving the city when the river comes rushing down. After all, there's no serious resistance so they can afford to divide their forces, and it makes sense for them to do all their *chevauchées* simultaneously. Also, coming from several directions, they can surround Choris before anyone has a chance to run."

She knows about stuff like that. "It's going to make getting to Auxentia difficult," I said. "Think about it. Every ship on the Middle Sea is going to be crammed with frightened people running away."

That hadn't occurred to her. "We'll be all right," she said. "We've got money."

"No, we haven't."

"We've got two pairs of gold shoes."

That hadn't occurred to me. "True," I said. "But I imagine it's going to be a buyer's market for trinkets and bling, so don't get your hopes up. I think we might do better to bide our time."

"You what?"

We were riding through what used to be the village. Its name was Eccan, but we never called it that, only the village, where servants were recruited, goods stolen from the house were fenced, that sort of thing. When I was a kid, it was a forbidden territory, gateway to the world, enticing and dangerous. On the night I ran away, I gave it a wide berth. All gone now, burned sunwise by professionals. Reduced to ashes, it was smaller than I remembered.

"Wait till the rush is over," I said. "The Sashan aren't going to invade Auxentia. It's non-aligned, no threat to them, nothing there they need. In due course they'll make a deal with the Auxentines, do what we tell you or else, and it'll be a buffer state between them and Blemya, like Antecyrene. Which means," I went on before she could interrupt, "there's no rush to get there and get the money out. It'll still be there in six months, or a year. By which time things will have calmed down and there won't be a desperate fight for a place on a ship."

"Mphm. What makes you think there'll be a ship?"

Oh, I thought. All right, a ship from where? Beloisa, Boc, Scona? Cinders and ashes by then. Or the military genius, cut off from support from home, could fall back on Auxentia and occupy it as a base of operations; just the sort of thing a military genius might do, more or less what Florian did in Orys, after he'd lost the rest of the known world. These days, nobody knows for sure where Orys was, though there are several theories. "Fine," I said. "You're probably right. And two pairs of gold shoes ought to get us standing room in a fishing boat, even in hard times."

Two days south of the ruins of my house, we were still in my country. I had a brainwave. My father used to have a small hunting lodge just inside the forest, an hour or so away from where we were. It was only used when he was out that way. The rest of the time it was closed up, but furnished and provisioned just in case he decided to go there on a whim. So, unless someone had beaten me to it and robbed me of my inheritance—

Nobody had. For all I knew, I was the last man alive who knew it was there. "This is great," she said, ripping open a trunk and pulling out an armful of clothes. "Good stuff, too. Where are the boots?"

I pointed to another trunk, then headed for the larder. Flour, biscuit, dried fruit, even a side of bacon; one of my father's many insecurities was a terror of being stranded out in the middle of nowhere with nothing to eat or drink. I filled two sacks, added a couple of bottles of a rather good Aelian rosé and went back into the main hall. She was standing on a chair, trying to reach the ornamental display of weapons on the wall. "We ought to have something," she said, when I looked at her. "A sword each, and a couple of spears wouldn't hurt. Would there be any armour lying about?"

No point trying to argue. I managed to keep her down to swords, daggers and a matched pair of bows, with a quiver of premium grade arrows to share between us. It's a question of weight, I told her. Every pound of iron we carry is a pound of food we can't. She appeared to take that argument at face value. "He had some nice stuff, your dad," she said. "Good taste."

"You should have seen his collection of miniature Blemyan ivory triptychs," I told her. "I never once saw him looking at them, but he was very proud of them."

One of the things he was always meaning to do but never managed to get round to was building a proper road to his southern boundary. But he spent a month's rent roll on building a gatehouse, where the road would one day be. The Sashan missed it by about six hundred yards – not surprising, since it was buried deep in brambles and withies, so you wouldn't notice it if you didn't know it was there. I insisted on taking a look, because it was only half finished when I left home, and I was curious to see what it had turned out like.

I can't remember the name of the architect offhand, but he'd done a good job. He'd used granite, because we had a quarryful of the stuff nearby, and he had a good eye for line. He'd managed to make it look bigger than it actually was, and if the rubbish hadn't grown up all round it, you'd have been able to see it from miles around. My father's name and titles in great big Robur capitals on the architrave, naturally, followed by his children, in order of birth date. My name had been chiselled out. The gateway itself was flanked by two boars, three times life size.

"Admit it," she said. "There's a tiny part of you that's thinking of coming back one day and owning all this."

I shook my head, though of course she was quite right. "The hell with it," I said. "Besides, on Sirupat I was a king. Poxy small fry like dukes weren't fit to polish my boots."

Talking of which, I was wearing a pair of his. They were a bit big, but I'd packed them out with straw. "No, but seriously," she said. "Stranger things have happened. The Sashan like ruling through puppets. Legitimacy and all that. Soon as things have settled down, you could do worse than send a discreet message to the governor, saying you might be interested."

The previous night I'd lain awake, composing just such a letter in my head. "Absolutely not," I said. "Once we leave here, I'm never coming back. You know what? The sight of the house all burned out was the prettiest thing I've ever seen in my life."

"If you say so," she said. She knows me too well.

Out of my father's country, into the fresh air. Our southern neighbour was Count Albeherz, who succeeded to the title eighteen months before I left. I didn't know him. He inherited from his uncle, having spent most of his life as a diplomat, schmoozing tribal chieftains in the north somewhere. He had an Aram princess as his trophy wife, and he collected greyhounds. That was all I knew about him.

"He probably wasn't there," I told her, as we surveyed the ruins of his palace. "My guess is, he's back in the wilderness, trying to get his in-laws to join the war."

"That might be interesting. The Aram like a good fight."

"Then they'll be fighting for the Sashan. More money, and after they've won they can help themselves to territory. No skin off the king's nose if they take over everything down to the sea." The possibility hadn't occurred to me before, but it made perfect sense. Aelia, Mezentia, the Vesani Republic, everything west of the Friendly Sea turned into grazing for the Aram Chantat, who never stay in one place for more than a week. The king would never have to give it a moment's thought. And the Aram don't hold with cities; they think they're unnatural and immoral. "None of our business," I said. "If my time in the profession taught me anything, it's that no good ever came of politics."

"You chose a good time to quit," she said. "If you hadn't, you'd be out of a job by now."

The Sashan trail went straight through Albeherz's country, which is slightly smaller than my father's, and below that was the Principate, the breadbasket of the West, held by the six Electors in trust for Holy Mother Church. When the Ostar left its banks and came tumbling down, it would sweep through the heart of the Principate, following and swallowing up the Green River and the Elbemyr; then there'd be a new lake in the Myr valley, curtains for the nine large towns there, and when that was full up, down through the gaps in the hills to Choris itself. "When we get to Braha Gate," I said, "we need to go east a bit, if we want to bypass Choris. That's assuming you're right about there being more than one army converging. If we hike up across the east Downs—"

"I'm way ahead of you," she said. "Braha Gate, then a dog's leg to Timois. Your dad's biscuits should see us there all right, if we're careful."

A few hours inside the Principate, some fool had decided to make a stand. I could see how his mind had worked. He had a good natural position, with the hills at his back and a forest on his left flank to hide his archers in, and a fold of dead ground half a mile away for his cavalry to jump out of, once he'd lured the enemy into attacking his deliberately weakened centre. He'd done everything right, but the Sashan had wiped the floor with him, and left his five thousand followers as a day out for the local crows. "About ten days ago," I told her. "We're closer to them than I thought. I don't think we should wait for Braha Gate. We want to turn off now."

"That's what the geometry says, is it?"

"Yes."

"I don't think so," she said. "I think, if we go wandering off, there's a risk we might get ahead of them, or run into one of the other armies. They'll have scouts and foragers out all over the place. If we stay behind them and slow down a bit, at least we know where they are."

Which made sense, and it was stupid of me to let my nerves get the better of my judgement. "That's all right," she said when I apologised. "We just need to stay calm and not do anything stupid, and when we get to Braha everything'll be fine."

*

If you think of life as a sequence of journeys – it's actually a pretty hopeless metaphor, but never mind that – you need to distinguish between the various types of journey, with the objective as your main criterion. There are journeys we make to get to a place we want to reach, there's the there-and-back trips that people like merchants and battlefield scavengers spend their lives making, there's the actor's provincial tour, meaning there's no work anywhere civilised, there's aimless wandering, and there's running away, a whole sub-category of journeys *from*, as opposed to journeys *to*. Most of my travelling has been there-and-back, and most of the rest has been decidedly from, usually with extreme prejudice. Other associated clichés deal with it being better to travel hopefully than to arrive, and the journey being more important than the destination. You can believe all that stuff if you choose to, and, while we're at it, would you be interested in buying the Echmen Imperial palace, which I'm in a position to offer you at a very competitive price?

Well, we had a destination, which made things simple. Simple as distinguished from easy. Heroes, for instance, tend to live simple lives. Slay the dragon and solve everybody's problems at a stroke. Killing a dragon isn't easy, but it's simple. Getting to Auxentia wouldn't be easy either, but at least I knew where I wanted to go, and I had a very clever friend to help me get there.

9

I woke up. Something was wrong. I couldn't move my arms and legs, and my eyes were open but everything was dark. There was something in my mouth that felt and tasted like dirty linen.

For God's sake, I thought, not again.

I tried to remember. Last night we camped out, same as we'd been doing for a week. We were beside the road, under a large crab-apple tree. No sign of anybody anywhere.

Made no sense; my father was dead, and any bounty hunter working for him must know that. No payday, therefore no point in grabbing me. Fan was safely tucked away in Ogiv, with a substantial sum of money by any criteria but not enough to fund a bunch of goons; besides, I'd saved her life and that had to count for something. I had other enemies, more than I could count, but a careful, precise snatch in the middle of the biggest war in living memory – who could do something like that? The Knights, the Sisters, but why? There was nothing anybody needed me for – alive – so it could only be revenge or retribution. Right now, the administration of justice would be at the very bottom of their list of priorities, with survival at the top. My other enemies: loads of them, as previously noted, but they'd have killed me in my sleep.

I was jolting about in a vehicle of some sort, but something rather special. It had springs, and it was moving quite fast; make that very fast. Not just a cart. A coach, or a carriage. Something like the Vesani State messenger service, or the Sashan royal mail.

And in any case, how the hell could they have found me? We'd been travelling light, two horses following a trail flattened by an army. The country we'd been passing through was deserted. We'd seen nobody, so there was nobody who could have seen us and told a bunch of goons where we were. We were in the middle of a war zone, with the jaws of a Sashan pincer movement closing just ahead of us. No private contractor, no matter how expensive, would agree to undertake a job in those conditions. You'd have your reputation to think of.

So how had they found me?

In the dark, unable to move, travelling fast in a smooth, expensive carriage; nothing else to do but think. You've probably had that sort of debate with yourself in the early hours of the morning – is the pain or the lump or the swelling what you think it is, or something else? Have they found out about me? What was she doing meeting a man in the middle of the day? The worst thing about it is the shortage of hard data; if you had all the facts, or access to an expert, you'd know, which would be better than this unbearable uncertainty, but the information at your disposal is incomplete, and you have no way of getting the data you need. The Antecyrenaeans have spent a thousand years and hundreds of thousands of lines of perfectly scanned hexameters conjuring up visions of the torments of the damned in hell, but I don't believe a word of it, because hell has to be the worst thing possible or it wouldn't be a deterrent, and none of the stuff they mention is in the same league as that overpowering, all-devouring anxiety—

How had they found me? Who knew where I was? Only one person. A person known to have worked closely with the Sisters, and the Knights, too. A person who'd just lost all her money, but who still had one valuable thing to sell. She knew where I was, just fine.

Go back and reconstruct how the choices had been made. Who suggested following the Ostar? Who suggested leaving the Ostar and heading south? If it had been me, had I made the suggestion acting on subtle hints and influences? Had I been led to that point on the road, under that tree?

At which point, counsel for the defence gets to his feet and starts his cross-examination. When and where is she supposed to have made this alleged deal with my enemies? She hadn't been out of my sight since – try and remember. We hadn't seen a living soul since – yes, but these people are *crafty*. They could have been following us since – I couldn't say, not having all the facts; but it was entirely possible that she'd got up while I was asleep and walked back down the track a hundred yards, and talked in the dark. I knew that was possible, because Gombryas did it. And falling asleep and waking up trussed like the proverbial chicken; not a problem if someone had put something in my food or my drink. Who had handled our last meal? I couldn't remember.

Yes, but why *here*, and why *now*? Made no sense. I was no more vulnerable in the Principate than I'd been at any other point on our journey. Yes, but if the rendezvous with the retrieval party was somewhere close by, it'd make more sense to bring me there of my own free will, given what a slippery, dangerous animal I could be when cornered.

All right, then. Why would she do it? Answer: for money. But she saved me from Gombryas and my father's goons. Yes, of course she did, because I was worth money to her. A lot of money. The big score.

It wasn't a bag over my eyes this time, it was a blindfold, wound so tight it gave me a headache. No need to take it off when they stuffed food in my mouth. I tried talking, but they knew precisely how to force my jaws open with their thumbs, like making a horse take the bit, and how to make me swallow; and then the gag went back in, straight away, no messing. Not just professionals: experts.

Think about that, since you haven't got anything else to do. Hired goons can be professionals, but where would they get enough practice to be experts? Suppose a really top-flight team of private contractors is lucky enough to get ten or a dozen gigs a year – unlikely, if only because the attrition rate is scarily high in that business, and hired goons don't tend to live long enough to acquire the really cutting-edge skills these people appear to have. But government men, the public sector, have the leisure and the job security to get really good at their trade, or craft. Practice, and only practice, makes perfect.

Someone going to a great deal of trouble, because they knew I was slippery and dangerous. Someone, therefore, who knew me well.

It horrified and sickened me to realise how easy it was for me to believe that she'd done it. That ought to be unthinkable, because I knew her too well (didn't I?). As well as I knew Gombryas. Better. No, I knew Gombryas very well indeed, and the thought had never crossed my mind until it happened.

What did I know about her? She'd been in love with me after the Sirupat thing, when I turned her down. She took the rejection quietly, with an ill grace, and not long after that we went our separate ways. When I went looking for my wife, she helped me and saved me from the enemy; I assumed she felt the same way about me at that time, but I didn't stop to gather or collate the evidence, because I never thought I'd need it for anything. But I knew that Stauracia had a very strong interest in money. Most of all, she wanted to collect a great deal of it: enough money to get out of the life she'd lived since puberty and stay out of it, safe, separate, immune from the world and its affairs and concerns. So it would make a sort of sense for her to cash in her biggest asset at a time when everything was going to hell all around her, especially after losing a million darics at Suda. And (I'd been thinking about it) would a million darics have been enough? Not sure about that. Define enough: I did some mental arithmetic and came up with a figure of two and a half million darics. With that much money, you could be pretty sure you'd be safe, no matter what.

So how could I possibly be worth two and a half million darics? For a moment I thought I'd come up with a winning argument, but that moment didn't last long. The king, I remembered: not the real king, but a king nevertheless, who I met once, who married my wife, and – as soon as I thought of it, I felt the weight of the truth crushing my windpipe – adopted my daughter.

Now then. Suppose the king was dead, but his daughter (adopted) was still alive. That wouldn't do at all. Here were the Sashan, forced by the stupidity of barbarians to put forth all their strength. Essential, therefore, that there should be no loose ends – pretenders to the throne, possible alternatives, no matter how improbable. Sashan history works that way. If the king is overthrown, it's always because he wasn't the real king after all. When he's driven out or killed, it's by the real king (spirited away as a baby, reared by wolves or a humble shepherd and his wife, recognised by the last loyal courtier, restored to his rightful throne in the very nick of time). So, suppose the king I met was the real king, or that it was suddenly expedient for him to have been the real king all along. But he's dead; but he has a daughter. There have, on rare occasions, been Great Queens of the Sashan, though on all the carved stelae and monumental mosaics they look like men and hunt lions from a chariot. It would therefore be necessary, verging on essential, to be able to prove that the Great King's daughter wasn't really his daughter. For which you'd need her real father. And for that, two and a half million darics would be a small price to pay.

In which case it drove a coach and horses through the argument that Stauracia would never betray me to my death, since I was needed very much alive – at least until my daughter was dead, and if someone else had got hold of her, to use as their ace of trumps, that could easily be a very long time.

If it was the Sashan, that would explain the fast coach with the excellent suspension, the expert goons and, most of all, the logic in snatching me in the heart of what was now undisputed Sashan territory – more so than in Sashan itself, where the military genius was prowling around defeating armies and burning down cities. If I was in Sashan and he got wind of me, he'd want me as a weapon; no, he'd want me dead. But here on my own turf, just down the road from my own property, the Sashan had absolute control on the ground. There'd be plenty of political officers and intelligence agents to strike a deal with, and all the resources and assets necessary for a neat, foolproof extraction.

The counsel for the defence didn't seem to have an answer to that argument; and the burden of proof in this case was the balance of probabilities rather the absence of reasonable doubt. I referred the question to the jury, and when they gave their verdict I found myself able to accept it.

In which case, nothing mattered any more.

Under such circumstances, time passes agonisingly slowly and very quickly. It was a pain in my head and chest and stomach that never let up for an instant, and the next thing I knew we'd stopped somewhere, and I was being carried, up a gangplank, on to a ship.

I hate being on ships. That was one sea journey I hardly noticed.

Nothing mattering any more is a strange feeling. You can't think of anything else except the pain, but since there are no longer any issues to be resolved or arguments to be presented and torn to shreds, the pain doesn't actually hurt. You live in it, like a squalid cell, but there's nothing it can do to you, because you're dead already. You can't sleep, because the thoughts hurt so much, but being awake is more like dreaming than anything else. You can't move, but if you could, you wouldn't bother. Lying still and quiet becomes your customary state and your natural environment. It would be better to be dead, with the light put out and the thoughts taken away, but it's not up to you when you die, so forget about it for now. It'll happen when it happens, and it really doesn't matter anyway.

With nothing much else to do with my time, I let myself

consider the fear of death, which is just another way of saying love. I've never been particularly scared of being dead, not until she loved me. It was more a case of being highly competitive and not wanting to lose. My brother Scynthius was like that. He *couldn't* lose; and when he did, it hurt him, because it was unnatural, it wasn't right, it offended every fibre of his being. Scynthius and the king, invincible by definition. I've fought against death the same way he fought against losing. Scynthius reckoned that he had to win because the best man always wins: there's a direct link between victory and worth. If he lost, it'd mean he was inferior, no bloody good, weak, useless. I suspect, thinking about it, that that was how he saw himself, and only an endless sequence of victories kept him going. If he didn't win, Dad would realise that he was no good and the disappointment would kill him.

I don't believe that the best man always wins, because I beat Scynthius once in a fencing match. But I recognise that I kept my life when it was forfeit, properly speaking, and I can't help feeling that there had to be some – not a reason, because then I'd be committed to believing in Fate and Destiny, and possibly even the Invincible Sun or the Eternal Flame, which I'd hate myself for doing. But if I'd kept my life when it should have ended, that suggested that my life was somehow worth something – a valuable possession; my father always got angry with me because I didn't treat my things right. He treats his stuff like it's so much rubbish, he'd complain to my mother: I despair of him.

So; I've misused my life, bashed it, battered it, used it as a hammer when really it's a saw. I haven't kept it clean or hung it up at night or polished it till it shone, but at least I haven't thrown it away, and I haven't let any bastard take it away from me. But fear of death – so what? The thought of being rid of my own company doesn't fill me with dread. If anything, the reverse.

Until Stauracia. I realised what I felt about her when I thought she'd gone for ever, and suddenly nothing mattered any more. All the colour was gone, all the flavour. The hell with it. It'd be presumptuous of me to assume that she'd feel the same way if I died, but it wasn't a risk I could allow myself to take. I had to stay alive, because of her.

Unless, of course, she'd stopped loving me. In which case, I was free again. The intolerable burden was gone, the wire of the snare biting into my leg, the steel spike pinning me to the ground. They say, don't they, that it's better to have loved and lost than never to have loved at all. Bullshit. Unless it's better to admit gracefully that you never were good enough to merit existence, because once you did something so bad it can never be forgiven. Not that it mattered, because nothing mattered any more. I was a free man, and I could choose, and I chose to give up without a fight. No point in wounding and killing perfect strangers just so I could jump out of a window and run for a few more years. They're just honest working men doing a job.

Besides, if I was right, I wasn't going to die, not straight away. The Sashan would parade me around for a bit, letting me be seen, and then they'd lock me up somewhere, and then they wouldn't need me any more, and two men would come into my cell in the early hours of the morning with twelve trachies' worth of rope, and that would be that. No skin off my nose.

If there's one thing I can't be doing with, it's self-pity. I felt ashamed of myself. After five days on the ship – fifteen feeding times, so five days, more or less – my mind was in roughly the same state as my trousers, and I really wished I could have peeled it off and thrown it in the sea. But I couldn't, so I lay still and put up with it. No choice.

Off the ship, another high-class coach; this one felt like it was going at a hell of a lick. I've only been in a Sashan mail-coach twice in my life. It's not an experience you'd ever forget, and it's not like anything else. You look out of the window and the countryside flows past you like a river, but you hardly feel a thing. The Sashan royal mail is the fastest thing on earth, over any distance greater than bowshot. The king's word, so they reckon, can reach any part of his incredibly huge empire in fourteen days or less, by *land*, not sea . . . The story goes that the Echmen emperor was planning to invade Sashan, so the Great King sent the emperor a rose, grown in his own garden in the royal palace. When the rose arrived, it was still fresh and blooming. The emperor looked at it and called off the war. Any human being who had the power to do something like that, he decided, must be as powerful as a god.

Then the coach stopped. I heard a door open, boots on foldaway steps. I was lifted up and carried. "Watch his head on the gatepost," someone yelled, in Sashan. I was carried up three flights of stairs and down two. It didn't matter, I told myself. This is the end, or the first step in a process leading to it, and I really don't mind a bit. I waited for the slight shudder that always follows when I lie to myself, but it didn't come. For the first time in my adult life, I wasn't the least bit interested in geometry.

They put me down, and started untying knots. It felt very strange, without the ropes pressing on me; I was afraid I might fall apart or unravel, without anything to keep me together. All the ropes were gone; I could've moved my arms and legs if I'd wanted to; the blindfold and the gag were still there, which was probably just as well. I was lifted up, and plunged into cold water. They were scrubbing me, with stiff brushes.

"I can't shave him with that thing round his mouth," someone said. The gag came off. A hand grabbed my jaw, and I felt a blade against my skin. I'd never been shaved by someone else before. It's a very strange sensation, though not unpleasant. Then someone washed my hair, and rubbed it dry with a towel.

"He'll do," someone said. The accent was Sashan middle-grade official; my washing and delousing was being supervised by a man of the fifth grade or above, which meant he was equivalent to a district magistrate or a colonel in the army. "No, don't put any of that stuff on him, they don't want him smelling like a tart's boudoir. But do something about his fingernails. They look like claws."

"His breath smells like shit," someone said.

"Scrub his mouth out," said the senior official. "Water and ashes ought to do it."

So they did that: ash first, then water. "How's that?" someone asked.

"You could bear to be in the same room with it," said the official. "Right, here we go. Let them know we're ready."

Someone walked away. "Get him on his feet," the official said. They tried, but my legs wouldn't take my weight. The floor was hard and smooth: tiles or stone slabs. "Fine," the official said wearily, "You'll just have to hold him up. Watch him, though, he's supposed to be a handful. Got a reputation for it. You, take that knife off your belt, if you don't want it stuck in your ear. No weapons within twelve feet of him, that's what it says in the briefing."

I managed not to smile. Not just professionals; Sashan professionals. They held me up, very strong hands gripping my arms, and I stood there for what seemed like a long time, not that it mattered. Then footsteps, and someone said, "They're ready."

"Fine," the official said. "Get the robe on him and let's go."

They lifted my arms and stuffed them inside sleeves. I felt cloth all around me, down past my knees, so a gown of some sort, or a monk's habit. "No, not the belt," the official said. "And remember, look sharp. I don't think he's in any fit state to do anything, but we aren't taking any chances."

"Gag back on?" someone asked.

"It says here no," the official replied. "All right, let's go. Straight down the hall, second left."

I tried to help out by walking, but I couldn't; I was only hindering them, so I stopped trying and let myself be carried. Straight down the hall proved to be a long way. Then we stopped and turned. About twenty more steps, then dead stop. Silence. Then they took the blindfold off.

Two weeks in the pitch dark; the light was unbearable. I closed my eyes. Fingers rolled my eyelids back. All I could see was dazzling white fire. "It'll take him a moment or so," I heard the official say.

The fire died down, and I could see shapes. For a moment I thought I'd never be able to force my eyes to focus. Then the shapes started to win the battle. Men standing round a big chair. Someone sitting in the chair. A woman.

"Hello, Florian," said a voice I recognised. My sister.

I tried to speak, but I'd forgotten how. There was something I had to move in my throat, I remembered that, but it appeared to be stuck solid.

"Daddy's dead, Florian," she said, "did you know that? And

poor Scaphio. There's just you and me left now. It's all over." I could see her, vaguely. If it hadn't been for the voice, I wouldn't have known it was her, just an outline surrounded by white light. "Do you know where you are?"

I could move my head. I shook it.

"This is my house," she said. "Mine and Siggy's. Mine now. I swore allegiance to the Sashan, so now I'm Grand Duchess regent and Electress of the Principality. The Sashan, bless them, are nuts on continuity and legitimacy, and there wasn't anyone else left. Which means I got it all back, and all I had to do was curtsey to the governor and say a few words after him. All that fuss over nothing."

Fuss. One way of describing it. If I'd been able to speak, I wouldn't have known what to say.

"You're going to die now," she said. "But first, there's something I want you to see. Doctor."

Someone came close and tilted my head back. He poured something in my eyes. It felt wonderful. I blinked a couple of times, then realised I could see his face quite clearly. Echmen, naturally. They're the very best doctors anywhere.

"Can you see me?" he asked. I nodded. "How many fingers am I holding up?"

I mouthed, two. "He's fine now," the doctor said, and stepped away.

"Show him," she said.

Someone came forward holding a jar. My guess is that it once held olives. He put his hand into it and pulled something out. I couldn't see what it was, because it was smothered in a pale reddish-gold liquid, which ran off it in streams and pooled on the floor. It smelled like honey.

"Go on," she said. "Show him."

He was holding whatever it was by a mass of long strands, plastered together with honey. It was somebody's head.

(Gombryas told me about that once. I'd asked him, what in God's name do you want thirty gallons of honey for? He explained that it was the best natural preservative that money can buy, for meat or anything similar. Just dump a bit of meat, or a choice cut of dead general, in a jar of honey until it's completely submerged, and it'll stay good practically indefinitely.)

I looked at Fan. She nodded to the man, who wiped away the honey with the palm of his hand.

"I might keep her," Fan was saying, "I haven't made my mind up yet. I hadn't realised, she was quite famous in some circles. You don't get many women generals."

I saw the scar, which was unmistakeable. If I hadn't seen it, I'm not sure I'd have recognised her.

"I'm definitely not keeping you," Fan went on. "You can go in the pigswill. They say pigs'll eat anything."

I said a moment ago that I don't choose to believe in Fate, or Destiny, or any form of god. I don't think that the Invincible Sun sat up figuring out incredibly complex patterns of geometry to govern my life, carefully interweaving them with thousands, hundreds of thousands of other patterns – no, wrong image, carefully meshing the teeth of my gears into an extraordinary machine, designed to carry out a very specific purpose. I reckon I have logic on my side. If there's a god, he'd have to be good, because an evil god would destroy the earth and all that therein is within a few hours of the act of creation. And I don't believe that a good god would build the sort of machine I've always found myself part of, or do geometry in which I could ever fit. If God was good, I'd never have been born. But I was, so he isn't, so he doesn't.

But I believe in men of learning, professors, academics; men who spend their entire lives studying an art or a science, and eventually perfecting their skill and knowledge to the point where they can command their subject absolutely, in order to do extraordinary things. My specialist subject is geometry. I've been learning it since I was sixteen. I'm rather good at it.

Is it possible, or credible, that I lived a life that compelled me to study geometry, and got so very good at it, all leading up to one particular moment? That would be opening the door to believing in something, and on balance I'd rather not, thank you so much. Not that choice has anything to do with it. It never does, in my experience.

I did the geometry.

The nearest weapon was fifteen feet away. But there was a straight line between me and my sister, four strides assuming she stayed still, and the nearest goon was four strides and a bit. I drew the lines and circles in my mind. It wasn't the sort of geometry I'd risk my life on under normal circumstances, and I wasn't convinced I'd got enough control over my body to do it, but what the hell. Under normal circumstances, the first and overriding priority would be my survival. Take that out of the frame and you suddenly find yourself with a great deal more scope, almost as though you'd been untied and ungagged and unblindfolded, after a lifetime of confinement.

I'd need time to ask her a question, and make her answer. That made it awkward. But what the heck, I thought. Besides, I'm quite good at this sort of thing.

When you need to move really fast, don't think about

moving. Just think about having got there. Here one moment, over there the next, nothing in between. It won't actually be like that, but the closer you can get to it, the better.

I felt her neck under my hands. She has a slim, graceful neck, luckily for me. I felt fingertip against fingertip, thumb against thumb. Her skin felt soft and beautiful under my fingers, like other skin I could remember. I looked into her eyes. She was terrified.

"One question," I said. "Were you there when it happened?"

"Yes," she said.

"Did I do it on purpose?"

"Yes."

Then I strangled her.

Some fool tried to interfere. He had his fingers in my eyes. It didn't matter, of course, but just in case, I kicked backwards with one foot and connected with something, and he let go. Meanwhile, my sister's life was coming to a close, there between my fingers. Every split second an opportunity – I could let go and she'll live, I could let go and she'd live – and then there was no choice any more. It seemed to me that I felt her life go past me, brushing against my cheek, but that was probably just my imagination.

Someone was hitting me. He'd already hit me two or three times, with something hard. I held on tight, just to be absolutely sure, and then I went to sleep.

10

I woke up and opened my eyes. What the hell am I still doing here? I thought.

I was lying on a bed, in a big, spacious room with elegant furniture. My head was splitting, which ruled out paradise because my head wouldn't hurt in paradise.

I sat up. I was still wearing the same robe, except that I could see it now. A monk's habit. Figures: the Sashan dress the condemned man in a habit before they execute him, for the good of his soul. I'd forgotten that until that moment.

In the corner of the room was a small man, sitting on a chair. I recognised him: the Echmen doctor.

"You're awake, then," he said.

"I think so."

"Try not to move about," he said. "It's all right, you're fine and you're perfectly safe. But if you stand up, you'll probably fall over and you might do yourself a mischief."

"All right," I said. "Why aren't I dead?"

He shrugged. "I don't know," he said. "Something political. I keep my nose out of politics."

"Very wise."

"Yes." He stood up. "I'm going to come over and examine you," he said. "Please don't throttle me. There's absolutely no need. You'll have noticed, you aren't tied up or anything."

"I promise," I said.

He peered at me, rolled back an eyelid. "Any nausea, dizziness, that sort of thing? I expect you know all the symptoms."

"I'm fine," I said. "My head hurts."

"The guard sergeant broke a chair over your head," the doctor said. "Took him five swipes. Naturally your head hurts."

One question. "Is she dead?"

He frowned slightly. "Yes."

So that was all right. "Can I lie back down again?"

"Sure. I can give you something for the headache."

"Thanks," I said, "but I'm not bothered about it."

"Suit yourself," he said. "Now, you stay there and don't do anything strenuous, and I expect someone'll be along in a bit. I'll tell them you're awake and fit to be talked to."

He left the room, opening and closing the door himself. I sat up and looked round. There was a window, and through it a view of distant mountains. Fan and Siggy's house, presumably.

There's that line in one of Saloninus's plays: *why, this is hell, nor am I out of it.* Maybe the science of jurisprudence has progressed to the point where they've figured out a worse punishment than death; that under certain circumstances, staying alive is infinitely more cruel.

Her face, with the honey dripping down. I really wish I'd died before I got around to remembering that.

The door opened and two men came in. Both Sashan. One

had soldier written all over him, though he was in civilian clothes, neat and unobtrusive. The other one was older, taller, thinner, more smartly dressed. The military governor and the political officer.

"How are you feeling?" the political officer said.

"All right," I said. "Who are you?"

"Colonel Mazaphernes," the political officer said, tilting his head at his buddy, "officer commanding the garrison. I'm secretary Atrabazus, representing the Sashan embassy in the duchy." He frowned at me, more or less the same way the doctor had done. "You've put us in a rather awkward position," he said.

"Sorry," I said.

The soldier said, "Officially you're under arrest for the murder of the Archduchess Phantis."

"Officially."

He nodded. "Unofficially, I don't think you've got anything to worry about. But I'd like to ask you not to leave the palace grounds, or talk to anyone without one of us present." His frown deepened. He wasn't enjoying this. "Cards on the table," he said, "we don't know if you're an enemy of the state or tomorrow's Very Important Person, though it looks rather like it's the latter, if you get my drift. We're waiting on confirmation and direct orders in writing, which will probably take another forty-eight hours. Until then, we'd be grateful if you'd cooperate. Absolutely no reason why you should," he added, with a sort of grin, "but I happen to be telling the truth. If I wasn't, you'd be in chains or dead. Think about it."

"I already have," I said.

"Splendid," the political officer said. "So essentially we're in limbo till the mail gets here. Won't be long and then we'll all know where we stand. Till then, the less fuss, the better. I'm sure you can understand that." He paused, then went on, "We, um, have something of yours. We don't know what you want done with it."

I looked at him. "Mine."

He shrugged. "Well, properly speaking, everything here is yours, as the Duchess' next of kin. But that all depends on what the despatches say, when they get here. But this item I'm talking about. I don't suppose you need me to be more specific."

"No."

"I talked to the priest," he went on. "As you know, the king believes in freedom of religion. You a religious man?"

"No."

He nodded. "Well, if you want to have a Sun-worshipper ceremony of any sort, we don't have a problem with that, but to be on the safe side, if you want one, it might be a good idea to do it before the mail gets here. There's a lot to be said for a fait accompli, after all. If it's all done and dusted, it can't be anybody's problem, can it?"

I really wanted him to stop talking. "Thank you," I said. "That's very considerate of you. But I really don't—"

"Fair enough. Would you like us to, well, just get rid of it for you? Respectfully, of course. A simple interment in the chapel grounds, something like that."

"Ideal," I said. "Thank you."

"Leave it with me," he said. "Apart from that, I don't think there's anything else, for now. I recommend that you stay put, get some rest, get back on your feet and all that. I gather you've had a pretty torrid time of it lately. Probably no bad thing to have a bit of a breather if you're going to be back on the road again shortly."

"Really? Where am I going?"

He gave me a you-know-better-than-that look. "You can have your meals in here, and a bath, that sort of thing. The servants will look after you. I can have some books sent up, if you like reading."

"No, thank you. Actually, yes, I'd like that."

"Anything in particular?"

"The collected comedies of Notker and Liutprand," I said. "And Carbo's farces, if you've got a copy."

Carbo was the name I used to write plays under. "Who?" he said.

Why? Because I was in a condemned cell once – long story, irrelevant – and the prison governor lent me Notker's comedies to read while I was waiting, and believe it or not, they helped. A bit like that medicine the Echmen brew out of poppies; the pain is still there, but you can sort of climb out of it, and walk round the side, and look at it objectively.

It still worked. The moment I closed the book, it all came rushing back, like floodwater, like a great river overwhelming a city. But while I was reading, it was content to wait patiently. So I read Notker's comedies of manners, and Liutprand's biting satires against a society that vanished with the walls that surrounded it a thousand years ago, and Ekkehard's honey-sweet romances, and even my own hackneyed kitbashes, of which the library proved to have a copy, much to everybody's surprise but my own. The food came three times a day, and I wish I'd been in a fit state to appreciate it. I didn't look to see if there were guards stationed outside the door or under the window.

On the third day, the political officer came to see me. He had a letter in his hand. He smiled at me.

"Good news," he said. "You're off on your travels."

"Where am I going?"

"I can't tell you that, obviously. But it's good news."

I looked at him. He seemed genuinely pleased about something, and I think he was probably a kind-hearted man, deep down, when it didn't interfere with business. "I'm leaving here, then."

"Yes. You're going for a trip on the Mail."

I nodded. "When?"

"In about half an hour, as soon as the documentation's in order. We'll need you to seal a couple of things, and swear an oath."

"Really?" I frowned. "Can you tell me—?"

"No. But wait five minutes and you'll know all about it."

He left, came back five minutes later. He had a dozen important looking men with him, all terrified. He gave me a Sashan clay tablet. "You can read Sashan?"

"No problem." I read it, and looked at him. "Seriously?"

"Just read what's written. Out loud."

So I solemnly and sincerely swore allegiance until death to the King, Brother of the Sun and Moon, Great King, King of Kings, Tenant-in-chief of the Eternal Flame, and promised to hold the duchy and the Electorate in perfect fealty to the king for the term of my natural life, and so on and so forth; and the important scared people kneeled down in front of me and kissed my hand, then stood up again, looking as though they'd just been made to eat spiders. "If we could hurry it along a little bit," the political officer murmured; the man kneeling in front of me pecked at my knuckles like a starling in a hurry and shot up again. "Splendid," the political officer said, "that's that done, and now we really ought to be making a move."

*

The political officer wasn't coming with me. Instead I rode alone in the mailcoach, with four soldiers on the roof and a twelve-man cavalry escort. They had a hell of a job keeping up with the coach, but they managed it as far as the first way station.

Continuity and legitimacy, Fan had said. It was enough to make a cat laugh, but I couldn't be bothered to argue, or speculate, or care. A night in the way station's VIP quarters, then back in the coach, with the countryside flowing by like a river and me sitting perfectly still and hardly feeling a thing. I happened to notice that we were travelling east; the sun set dead ahead of us, so I couldn't avoid the conclusion. Entitled, Stauracia had called me once. Clearly she hadn't known the half of it.

Four days on the road, then a horrible ship. But this ship was different. It skimmed across the sea as though it wasn't there, and I barely felt it move. I didn't know ships could go that fast. We were out of sight of land most of the time, so I had no idea where I was, and I couldn't summon up the energy to figure anything out. As far as I was concerned, geography was irrelevant as geometry. You are where you are, and all places are basically the same.

Another mailcoach waiting for me at the dock. It looked identical to the one I'd just been in. No cavalry escort this time, because we were in the king's country, so no need. That made me smile, because last I heard, at least a third of the western provinces were under the control of the Aelians and their military genius. But every Sashan knows that no harm can come to a loyal subject once he's inside the king's country, and I'd just sworn an oath that made me officially Sashan, so that was all right. More countryside flowing past, more way stations, all identical down to the width of the doors and the height of the windows.

I was asleep, and they woke me up. "We're here," they said.

It was pitch dark. "Where's here?" I asked. They didn't answer. I got out of the coach. There was a man with a small lantern, throwing just enough light to show me a few yards ahead: a paved courtyard, polished granite. Somewhere rather grand, therefore, but in Sashan that doesn't really help you very much. I followed the lantern. After a bit we went under an arch, through a big doorway and out the other side into a quadrangle. It was lit with big oil lamps, so I could see tall stone buildings, walls covered in frescoes, the Great King spearing lions from the back of a chariot. I'm not sure if there are any lions in Sashan any more, but the Great King slaughters cartloads of them nonetheless, whenever he can spare a moment from affairs of state.

A very big building with an impressive gateway, flanked by human-headed bulls twelve feet tall. The gate was gilded bronze, beautiful, embossed with the king gutting and slicing Echmen heavy dragoons. I stopped dead, and the man behind me walked into me and trod on the backs of my heels. "Excuse me," I said.

"What?"

"This is probably a stupid question, but what's the name of the king?"

Someone knocked on the gates. They swung open, and golden light flooded out. "This way," the man behind me said. "Mind the step."

Last I heard, the king's name was Bardiya. He'd been the king for forty-odd years, ever since he succeeded his uncle, or his great-uncle. That would make him around eighty in human terms. Of course, the king doesn't age; he just gets taller and stronger, like an oak tree.

We were in a vast entrance hall, big enough to graze forty sheep for a month if the floor was covered in grass rather than unspeakably valuable Echmen silk carpets. Twelve polished porphyry pillars held up a roof seething with the most exquisite abstract motifs in gold and silver mosaic. On the walls were frescoes, the king leading a procession of gods and terrifying lion-headed angels, so beautiful that I couldn't help looking at them, in spite of everything. In the middle of the hall was a fountain, tinkling softly. It was as bright as day, thanks to about a thousand silver lamps, burning rose-scented oil.

"Vistam," whispered someone in my ear. "His name is Vistam."

Everything made sense and I smiled. I was about to meet a friend. Of course, it could easily be that the friend was about to have me killed, but I didn't mind that. He'd do it as nicely as possible, and if my death was any help to him, he was welcome to it.

Two men were carrying a chair. It was made of ivory, with legs that curved like a strung bow. They put it down and a third man settled a cushion on it. He had another cushion, which he put on the floor, about ten feet from the chair. Someone nodded at the cushion; that's for you, he didn't need to say.

Well; I was still a bit stiff from sitting in the mailcoach. I sat down on the cushion, which was crimson silk, embroidered with lions eating gazelles in gold thread. Nothing happened for a bit, and I amused myself by gawping at the artwork.

I met a man called Vistam once. His real name was Balas, just as my real name is Florian, but very few people would ever call him that. He was married to my wife, but when she screamed at him to have me killed he'd taken no notice, because I'd told him the truth and he'd believed me.

Trumpets sounded. The acoustic in that room was amazing, and the noise made my ears sting. Someone grabbed me by the scruff of the neck and shoved me face down into the cushion, then dropped down beside me, flat as a corpse. The trumpets stopped. Someone said, "Rise." I stayed where I was.

I heard a pair of hands clap three times. The man lying next to me scrambled to his feet and I heard him walk away quickly. Nothing for about twenty heartbeats; then a voice I recognised said, "You can get up now, it's just us."

I got to my knees and looked at him.

For a moment, I recognised him only as the king. The king, as everybody knows, is seven feet tall and strong as a bear. He has shoulder-length black hair, curled in ringlets, and a beard down to his waist, also curled. He wears a robe of cloth of gold, elbow-length so as to show off the forearm muscles, with an ivory-hilted sword in an ivory sheath stuck in his belt. On his feet are purple boots. "You look awful," he said. "Haven't they been looking after you properly?"

"I'm fine," I said. "Your majesty."

"Oh, skip all that." He stood up, walked a long way and came back with another chair. It was identical to the one he'd been sitting on. I hesitated. "Come on," he said, "it won't bite you."

I got up and sat on the chair. "Congratulations," I said.

He grinned. "You're joking," he said. "I liked it much better back in Hetsuan. But there you go. Uncle Bardiya finally managed to piss off practically everybody who mattered, so here I am, like it or not." He sighed. "Hell of a fuss," he went on. "And the war, of course. Properly speaking, it's all my fault."

"To smooth your accession."

He nodded. "I didn't actually suggest it or anything like that," he said. "Not up to me. The idea is, if there's suddenly a war, nobody's going to stop and ask what happened to the old king or where I suddenly appeared from. Politics," he added, with a sad smile. "Also tradition. Every time there's a new king, there's a war. To give me something to win, so everybody knows I'm the real thing. Bloody stupid way to carry on if you ask me, but nobody did, so the hell with it."

I looked at him. He nodded.

"I know," he said. "And, yes, the war's going really badly. Nobody around here would admit it if you pulled their fingernails out, but the fact is, that Aelian lunatic is about thirty miles south of here with an army of forty thousand men, and nothing between him and us but two cavalry regiments and the Royal Artillery. Fortunately, we managed to cut his supply lines, so his men haven't eaten for a week. Also, there's a big river in the way." He looked at me. "You've just come from out west," he said. "What's happening there? I get the reports, but I've found that in this place you've got to take what they tell you with a pinch of salt."

"You're winning," I told him. "Your armies are about to surround Choris Anthropou."

He nodded. "Bad business, that," he said. "They tell me I've got to make an example of it. I'm not supposed to tell anyone this, but—"

"Then don't," I said. "The plan is to divert the Ostar and flood Choris."

His eyes widened a little bit. "They know, then."

I shook my head. "I figured it out for myself," I said. "Maybe they have, too, I don't know. If they have, there's absolutely nothing they can do to stop it."

He breathed out, relieved. "Me neither, unfortunately," he said. "I have to do something special, you see. The big gesture." He wasn't happy. "Everything's gestures in this job. Stupid, really. The only way out of it would be if they recall that maniac Tisander in time to rush home and try and save Choris. Trouble is, they don't have a communications system as good as ours. I'd offer to let them use the Mail, but I don't suppose they'd agree. So, by the time they can get word to the maniac, Choris will probably be under water. Ridiculous, but that's politics for you."

"You could try," I said.

His face changed. He was my friend, but he was the king. "Not up to me, unfortunately," he said. "Not the done thing, second-guessing the joint chiefs of staff. Besides, the Aelians have slaughtered about a million people since they got here; not just soldiers, ordinary men and women, kids. They shouldn't have done that. There was no need."

"And you're the king," I said.

"Yes, worse luck. So I've got to do something about it. And it means Choris and Aelia will never threaten us again. I know that sounds like politics-speak, but a million dead civilians – we don't do things like that, not unless some idiot makes it unavoidable." He looked past me for a moment, then back at me. "I read about you in the reports," he said. "On Sirupat. There was going to be a war then, but you stopped it."

"I thought I did."

He nodded. "Trouble is," he said, "if we'd had the war then, we'd have won it easier and quicker, and a million Sashan civilians wouldn't have died, and I wouldn't be obliged to drown Choris Anthropou. So, probably better for all concerned if you hadn't interfered. Also, I'd still be in Hetsuan, growing my own vegetables. But you weren't to know. As far as you were concerned, you were doing the right thing. Good on you for that."

"Thank you."

He shrugged it away. "Anyway," he said, "I heard about your sister."

I looked him in the eye, then looked away.

"No offence," he went on, "but she sounds like a dreadful woman. Murdered her own husband, I ask you. Reinstating her was the governor's idea, not mine. Just as well I heard about it when I did, or you'd be stuck up on a pike somewhere right now." He paused. "I read something about a friend of yours. I'm sorry."

"Yes."

"I'm sorry," he repeated. "It's horrible when things like that happen, and unfortunately there's nothing anyone can do, once it's done." He was quiet for a moment, then went on: "I'm reinstating you as duke. Is that all right with you?"

"As duke."

"Your father's heir. It's what we usually do, when there's a legitimate successor we can trust. That's as well as your sister's properties, of course. You'd be doing me a favour. Two strategically important buffer states, and all that. It won't make up for anything, needless to say, but nothing ever would. And, like I said, you'd be helping me out."

"How's Apoina?" I asked.

He didn't answer straight away. "Blooming," he said. "She likes being queen."

"And—?"

"She's fine, too. Actually," he went on, "I wanted to talk to you about that."

I closed my eyes, but only for a moment. "Go on."

"The thing of it is," he said, "it doesn't look like Poina and I can ever have kids of our own. My fault, presumably, but there you go. So, all things being equal, when I die, your – well, our daughter is going to be the heir to the throne. Which means, of course, that she can't be your daughter any more, she's got to be mine."

I nodded. My daughter hates me. She believes I want to kill her. "So you need me out of the way."

He was genuinely shocked. "Don't be an idiot," he said. "Nobody knows except you, Poina and me, or at least nobody I know about." He frowned. He wasn't happy about what was coming next. "At least, as long as I'm alive. If I go on before you do, that'd be different. Can't take the risk, is what I'm saying. Now I'm, what, eight years older than you, but we're a long-lived family if we get the chance, I mean, look at my loathsome uncle, eighty-two and still going strong when they did for him. You'll be fine, I'm sure of it. Meanwhile, your daughter will get to be the Great Queen." He shrugged. "I don't know if you reckon much to family, given the life you've led, but we Sashan put a lot of store in that sort of thing. And I think she'd enjoy it. There are times when I think she's more Sashan than the rest of us put together."

"That's a good thing," I said.

He smiled. "I think so," he said. "It's different for me. I had all those years in Hetsuan, I know there's another world and another way of doing things. She never saw it like that. She hated Hetsuan. All she ever wanted to be was a princess.

What was rightfully hers, and all that nonsense. Of course, she thinks she's my daughter, so what can you expect?"

I laughed. "Entitled."

"Sorry?"

"A word a friend of mine was very fond of," I said. "But why not? If she's happy, that's all that matters."

"I think she will be," he said. "Don't ask me how, stuck doing this job, but there it is. It's a good thing we're not all made alike." He was looking straight at me, the king's gaze, Brother of the Sun and Moon. "Are you all right with all that?"

"Yes."

"No, but really. I don't want to make you do anything you're not comfortable with. If you'd rather, I can make you governor of one of the provinces out east. Revoltingly hot out there, but peace and quiet and you can do what you damn well like as far as I'm concerned. I owe you something nice, bearing in mind Poina and everything. Up to you entirely."

"Thanks," I said. "But it'd make more sense for me to be the duke. I'm—" I managed not to laugh. "I'm entitled, after all. Continuity and legitimacy. Good for business."

"That's how we've always seen it," he said. "Basically, people like things to stay the same."

"There aren't any people left in my duchy," I said.

"There will be," he said. "We'll ship them in from Agbatana. There's been a hell of a famine there the last couple of years, I've got about ninety thousand families desperate for somewhere to go."

"Where's Agbatana?"

"North-east," he said, "second in from the Echmen border. Too hot in summer, too cold in winter, ghastly place. Your neck of the woods will seem like the earthly paradise. And you'll do a grand job of looking after them, I'm sure. And I'll settle a load of my veterans in your sister's country. If that's all right with you, of course."

Continuity and legitimacy, in the Sashan sense. "I'll do my best," I said.

"Course you will. Your file says you're good at looking after people. In the blood, presumably."

My father; his possessions, his home, and his people. I wasn't sure I could ever care for possessions, not after Gombryas and his devoted love for his collection. The other two, however, ought to be possible, if I set my mind to it. "Thank you," I said.

"Think nothing of it." He smiled. "I reckon I owe you, for Eudocia. Your daughter," he reminded me. "Of course, we can't call her that any more, it being an Aelian name, so from now on she'll be Dastana, after my mother. I really do love that kid," he added. "She's sweet and smart and a lot of fun. Takes after her mother, of course, but I reckon the smarts come from you. You should be proud of her."

Not that I'd ever get to meet her. "I had nothing to do with it," I said. "If she's turned out well, that's you and Apoina."

He accepted that with a smile. "Anyway, like I said, I owe you. Besides, you're all right. And it's nice to have someone I can talk to, you know, like this. It gets a bit wearing at times, being the brother of the Sun. Poina and Docia are wonderful, of course, but they're, you know, women." He grinned. "So, the occasional state visit, when we can find the time. You won't mind that, will you?"

"I'll look forward to it."

"Grand." He nodded; all done and dusted. "Right," he said, "you'd better be getting back to your duchy, and I suppose I'd better get on with being king. It's a great job, actually, I love it, but you never get a moment to yourself." He clapped his hands three times. "You'd better get down on the floor," he said. "Protocol and all that."

I stood up and put the chair back where he'd got it from. "Good man," he said, "I'd forgotten about that." Then I fell on my face before the King of Kings, just in time before the chamberlains arrived.

We won the war, it goes without saying, but it was actually a close-run thing. General Tisander, the maniac Aelian, actually broke through and drew his army up in front of the gates of the Royal City. But he didn't have enough men, his supply line was in shreds, he'd left his artillery and siege train ninety miles to the south and his army was just starting to show signs of mountain fever. He walked up to the gates with a bow in his hand and shot an arrow over the ramparts, as a gesture, then turned away and led his forces to the nearest seaport, where the fleet was waiting to take him back to Aelia. He never got there. A storm sank the fleet in the middle of the Middle Sea, and since he was sailing out of sight of land, to save time, there were only a handful of survivors. Tisander wasn't one of them. The war was over.

Just in time, thanks to the superhuman efforts of the Royal Engineers, to save Choris, though not the other cities to the north. They built a dam in five days flat, the sort of thing only the king could achieve, so he got to make his gesture after all; and these days the river flows round Choris on two sides, making it possible to irrigate the plains and grow enough food to ensure a continuous supply and low prices that even the poor can afford. The king worked his miracle, it was better and more memorable than the original one, and a quarter of a million people didn't drown. They love the king in Choris these days, which is only right and proper.

Continuity and legitimacy. The western shore of the Friendly Sea is now almost completely repopulated, and the people who live there like it just fine. They came from places that were overcrowded, hot, ruled by cruel noblemen and hereditary tyrants and prone to continuous cycles of drought and flood, into a land flowing with milk and honey. My lot, the Agbatanes, are the proverbial salt of the earth. They're good farmers, hard workers, sensible, peaceful, happy that they've ended up in a better place, and it doesn't hurt that their duke is known to enjoy the king's special favour. My other lot, in Fan's country, are mostly ex-soldiers, enjoying their forty-acres-a-head pensions after twenty years in the service. Mostly I leave them to themselves, which is fine; their officers are settled there with them, on two hundred acres apiece, so everybody knows what to do and who to turn to if things go wrong. The Sashan have a genius for stability. There are – genuinely – no wars inside the king's borders. Of all the bad things I've seen in my life, war is the worst of all.

I knew a one-armed man once. He lost it in a battle. When he realised what had happened to him, he didn't want to go on living. It was his right arm, and he was right-handed. I met him again years later. He was settled, doing quite well, making a good living dealing in hides and pelts. He had a wife and two sons, a nice house, friends, well-respected in the trade, a lot of people who depended on him. So, I said to him, it's just as well you didn't die after the battle. He looked at me. No, he said. I wish you'd left me there. It's just not the same without it.

It's not the same without her. These days I'm everything I was born to be. I have everything I'm entitled to. I stopped calling myself Saevus years ago; I'm Florian now. I even think of myself as Florian, which is something I never thought I'd do again.

It pleases me to think that, if I live that long, my life and the king's will end together. It'll be organised, of course, with typical Sashan efficiency. There'll be a list, drawn up by the senior council, discussed and approved by a sub-committee; these people will not survive into the next reign. Usually the names on it are illegitimate kids, second cousins, senior officials who know too much, generals of questionable loyalty. If the king is seriously ill, men are briefed and sent out on the Mail, ready to act as soon as the Mail brings word that the king is dead. I've made my own arrangements. When the men arrive, I've ordered, the cook and the household staff are to get them something nice to eat and drink, after their long journey, and make up the best guest rooms for them, and there's a present of money for after they've done the job, to remember me by. The First Emperor's bodyguard insisted on dying with their lord (that's true, because it's in a Sashan history book) and they regarded it as a privilege to be allowed to do so. I've seen their golden armour with my own eyes, and the lesson wasn't lost on me. The Sashan believe that the king has a court in heaven when he gets there, like the one he had on earth but much bigger and better, and immortal lions to hunt among the stars. I don't believe that. But I believe in the king, because he's my friend, and there are no wars in his country.

The Royal Treasury allotted me a million darics to rebuild my father's house. I spent it on two new bridges, three watermills, half a dozen decent roads and a poor-relief fund. I got a letter of reprimand from the palace, telling me that the king's tenant represented the king, and it was disrespectful for him to live in anything less than magnificent splendour. On the back of it, in rather sloppy handwriting, was written: Good on you, splendid idea, A and E both well, your friend Balas. Not long after that, I got another grant from the Treasury, a hundred thousand darics, to buy a pack of hounds in case the king ever came out my way to hunt lions. I used it to hire five Echmen doctors, to train up local kids who showed promise. Now there's best part of a hundred of them, so anyone in my country can get to one and be seen to, and I pay the bills. It was all the king's idea, of course, as witness the fact that they're starting to do it all over the Empire. Meanwhile I live in my father's magnificent hunting lodge, where Stauracia and I found the stash of food.

I have no illusions about the Sashan. I don't hate them, even though they slaughtered my countrymen and left the ones they didn't kill to starve, just as my countrymen slaughtered a million Sashan. But it was the war that did that. The Sashan didn't start the war, and I didn't deliberately murder my brother.

But it's a civilisation built on lies, and there's about as much truth in it as there's silver in a late Republic Mezentine stuiver: one part silver to ninety parts copper, because of inflation, because of the war. The silver rises to the surface in the melt, so when it's issued the coin is white and shiny. A few weeks later, the silver's all rubbed off. Before too long there'll be a king who isn't the king's son, isn't Sashan, isn't even a man; but s/he will still hunt lions and slaughter the enemy and be the Brother of the Sun and Moon – all lies, of course, and her strength and power and wisdom will be as frail as a sheet of silver foil. The Sashan can be as cruel and vicious and unjust as anybody else. They frequently are, but there are occasions when they choose not to be, mostly because it's more productive to be kind and fair. You get more wool off well-fed sheep than starving ones, and fat sheep don't break out and go wandering off, and dead sheep are no use to anyone, except my former colleagues the crows. It amazes me how simple that is, and how few people have ever figured it out.

I have no interest in the truth. It's usually depressing and it rarely does anyone any good. Just before she died, Fan told me she was there and she saw me do it. I have no idea if that was true, or whether she was just being spiteful. To the Sashan, the truth is a fluid, living thing, not a quill-mark stuck in clay and then baked rock-hard. Now that I've outlived all the witnesses and the house isn't there any more, I'm in a position to declare the truth absolutely. It wasn't my fault. It was an accident. All the harm and evil that came of it was other people's doing, not mine.

The war, my Agbatane countrymen tell me, wasn't such a bad thing after all. If it hadn't been for the war, this wouldn't be Sashan territory, under the king's peace, and we'd still be living in godforsaken Agbatana, and half the children you're looking at right now would never have been born, and two out of three of them would've died in infancy. War's all right, they tell me, if it's a good war. It's just a way of getting things done, a means to an end, a tool like any other. At which point I generally change the subject, because there's a certain amount of truth in what they say, and I think you probably know by now how I feel about that.

So much, then, for the big score. It turned out to be more than I could ever have dreamed of, everything I was entitled to, nothing I deserved, and I'd trade the lot in a split second for one more day with her, or even a chance to say goodbye.

Irony, or the king moving in mysterious ways. But it doesn't matter. My life is all about other people now; looking after them, trying to do what's best for them, gently heading them off from straying over cliffs. That makes me sound altruistic and practically a saint, but that's misleading. I do it because my friend wants me to and he was kind to me, and because I have nothing better to do, and I never liked myself much anyway.

I miss her. The absence of her is a positive, substantial thing, and I take it everywhere I go, like my shadow. The brighter the light, the more clearly I see her absence. On the back of an official letter, my friend wrote: you ought to find a nice girl and get married again, would you like me to send you one? He wrote it in Aelian, which is now practically a dead language. On the back of my reply I wrote, thanks but no thanks. I don't doubt for a moment that the king could go down to the Underworld, wrestle with Death and bring Stauracia back to me, but it'd be a lot to ask and he's a busy man.

She always had the last word. It wasn't always the best word. Sometimes, when I'd come out with a particularly neat and witty line, it'd just be *shut up* or *fuck you*. I wish she could have it now. I have nothing at all left to say.

extras

orbit

meet the author

K. J. PARKER is a pseudonym for Tom Holt. He was born in London in 1961. At Oxford he studied bar billiards, ancient Greek agriculture and the care and feeding of small, temperamental Japanese motorcycle engines. These interests led him, perhaps inevitably, to qualify as a solicitor and immigrate to Somerset, where he specialised in death and taxes for seven years before going straight in 1995. He lives in Chard, Somerset, with his wife and daughter.

Find out more about K. J. Parker and other Orbit authors by registering for the free monthly newsletter at orbitbooks.net.

if you enjoyed
SAEVUS CORAX GETS AWAY WITH MURDER

look out for

THE EIGHT REINDEER OF THE APOCALYPSE

by

Tom Holt

Welcome to Dawson, Ahriman & Dawson! *

The team of commercial sorcerers at Dawson, Ahriman & Dawson can help with any metaphysical engineering project, large or small. (Though by definition, they all tend to be pretty large.)

---

* By reading beyond this point you agree to comply with certain terms and conditions that are mostly reasonable but confidential. The management reserves the right to terminate any employees or clients, human or otherwise.

They can also create massive great puddles of chaos that might one day swallow up the entire universe.

Take, for example, the decision to recruit a certain bearded fellow whose previous work experience mainly involves reindeer and jingle bells. It might have seemed like a good idea at the time, but is he really the best person to save the world from Tiamat the Destroyer, who has literally gone ballistic?

Find out today in Tom Holt's brilliantly funny new novel set in the world of The Portable Door *(now a delightful movie starring Patrick Gibson, Sophie Wilde, and Christoph Waltz).*

Dasher

A dark and stormy night, a deserted country road, a solitary female motorist driving an elderly, unreliable Toyota. What could possibly go wrong?

Total failure of the car's electrical systems, for one thing. The engine died, all the lights went out, the radio lapsed into silence, the car coasted to a halt and just sat there. Bother, thought Alice, or words to that effect. She reached in her pocket for her phone. Nothing, dead as a stone. She could only tell that it was there because she could feel it in her hand.

The scenario, she couldn't help thinking, was not entirely unfamiliar; except, of course, that stuff like that didn't actually happen, and there's absolutely no such thing as—

She cried out and closed her eyes, a fraction of a second too late. The brilliant white light all around her was painful, unendurable. "Oh come on," she screeched at it. She could feel its warmth on her skin.

The car was floating, as if on water. She risked opening one eye, just a bit, but all she could see was dazzle. A scooped-out feeling in her tummy suggested that the car was rising, none too steadily, as though a magnet had clamped to the roof and a winch was reeling her in. Terror flooded her, as if she'd left the window open in a car wash, together with the soft, scornful whisper of a tiny voice in the back of her head; this can't be happening; this is silly.

A gentle shudder coming up through the floor via the shock absorbers. Not moving any more. A firm but not deafening metallic clunk. I'm dreaming all this, she told herself. Gentle forward motion, causing the seat belt to press lightly on her collarbone, contradicted her. Not a dream.

A tapping noise; close, insistent. Something banging against the driver's side window. She ignored it. It grew louder. It was similar to the sound of a knuckle, but that bit clearer and sharper. It wasn't going to go away. She opened her right eye, looked and screamed.

The reason, she later realised, why the knocking didn't sound quite right was that human knuckles are covered in skin, whereas the tapper at her window had scales: small ones, about thumbnail size, a sort of iridescent greeny-gold. It wasn't the scales she had a problem with, or the head being a third bigger than the body. It was the eyes: clusters and clusters and clusters of them, on long stalks.

She had no cogent reason to believe that if she shrieked loud enough, the monster would back off, she'd be put back where she'd been taken from and none of this would ever have happened. It was, she'd have cheerfully conceded, a long shot, at best. But she couldn't think of anything else to do, so she gave it a go.

It didn't work. The monster kept on tapping.

Somewhere inside her head, a voice said: anyone or anything capable of this level of technology isn't going to be defeated by a car door. She stopped screaming and pressed the window wind-down button. It didn't work, of course. Then it did.

The monster lowered its head, though it took care not to let any part of its anatomy actually enter the car. It was, she realised, respecting her personal space. Earth?

The voice was inside her head, but she knew beyond a shadow of a doubt that it hadn't come from her. Telepathy, it said. This is Earth, right?

She discovered that you can't lie to a telepathic species. Yes, said her mind, a moment before her lips could shape the word No. Oh well.

Parcel for you.

Excuse me?

Parcel for you. Delivery.

Understanding gradually seeped through her, like melting ice dripping off a roof. Oh, she thought, right. Do you need me to sign for it?

A sea-blue laser beam hit her between the eyes. No need, we scan. Have a nice 9.16030534351145-times-the-half-life-of-Silicon-31.

You what?

Something scrabbled in her mind for the right word. Day. Have a nice day.

The monster's hand – nine-fingered and absolutely not something she wanted to think about, though she had a nasty feeling she would, every day for the rest of her life – came through the window, holding something about the size of a small cushion, wrapped in a shiny grey polymer. Somehow she forced herself to take it. The hand let go and withdrew. Her window wound up, all by itself. The monster took a step back, and she couldn't see it any more, because of the dazzle.

The car was moving again, sinking this time. She heard the same soft clang she'd heard before, and felt a faint jar as the car stopped. Two seconds later, the terrible light went out. Five seconds after that, her car engine purred smoothly into life and the headlights and radio came on. You are my sunshine, it sang at her. She switched it off.

In her lap was the parcel. She turned on the interior light and stared at it. Just a parcel; and on it was a label. The label had signs on it, squiggles. She'd never seen anything remotely like them in her life, not even late at night after eating Limburger cheese. She discovered she could read them, quite easily. Telepathic reading, for crying out loud.

Q'xxw^etrqegr-3885/8a8!83/Z'ggwerq!tgr, Esq.
Unit 17, Sfhyoynxxxxx!xxyx Plaza,
ZZZxZ,
Alpha Centauri
– and underneath, a series of boxes, one of which was ticked:
Not at home; left with neighbour.

"I see," said Mr Sunshine, pursing his lips. "Did you bring it with you?"

Alice nodded. "I haven't opened it."

"Of course not," said Mr Sunshine. "It wasn't addressed to you."

"I hadn't thought about it in quite those terms," Alice said. "But, no, you're right, it wasn't. Look—"

Something nudged her kneecap. She was about to open her mouth and let fly when she realised it was one of the drawers of Mr Sunshine's desk. It was trying to open. Mr Sunshine saw the look on her face and smiled. "That's just Harmondsworth," he said. "Stop it, Harmondsworth." The drawer stopped nudging. "It means he likes you," Mr Sunshine said. "You were saying."

She looked at him. She saw a big man, somewhere around seventy, with a bald head rising up through a fringe of snow-white hair like a volcano surrounded by jungle. The sleeves of his shirt – white with a pale red and green check, the sort of thing you still see occasionally being worn by old-fashioned chartered surveyors in market towns – were rolled up, revealing powerful forearms with a few faint scars and liver splodges. His thick spectacles magnified pale blue eyes, topped by dense hedges of white eyebrow. "Sorry," she said, without really knowing why.

"That's perfectly all right. You were going to ask me something."

Far below, traffic swirled, but she couldn't hear it. "What am I supposed to do with it?" she asked.

"The parcel."

"Yes."

Mr Sunshine leaned back in his chair and rubbed his upper lip with the ball of his thumb. "You know," he said, "I'm not sure I'm quite the right person to help you with this. It sounds more like a science thing."

"It's weird shit," Alice said. "My friend told me, weird shit is what you do."

"Not that kind of weird shit," Mr Sunshine said gently. He picked a business card off his desktop and handed it to her. "Read that," he said.

DAWSON, AHRIMAN & DAWSON
Commercial and Industrial Sorcerors,
Thaumaturgical & Metaphysical Engineers
Edwin Sunshine – Consultant

"Some of our practice does overlap with science," he went on, "a bit, the trailing edges of the Venn diagrams barely touching. But flying saucers and space aliens—" He shrugged, very slightly. "You might be better off talking to NASA," he said. "Or the Air Force."

She felt as though the roof had just caved in on her. "You don't believe me," she said. "You think I'm—"

"Entirely truthful and as sane as I am," Mr Sunshine said. "In fact, I don't just think that, I know."

Something about the way he said it made her shudder. "Thank you," she said, in a tiny voice.

"But that doesn't alter the fact that this isn't really my field of expertise. Basically, anything where E equals mc2 isn't our bag. We're more sort of—"

A tiny starburst of golden flowers appeared from nowhere in front of her eyes. They hung in the air twinkling, then vanished, leaving behind a faint scent of lavender mixed with burnt gunpowder.

"Ah," she said. "Right. But I don't know any scientists, and if I did they'd laugh like a drain or have me locked up, and my friend Carol said—"

The name seemed to carry weight with Mr Sunshine. "I suppose I could have a word with one of my partn—" He stopped short and flushed. "One of the partners," he said. "She's had a certain amount of experience in spatio-temporal dynamics. If she can't help, she probably knows someone who can." He frowned, as though listening to someone raising an objection. "It can't hurt," he said. "Of course, there's the question of money. I'm afraid we're rather expensive."

"Money?"

"Well, yes."

"I've got money," Alice remembered. "What sort of figure are we talking about?"

Mr Sunshine took back the card, turned it over and wrote something on the back with a pencil. He showed it to her. It was as though there was a part for a zero in a Harry Potter movie, and all the noughts in the world were queuing up to audition. "Oh," she said.

Mr Sunshine looked at her. "Quite," he said. "Of course, if you'd gone to JWW or Zauberwerke or one of the big City firms, you'd be looking at twice that, and they don't do free initial interviews like we do. Even so—" He opened a drawer, reached in and took something out. "Not exactly cheap. Still, anything worth having very rarely is."

The thing he'd taken from the drawer was a tatty old purse. Alice looked at it. Her grandmother had had one just like it, many years ago. "How long did you say you'd known Carol?"

"We were in the same class at junior school."

"Ah." Mr Sunshine nodded. Then he made a show of looking for something – shuffling papers on the desk, moving his chair a few inches, glancing round at the floor. "Stupid of me," he said. "I seem to have lost a bottomless purse. I had it a moment ago."

"A—?"

Mr Sunshine rolled his eyes. She picked up the purse and opened it. Out of it tumbled a heap of cut diamonds, more or less enough to fill a soup bowl. She put down the purse and scooped the diamonds into her lap, then picked up the purse again. "Is this it?"

"Yes, that's the one." Mr Sunshine smiled, took it from her and put it back in his desk. "Silly me, I'm always losing things," he said. "About the money."

She piled the diamonds back onto the desk. "Would these do?"

"You dropped one."

He was right, she had. She retrieved it and added it to the pile. "That'll do nicely," Mr Sunshine said. "It's always nice when people give you the exact money. It saves having to fiddle about with small change."

She tried to remember exactly what Carol had said about Mr Sunshine. He's nice, she'd said. A bit weird, but nice. She shivered. "So you'll—"

He nodded. "No promises," he said, "but I'll do my best. And like I said, Gina will probably know someone who knows about this sort of thing. Let's see it, then."

"Oh, the parcel." She picked up the carrier bag from the floor. "It's in here."

Mr Sunshine had suddenly gone very still and very quiet. "In there. No, don't take it out," he said. "Just leave it in the bag, would you?" He dipped his fingers into his shirt pocket and produced a magnifying glass. It was jet-black. He peered at the bag through it, then put it away. The look on his face was the most disconcerting thing she'd seen all morning. "Now that's not something you come across every day," he said, and his voice was ever so slightly shaky. "You know, I think we might be able to help you after all. You wouldn't mind leaving that with us for a day or so? I'll give you a receipt."

"Sure," said Alice. She tried to hand it to him, but he gestured to her to put it on the desk. "Keep it. Please."

"No," Mr Sunshine said, "I don't think I will, thanks all the same. Just a temporary loan, while we run some tests, that sort of thing." He wiped his forehead with the back of his wrist. "Just routine stuff."

if you enjoyed
SAEVUS CORAX GETS
AWAY WITH MURDER

look out for

SIXTEEN WAYS TO
DEFEND A WALLED CITY

by

K. J. Parker

K. J. Parker's new novel is the remarkable tale of the siege of a walled city and the even more remarkable man who had to defend it.

A siege is approaching, and the City has little time to prepare. The people have no food and no weapons, and the enemy has sworn to slaughter them all.

To save the city will take a miracle, but what it has is Orhan. A colonel of engineers, Orhan has far more experience with bridge-building than battles, is a cheat and a liar, and has a serious problem with authority. He is, in other words, perfect for the job.

Sixteen Ways to Defend a Walled City *is the story of Orhan, son of Siyyah Doctus Felix Praeclarissimus, and his history of the Great Siege, written down so that the deeds and sufferings of great men may never be forgotten.*

1

I was in Classis on business. I needed sixty miles of second-grade four-inch hemp rope—I build pontoon bridges—and all the military rope in the empire goes through Classis. What you're supposed to do is put in a requisition to Divisional Supply, who send it on to Central Supply, who send it on to the Treasurer General, who approves it and sends it back to Divisional Supply, who send it on to Central Supply, who forward it to Classis, where the quartermaster says, sorry, we have no rope. Or you can hire a clever forger in Herennis to cut you an exact copy of the treasury seal, which you use to stamp your requisition, which you then take personally to the office of the deputy quartermaster in Classis, where there's a senior clerk who'd have done time in the slate quarries if you hadn't pulled certain documents out of the file a few years back. Of course, you burned the documents as soon as you took them, but he doesn't know that. And that's how you get sixty miles of rope in this man's army.

I took the overland route from Traiecta to Cirte, across one of my bridges (a rush job I did fifteen years ago, only meant to last a month, still there and still the only way across the Lusen unless you go twenty-six miles out of your way to Pons Jovianis) then down through the pass onto the coastal plain. Fabulous view as you come through the pass, that huge flat green patchwork with the blue of the Bay beyond, and Classis as a geometrically perfect star, three arms on land, three jabbing out into the sea. Analyse the design and it becomes clear that it's purely practical and utilitarian, straight out of the field operations manual. Furthermore, as soon as you drop down onto the plain you can't see the shape, unless you happen to be God. The three seaward arms are tapered jetties, while their landward counterparts are defensive bastions, intended to cover the three main gates with enfilading fire on two sides. Even further more, when Classis was built ninety years ago, there was a dirty great forest in the way (felled for charcoal during the Social War, all stumps, marsh and bramble-fuzz now), so you wouldn't have been able to see it from the pass, and that strikingly beautiful statement of Imperial power must therefore be mere chance and serendipity. By the time I reached the way station at Milestone 2776 I couldn't see Classis at all, though of course it was dead easy to find. Just follow the arrow-straight military road on its six-foot embankment, and, next thing you know, you're there.

Please note I didn't come in on the military mail. As Colonel-in-Chief of the Engineers, I'm entitled; but, as a milkface (not supposed to call us that, everybody does, doesn't bother me, I like milk) it's accepted that I don't, because of the distress I might cause to Imperials finding themselves banged up in a coach with me for sixteen hours a day. Not that they'd say anything, of course. The Robur pride themselves on their good manners, and, besides, calling a milkface a milkface is Conduct Prejudicial and can get you court-martialled. For the record, nobody's ever faced charges on that score, which proves (doesn't it) that Imperials aren't biased or bigoted in any way. On the other hand, several dozen auxiliary officers have been tried and cashiered for calling an Imperial a blueskin, so you can see just how wicked and deserving of contempt my lot truly are.

No, I made the whole four-day trip on a civilian carrier's cart. The military mail, running non-stop and changing horses at way stations every twenty miles, takes five days and a bit, but my cart was carrying fish; marvellous incentive to get a move on.

The cart rumbled up to the middle gate and I hopped off and hobbled up to the sentry, who scowled at me, then saw the scrambled egg on my collar. For a split second I thought he was going to arrest me for impersonating an officer (wouldn't be the first time). I walked past him, then jumped sideways to avoid being run down by a cart the size of a cathedral. That's Classis.

My pal the clerk's office was in Block 374, Row 42, Street 7. They've heard of sequential numbering in Supply but clearly aren't convinced that it'd work, so Block 374 is wedged in between Blocks 217 and 434. Street 7 leads from Street 4 into Street 32. But it must be all right, because I can find my way about there, and I'm just a bridge builder, nobody.

He wasn't there. Sitting at his desk was a six-foot-six Robur in a milk-white monk's habit. He was bald as an egg, and he looked at me as though I was something the dog had brought in. I mentioned my pal's name. He smiled.

"Reassigned," he said.

Oh. "He never mentioned it."

"It wasn't the sort of reassignment you'd want to talk about." He looked me up and down; I half expected him to roll back my upper lip so he could inspect my teeth. "Can I help you?"

I gave him the big smile. "I need rope."

"Sorry." He looked so happy. "No rope."

"I have a sealed requisition."

He held out his hand. I showed him my piece of paper. I'm pretty sure he spotted the seal was a fake. "Unfortunately, we have no rope at present," he said. "As soon as we get some—"

I nodded. I didn't go to staff college so I know squat about strategy and tactics, but I know when I've lost and it's time to withdraw in good order. "Thank you," I said. "Sorry to have bothered you."

"No bother." His smile said he hadn't finished with me yet. "You can leave that with me."

I was still holding the phony requisition with the highly illegal seal. "Thanks," I said, "but shouldn't I resubmit it through channels? I wouldn't want you thinking I was trying to jump the queue."

"Oh, I think we can bend the rules once in a while." He held out his hand again. Damn, I thought. And then the enemy saved me.

(Which is the story of my life, curiously enough. I've had an amazing number of lucky breaks in my life, far more than my fair share, which is why, when I got the citizenship, I chose Felix as my proper name. Good fortune has smiled on me at practically every crucial turning point in my remarkable career. But the crazy thing is, the agency of my good fortune has always—invariably—been the enemy. Thus: when I was seven years old, the Hus attacked our village, slaughtered my parents, dragged me away by the hair and sold me to a Sherden; who taught me the carpenter's trade—thereby trebling my value—and sold me on to a shipyard. Three years after that, when I was nineteen, the Imperial army mounted a punitive expedition against the Sherden pirates; guess who was among the prisoners carted back to the empire. The Imperial navy is always desperately short of skilled shipwrights. They let me join up, which meant citizenship, and I was a foreman at age twenty-two. Then the Echmen invaded, captured the city where I was stationed; I was one of the survivors and transferred to the Engineers, of whom I now have the honour to be Colonel-in-Chief. I consider my point made. My meteoric rise, from illiterate barbarian serf to commander of an Imperial regiment, is due to the Hus, the Sherden, the Echmen and, last but not least, the Robur, who are proud of the fact that over the last hundred years they've slaughtered in excess of a million of my people. One of those here-today-gone-tomorrow freak cults you get in the City says that the way to virtue is loving your enemies. I have no problem with that. My enemies have always come through for me, and I owe them everything. My friends, on the other hand, have caused me nothing but aggravation and pain. Just as well I've had so very few of them.)

I noticed I no longer had his full attention. He was peering through his little window. After a moment, I shuffled closer and looked over his shoulder.

"Is that smoke?" I said.

He wasn't looking at me. "Yes."

Fire, in a place like Classis, is bad news. Curious how people react. He seemed frozen stiff. I felt jumpy as a cat. I elbowed myself a better view, as the long shed that had been leaking smoke from two windows suddenly went up in flames like a torch.

"What do you keep in there?" I asked.

"Rope," he said. "Three thousand miles of it."

I left him gawping and ran. Milspec rope is heavily tarred, and all the sheds at Classis are thatched. Time to be somewhere else.

I dashed out into the yard. There were people running in

340

every direction. Some of them didn't look like soldiers, or clerks. One of them raced toward me, then stopped.

"Excuse me," I said. "Do you know—?"

He stabbed me. I hadn't seen the sword in his hand. I thought; what the devil are you playing at? He pulled the sword out and swung it at my head. I may not be the most perceptive man you'll ever meet, but I can read between the lines; he didn't like me. I sidestepped, tripped his heels and kicked his face in. That's not in the drill manuals, but you pick up a sort of alternative education when you're brought up by slavers—

Sequence of thoughts; I guess the tripping and kicking thing reminded me of the Sherden who taught it to me (by example), and that made me think of pirates, and then I understood. I trod on his ear for luck till something cracked—not that I hold grudges—and looked round for somewhere to hide.

Really bad things happening all around you take time to sink in. Sherden pirates running amok in Classis? Couldn't be happening. So I found a shady doorway, held perfectly still and used my eyes. Yes, in fact, it was happening, and to judge from the small slice of the action I could see, they were having things very much their own way. The Imperial army didn't seem to be troubling them at all; they were preoccupied with fighting the fire in the rope shed, and the Sherden cut them down and shot them as they dashed about with buckets and ladders and long hooks, and nobody seemed to realise what was going on except me, and I don't count. Pretty soon there were no Imperials left in the yard, and the Sherden were backing up carts to the big sheds and pitching stuff in. Never any shortage of carts at Classis. They were hard workers, I'll give them that. Try and get a gang of dockers or warehousemen to load two hundred size-four carts in forty minutes. I guess that's the difference between hired men and self-employed.

341

I imagine the fire was an accident, because it rather spoiled things for the Sherden. It spread from one shed to a load of others before they had a chance to loot them, then burned up the main stable block and coach-houses, where most of the carts would have been, before the wind changed direction and sent it roaring through the barracks and the secondary admin blocks. That meant it was coming straight at me. By now, there were no soldiers or clerks to be seen, only the bad guys, and I'd stick out like a sore thumb in my regulation cloak and tunic. So I took off the cloak, noticed a big red stain down my front—oh yes, I'd been stabbed, worry about that later—pulled off the dead pirate's smock and dragged it over my head. Then I pranced away across the yard, looking like I had a job to do.

I got about thirty yards and fell over. I was mildly surprised, then realised: not just a flesh wound. I felt ridiculously weak and terribly sleepy. Then someone was standing over me, a Sherden, with a spear in his hand. Hell, I thought, and then: not that it matters.

"Are you all right?" he said.

Me and good fortune. How lucky I was to have been born a milkface. "I'm fine," I said. "Really."

He grinned. "Bullshit," he said, and hauled me to my feet. I saw him notice my boots—issue beetlecrushers, you can't buy them in stores. Then I saw he was wearing them, too. Pirates. Dead men's shoes. "Come on," he said. "Lean on me, you'll be fine."

He put my arm round his neck, then grabbed me round the waist and walked me across to the nearest cart. The driver helped him haul me up, and they laid me down gently on a huge stack of rolled-up lamellar breastplates. My rescuer took off his smock, rolled it up and put it under my head. "Get him back to the ship, they'll see to him there," he said, and that was the last I saw of him.

Simple as that. The way the looters were going about their business, quickly and efficiently, it was pretty obvious that there were no Imperial personnel left for them to worry about—apart from me, lovingly whisked away from danger by my enemies. The cart rumbled through the camp to the middle jetty. There were a dozen ships tied up on either side. The driver wasn't looking, so I was able to scramble off the cart and bury myself in a big coil of rope, where I stayed until the last ship set sail.

Some time later, a navy cutter showed up. Just in time, I remembered to struggle out of the Sherden smock that had saved my life. It'd have been the death of me if I'd been caught wearing it by our lot.

Which is the reason—one of the reasons—why I've decided to write this history. Under normal circumstances I wouldn't have bothered, wouldn't have presumed—who am I, to take upon myself the recording of the deeds and sufferings of great men, and so on. But I was there; not just all through the siege, but right at the very beginning. As I may already have mentioned, I've had far more good luck in my life than I could possibly have deserved, and when—time after time after time—some unseen hand scoops you up from under the wheels, so to speak, and puts you safely down on the roadside, you have to start wondering, why? And the only capacity in which I figure I'm fit to serve is that of witness. After all, anyone can testify in an Imperial court of law; even children, women, slaves, milkfaces, though of course it's up to the judge to decide what weight to give to the evidence of the likes of me. So; if luck figures I'm good enough to command the Engineers, maybe she reckons I can be a historian, too. Think of that. Immortality. A turf-cutter's son from north of the Bull's Neck living for ever on the spine of a book. Wouldn't that be something.

orbit

Follow us:

f **/orbitbooksUS**

𝕏 **/orbitbooks**

▶ **/orbitbooks**

Join our mailing list
to receive alerts on our
latest releases and deals.

orbitbooks.net

Enter our monthly
giveaway for the chance
to win some epic prizes.

orbitloot.com